THE
FRONTIERS SAGA
EPISODE 15

THAT WHICH
OTHER MEN
CANNOT DO

Ryk Brown

CHAPTER ONE

"You're not wheeling me out in that thing."

"But, Admiral..."

Admiral Galiardi's expression silenced his young assistant's objections. The admiral straightened his suit jacket as he prepared to leave the hospital room he had occupied for months now. "A wheelchair says disabled," the admiral explained as he reached for his cane. "A cane says determination."

"And what does losing one's balance and falling, all on global network coverage, say?" his assistant wondered aloud.

A disapproving glance was his assistant's reward. "You can be replaced, Dacosta."

"I'm only offering alternative points of view, Admiral."

"Just get my bag," the admiral replied. He paused for a moment, considering the young man's words. "Perhaps you should walk on my left," he conceded. "Just in case."

———————

Minutes later, Admiral Galiardi and Mister Dacosta stepped through the main doors of the rehabilitation facility and into the morning sunshine. The admiral paused long enough to look around. Despite all efforts by the people of Geneva to repair the damage, it was still quite apparent they had suffered greatly. He knew from images that had recently begun to flow, after the global networks had been reestablished, just how bad the damage had been, worldwide. By comparison, the people of Geneva had been fortunate.

Unfortunately, the crowd was much smaller than he had hoped. He had not expected crowds of well-wishers, nor throngs of reporters clamoring to get a few comments from him. However, he had expected more than the two or three, somewhat disinterested, junior reporters who were waiting to hear what he might have to say.

"Admiral Galiardi!" one of the reporters called out as he spotted the admiral and his assistant. "How are you feeling, sir?" he asked, as he moved into position, his camera-operator right behind him.

"I'm feeling very well, thank you," the admiral replied.

"Sir," the reporter followed quickly, not giving the other two reporters who were moving in behind him a chance to ask their own questions. "How do you feel about the Alliance's policy of clearing all Jung forces within twenty light years of Sol?"

"I think it's a dangerous tactic, considering the odds are in the Jung's favor."

"Can you elaborate?" the reporter continued.

"It is believed that the Jung outnumber the Alliance by nearly one hundred to one," Admiral Galiardi explained as he made his way carefully down the steps toward his waiting vehicle. "If the Jung manage to coordinate even half those ships into a concentrated attack, Earth would not stand a chance."

"But the stated purpose of the Jung-free zone is to buy the Earth time to prepare for such an attack. If the Jung truly do outnumber us, then wouldn't that time be..."

"You don't prepare to defend yourself against an attack by superior forces by committing acts of aggression against said forces," the admiral insisted,

2

interrupting the reporter. "Patrol and intercept inbound forces...yes. You can even destroy them if necessary, but going out and attacking forces just because they are within a certain distance from you?" The admiral stopped at the open car door and turned back toward the reporters. "If you were the Jung, how would you react?"

* * *

President Scott sat quietly behind his desk, watching the netcast of Admiral Galiardi's release from the rehabilitation facility in Geneva.

"Who is he kidding?" Mister Pagni, one of the president's advisors, wondered. "He knows as well as anyone that those forces are best dealt with *before* they are en route for Sol."

"But the public doesn't," Miri commented.

"But *he* does," Mister Pagni reminded them.

"He doesn't care," President Scott muttered. "He's just taking a side opposite that of the Alliance."

"Do you think he's going to make a play to reestablish the Earth Defense Force?" Miri wondered.

"I don't think he'll take it that far," her father replied. "After all that the Alliance has done for us, there's no way he'll get public support to leave it."

"His claims that your son overstepped his authority when forming the Alliance could have some legitimacy to it," Mister Pagni admitted. "An argument could be made..."

"In what court?" President Scott wondered. "We're still operating under martial law, remember? Disputes are being handled by local magistrates using common-sense justice, and there are no appeals, no higher-up courts in the chain in which to seek an overturn. There probably won't be for

3

years." The president sighed. "No, he is just trying to get attention."

"For what reason?" Miri wondered.

"I don't know," President Scott admitted. "But I'm sure we'll find out soon enough."

* * *

Nathan peered out the window of the shuttle as it circled the field to turn into the wind before setting down. What had once been a Jung fighter base and a symbol of Jung dominance over the Tannan people, had instead become a symbol of defiance against that very same empire. Tracks weaved in and out of rows of oversized hangars, forming a makeshift assembly line that would have taken months to build from scratch. Instead, the entire facility had been put together and had begun building Cobra gunships in only forty days. And now, only a month after production had begun, the first gunship was about to roll off the assembly line.

The shuttle finished its approach turn and descended to a gentle touchdown alongside several other Tannan shuttles. The steward popped the door and extended the boarding ramp as the shuttle's engines wound down. Nathan rose from his seat, turning to face the Ghatazhak sergeant sitting behind him who had been assigned as his security escort for this trip. "Would you like to go first?"

"Not necessary, sir," the young sergeant replied confidently. "I called ahead. The area is secure."

"I would hope so," Nathan muttered as he turned to head forward. It wasn't that he didn't like the sergeant, it was just that his very presence served to remind him of the loss of his previous bodyguard, and friend, Sergeant Weatherly. Telling the young marine's mother of his death had been the hardest thing Nathan had ever done. He could have written the standard letter, the same one he had sent to the survivor's of every crewman he had lost over the last year and a half, but he had chosen not to. Not with Jerome. He didn't know the others, except by name. He had known Jerome. He had met his mother, his sister, his nephews...all of which made it more important that he had delivered the tragic news in person...and also made it even more difficult.

A year and a half. Had it really been that long? It seemed like he had only taken command recently, despite the many battles he and his crew had faced. Although these days he felt like the captain, there were still times when he felt like he did not belong in that chair.

Nathan stepped through the hatch, pausing at the top of the ramp to look around the field. It was a busy place, with vehicles moving all about, and people busy at their jobs. He headed down the ramp as a small open-top transport vehicle pulled up with two people inside...a driver, and a familiar blonde-haired woman smiling broadly at him as his feet touched the pavement.

"Captain Scott," Abby greeted. "I trust you had an uneventful trip?"

"Yes," Nathan replied with a grin, "all twenty minutes of it."

Abby rose from the vehicle and hugged Nathan. "It's good to see you again, Nathan. I thought you were coming in the Mirai?"

"It landed at Lorrett, so I took a local shuttle over."

"Why Lorrett?" Abby wondered.

"Jessica is visiting Synda," Nathan explained as he climbed into the backseat of the vehicle.

"Synda lives in Lorrett?" Abby wondered, somewhat surprised. "I thought all Terrans lived in either Aronelle or Visanori?"

"Apparently not," Nathan said as the Ghatazhak sergeant took his seat next to him. "This place is quite impressive, Abby," he said as the vehicle pulled away and headed toward the last hangar at the far end of the base. "I see you took to your additional responsibilities with your usual vigor."

Abby turned and smiled back at Nathan. "You know, I hated working on that asteroid base, just like I hated working on the Aurora. No sunlight. No fresh air. It's just not natural."

"I know what you mean."

"This place, on the other hand, is great. It's only a thirty minute commute from home, five if I catch the worker shuttle."

"Are you still living in the camps?"

"Yes," Abby answered. "We thought about moving to Aronelle, but it's further away. Besides, now that so many Terrans have moved out of the camps and into the cities, conditions have become much better. And the children really like the camp for some reason."

"What about your husband?" Nathan asked. "Last I remember he wasn't too fond of them."

"He started a small farm on the edge of the camp. He's always been a bit of a gardener. He plans to open a small produce stand after his first harvest a few months from now."

The vehicle pulled to a stop at the corner of the building. Nathan and the Ghatazhak sergeant stepped out and followed Abby around the corner of the building. There, in front of him, was the first Cobra gunship. It was sitting on a massive carriage

6

on the same set of tracks that had carried it through each assembly building, as it went from frames being welded together, through nine more assembly stations, until it finally had rolled out of the last hangar as a complete ship.

"I can't believe you built this in only thirty days," Nathan exclaimed as he gazed up at the gunship. "You know, it took over two years to build each scout ship back on Earth."

"I remember," Abby replied, "but we didn't have Takaran fabricator technology back then, either."

"But someone still has to assemble all the parts. And don't those parts take time to make?"

"Some of them, yes," Abby agreed. "But we started making parts long before the facility was ready. And the Tannans made huge sacrifices, retasking most of their fabricators to help build up a stockpile of components prior to the start of production. You wouldn't believe how much the population has been behind this effort. It's almost as if it's therapeutic for them."

"I'm not surprised." Nathan continued examining the gunship. "It's a bit different than I expected."

"The sides were trimmed up to be made straight, so they can attach additional weapons pods, missiles, or even KKVs to the outboard edges."

"Are those quads directly manned?" Nathan wondered, noticing the windows behind the guns.

"Yes, they are," Abby replied. "We thought about making them remotely operated from the flight deck, but that entailed considerable changes to the flight deck itself, as well as additional targeting sensors. Direct operation was simpler to implement."

"And more dangerous for the operator," Nathan commented. "Not much of a field of fire, though."

"The entire gun structure extends nearly two meters, giving both guns overlapping fields of fire above and below, as well as forward."

"And hangs the gunner's ass out as a target," Nathan argued. "One good rail gun round and he's done for."

"These ships are shielded, Nathan," Abby reminded him. "And if their shields fail everyone on board is done for. Their hulls aren't armored like the Aurora's."

"Good point." Nathan looked the gunship over one last time, from stem to stern. "Yup, she's a good looking ship, Abby." He turned to look at her again. "So, when is the launch ceremony?"

"Three days. Captain Nash wants time to double-check all the systems before the first launch."

"That's going to be a hell of a sight," Nathan declared as he looked up at the gunship again. "Yup, a good looking ship, indeed."

* * *

Vladimir stood at the railing of the fourth dock tier, clutching the railing and fighting to keep his mouth shut. Before him, the Aurora floated in the middle of the fully pressurized dry dock, deep inside the Karuzara asteroid base. It hung there, slightly above him, unmoving, held in its position only by a collection of fragile-looking mooring arms, and four boarding tunnels. All about her, long manipulator arms, their bases moving along tracks attached to the rock walls of the cavern, moved technicians and materials about the outside of her hull, placing each where they needed to be with exact precision. There were more than a thousand technicians working on his ship at the moment, a few hundred of which were working on the outside alone. Men were floating about, maneuvering from one position to the next with thruster packs. Others walked on the outside of the hull, their mag-boots keeping them from drifting away. Work platforms flew about, moving men from place to place. It was all a well choreographed dance, but it looked like chaos. He had quickly realized that it was impossible for him to keep track of everything that was being done to his ship. He simply had to trust that those in charge of each project knew what they were doing.

That was the hard part. Vladimir had never been good at letting others do the work. He had always been the type to roll up his sleeves and do it himself. Now, he was utterly helpless, being used as a 'consultant' whenever something about his ship was found to be not quite to specs, requiring an explanation from him. It wasn't that he himself was not qualified. After all, no one knew the Aurora better than he. It was just that the scope of what was being done was too large for *any* one person to manage.

They had been in dry dock for all of nine days now, and there were already more openings in the Aurora's hull than ever before. At the morning review, he counted at least fifty places where one could exit the ship directly, *without* going through an airlock...sometimes even without going through a hatch. And this was a space ship. And now, they were about to open the biggest hole of them all.

He stared up at the underside of the bow of the ship as four spidery arms, stretching out from tracks directly below him, pulled the last four hull panels away from the Aurora's underside, leaving a massive rectangular gap in her. As the panels were lowered away, Vladimir could see into the opening in the hull, revealing the technicians inside who had just disconnected the outer hull plates. Deeper inside, beyond those technicians, he could see the four, long tunnels, which had been created inside his ship by removing dozens of bulkheads, that would house the four, massive, mark five plasma torpedo cannons that would be installed sometime next week.

He glanced downward as the four manipulator arms placed the hull panels onto flatbed haulers on the deck below. The panels would be hauled away and recycled, their materials feeding one of the dozens of fabricators in the shops surrounding the dry dock. Those fabricators would then make new panels that would accommodate the new plasma torpedo cannons, as well as many other components used in the Aurora's refit.

"Not an easy thing to watch, carving up your ship like that, is it?" Marcus commented as he stepped up beside Vladimir at the railing.

"No, it is not."

"Have you had a chance to walk the hull, stem to stern?"

Vladimir looked at the Aurora's chief of the boat. "Why would I want to do that?" he wondered. "That's fourteen hundred meters."

"It's an opportunity you likely won't get again," Marcus said. "You should give it a go. But I'm warning you, zero gravity aside, it's a steep climb up the main propulsion section. And I'd steer clear of the heat exchangers as well. They're still pretty warm, even though the ship's internal heating is being pumped out to the Karuzara's exchangers."

"I think I'll pass," Vladimir replied.

"But you're her chief engineer. You of all people should want to walk her outsides."

"It would be too painful," Vladimir insisted, "seeing all the holes in her hull. I'm already having nightmares that we launch and they didn't seal the hull up properly."

"Yeah, I guess I see what you mean." Marcus patted the lieutenant commander on the back. "Maybe after they're done with the exterior modifications. Hell, you can inspect every seal, if you like. Might make you sleep better."

"I just might do that," Vladimir agreed, "*if* I make it through this refit."

Marcus chuckled. "Maybe you should have gone with the captain...taken a vacation away from the ship."

"I went down to Earth," Vladimir told him. "I didn't last two days. I couldn't stand not knowing what was going on here, even if I don't have any control over it."

"Try not to worry, sir," Marcus said, trying to ease Vladimir's concerns. "They did a pretty good job on the Celestia, didn't they? I mean, she hasn't sprung a leak yet, has she?"

"Yet," Vladimir replied, one eyebrow raised in suspicion.

* * *

After a twenty minute ride from the Lorrett spaceport, Jessica found herself standing on the front steps of a traditional Tannan home. It was modest like all the rest, built from wood and clay bricks molded from Tannan soils, and painted an off-white color. Like all the buildings of Lorrett, it was positioned so as not to interfere with the surrounding forest and geography. The Tannans had a great respect for the natural landscapes of their world, and generally went to great pains to avoid disturbing what was there before them. Especially when it came to forests. So much of Tanna was relatively bare, desolate and dry, with only scrub brush and rocks. Wherever there was flowing water on the surface of Tanna, there were forests, and where there were forests, there were Tannans.

Jessica knocked on the heavy, wooden door. Her mouth fell agape when it opened, revealing Synda and her rather sizable belly. "Oh my God," Jessica exclaimed. "Are you pregnant?"

Synda put her arms around Jessica, embracing her. "Five months," she replied as she pulled away.

"Five months?" Jessica was having a hard time hiding her disbelief. "I knew you met someone, but..."

"Yeah, I know," Synda replied, understanding her friend's surprise.

"Same guy, right?" Jessica asked as Synda led her inside.

"Same guy. His name is Terros."

"Yeah, I remember," Jessica said as she entered the living room. She looked around at the small but comfy room. "This is nice, Synda."

"It's small, but it's in a nice area, and there is an extra room for the baby."

"Beats the hell out of the camps," Jessica insisted.

"Yes, it does."

"I take it you two are serious, then."

Synda pulled a necklace out from under her blouse, dangling it in front of her for Jessica to see.

"What's that?" Jessica wondered.

"It's a wedding necklace," Synda explained, "at least that's what I call it. The Tannans have a name for it. *Welta-norbay-something...* I can't remember. Every year, you add a piece to it. After ten years, a couple of links are taken and made into wedding bands, and the rest goes on display on your living room wall. It becomes a symbol that your union has survived the test of time and will likely last forever."

"I never heard of such a thing," Jessica said as she sat down on the couch.

"Apparently it is a very important custom to the Tannans. In fact, they don't have a wedding ceremony like we do. Their big ceremony comes when you reach the ten year mark." Synda struggled to sit down next to Jessica. "We tried to invite you to the wedding, but they said you were on assignment somewhere and couldn't be reached."

"Yeah, I've only been back about a month." Jessica winced as she watched her friend struggle just to sit down. "Are you sure you're only five months? You look like you're ready to pop."

"Twins."

"Seriously?"

"Yup. Girls. And I didn't even *want* a family, remember?"

"Then why?"

"I honestly don't know," Synda admitted. "Something in me changed after I met Terros. It's like the last few pieces of the puzzle of who I really was suddenly fell into place, and it all made sense to me."

"Well then, that's great," Jessica said. "Really, that's wonderful. I'm happy for the both of you." Jessica paused to look about. "Is he home?"

"No, he's at work. He works as a translator at the gunship plant."

"Then he speaks English."

"He does now," Synda laughed. "He didn't speak it very well when I first met him, but he's a fast learner. In only six months, I've got him speaking like a native. That's how we got this house...it came with the job."

"Will he be home soon?" Jessica asked. "I'd love to meet him."

"He only left an hour ago. They work long shifts. When he comes home, he barely has time to shower and sleep before returning to work. Everyone there works hard. They are trying to produce ships as quickly as possible. Terros says that once they have thirty or forty of them built, the pace will probably slow down a bit, but I don't know."

"He's probably right. The purpose of those gunships is to defend Tanna, since the Alliance doesn't have any ships that can get all the way back to Tanna on short notice."

"But can gunships really stand up against Jung ships?"

"A handful of gunships can probably take down anything up to a battleship, and maybe even a battleship, if there are enough of them *and* they fight in packs," Jessica insisted. "Of course, they wouldn't stand a chance against a battle platform, but from what we've seen those are reserved for more densely populated systems nearer the core. I doubt you're going to see one all the way out here."

"Wouldn't it have been better to build something bigger, then?"

"And what would happen if you spent a year building a frigate, or two years building a cruiser, and while you were building it, a single Jung frigate came along? They could wipe you out with ease. At

14

least with twenty or thirty gunships, you have a chance."

"That's what Terros said."

"Sounds like a smart guy," Jessica said.

"Yeah, I think you'll like him." Synda shifted positions on the couch. "So, what brings you to Tanna?"

"What, I can't just come to visit?"

"Of course you can, but I know you better."

"Captain's orders."

"Captain Scott ordered you to visit me?"

"Not exactly. He ordered me to take a vacation. Said I was getting out of line and such. He thinks I'm suffering from post incident stress disorder, just because I mouthed off and threatened to kick a Ghatazhak's ass."

"You threatened to kick a Ghatazhak's ass?" Synda asked, her eyes widening in disbelief.

"It was only Telles. He wouldn't have done anything."

"You threatened to kick the Ghatazhak commander's ass?" Synda shook her head. "I think your captain's right."

Jessica shrugged. "Who knows, who cares. I didn't argue. The Aurora's in dry dock for a couple months anyway, and I get a chance to visit you and my brother."

"Your brother?"

"Robert. He's in charge of training the Tannan gunship crews."

"I thought he just had the same last name," Synda said. "I saw him being interviewed on a netcast the other day. I didn't realize you two were related. He looks too old to be your brother."

"He was first, I was last. Big family. He enlisted when I was just out of diapers."

"Jesus," Synda said, grabbing her belly.

Jessica's eyes widened. "What is it?"

"I'm hungry again."

"Crap, don't scare me like that," Jessica protested.

"I just ate an hour ago," Synda exclaimed. "Seems like all my time these days is spent in either the kitchen or the bathroom." Synda moved to the edge of the couch in preparation to stand. "Are you hungry? I'm getting pretty good at making traditional Tannan foods."

"You're cooking now as well?"

"Yup. Help me up."

* * *

Josh and Loki stood gazing at Falcon One, the first, fully completed Super Falcon. It was the same ship Josh had test flown a few weeks ago, but now, *all* of its modifications had been completed.

"You know something," Josh began, "I think it looks even better than before."

Loki slowly turned his head to look at his friend. "It *looks* better?"

"Yeah. You don't think so?"

"Only *you* would worry about how it looks," Loki muttered.

"Hey, it was damned embarrassing flying around in that harvester all those years..."

"Josh..."

"I mean, *nothing*, and I do mean *nothing*, is uglier than that harvester."

"Josh..."

"A flying garbage truck...that's what it looked like."

Loki looked at his crew chief. "Just ignore him."

16

"I usually do," the crew chief replied.

"Look, they closed off the air intakes underneath," Josh noticed as he moved closer to their ship.

Loki moved around the Falcon to his right, walking around the wingtip as he scanned the aft upper fuselage. "I can't believe you got four mark two's in her."

"Actually, they're more like mark two point five's," the crew chief replied. "They're mark three's cut short. Same amount of power per shot, but only about a third of the useful range."

"I thought there wasn't enough room in the old atmospheric engine compartments to hold the mark three plasma generators?" Loki commented. He looked more closely at the underside of the aft end of the ship. "You widened the fairings a bit, didn't you?"

"Yes, sir, we did."

"What about the heat?" Loki wondered. "How many shots can she fire in succession?"

"If you dial them down to mark two power levels, you can fire all you want. If you crank them up to full power, you can fire a single burst of triplets per cannon per minute. Much more than that and you'll likely overload the heat exchangers. We're working on a new heat exchanger design that would fit in the wings, but it's still in the idea phase right now."

"Jeez! This bay is huge!" Josh exclaimed from underneath the Falcon.

"With the removal of the atmospheric engines, we were able to combine both weapons bays. We're working on the different modules for that bay now. The first one will be ready for testing in a few days."

"The missile system?" Loki wondered.

"Yes, sir. Four anti-ship, eight medium-range

interceptors, or twelve air-to-surface missiles, depending on the mission. We're also making one that can carry twenty dumb bombs," the crew chief explained. "They're also making a cargo pod, passenger pod, a search and rescue pod, and a sensor pod for recon missions. Fact is, that bay is so big we can pretty much do anything with it."

"How are you going to get the pods into here?" Josh wondered as he climbed out from under the Falcon and joined them. "It's not like we can jack her up higher off the deck."

"They're building special loading elevators into the decks of the Aurora, the Celestia, and here. They'll park the pod on the platform, lower it down enough for the Falcon to drive over her, then raise it up from underneath and plug it in."

"I gotta say, I wasn't too excited about the side-by-side cockpit idea," Josh said as he moved around the nose of the ship, "but it looks pretty good."

"Would you like to take a look inside?"

"Standard module?" Loki asked, his anticipation showing.

"Standard module fully installed," the crew chief beamed.

Loki smiled then headed for the boarding ladder at the leading edge of the port wing, near the fuselage. Josh was already moving up the boarding ladder that led directly to the side of the cockpit, its gull-wing canopy doors already wide open.

"How the hell are you supposed to get into the back from here?" Josh wondered as he climbed into the pilot's seat.

"You lean the seat back and grab the handle above your head and slide back. Then swing your feet around," the crew chief explained. "It's a bit tricky in normal gravity, but during flight the cockpit is only at half-gravity, so it'll be easier."

"Why the gull-wing canopy doors?" Loki wondered.

"Not all of the cabin modules we're planning include access from the cockpit aft. So we needed a way for the flight crew to get in and out in those cases."

Loki looked at the recessed rim around the topside access hatch to the cabin module. "Is this a docking collar recession?"

"Yes, sir." Again, the crew chief beamed with pride. "You can change crews in space without depress."

"Very nice," Loki replied as he climbed down the short ladder into the aft cabin. He paused as his feet touched the deck and did a complete turn, scanning the small cabin. There was a small terminal and seat in the forward starboard corner of the cabin, just behind the copilot's seat. Along the wall behind it was a small galley area, complete with a washbasin and a food prep system. In the aft port corner, there was a rather comfortable looking seat, with plenty of room to stretch one's legs and relax. He reached down and lifted the seat, finding the toilet underneath. Above the seat was a hatch that opened into a bunk compartment. There was a similar hatch on the opposite side, and two lockers built into the aft bulkhead between them, both of which were quite deep. The lockers themselves could be pulled out, giving them access to the cabin's environmental systems located behind and underneath the two bunks.

The crew chief squatted on the wing just outside the hatch, looking inside as Loki explored. "Standard cabin, accommodations for two, for up to three weeks."

"This is going to make those long cold-coasts so much easier," Loki exclaimed.

"How soon do we get to take her up?" Josh asked from the cockpit, calling back over his shoulder.

"We were hoping you'd log some hours on her straightaway," the chief told them. "We've got seven more to overhaul and modify. The sooner you two can shake the bugs out, the less re-modifying we're going to have to do to the rest of them."

"I can already tell you one problem," Loki said. "No coffee maker."

"Open compartment fourteen, just above the basin," the chief told him.

Josh twisted in his seat to look down behind him into the cabin as Loki opened the compartment, then turned to smile at Josh. "Outstanding," Josh exclaimed. "No more cold coffee on the cold-coasts."

* * *

Nathan looked at the numbers on the home in front of him. They were the right numbers, but it was not the same house he had been to before. In fact, it was at least twice the size of the modest little residence he had visited ten months earlier. He had seen the correct street name carved into the curb, so he had to be in the correct place.

Two young men came out of the front door and walked toward him.

"Excuse me," Nathan said to the young men. "Is this where Mister Dubnyk lives?"

"You mean, Captain Dubnyk?"

"Uh, yes," Nathan replied.

"Yes, it is," the man replied, after which he and his associate continued on their way.

Nathan looked at the house, examining it more closely. "Business must be booming," he said to his Ghatazhak escort as he continued to the front door.

After knocking, the door opened, and a young woman appeared in the doorway. "Do you have an appointment, sir?" she asked, eying them both with suspicion.

"No, I'm afraid we do not," Nathan apologized. "However, I suspect that Captain Dubnyk will want to see us."

"The captain is very busy, I'm afraid..."

"Please, if you'll just let him know that Captain Scott is here, I would appreciate it greatly. We have come a long way."

"Of course," the woman acquiesced, stepping back and closing the door.

"I didn't think we would need an appointment," Nathan commented as they waited.

"I believe this residence was once two separate buildings," the Ghatazhak soldier said as he walked to the side of the porch, inspecting the front of the building. "There was once a path over there, just like the one on which we approached. It has been removed, as has the platform to which it once led."

"That would explain things," Nathan realized.

The door opened again, and the young woman reappeared. "My apologies for the delay, Captain. Please, come in."

The Ghatazhak soldier stepped forward, determined not to allow the captain to enter without first ensuring his safety.

"I'm sorry, I was instructed to only allow Captain Scott inside," the young lady said firmly.

"I am responsible for the captain's safety," the soldier insisted.

"It's all right," Nathan told his bodyguard.

"No one is ever in any danger in Captain Dubnyk's home," the young woman reassured him.

"There, you see?" Nathan said. "Everything will be fine."

"Captain, I am under strict orders…"

"I'll leave my comm-set open, alright?" The sergeant was not smiling.

The Ghatazhak sergeant touched the side of his helmet, causing his visor to drop down and his tactical display system to activate. He swept his head from side to side, scanning the interior of the building. "There are at least seven more persons in the building," he reported. "I do not detect any weapons. However, there are several locations within the structure which my systems are not able to penetrate, all of which are large enough to contain hidden weapons."

"Give me your side arm, then. Will that make you feel better?"

"Do you know how to use it?"

"I think I can figure it out," Nathan assured him.

The Ghatazhak soldier removed his belt and holster, handing it to the captain. "It will power up when it is drawn from its holster." He looked sternly at the captain. "There is no safety."

"Thanks for the warning, Sergeant," Nathan said as he strapped the weapon to his hip.

"Captain Dubnyk does not allow guests to carry weapons into his home," the young woman warned.

"I'm afraid he doesn't have much of a choice, this time," Nathan told her. "It's either I come in with a weapon, or my friend here comes in with *all* his weapons *and* his bad attitude. I'm pretty sure that

Captain Dubnyk would prefer that it was just me and one little gun."

The woman sighed in resignation. "Very well. Follow me." The young woman stepped aside, allowing Nathan to enter.

The interior of the house was also not as Nathan remembered. The last time he had visited Captain Dubnyk, his home had been small, sparsely furnished, with little in the way of decoration. It had also been poorly kept and in disarray. This time, it was the complete opposite. The interior was well decorated in traditional Tannan stylings, and it was spotlessly clean and tidy.

Nathan was led into a small sitting room just off the main entry foyer.

"If you'll please take a seat, the captain will be with you in a moment. He is just finishing up his afternoon teachings."

"Teachings? What does he teach?"

"History, religion, philosophy," she replied, "the captain is a *very* wise man. He has lived over a thousand years, you know."

"Yes, I am aware." *Most of it in suspended animation,* Nathan thought to himself as he took his seat.

"Can I get you anything?" the young woman asked. "Something to eat or drink? Some spiced tea, perhaps? It is a wonderful blend that we grow in the garden here. It goes very nicely with the tarts I made this morning."

"No thank you, I'm fine."

"Very well. It will just be a few minutes," the young woman assured him. She nodded politely and excused herself.

23

"How are you doing out there, Sergeant?" Nathan said in a near whisper over his comm-set.

"*I am fine, Captain. Further scans confirm my original assessment. This structure is actually two structures that were recently joined. There has also been considerable remodeling done to the interior in recent months.*"

"How can you tell?"

"*My sensors can detect weaknesses in the structure,*" the sergeant explained. "*Newer construction tends to be stronger, due to better methods and newer materials. There are a total of four exits. One on each face of the building. There are also many windows through which one can exit, none of which appear to have been reinforced. Should you need to exit quickly, it should not be difficult. Furthermore, the front door has only a single locking bar, which my weapon will handle with ease. I can be inside in seconds if needed.*"

"Thank you, Sergeant. I'm sure that won't be necessary. Captain Dubnyk is not a violent man."

"*I have read the files on Mister Dubnyk,*" the sergeant replied. "*The only conclusion I was able to come to was that he is intelligent, and is willing to do whatever is necessary to stay alive. Those two attributes alone make him dangerous, in spite of his advanced age. Other than that, we know alarmingly little about him, which makes him even more suspect as a threat.*"

"I'll keep that in mind," Nathan replied.

The young woman reappeared. "Captain Scott, if you will please follow me, Captain Dubnyk will see you now."

Nathan rose and followed the young woman down the corridor.

"*Captain,*" the sergeant called over the comms, "*It appears you are being led to a large room at the end of the corridor. There are seven men in the room. Six of them to your left as you enter, and one of them to your right. I believe the one to your right will be Dubnyk, as the other six persons are facing him. I still detect no weapons.*"

Nathan refrained from answering the sergeant as he continued to follow the young woman down the corridor. He was not sure if she was aware of their comm-link, and he felt no need to advertise the fact.

The young woman opened the door at the end of the corridor and stepped into the room, holding the door open for Nathan. He followed her in, and found exactly what his sergeant had described. Six men to the left, and Captain Dubnyk to his right. The room was tastefully decorated, with rich tapestries on the walls and floor. Captain Dubnyk sat in a comfortable, overstuffed chair on one side of the room, and the rest sat in more modest chairs arranged in a semi-circle facing the captain.

"Captain Scott," Mister Dubnyk greeted in earnest. He gestured to the young woman who had escorted the captain in, and she quickly moved to his side to help him rise from his chair. "I did not think I would see you again," he continued as he took a few shaky steps toward Nathan to greet him properly. He reached out to shake his guest's hand.

Nathan took the old man's hand. Mister Dubnyk's grip was weak, but his hands did not tremble as much as before. Nathan shook his hand gently. "I am happy to see that you are doing so well," Nathan greeted. "When I approached, I was positive that I had made a wrong turn somewhere."

"Ah, yes. I was fortunate to acquire the residence next door when the owner passed."

"How have you been able to afford so much in so little time?" Nathan wondered.

"Please, Captain, won't you sit?" Dubnyk said, as he gestured to one of the young men to give up his seat.

"I hope I'm not interrupting?"

"Not at all, not at all," Dubnyk insisted. "What better opportunity for my students to learn about history than to meet a man who is making it day in and day out."

"I think you are exaggerating my contributions, Mister Dubnyk."

"The good captain is too modest," Mister Dubnyk told his students.

"I would feel better if only you and Mister Dubnyk were in the room, Captain," the sergeant said over the captain's comm-set.

"I wasn't expecting an audience, I'm afraid," Nathan told Mister Dubnyk. "Perhaps we could talk in private? I promise I won't take too much of your time."

"Nonsense, Captain. I am always available for you. I have already cleared my calendar for the afternoon. I gave the order as soon as I was made aware of your arrival." Mister Dubnyk looked at his students. "Please, gentlemen, the captain and I have much to discuss. We will continue your lessons tomorrow morning, at the usual time."

Nathan nodded at the young men as they rose from their chairs and left the room. "They are all so young," he commented after the last of them had left the room.

"The young are usually the most eager to expand

their horizons. They are at the age when all the world is a mystery, and life has not yet locked them into the daily routines and responsibilities that so often hamper one's continued personal growth."

"And their parents approve of your teachings?"

"On the contrary, Captain," Mister Dubnyk said, surprised by Nathan's accusing tone, "they encourage it. I am helping to broaden their understandings of humanity through the teachings of history. Being a student of history yourself, I would expect you to understand the value of its lessons more than most."

"History can be both objective *and* subjective," Nathan pointed out.

"Ah yes, the old 'history is written by the victorious' argument. I suppose there is some truth to the matter, as well as your assertions. But that is where philosophy comes into play, is it not? We present the facts, the objective aspects of a historical event, and then we look at them subjectively as we try to understand the how and why of the events. It is in the *analysis* of those objective facts wherein the *value* of history's lessons lie." Mister Dubnyk chuckled. "If nothing else, Captain, I am keeping restless young men off the streets of Klondell and out of trouble."

Nathan smiled wryly. "Why do I feel like I'm being given a sales pitch?"

"My apologies," Mister Dubnyk replied. "I have had to defend the value of my teachings on more than one occasion. I am running a business, after all."

"And a quite lucrative one at that," Nathan replied.

"Yes, I have been fortunate in that regard. As I

said during your last visit, the Tannans love their stories, and there is so much they do not know about the past. Their own history has been nearly erased on two separate occasions...first by the bio-digital plague, and then by the Jung centuries later. There is a great void in their own cultural history that is dying to be filled. *That* is where *I* come in. In exchange, I accept whatever remuneration my customers are willing to bestow upon me. Some are even willing to pay for regular sessions, like those young men who just left."

"And how many *students* do you have?" Nathan wondered.

"A few dozen, I suspect. My assistant, Fayla—the young woman who greeted you—she keeps track of such things."

"You can even afford an assistant?"

"A sad story, one of many, I'm afraid. She lost her father. He was serving on the Jar-Keurog when it was destroyed. Her mother died when she was young. She had nowhere to go, so I took her in. She has become quite indispensable to me. Almost like a daughter, really. She takes care of me, and in exchange, I share everything I have with her."

"And the others? Are they lost souls as well?"

"A few others might fit that description, each in their own unique way, I suppose. I do have some students who regularly exchange labor for lessons. In fact, most of the remodeling of my home was accomplished by such arrangements."

"Quite the enterprise."

"It has worked out well for me here on Tanna. That is why you pop in periodically, is it not, Captain? To check on my well-being?"

"Perhaps."

"Or is it my magnetic personality that draws you back time and again?"

"Let's stick with the 'well-being' thing."

"Of course," Mister Dubnyk replied with a smile. "I trust you are in good health?"

"Indeed, at least for a man of a thousand. From what I hear, you are doing quite well for yourself as well, Captain. How many systems have you liberated now? Eight?"

"Two, actually," Nathan replied, "and I had a bit of help."

Mister Dubnyk looked confused. "I was under the impression that it was far more."

"This system, and Sol. All those that followed were liberated under the command of Admiral Dumar of the Alliance."

"But you did lead the attacks, did you not?"

"Yes, I did."

"Then it is your name that history will remember," Mister Dubnyk insisted. "People like to hear stories of those who led the battles, not those who made the decisions to send others into battle."

"I'm not sure that my history professors would agree with you."

Mister Dubnyk leaned forward in his chair. "Tell me, Captain, to whom does the child whose father was killed direct their hatred? At the general who gave the order to attack, or at the man who pointed the gun and pulled the trigger? Make no mistake, Captain, you are the one who will be remembered in the centuries that follow. Of this I am quite certain."

"As I have no control over how future generations judge my actions, I am quite content not worrying about their judgments," Nathan replied.

"A bold statement," Mister Dubnyk observed. "Some might call it disconcerting, as well."

"How so?"

"*I* know that you consider the consequences of every order you give, however, others may not. Take Kent, for example. How many millions died because of your failed attempt to remove the Jung from the Alpha Centauri B system?"

"And how many more on Earth might have died had we *not* eliminated those forces?" Nathan asked.

"That question can never be answered with any amount of certainty," Mister Dubnyk replied. "I am not condemning your actions, Captain, nor am I agreeing with them. I am merely pointing out the value of such historical analysis. Each and every one of us must make similar decisions on a daily basis. Perhaps not on such a grand scale, of course, and most likely few of us must make decisions of life and death for others in our entire lifetimes. But knowing of others who have been forced to make such decisions, and contemplating their reasons, good or bad, can help prepare us to make our own decisions in a more timely and responsible manner." Dubnyk again looked at Nathan, studying him intensely. "Or have I given you more credit than you are due?"

"How do you mean?" Nathan asked.

"When you attack Jung forces, when you destroy ships, when you take lives, when you put the lives of innocents at grave risk... *Do you consider* the possible consequences, or do you simply dismiss such potential outcomes as acceptable losses, given what you consider to be the dire nature of your own situation?"

"An interesting question," Nathan admitted. "I do consider the possible consequences, to an extent.

But as I took an oath to defend my people, and by extension the people of any world who choose to join our Alliance, I have to accept those consequences, and not allow the horror of their nature to dissuade me from meeting the responsibilities entrusted to me."

"Very well put," Mister Dubnyk congratulated, sitting back in his chair again. "Very well put, indeed. But, do you actually believe that?"

"If I did not, I would resign my position," Nathan insisted.

"Would you?"

"Yes."

Mister Dubnyk leaned his head to one side, rubbing his cheek. "I wonder. Power and authority can be quite addictive. You know as well as I that history is replete with those who violated their own ethics in order to maintain the position."

"As well as those who did not," Nathan countered. "Although history rarely remembers them with equal interest."

"Indeed, acts of great horror are far more memorable, it seems. So tell me, Captain," Mister Dubnyk continued, "how do you wish history to remember you?"

"To be honest, I would be quite content if history were to completely forget about me."

Mister Dubnyk chuckled. "There is little chance of that, Captain. For better or worse, your name will likely be known for many years to come. Perhaps not by all, but by many. Of that I am certain. The question remains, however, if you can live with their judgments?"

"As I said before, their judgments do not concern me. The only judgments that concern me are my own, of myself, as I am the only one who must live with my decisions."

"You are grossly mistaken in that regard," Mister Dubnyk argued. "Millions of us have to live with your decisions, as well as the decisions of your superiors, whether we like it or not. Your Alliance has taken it upon themselves to decide which of us lives, and which of us dies. Your Alliance believes that they have the right to dictate to the Jung where they can and cannot position their forces, and whether or not they have the right to conquer others."

"You believe the Jung are justified in what they do?" Nathan wondered in disbelief.

"Not at all. However, I strongly suspect that *they* feel they are justified, otherwise they would not have taken such actions."

"And the rest of us should just accept whatever the Jung do because they feel they are acting within their rights?"

"I believe you're missing the point, Captain," Mister Dubnyk said. "There is no absolute right and wrong, here, for right and wrong are subjective as well. What is right for you may be wrong for me, and vice versa. The Jung have committed no crimes, at least not in their eyes. Now, if they had done something that *they* felt was wrong, but did it anyway, then *that* would constitute the commission of a wrongful act, but still, not necessarily a crime. You see, there is no accepted, universal set of rules. No agreed upon system of order against which to measure the actions of each and every one of us. Because of this, there can only be chaos, at least at the universal level. Sure, we can have little pockets of order, here and there, but because of the inconsistencies in our interpretation of right and wrong, order and disorder, chaos will always exist. It is the natural state of humanity."

"There is one common human belief," Nathan began.

"Ah, yes, that which is taught by all of man's religions. 'Do unto others as you would have them do unto you.' Also one of the least followed teachings of humanity, I might add. A better lesson might be to expect that others will do unto you what they must in order to survive. That is what I have come to expect over my many years of life."

"Perhaps your opinions are somewhat jaded by your own experiences?"

"Influenced, yes, but not jaded. I have seen humanity at its best *and* at its worst, Captain. I have seen the good and the bad, and the bad usually win. And do you know why?"

"No, but I expect you are about to tell me," Nathan replied.

"Because the bad are generally the stronger. They have the strength to pull the trigger. They simply see what they want, identify what is preventing them from obtaining it, and take action. To the bad, the 'right' is that which gets them what they want, and the 'bad' is that which is in their way. This is precisely why the Jung have been so successful. It is also why you will never defeat them. You are not willing to be as strong as them."

"You mean, as evil as them."

"Evil, just as beauty, is in the eye of the beholder," Mister Dubnyk insisted. "If you do not believe that the end justifies the means, you cannot win the ultimate victory."

"I'm not sure it is that simple," Nathan argued.

"Ah, but it is, my dear Captain," Mister Dubnyk

laughed. "It truly is. The sooner you see that, the better off you will be."

* * *

"One minute to first target," Luis reported from the Celestia's tactical console. "All cannons show hot and ready to fire, parallel pattern, single shots, range will be twelve-fifty."

"Very well," Cameron replied. "Shields up, Lieutenant. I don't want any debris bouncing back at us."

"All shields at maximum," Luis confirmed. "Thirty seconds."

"Contacts?"

"Board is clear," Ensign Kono replied.

"Comms, broadcast a warning, all directions, all frequencies," Cameron ordered.

"Aye, sir," Ensign Souza replied.

"Weapons free, Lieutenant. Fire when ready."

"Weapons free, aye. Fifteen seconds."

Cameron looked down at the new, clear touchscreen to her right and tapped the controls. She glanced over at the large, clear, display screen to the right of her helmsman, which was also new. The view from the starboard cameras came up on the screen, showing a rather large asteroid passing to starboard about twelve hundred meters away. She tapped another button on her touch screen and the view on the right screen swapped with the forward cameras currently displayed on the main view screen, bringing the starboard camera view to the main screen that wrapped around the front half of the bridge.

"Five seconds," Luis reported.

Cameron watched and waited, her eyes, just like everyone else's on the bridge, glued to the main view screen and the image of the asteroid as it passed by at a slow speed.

"Firing."

On the right side of the main view screen, balls of red-orange plasma streaked away from the newly installed broadside cannons at the aft end of the Celestia. Each of the eight cannons on the starboard side fired at a rate of one shot per second, with each pair of cannons alternating their fire. The result was waves of quadruple shots of plasma energy that tore into the side of the asteroid, blasting deep into its rocky surface and sending debris blasting out into space in all directions. The barrage continued for several seconds, until finally the asteroid—which although larger than the Celestia was still small by comparison to most asteroids in the Ross 154 system—came completely apart.

"Holy crap," Luis exclaimed. "Uh, target is definitely destroyed, sir."

"Heat levels?"

"Nowhere near the maximum safe operating temps," Luis replied. "We could've kept that fire rate up for at least a full minute, maybe longer." He looked down at his display again. "Twenty seconds to port target."

Cameron tapped her touchscreen again, calling up the port camera onto the main view screen. "Shields?"

"Still at full strength," Luis replied.

"Let's try triplets on the port cannons," Cameron suggested. "Sustained max fire rate. Let's see how their heat exchangers handle the increased load."

"Triplets on all eight port cannons, max sustained rate, aye," Luis replied. "Five seconds to target."

Again, all eyes were focused on the main view screen.

"Firing."

Triple shots of plasma energy began streaking away from the Celestia's port cannons, drawing an intense red streak from the left side of the main view screen to center, disappearing into a red fireball as they struck the surface of the second asteroid. More triple shots followed, a trio every second, for nearly thirty seconds, until finally, the second, larger target asteroid also came apart, sending large chunks of debris in all directions, including a few that slammed into the Celestia's port shields. The ship rocked slightly from the impacts, jostling the crew in their seats just enough to let them know of the impacts.

"Multiple impacts, port shields, upper and lower, stern pairs," Luis reported. "Shield strength holding."

"Damage reports?" Cameron wondered.

"Damage control reports no damage," Ensign Souza replied.

"Ensign Kono?" Cameron called as she rotated her chair to port.

"Second target is completely destroyed, sir."

Cameron continued rotating to her left to look at her tactical officer behind her, a satisfied look on her face. "What do you think, Lieutenant?"

"I think we're going to rip open a few Jung ships, sir," Luis replied with a grin.

* * *

Nathan stood in the Mirai's main salon, staring out the large windows on the starboard side, as the ship passed under the Cetian orbital shipyards. The facility was similar in design to the orbital assembly platform that had been used to build both the Aurora and the Celestia, as well as the six Defender-class ships that had come before them. However, the Cetian shipyards were more than twice the size of the Earth's old facility, with four assembly bays, each of which was twice the size of the OAP's.

Another difference was the bays themselves. The Earth's facility used trusses to form the assembly bays, with all the shops and operational facilities in the main pressurized structure located between the two bays. The bays of the Cetian shipyards were solid on either side, with open truss frameworks on the top and bottom of the bays. Each bay had their own shops, their own flight operations areas, their own command and control, and their own housing areas. In fact, each bay, if detached from the others, could continue to operate on its own.

"The Jung never do anything small, do they," Jessica commented as she entered the compartment and joined Nathan as he continued staring out the overhead windows at the shipyards slowly moving over them.

"Nope, they sure don't."

"I heard that the Jung had been planning on adding another four bays to this facility," Jessica added. "They've already begun component production for a fifth bay on Sorenson. Of course, that's stopped for now."

"Probably best to concentrate resources on what they've already got," Nathan muttered as he watched the last bay slide out of view. He turned to look at Jessica. "Those bays are so big, you could probably build two Explorer-class ships in there at the same time."

"That's what they did with the frigates," Jessica

said. "Gerard told me that the two that are in there now were the last of a batch of eight that were under construction."

"Where did the other six go?" Nathan wondered.

Jessica moved to the nearest couch and made herself comfortable in her usual unceremonious style. "As far as we know, all six of them were still in the system when we first attacked, so we probably destroyed them. He also said that although the Cetian shipyards are large enough to service battleships, their primary focus *was* to build frigates. In fact, all of the support facilities and component manufacturing plants on Sorenson are designed to build frigates as well. They could retool to build just about anything, I suppose."

"Dumar wants to keep them building frigates, but with Takaran weapons and shields, and our jump drives."

"I'd have to agree," Jessica replied. "The Cetians can crank a frigate out in a single year. Can you imagine? Eight frigates, all with plasma cannons, shields, and jump drives, in only a year?"

"That's if we can keep the Jung from coming back and wiping the shipyards out before then," Nathan reminded her. "That's got to be at the top of their agenda."

"Well, since there currently aren't any Jung forces within six months of here, if we keep the detection patrols going, the odds are in our favor," Jessica said. "Besides, if the Jung do come back to Tau Ceti, they'll come back in force, and likely glass everything. In that case, losing the shipyards will be the least of our worries."

"Good point," Nathan conceded as he sat down. "So, why are we here, again?"

"I'm meeting with Telles and a rep from the new Cetian security forces to conduct a security review of the facility."

"You and Telles are okay?"

"Uh, yeah," Jessica replied, giving him a strange look. "Why wouldn't we be?"

"Well, you did get in his face...twice. You even threatened bodily harm...on a superior officer, I might add."

"I was just trying to make a point."

"Risky way to make a point," Nathan said. "You didn't really think you could take Telles, did you?"

"Of course not," Jessica admitted. "I may be crazy, but I'm not stupid. It was all for emphasis."

"Like how you tried to 'emphasize' your point on the bridge that day?"

"Exactly."

"Some might call it insubordination, you know."

"Some, but not you."

"Dumar asked if I wanted to take corrective action," Nathan told her, "offered to back me if I did."

Jessica sat up straighter, one eyebrow going up. "And?"

"I told him that you'd been through a lot recently..."

"I don't have post-incident stress dis..." Jessica protested.

"I never said you did," Nathan replied, cutting her off. "I just said I thought you deserved a little leeway, that's all. He *did* insist that I speak to you about it, though."

"What the hell?"

"Look, Jess, we've got a lot of new volunteers coming in, most of which have zero military training.

We have to set an example for them. A *good* example, not mouthing off and picking fights."

"I'm fine," Jessica insisted.

"I know you are...one friend to another. But as your CO, I have to tell you to knock the shit off, or else."

"Or else, what?"

"Or else I'll make you eat molo at every meal," Nathan replied, a smile creeping onto his face.

Jessica laughed. "In that case, I'll try to straighten up and fly right...sir."

"*Attention, all hands. Prepare for docking,*" the copilot's voice called over the ships intercoms.

"Gotta say, I rather like this luxury shuttle," Jessica commented as she leaned back on the couch again. "Too bad she's got a jump drive. Leaves you no time to enjoy the amenities. You should ask the admiral if Alliance captains are going to get their own personal luxury shuttles."

"I did," Nathan replied. "He laughed."

"How did your visit with Dubnyk go?" Jessica asked.

"Fine, I guess. It was weird, though. He's doing a lot better than I would have thought. He's expanded and upgraded his residence, and has a lot of regular 'students' now."

"'Students?'"

"Yeah, I thought it was a strange choice of words as well," Nathan said. "Especially when you see how they hang on his every word."

"What can he possibly be teaching them?"

"History, philosophy, that kind of thing," Nathan explained. "Best I can tell, they just sit around and speculate on the causes and effects of events in the past. Dubnyk makes like it's some kind of deep intellectual exercise, one that helps young minds grow and become more enlightened. I think it's just a way for him to keep them coming back for more, so as to keep his accounts full."

"Whatever works for him, I suppose," Jessica said. "Personally, I don't know why you keep going back to see him."

"I don't know," Nathan replied. "I suppose I feel like I have to check up on him from time to time, like I'm responsible for his welfare, or something."

The ship shuddered slightly as it made contact with one of the Cetian shipyard's many docking arms.

"Well, you're not, you know," Jessica told him. "You rescued him from certain death. That's enough. Your responsibility for him ended once you put him off the ship."

"*Attention, all hands. We have hard dock,*" the copilot's voice announced over the intercoms.

Jessica rose from her seat. "Shall we go and take a look around?"

"I don't know," Nathan replied. "Are you going to be on your best behavior, or are you going to challenge Telles to a duel at twenty paces?"

CHAPTER TWO

"How was your tour?" Cameron asked as she sat down next to Nathan at the conference table in one of the Karuzara's briefing rooms.

"Interesting," Nathan replied. "The Jung sure know how to build a shipyard, that's for sure."

"The place was enormous," Jessica added from Nathan's other side. "Security is going to be a breeze, though. They've got cameras and sensors everywhere. You can't get within a hundred kilometers without them knowing, and every point of entry is remotely monitored and controlled. The place even has its own point-defense system. Not big enough to defend against a full-scale attack, but more than enough to defend against an unauthorized boarding attempt. My biggest concern is the workers. Most of them are registering as dirty on Doc Galloway's Jung-bug detector, although very few have enough nanites in them for the Jung to turn them into saboteurs. They've tagged those who do with tracking chips and refused them entry for the time being, until they come up with a way to remove the nanites that doesn't cause excruciating pain. Unfortunately, if they find too many with high nanite counts, it's going to cut into their workforce and slow things down."

"Any word on how long that will take?" Cameron asked.

"Nope. All I know is that they are working on it," Jessica replied. "I just hope they come up with something soon, because we're finding a few among our people as well, especially among the newest volunteers from Earth."

"If the Jung are not close enough to link to any person's nanites, then those carriers aren't a threat, are they?" Nathan suggested.

"Theoretically, no, but do you want to bet the ship on that assumption? For all we know, there could be Jung spies all over the place, each of them with their own personal bug-control device."

"Could we block their signals somehow?" Cameron wondered.

Jessica shook her head. "Galloway says that we can jam the communications between the nanites within the host body, which would isolate them, but she doesn't know if that will have any negative effects on the host, since the nanites *are* acting to help maintain the host's health to some extent. She just isn't sure as to *what* extent. She really needs to figure out how to reprogram them so that *we* control them instead of the Jung. Then we can give them orders to vacate as we replace them with Corinairan nanites."

Admiral Dumar entered the briefing room, followed by the Karuzara's station manager, Mister Bryant, along with three other men whom Nathan did not recognize.

"Attention on deck," the guard ordered. Everyone in the room immediately rose to their feet and came to attention.

As the admiral and his entourage moved to the head of the table, two more people entered the room. President Scott and his daughter, Miri.

Nathan remained at attention, though he was surprised to see them. He had visited them both just over a week ago, and neither had mentioned that they would be traveling to the Karuzara. His sister had mentioned, however, that she had taken over the role as their father's personal assistant, since his former assistant had a significant level of Jung nanites in his system. It was a scenario that had been occurring all over the Earth, as well as on Alliance vessels and stations. In fact, the more Jung nanite detectors that were built and distributed, the more they discovered Terrans infected with nanites.

Admiral Dumar stood at the head of the table until President Scott and his assistant reached their seats at the opposite end. "As you were," he finally ordered, taking his seat. "Let it be noted that Captains Poc and Nash are unable to attend, due to the demands of their current assignments." The admiral looked at the faces of everyone sitting around the conference table, then turned to the man sitting to his left. "Before we begin, I'd like to welcome Mister Aberdin. He is the director of operations for the Cetian orbital shipyards."

"Thank you, Admiral," Mister Aberdin replied, his Cetian accent barely noticeable.

The admiral turned his attention back to the rest of the people at the table. "This meeting has been called to discuss the current state of the Alliance forces in the Sol sector, and to consider our plans going forward. I have asked President Scott to attend this meeting, as he is the current leader of the Coalition of Nations on Earth. Before we begin our discussions, I shall ask each of you as to the status of your departments." Admiral Dumar turned again to Mister Aberdin. "Mister Aberdin?"

"The Cetian orbital shipyards are back in full operation once again. We have had to restrict many of our technicians and specialists from returning to work, due to the high concentrations of Jung nanites in their bloodstreams. However, since we are only operating three of our four assembly bays, we are still able to meet the minimum staffing levels for those three bays. Unfortunately, due to the number of modifications that we are being asked to perform on the frigates as well as the battleship, work is progressing at a reduced pace on the two frigates that have yet to be completed. As it provides the best possible defense for the Tau Ceti system, we have been concentrating our efforts on repairing and modifying the captured Jung battleship, per your request."

"How long until the frigates can be completed at your current staffing levels?" Admiral Dumar wondered.

"At current staffing levels, approximately six to seven months," Mister Aberdin replied. "At full staffing levels, possibly as little as four months."

"Can replacements be trained using Cetians with lower nanite concentrations?" the admiral asked.

"Building ships in space requires highly trained technicians. It takes many months," Mister Aberdin explained.

"Hopefully, we will have an efficient way to remove the Jung nanites long before then," the admiral commented before turning to the next person. "Captain Taylor?"

"The testing of our new broadside cannons yesterday went quite well," Cameron began. "We still have a lot of work to do on our inner decks, including the new fighter launch operations deck, the conversion of the old fighter launch tubes into their new configuration, and the installation of the additional elevator systems between the main flight deck and the new hangar deck below. We are also preparing to install the secondary jump field generators and energy banks, once they are made available to us. However, all our weapons systems are fully functional, as well as our shields, and all flight systems. We are combat ready, sir."

"How long until the remainder of your internal modifications are completed?" the admiral asked.

"Latest progress reports estimate thirty days," Cameron replied.

"Captain Scott?" the admiral turned his attention toward Nathan.

Nathan leaned forward in his seat, placing his arms on the table. "The Aurora is currently in dry dock. Her nose has been opened, and installation of our mark five plasma torpedo cannons has begun. Repairs to the outer hull are nearly completed, and the installation of sixteen mark one plasma turrets on the underside of the hull has also begun. Reports from the dry dock manager and Lieutenant Commander Kamenetskiy indicate that everything is progressing according to plan, and that we should be ready to leave dry dock on schedule in fifty-five days. After that, another thirty days until all internal modifications have been completed, during which time the Aurora will, of course, continue to be combat ready."

Nathan leaned back in his seat as Jessica moved forward slightly, expecting to be called next. However, the admiral instead addressed Captain Roselle who sat just beyond Mister Bryant to the admiral's right.

"Captain Roselle, how goes the work on the Jar-Benakh?"

"We started installing the antimatter cores

recovered from the engagement with the Eridani forces this morning. Those should all be online in about four days, at which time we will be back to full operating power," Captain Roselle reported. "Repairs of the decks damaged by Scout Three's escape jump and the subsequent Ghatazhak boarding will be completed tomorrow, after which we'll start repairs on the outer hull in that area. Also, we're starting the process of converting all the controls and displays on board from Jung into English. Most of the control consoles are touch screen and are easily reconfigurable. An operator will be able to choose either language, in fact. Anything that is hard-labeled will get secondary labels in English. As far as our combat readiness, we can fight as we are, but we'd be hard pressed to do anything other than basic maneuvers and firing our weapons. We simply don't have the crew. When we begin switching out our big rail guns for big plasma cannons next week, we will do so one at a time, as requested, so that we will be able to respond to defend the Tau Ceti system if need be."

"How long until you have more adequate staffing?" the admiral asked.

"Well, we have the same problem as Mister Aberdin," Captain Roselle explained. "A lot of the qualified Cetians volunteering for service have unusually high concentrations of Jung nanites, so we have to turn them away. It'll be a lot easier once we find a way to remove those little bastards. Regardless, I expect we'll have at least one full shift manned and trained by the time we are ready to leave the shipyards, so, as long as you don't send us on any long-duration missions, we should be okay."

"Admiral," Mister Aberdin interrupted, "if I

may, once the Jar-Benakh is completed, many of the technicians currently working on her might be available to serve as crew, at least until such time as additional crew can be secured."

"We'll keep that in mind, thank you," Admiral Dumar replied, as his gaze shifted to the next man after Roselle. "Ensign Tillardi?"

"We managed to correct the code that caused the Aurora's jump KKVs to miss their target. It wasn't so much an error as it was a couple of unnecessary subroutines designed to double-check course and speed prior to committing to the final jump to the engagement point. The additional code caused just enough of a delay so as to put the weapons far to the edge of the impact envelope. When the battleship dropped out of FTL and initiated a turn toward the incoming weapons, the weapons missed. The closest one missed by only a few meters at the most. However, the code has been altered, and subsequent tests simulating the exact same conditions have resulted in strikes in every simulation run. We did manage to receive confirmation that all four weapons self-destructed as designed, once they had determined that they missed their targets. It took a while to pick up their signals, but we eventually found them. Future versions will release a marker buoy just before detonation that will not only record the weapon's destruction for verification purposes, but will also transmit a signal to enable us to retrieve verification more quickly."

"Good idea, Ensign," the admiral agreed. "I have to say, that was possibly the longest ten days of my life."

"All of ours, sir," Tilly agreed.

"Then you are ready to begin production?"

"Yes, sir. Once the assembly line is up and running, we should be able to push each conversion through in ten days, with two days at each station. So ten days after production begins, we will be rolling jump KKVs out the door at a rate of one every other day."

"And how soon will the production facility be ready?" Dumar asked President Scott.

"Barring any problems or delays, it should be ready to begin production in just under two weeks."

"Very well." The admiral turned back to Ensign Tillardi. "Good work, Ensign. What about the jump missile project?"

"That one is a bit trickier," Ensign Tillardi said. "The Jung missiles are smaller than ours, so there is less room for the jump drive. Our plan is to reduce the size of the propellant tank enough to house the mini-jump drive and energy storage. However, because of the space limitations, we can only fit a single energy cell. Unfortunately, they will only have a jump range of about three million kilometers. That means the attacking ship will have about ten seconds after jumping in to get those missiles locked on target, launched, and jumping toward their target, before the target detects the attacking ship's presence and goes to general quarters and raises her shields."

"Will shields stop those missiles?" Cameron asked.

"A few of them, even the nukes, yes. The battleships, definitely. It would take at least eight simultaneous nukes hitting the same shield segment at once to bring one of their shields down. Even more for a battle platform. A lot more."

"What if you reduce the propellant storage even more?" the admiral asked.

"There's barely enough left over to make final course corrections between arrival and impact as it is," Tilly explained. "The Jung missiles are smaller because a lot of their acceleration is provided by their launchers. They only burn for about fifteen seconds after launch. The remaining propellant is used for course corrections."

"Can you strap the energy cells on the outside of the missiles?" Nathan wondered.

"Yes, but then we'd have to completely revamp the launchers, as they're made to launch the missiles as designed. And we were planning on pulling stock launchers to outfit the Aurora and the Celestia. Two from the Jar-Benakh and one from each frigate."

"Can they spare them?" Cameron asked.

"We've got eight of them," Captain Roselle said. "I think we can spare a couple, especially if the impact percentage will be higher. We won't need to fire as many at a time."

Admiral Dumar sighed impatiently. "Is this a viable concept or not, Ensign?"

"Yes, sir, I believe it is."

"How soon will you know?"

"We're using components left over from the jump KKV prototypes, so it shouldn't take us more than a couple of weeks to get the prototypes ready for testing. Three weeks at the most."

"I prefer the least," Dumar replied flatly, one eyebrow raised.

"Yes, sir."

"Miss Ta'Akar?" the admiral said, looking to Deliza next, seated next to Ensign Tillardi.

"The final modifications to Falcon One have been

completed, and yesterday's initial test flights were a success. We did uncover some minor modifications that need to be made, but nothing that will put us behind schedule. We'll be doing more test flights over the next few days, but in the meantime, we will be proceeding with the modifications of the remaining Falcons. We believe that we will be able to get a total of eight Super Falcons operational. The last two will require the acquisition of additional engines. Captain Navarro has his people working on that back in the Pentaurus cluster."

"Perhaps he can find some more on Palee?" Dumar suggested.

Deliza shook her head. "Doubtful, between your first buying spree and the follow-up ones my father's people made, Palee has been picked clean. We'll probably have to head further out."

"I'm sure Navarro will find something," Admiral Dumar said. "What about the Super Eagle program?"

"The first prototype should be ready in a little over a week."

Admiral Dumar looked at President Scott, silently requesting an answer.

"The Eagle plant will be operational in three weeks," the president said.

Deliza looked at President Scott, then at Admiral Dumar at the opposite end of the table, her eyes wide with shock. "Admiral, we haven't finished the computer simulations yet."

"It takes time to build airframes from the ground up," Admiral Dumar explained patiently.

"That's my point," Deliza exclaimed. "Maybe we should wait until we've flown the prototype before we start setting up for production. What if we have to make a major change in the airframe?"

"The plant already existed, as did the dies and molds for the Eagle's hull and control surfaces," Admiral Dumar told her. "If you are unable to make the Super Eagle concept work, we will just build regular Eagles."

"But what if I *can* make it work, but I need to modify the airframe to do so?" Deliza wondered.

"It would be better if that were not the case," Admiral Dumar admitted.

Deliza's head went down slightly. "No pressure," she mumbled to herself.

"Doctor Sorenson, how are things going with the Cobra project on Tanna?" Admiral Dumar asked next.

"The first Cobra gunship rolled out yesterday. It's undergoing a rigorous preflight right now, and will launch on schedule the day after tomorrow. Captain Nash will spend a few days in flight trials, and then it will go into service as a trainer for the Tannan Cobra crews. We should see a new gunship rolling out every five days, and entering service five days later."

"You're producing a new gunship every five days?" Jessica exclaimed in disbelief.

"Actually, it takes about a month to assemble one. Each ship spends three days in a station, and there are ten stations overall. The Tannans have really dug in hard on this project. The gunships are a symbol of pride for them. They finally feel like they are standing up against the Jung. They work day and night. People who aren't qualified to work the line help out by providing food for the workers, or by helping take care of their families while they are busy working. It's an amazing thing to watch."

"Then everything is on schedule?" the admiral asked.

"Yes, sir. The first twelve gunships will be in service, fully crewed, within two months. In addition, the docking facilities on the asteroid base will be ready in another week. They'll be able to dock at least twenty gunships there by the time the first twelve are ready."

"Very well," Admiral Dumar replied. He took a moment to reflect before continuing. "So, it looks like we're finally starting to get some significant forces going here. Which begs the next question... What are we going to do with them?"

"I believe that is why I was asked to attend this meeting," President Scott said. "Some of you may have seen the news report of Admiral Galiardi's release from the rehabilitation facility. He was somewhat vocal as to his opposition of the Alliance's efforts to clear a twenty light year sphere around Sol of Jung forces. He was also opposed to taking on more members into this Alliance."

"Then he's really not going to like what I'm proposing we do next," Admiral Dumar mused.

"Which is?" the president wondered.

"I want to extend that Jung-free zone out to thirty light years."

The room went silent, as all eyes turned toward the admiral.

"It's not that I am opposed to the idea," President Scott began. "However, there may be others who are... Others with considerable influence."

"Such as Galiardi," the admiral said.

"And others... Others who will listen to the admiral."

"You're talking about eleven more worlds,"

Jessica said, her eyes coming up from her data pad on the table. "Every one of which has a battle group, and every one of which is already aware of the threat the Alliance represents, at least to some degree. So, they're all going to be on alert status."

"That makes it a bit more of a challenge," Nathan muttered.

"Perhaps," Admiral Dumar admitted, "then again, perhaps not. We do have more ships, and we do have better weapons than before, as well as shields. If we can crank out enough JKKVs, we should be able to clear all eleven of those Jung-held systems within four months."

"The Celestia won't be fully operational for another month," Cameron reminded the admiral. "The Jar-Benakh and the Aurora for at least two. The frigates more like six. Not to mention the training of their crews."

"We'll have enough KKVs to strike the first system by the time the Celestia is fully operational," Admiral Dumar said. "You'll also have four Super Falcons and at least as many Cobra gunships, either of which could probably deal with the frigates on their own. Same as before. Strike the battle platform and battleship with JKKVs, then go in and clean up the rest."

"It's not the same as before, Admiral," Cameron disagreed. "Those ships aren't going to be cruising lazily along as if nothing is wrong. They're going to be randomly changing course and speed, and they're going to have all their shields at full strength, every minute of every day."

"None of which matters, as long as at least a few jump KKVs hit them," the admiral replied.

"And if they don't?"

"Then you abort the attack. Since they are already on alert, you've lost nothing by the attempt, except a few JKKVs."

"And then what?" President Scott wondered. "After you extend the Jung-free zone out to thirty light years, what next? Forty? Fifty?"

"If need be, yes," Admiral Dumar replied.

"The Jung will not sit idly by while you destroy their ships, one battle group at a time," Commander Telles said. "Nor will they increase their defenses, or double up the number of ships in each group. Instead, they will assemble a vast fleet and send it toward Earth, with the intention of destroying it once and for all."

"And what would you suggest, Commander?" President Scott wondered.

"You must strike them in the heart. You must strike their homeworld."

"You're not suggesting that we glass the Jung homeworld?" the president wondered.

"Not at all," Commander Telles replied, "as I know none of you would be willing to resort to such measures. Besides, it would likely escalate the conflict considerably. However, you *could* attack their fleet. Destroying a substantial portion of the Jung homeworld's defenses, and with only a handful of ships, would send a strong message to the Jung. If their leaders are subject to the same kind of public pressures as most world governments, they may rethink their plans of conquest."

"There's only one problem with that plan," Jessica said. "We still don't know where the Jung homeworld is located."

"Then you must find it," Commander Telles insisted. "In the meantime, the admiral's plan to expand the Jung-free zone is sound, as it increases the amount of time that you have available to increase your forces."

"Some will side with Galiardi," President Scott warned. "They'll argue that we are provoking the Jung, forcing an escalation in the conflict."

"It is only a matter of time before the Jung either capture a jump drive, obtain usable scans of one, or simply develop one of their own," Commander Telles pointed out. "To believe otherwise would be foolish."

"Recent events would support the commander's assertions," Admiral Dumar agreed. "If the Jung do develop a jump drive, it will take them several years to install working prototypes in even a few ships. Removing Jung assets from nearby systems, and perhaps even the entire Sol sector, will not stop them from coming. However, it may give them cause to reconsider their plans. We can build weapons, we can build ships, and we can train crews. But not without time. The only way to acquire that time is to continue expanding the Jung-free zone as much as possible."

"We have already killed hundreds of thousands of Jung troops and ship crews," President Scott said. "When I consider that fact, I start to wonder if Galiardi isn't right."

"He probably is," Commander Telles replied. "But that is not the point. The fact is that the Jung have already killed millions of your people. Not just ship crews and troops, but civilians. Innocent men, women, and children, all of whom were not a threat to the Jung. The *point* is that the only thing the Jung respect is strength. You must show them your resolve. You must make them aware, beyond a shadow of a doubt, that continuing their campaign will exact an enormous cost on their society, one that they may not be able to bear. *That* is how you will dissuade the Jung from pressing their attacks."

President Scott took a deep breath, letting it out in a long, slow sigh. "Continue preparations for your plans to extend the Jung-free zone further, Admiral," he finally said. "I will convince the other leaders of Earth, as well as the other member worlds of the Alliance, to support your plan. It will not be easy, but I will do my best to get their support."

Nathan couldn't help but remember Captain Dubnyk's words. *A war is what you have started, and a war is what you shall have to fight.*

* * *

"*One minute to the summit,*" the controller's voice called over the comms.

"Copy that," the copilot replied. He glanced to his left at Captain Nash. "All checklists are complete, sir. The ship is ready for launch."

Captain Nash sighed. "Hell of a way to launch a ship...pushing it up a hill and then letting it roll down the other side. Reminds me of the roller coasters I used to ride when I was a kid."

"Roller coaster?" the Tannan copilot echoed, unfamiliar with the term.

"Little trains that rolled really fast around a track full of loops and twists and turns."

"Interesting. Was it an enjoyable experience?"

"Scared the hell out of me, every single time."

"*Twenty seconds to summit.*"

"Launch jump is plotted and ready," the copilot reported. "Jump drive is fully charged, and all jump systems show green. All engines are online and ready to fire."

"Control, Cobra One," Captain Nash called over the comms. "We are go for launch."

Nathan stood on the dignitary's viewing stand at the Cobra gunship compound on Tanna. Before him were the hundreds of Tannan and Terran technicians who had built Cobra One, each of them watching with bated breath. Behind him, thousands more gathered to watch the launch of the first gunship that would be used to protect their world.

Nathan looked to his right at Jessica, Cameron, and Vladimir. It was rare for all four of them to meet away from their ships. They had been through so much together over the last five hundred and twenty-three days, more than any of them could have possibly imagined upon graduation from the EDF Academy nearly two years ago.

Nathan looked to his left, at Admiral Dumar, Commander Telles, and President Scott. He had been through nearly as much with each of them. In fact, the people standing beside him at the moment were among the ones he trusted most. It seemed fitting that they were gathered here, to witness what was surely the result of all that they had fought and struggled for...together.

His focus joined that of his friends, on the distant gunship as it reached the top of the long hill that it had spent the last hour climbing.

"What happens if it doesn't jump?" Jessica whispered, leaning in closer to Nathan as she spoke.

"It will jump."

"But what happens if it doesn't?"

"Nothing. It just rolls down the other side of the launch hill," Nathan assured her. "Then it spends the rest of the day making its way back here to figure out what went wrong."

"Good to know," Jessica said.

"Don't worry, it will jump."

The gunship paused at the summit for a moment, then began slowly rolling down the long grade on the other side. It quickly picked up speed, continuing to accelerate until it reached the bottom of the hill and rolled out across the level ground. Seconds later, it reached the small hill at the other end of the grade, causing it to angle upward toward the distant sky. It slowed as it started upward, to the point that Nathan was unsure if it would even reach the top of the launch ramp. As it crested the next summit, the gunship became enveloped in blue-white light. In a split second, the light turned into a brilliant blue-tinged flash, then the gunship disappeared. The carriage that had carried the first gunship through all ten assembly bays, and then finally to its ultimate launch point, was left behind to roll down the opposite side, its mooring arms cleanly severed by the gunship's jump fields.

Nathan instinctively looked skyward along the perceived track of the departing gunship, as if he expected to see another distant flash indicating that the ship had safely reached orbit. But there was nothing in sight.

The rest of the crowd—dignitaries, technicians, and spectators alike—held their breath, as they waited for confirmation. Finally, after a few agonizingly long seconds, their confirmation came.

"*Control, Cobra One,*" Captain Nash's voice called triumphantly over the loudspeakers. "*Jump complete. We have a good burn on the mains, and we'll be settling into stable orbit in three minutes, thirty seconds."*

The crowd erupted into cheers.

Captain Nash smiled from ear to ear as he reached out to shake his copilot's hand. "Nice work, Rano."

"Was it as scary as a ride on your roller coasters, Captain?" his copilot wondered.

"Ten times worse, my friend. Ten times worse."

* * *

"Whoa," Josh said as he entered hangar bay zero deep in the Karuzara asteroid base. He turned to look at Deliza and Loki. "Okay, that is hands down the coolest ship I have ever seen." He turned and continued toward the prototype Super Eagle. "You changed it a little, didn't you?"

"Trimmed the wing roots back and thickened them up a bit to make more room for the upgraded maneuvering thrusters," Deliza explained.

"The tail is different, too."

"Increased the forward angle to reduce drag. Since you'll be jumping down from orbit instead of letting atmospheric friction slow you down, we needed to increase the slope so the tail didn't get torn off when you come out of the jump."

"They also blended the wing and the stabilizer," Loki pointed out.

Josh moved around the port wing root and around the back, looking over the tail. "You widened the space between the stabilizers as well."

"The new engines have a greater range of thrust vectoring, so we had to in order to give you more maneuverability."

"How's that going to affect her pitch response?" Josh wondered.

"Considerably reduced at lower speeds, but the flight computers will compensate, so you won't be able to tell."

"I will if the flight computers fail," Josh said.

"Not likely, as there are two backups. Besides, it's worth it to give you better turn rates, especially in space."

"Inertial dampeners?"

"Of course," Deliza replied.

"But they are not fully compensating," Loki warned.

"Why?"

"Uses too much power, and too much room."

"How much?" Josh asked, a suspicious look on his face.

"They auto-adjust," Deliza replied. "The greater the force, the more they compensate. You will feel it, but you'll never pull more than a few Gs...at least under normal flight parameters."

"Princess, there's nothing *normal* about the way I fly things," Josh reminded her. "You should know that by now."

Deliza sighed. "The inertial dampening systems will protect you up to about fifty Gs. At fifty Gs, you'll feel five. Every G above fifty will be directly added to what you feel, so fifty-one Gs will feel like six Gs, fifty-two will feel like seven, and so on. But the Super Eagle's max acceleration is only thirty-two Gs, at which point you will feel about three Gs, so you should be fine."

"Weapons?" Josh asked as he moved around the far side of the Super Eagle.

"Half-length mark two plasma cannons, one on each side, where the air intakes used to be. Effective full power range of five kilometers. They can also be angled down twenty degrees so that you can execute ground attacks while flying level. When operating in the atmosphere, you can fire at a rate of five shots per second, for as long as you want, since they are being air-cooled. In space, however, that fire rate is limited to no more than thirty seconds, after which you need to wait another thirty seconds for the plasma generators to cool down. You can also set them to fire once per second, and alternate between the cannons. That way, you can maintain fire for several minutes."

"We can't put more heat exchangers somewhere?" Josh asked.

"There's no place to put them."

Josh turned to look at Deliza and Loki as he climbed up the boarding ladder. "I guess the Eagle pilots are going to have to learn to shoot like a Ghatazhak."

At the top of the ladder, Josh paused to look inside the cockpit. "Are you sure this thing is ready to fly?"

"That's all just temporary," Deliza replied defensively. "We still haven't settled on the final cockpit layout. That's one of the things we need your input on, after you fly her."

"Just as long as none of the controls fall off in my lap while I'm flying her," Josh muttered as he climbed into the Super Eagle's cockpit.

The crew chief climbed up the ladder and made sure that Josh was securely fastened into his flight seat. "You're good to go, Ensign. I checked her out myself," he assured Josh as he handed him his helmet.

"It's a little snug in here," Josh commented.

"That's because you're wearing a pressure suit," the crew chief replied.

"Of course I'm wearing a pressure suit."

"This bird wasn't designed to be flown with a pressure suit."

"Then why am I wearing one?" Josh wondered.

"Because it's a prototype, and it's her first flight," the crew chief explained. "And because there is no ejection system yet," he added as he pushed Josh's visor down, sealing him inside his suit. He gave him a thumbs-up sign and then climbed down.

"Hey, Princess, you might have told me there was no ejection system in this bird," Josh called over the comms.

"*Don't worry, there will be one in the final cockpit design,*" Deliza assured him. "*In fact, the entire cockpit will eject from the airframe and act as a lifeboat.*"

"I'd rather wear a pressure suit."

"*Sorry, the cockpit isn't as roomy as a Falcon's. However, the canopy is much stronger than the old ones on the Falcons.*"

"That's good to know," Josh replied as he powered up his systems. "Reactors are hot, power is coming online." Josh looked about his consoles as his fighter came to life. "Wow, this thing fires up quickly. I've already got green lights across the board, here." He looked outside as the crew chief gave him another thumbs-up, followed by a salute. Josh returned the salute and started his ship rolling forward into the open airlock. "Karuzara Control, Super Eagle, ready for departure, bay zero."

"*Super Eagle, Karuzara Control. Clear for direct departure, bay zero. On departure, fly one seven zero, four up relative for Earth orbit intercept. Speed* restriction of one five zero until clear of Karuzara control zone. Be advised your test area is clear of all traffic."

"Super Eagle, cleared for departure, bay zero, one seven zero and four up. I copy area is clear of traffic." Josh paused a moment, smiling. "I'll try and keep her below one five zero."

A few minutes later, Josh found himself outside of the asteroid base and accelerating, as he put the Super Eagle through a series of basic maneuvers. "Hell, this thing is really snappy."

"*Snappy?*" Deliza asked, unsure of what he meant.

"Yeah, snappy...as in, responsive," he explained as he rolled the ship on its longitudinal axis, while yawing it around its vertical axis. He continued the maneuvering, starting and stopping the movements periodically, to get a feel for how well the ship responded to each of his control inputs.

"*You should be coming up on your jump interface point in one minute,*" Loki warned. "*Just select the location and altitude you want to be at when you come out of the jump and then tap the auto-adjust button. The flight control computers will momentarily take control and put you on the right heading and speed. Once you're on the numbers it will initiate a five count to the jump, and release the controls to you. If you deviate from the jump plot during the five count, the system will abort the jump automatically. You can also do a manual abort by pushing the auto-flight disengage button, which works as the jump abort when you're in the five count.*"

"Got it," Josh replied. He tapped the map display, slid it over with a swipe of his finger, and then zoomed in with a double tap. He then placed his finger on the display where he wanted to arrive. An icon appeared, along with a number beside it indicating the selected arrival altitude of five thousand meters. Josh twisted the knob next to the navigation display, lowering the target altitude to one thousand meters, again, smiling. "You know, this all would have been easier if I could've spent some time in a sim before the first flight."

"*There wasn't time,*" Deliza replied. "*Besides, I thought you were the best.*"

"I'm just sayin'."

"*Uh, don't you think a thousand meters is a bit on the low side for your first jump into the atmosphere,*" Loki suggested, "*in a prototype?*"

"I'd be jumping in lower than that in combat."

"*You would, but no one else would be.*"

"She'll be fine," Josh insisted. "Right, Princess?"

"*Uh...right?*"

"*Remember what Prechitt said, Josh?*"

"Hey, I followed the speed restriction on departure." Josh heard a warning tone and glanced down at his console as the five-second countdown to jump began. "Jumping in three... Wings deploying... One......"

The canopy of the Super Eagle turned opaque.

"Jumping."

The ship suddenly slowed, pushing Josh forward against his shoulder restraints as the fighter found itself in the thick atmosphere of Earth. His canopy cleared as the ride became rough, and he felt the familiar sensation of atmospheric pressures against his control surfaces being translated back to his flight control stick.

"Jump complete!" he reported as he pulled back on his flight control stick to bring his nose up and level off. "Altitude holding at six hundred meters. Speed is four thousand KPH and falling. Initiating decel burn."

Again Josh was thrown forward into his shoulder restraints as the Super Eagle's forward-facing deceleration thrusters fired, causing his speed to fall off quickly. "Three thousand!" he reported, struggling against the deceleration forces. "Two thousand!" Josh felt the inertial dampeners finally starting to kick, as the pressure of his restraints against his shoulders began to ease up. "One thousand! We're subsonic. Killing decel burn and deploying speed brakes." Josh pulled back the throttle on his left to zero, as he tapped the speed brake button on the side of his flight control stick. "Might want to program the inertial dampeners to anticipate the load better when we jump in."

"Hopefully, most pilots will jump in a little higher, and a little slower," Loki replied.

The Super Eagle's nose immediately tried to rise as the panels on the top and bottom of the its wing roots, as well as the sides of the fuselage, deployed to increase the ship's drag and help slow it further. He countered the effect with a little nose-down pitch, and then reset his thrust to be directed aft. "Speed is five hundred KPH and falling. Nav-com has a lock on Porto Santo. Four hundred." Josh tapped the button to retract his speed brakes, and then eased his throttle back up. His engine whined as it spun back up to provide the thrust needed to maintain the Super Eagle's airspeed in the atmosphere. "Speed brakes retracted. Powering up. Speed holding at three-fifty." Josh activated his second radio set, adding it to his comms. "Porto Santo Control, Super

Eagle. Inbound for landing from the southwest, two zero kilometers, and I have your weather link."

"*Super Eagle, Porto Santo Control. Enter left base runway zero one. The pattern is empty, and you are cleared for the option.*"

"Super Eagle copies, left base for zero one, and cleared for the option."

"*No options, Josh,*" Loki insisted. "*Just put her down and let the techs look her over. You can have your fun later.*"

"Party pooper," Josh replied.

* * *

Captain Nash looked over the group of men assembled in the training hangar. "Today, you will start your flight training." He gestured to the apparatus behind him. "This simulator is an exact duplicate of the interior of the Cobra gunships that you will be operating. Everything inside looks and acts the same. It even feels the same. The only difference between this and the real thing is that this never leaves the ground. It is a full-motion, gravity-assist, simulation environment. That means when you fire the simulator's starboard thrusters, your body will feel like it wants to slide to the right. If you are not secured, you will do exactly that. There is another difference as well. You won't die in here. This is where you want to make your mistakes. *This is where you want to learn from those mistakes, not* up there, where you *can* die. Do not be afraid to ask questions. Do not be afraid to make mistakes."

Captain Nash looked at the faces of the men again. Some of the members of the first group of volunteers had piloting experience, and some of them even had time in space, either working for the Jung or on Tannan jump shuttles running back and forth between Earth and Tanna. But this group was the only one. The groups that would follow had neither.

"You twenty men will become the first Cobra pilots. You will work in teams of two, taking turns acting as pilot and copilot. For now, the functions of your weapons officer, systems engineer, and gunners will be performed by the simulation. We want you to concentrate on one thing, and that is flying the Cobra gunship."

Captain Nash paused long enough to clear his throat. "Although all twenty of you will learn to pilot the Cobra gunship, only ten of you will become pilots. The other ten will become copilots. Those becoming pilots will also serve as captain in command of their gunship. Those becoming copilots will become executive officers, and will act as second in command."

Captain Nash turned and looked at the simulator as he spoke. "This simulator, and the one in the next hangar, will be operating twenty-eight hours per day, every day. Each team will conduct two flights per day. When you are not in the simulator, you will be either reviewing your previous flight, preparing for your next flight, or eating, sleeping, or shitting." Captain Nash smiled for a moment. "And yes, we will allow you to shower on occasion."

"While you are working your asses off in here, those men training to be your crews will be doing the same in the simulator next door. In thirty-eight days, we will have ten gunships in operation. I have to have ten crews ready for action by then. In eight days, we will have a total of four gunships in operation. At that time, we will begin flying in real gunships, in space. So you people have your work cut out for you."

Captain Nash turned back to the podium, placing his hands on top of it. "Like I said, make your mistakes here, in the simulator. I do not want you crashing the real things."

Captain Nash looked down at his data pad. "Annatah and Jahansir. You're up first. Lucco and Harral will be second. The rest of you take a look at the flight schedules on the training board to see your report times. That is all."

The men dispersed into small groups as most of them made their way to the training board on the far wall. Two men approached Captain Nash. He looked at them. "Annatah and Jahansir, right?"

"I'm Annatah," the man on the right said. "He's Jahansir."

"Climb aboard, gentlemen," Captain Nash ordered.

Lieutenant Commander Rano waited until the men had stepped through the hatch into the simulator before speaking. "Do you really think we can train them to fly the gunship in only a few weeks?"

Captain Nash shrugged. "I don't know. It took me six months. Hopefully they're smarter than I was."

* * *

"*Super Eagle, Porto Santo Control. Clear for takeoff and straight out departure runway zero one. Cleared to jump at ten kilometers out, and one kilometer up.*"

"Porto Santo, Super Eagle, taking zero one straight out," Josh replied as he crossed the runway boundary line and turned to line up with its centerline. "Clear to jump at ten out and one up." He disengaged the auto-taxi system, then advanced his throttle to fifty percent, causing his fighter to lurch forward. "Super Eagle, rolling," he added, as his ship accelerated down the runway. He glanced at his console, checking his power plant displays and flight systems status displays, ensuring that everything was in order before pulling back ever so slightly on his flight control stick. The Super Eagle's nose lifted up a couple degrees, and the fighter took to the air, climbing slowly away from the runway below. A touch of a button and his landing gear disappeared into the ship's underside, the gear doors closing over them. "Super Eagle, wheels up." When all three gear lights went off, he pushed his throttle to the stops and pulled back hard on his flight control stick. The Super Eagle responded instantly, pointing straight up and accelerating toward the clear blue sky above.

The force of the Super Eagle's Corinairan-built engine pushed Josh back in his seat with far more force than he was generally accustomed to. "Damn!"

"What is it?" Deliza asked, her voice coming over the comms from her monitoring station in the Black Lab on Karuzara.

"You weren't kidding when you said the dampeners would only partially compensate," Josh replied in a strained voice.

"Too much?" Deliza wondered, her voice sounding genuinely concerned. *"We might be able to allocate additional power from the weapons systems when they are not armed..."*

"No, it's okay," Josh interrupted. "I just wasn't expecting it to be that much, is all." He eased his throttles back as he brought his nose back down, settling into level flight. "Damned thing climbs like a rocket, that's for sure," he said, this time without the additional effort. "I was only vertical for five seconds, and I'm at five-five already. That means vertically this thing can get to space in what, three minutes?"

"*About that,*" Deliza confirmed, "*but more likely you'd be on a forty-five-degree climb, not straight up. Far more energy efficient since you'd still have to pitch over and accelerate in order to attain...*"

"Ya, ya, ya." Josh pulled his throttle back to zero thrust, allowing his airspeed to drop off as he added upward pitch to maintain level flight. "I'm going to jump down to five hundred meters at minimum cruise speed."

"*Why?*" Deliza wondered.

"*That's not in the flight plan,*" Loki chimed in.

"Hey, we're supposed to be testing the jump systems on this flight, right?"

"*Yes, but...*"

"Then why waste time flying down to five hundred meters when we can jump down to five hundred meters?"

"*Because until the jump system has been fully tested, it's safer to...*"

"It was safe enough for me to jump from orbit down into the atmosphere, wasn't it?" Josh said as the Super Eagle began to buffet slightly. "Selecting a jump to five hundred meters altitude on a forty-five down," he announced as he pitched his nose down. "Auto-jump is armed. Activating." Josh took his fingers off the flight control stick, allowing the Super Eagle's automated flight control systems to take over, keeping the ship on a perfect course as the jump drive quickly made the calculations to put the ship exactly where Josh had indicated. Only two seconds after he had activated the auto-jump system, his canopy turned opaque for a split second to protect his eyes from the jump flash. In that second, his ship dove from an altitude of five and a half kilometers, at a forty-five-degree angle, down to an altitude of half a kilometer—*automatically*—all without the assistance of a copilot behind him managing the calculations. Two spins of a knob, two touches of a button, and a little movement of his throttle and his flight control stick afterward, and Josh was now several kilometers further along his course and five thousand meters lower...and it had taken him all of five seconds to get from the *thought* to the *result*.

"Damn," Josh exclaimed as his fighter leveled off again and the G-forces subsided. "This thing is sweet." He dialed up another jump. "Let's try single-click, on-demand jumps, shall we?"

"*Josh...*" Loki began, in his usual cautionary tone.

"Ease up," Josh interrupted. "Just let me play a bit, then we'll get to your flight plan, I promise." He tapped his navigation map display a few kilometers ahead of his current position, placing a target icon. He then executed a snap turn to his left, changing his ship's course by forty-five degrees to port. A press of the jump trigger button on his flight control stick, and his canopy cycled opaque and then clear again. He glanced at his map, noting that the target icon had moved to the right side of his display. "This is so cool." He executed another snap turn, this time changing course ninety degrees back to starboard. Another touch of the jump button, and the targeting icon was directly in front of him again, but only a few hundred meters away. "Guns, guns, guns," he said with a smile. "That would be a kill, boys and girls."

"*Are you done yet?*" Loki asked impatiently.

"Nope." Josh pulled his flight control stick back, bringing the Super Eagle's nose straight-up vertical once more. As his airspeed quickly fell away, he dialed in a jump distance of three kilometers, then tapped his jump button. Another cycle of the canopy to opaque and back to clear, and he was three and a half kilometers above the Atlantic. With his power at only enough thrust to maintain minimum cruise speed in level flight, his airspeed quickly fell away, as did his rate of climb. Just before he came to a stop, he tapped the jump button again, jumping another three kilometers toward space. As his canopy turned clear again, he glanced at his flight displays. He was seven kilometers up, and his speed had fallen to zero. His ship seemed to hover in mid-air for a moment, its nose pointed straight up. He felt the Super Eagle begin to slide backwards, its energy no longer sufficient to counteract the Earth's gravity. With considerable finesse, he manipulated his flight controls to keep his ship pointed straight up as the fighter slid straight down, back toward the vast ocean below. Five KPH...ten, then twenty. Finally, while still falling tail first, he tapped the jump button again, jumping the Super Eagle, tail-first, down to three thousand meters above the planet. He pitched back over, bringing his ship into another forty-five-degree dive, and executed one last jump. As his canopy cleared again, he leveled off, added enough power to maintain level flight, and glanced at his navigation map once more. "Guns, guns, guns," he said again, a grin stretched from ear to ear.

"Are you done showing off?" Loki asked.

"For now," Josh replied. "Screw the Falcons," he added. "I wanna fly Super Eagles."

* * *

"He's got a good point, though," Cameron said, as she picked at her salad.

Vladimir said nothing, only shoveled another fork full of food into his mouth and watched Nathan with an expectant look on his face.

"Sure, he's got a point," Jessica chimed in, "he's just a year too late with it, that's all."

Vladimir looked at Jessica, then back at Nathan. "You have nothing to say?" he wondered, still chewing.

Nathan shrugged. "They are both correct. However, it doesn't really matter. Even if we stopped all offensive actions and took a purely defensive posture from this day forward, the Jung would still come at us with whatever forces they deemed necessary. The only reason that Earth is still alive today is because the Jung haven't yet figured out how *many* ships they *need* to send, in order to finish the job...and that's only because of the communications delay inherent with traditional FTL communications. They simply don't have adequate information...*yet*."

"Eventually, they will," Jessica said.

"Did it ever occur to anyone that a *cease-fire* might be a good thing?" Cameron wondered.

"It would be nothing more than a stalling tactic," Nathan insisted.

"During which time the Jung would rally their forces," Jessica added. "Probably stack them up at various locations, all within a few days FTL of us."

"Exactly," Nathan agreed. "And when the time

is right, they'll attack with enough force to destroy us...or at the very least, send us running back to the Pentaurus cluster, with our tails between our legs."

"The stalling tactic can work in our favor as well," Vladimir pointed out, speaking in between bites. "We can build more ships, create better weapons, train more people..."

"We can never match the Jung's industrial capacity," Nathan told him. "That's how wars are won, you know. By factories and farms. That's why we must continue to destroy their ships and their factories."

"But what if you're wrong?" Cameron said, reaffirming her point. "What if we *could* coexist peacefully with the Jung?"

"It will never happen," Jessica insisted.

"How can you say that?"

"Just look at the facts, Cam," Jessica replied. "We have the jump drive. We have superior energy weapons, and shields. What we *don't* have is the infrastructure to *build* what we need...to take advantage of our technological edge. That's *exactly* what Dumar is trying to do with this lull that he's created by clearing the Jung from the twenty light year sphere around Sol. We've got a year, two at the most, until the Jung figure all of this out for themselves, move their ships into position, and take us out. Every ship we destroy is one less ship that can attack us. Every system we liberate is one less industrial base to support the Jung, and possibly one more that can support us. Because of the liberation of Tau Ceti, we could have eight more jump frigates added to our fleet in just two years' time. Probably less, given that we have Takaran fabrication technology."

"A war is what you shall have to fight," Nathan muttered to himself.

The others at his dining table stopped and looked at him.

"Something Dubnyk once said to me." Nathan took a drink from his glass. "Seems he was right."

Vladimir shoveled a spoon full of potatoes into his mouth as he spoke. "Why do you keep going back to see that old man?"

"Because our captain is a history geek," Jessica teased, "and that old fart is a walking, talking museum exhibit, straight out of the twenty-fourth century."

"Seriously, Nathan," Cameron pressed, "why *do* you keep going back to see him?"

"I don't know," Nathan admitted. "Jessica's probably right. I suppose I find him a curiosity."

"You just feel responsible for him," Vladimir snorted as he chewed.

"A little of that too, I suppose," Nathan admitted. "He's got an unusual knack for seeing the big picture... and I mean *really* big. It must have something to do with him having seen humanity from two vastly different points in time. His perspective is unique. No one has ever lived through such horrific events, and then lived long enough to see the outcome a thousand years afterward. How can one *not* wonder what he thinks?"

"I thought we were talking about Galiardi?" Vladimir said as he raised his glass to wash down his food. "How did we end up on Dubnyk?"

"*Galiardi*, on the other hand... Him I do *not* find interesting," Nathan said.

"Then you don't agree with him?" Cameron confirmed.

"No, I *do* agree with him," Nathan replied. "I *do* think we are provoking the Jung to come at us with even more force. I just think they would still do so, whether we provoked them or not. That being the case, I don't see any reason *not* to continue our offensive."

"Then why not take it all the way?" Cameron suggested. "Why not just attack the Jung homeworld?"

"Because we don't know where it is," Jessica reminded her.

"I was speaking hypothetically."

"And I was being sarcastic."

"*If* we knew where the Jung homeworld was located, I would *not* be opposed to attacking it, directly," Nathan admitted.

Again, the room fell silent.

"It's not like they don't have it coming," Jessica mumbled as she took another bite of her meal.

"An 'eye for an eye' is not always the right answer," Cameron said.

"Maybe not, but it would be fair."

"It's not about right and wrong," Nathan said, "nor is it about fair and unfair. It's about survival, plain and simple."

"That's right," Jessica agreed, "and the Jung think they have a greater right to survive than we do."

"Don't we all?" Vladimir said as he scooped up another fork full of food. He noticed the silence, and looked up. "Well, don't we?"

"He's right," Nathan agreed. "It's part of our nature...to survive."

"Then why do you all look so surprised?" Vladimir wondered.

"Maybe because it's the first thing you've said without your mouth full of food," Jessica laughed.

CHAPTER THREE

"Captain on the bridge!" announced the guard at the ready room hatch as Cameron passed by him.

"Report," she barked as she made her way to the center of the Celestia's bridge.

"Twelve contacts jumped in thirty seconds ago," Ensign Kono reported from the sensor station. "Appeared two million kilometers out."

"All departments report general quarters," Luis reported from the tactical station.

"Targets ID as combat jumpers," Ensign Kono added.

Cameron turned to look at her tactical officer. "I thought we only had eight CJs left?"

"Last I heard," Luis replied, "and I show them all still at Porto Santo. Nothing on the arrival schedules, either, sir."

"I'm getting Corinairan IDs and codes coming in now, Captain," Ensign Souza announced. "Their ID codes are valid. Receiving transmission. They were sent by the Corinari. Their flight leader is requesting clearance into Porto Santo, to deliver his ships and crews to Ghatazhak Command."

"Why weren't they on the delivery schedule?" Cameron wondered.

"I can ask, but at their current range it will take at least twenty minutes to get a response," Ensign Souza explained.

"Stand by on that," Cameron ordered. "Mister Hunt, take us out of orbit. Plot an intercept course and jump out to meet them. Arrival distance of one thousand kilometers."

"Leaving orbit, aye," Mister Hunt answered from the helm.

"Plotting intercept jump," the ship's navigator added.

"Shall I stand down from general quarters?" Luis asked.

"Negative," Cameron replied. "They're probably friendlies, but better to err on the side of caution, Lieutenant."

"Aye, sir."

"Leaving orbit," the helmsman reported.

"Intercept jump plotted and ready," the navigator added.

"Very well, Mister Sperry," Cameron said. "Let's go out and say hello."

"Jumping in three......two......one......"

The Celestia's bridge lit up for a split second as the ship jumped from high Earth orbit to the inbound flight of combat jump shuttles, some two hundred million kilometers away.

"Jump complete," Mister Sperry reported.

Cameron tapped the control panel on the right of her command chair, changing the magnification settings on the spherical main view screen that enveloped the forward half of the bridge itself. Before them were twelve Corinairan utility shuttles, all of them modified into combat jump shuttles.

"I have the lead ship, Lieutenant Aday, on comms, Captain," Ensign Souza reported from the Celestia's communications station.

Cameron tapped her comms control. "Lieutenant Aday, this is Captain Taylor of the Celestia. Your flight was not on the arrival schedule."

"*Apologies, Captain,*" the lieutenant replied over the loudspeaker. "*That's why we jumped in from a* distance. We were dispatched in secret by the prime minister, at the request of Captain Navarro of the Avendahl. He wanted to replace the combat jumpers lost during the liberation of Tau Ceti, but did not want it to be public knowledge that Corinair was still sharing resources with Alliance forces in Sol. Something about keeping the 'Nobles of Takara' in the dark about our force strength."

"I understand," Cameron replied. "I take it things are still a bit tense, then?"

"Yes, sir. Just a bit. The nobles haven't taken any overt actions as of yet. However, they don't really have the firepower to take on the Avendahl. Word is they aren't looking to stir up any trouble outside of their own system, but not everyone is convinced that's the case. I have orders from Captain Navarro for the transfer of my ships and crew over to Commander Telles of the Ghatazhak. I'm transmitting them now."

Cameron turned to look at Ensign Souza, who nodded his head to confirm receipt. "Ensign Kono?" Cameron said, looking to her sensor operator.

"I show standard armaments for combat jumpers. Crew of three, loaded with supplies. Looks to be spare parts, mostly. Four of the jumpers are carrying additional passengers. Ground crews, most likely. No side arms."

"All their weapons and shields are powered down," Luis added.

"Very well." Cameron keyed her mic again. "Lieutenant. You're cleared to Porto Santo, via a jump to high Earth orbit. We'll transmit approach frequencies and jump waypoints. You may follow us to Earth."

"Thank you, sir. Aday, out."

"Comms, dispatch a jump comm buoy and notify

Alliance Command *and* Ghatazhak Command," Cameron directed.

"But, you'll ruin the surprise," Luis joked.

"If I know Commander Telles, he doesn't care much for surprises," Cameron replied.

* * *

"We simply do not have the resources to continue liberating additional worlds," Admiral Dumar argued. "We are down to only four hundred troops, and the number of ships that can deliver them has also been greatly diminished."

"Did you not just receive an additional twelve combat jump shuttles?" the Coporan representative reminded the admiral.

"Yes, and although they are formidable ships, each of them can only carry five Ghatazhak soldiers. Even if we used all twenty ships now at our disposal, that would only put one hundred men on the ground."

"But you also have utility shuttles, and cargo shuttles, and...what did you call them? Boxers?"

"Boxcars," the Admiral corrected. "Utility shuttles can normally only carry ten fully outfitted Ghatazhak. Cargo shuttles, fifty."

"And your boxcars? Can they not carry hundreds?"

"At least," the admiral admitted. "However, the boxcars are our best means of moving equipment and supplies between worlds. Committing them to combat actions puts them at risk. We lost two of them on Kohara."

"We have many cargo ships in the Tau Ceti system," President Kanor reasoned. "And we have shipyards. If we were to outfit some of those ships with jump drives, they could take over the role of interstellar cargo, thus freeing your boxcars for combat actions."

"Of course, but we still need men," the admiral replied. "Men with guns, and who know how to use them."

"We may not have ships, or weapons, but one thing we do have are men," the representative from Pylius stated. "Men full of hatred for the Jung, I might add. If they could be trained to fight, perhaps by your Ghatazhak..."

"That would take months, perhaps longer," the admiral said, waving his hand dismissively.

"I'm not suggesting you train them to be as mighty as your Ghatazhak," the Pylian representative countered, "just that you train them to shoot straight and follow orders. My people have always been willing to fight. We have just never had the tools, nor the opportunity to do so. They will line up by the thousands, I assure you."

"And they will die by the thousands, I assure *you*," Admiral Dumar replied.

"As they will if the Jung return, and in greater numbers."

Admiral Dumar sighed.

"There is something else we must consider," President Scott said. The other men at the table turned to look at him. "You have all been discussing if we *can* continue to liberate Jung-held worlds. Perhaps what we *should* be discussing is whether or not we *should* be liberating them."

"I believe that goes without saying," the minister from Weldon scoffed.

"Odd statement, coming from the world who most protested being liberated without consent," President Scott replied.

"That was then, this is now," the minister answered.

"There are those on Earth who feel that we are provoking the Jung by attacking their forces and liberating their worlds. There are those who say that we are no better than the Jung by doing so."

"*We* don't destroy entire societies in order to make them more *manageable*," the Tannan minister sneered.

"Or entire worlds simply to send a *message*," President Kanor added.

"Gentlemen," Admiral Dumar interrupted, "let us not stray into ethical debates, as the question is one of practicality, not morality. Let us assume, for the moment, that we had the forces needed to liberate every Jung-controlled system we wished. The question of whether we *should*, or should *not*, must be decided based on necessity, not ethics. What do those systems have to offer us? Is it worth the losses that we might face?"

"You're wrong, Admiral," President Scott argued politely. "The question *is* one of ethics. It always has been. You can tell yourself that you liberated Tau Ceti because of their shipyards, Tanna for their propellant refineries, or Pylius for their thousands of able young men ready to pick up arms against the Jung. But what of Kalita? What of Copora? Neither of them had anything to offer the Alliance."

"Their proximity to Earth was the justification for their liberation," Admiral Dumar insisted.

"Nonsense," President Scott replied. "That may have been the reason you took out the Jung ships in those systems, but you destroyed the Jung surface forces because it was the right thing to do."

"Only because leaving them intact might pose

unexpected complications at a later date," Admiral Dumar replied.

"Such as?"

"Such as a population that might be punished at the hands of those very forces left on the surface," the admiral argued. "Which, I might add, is precisely what occurred on Kohara during the two weeks immediately following the defeat of the Jung's space forces in Tau Ceti. So you see, Mister President, as much as you'd like to *think* of liberation as the morally *right* thing to do, it is still a matter of practicality."

"Yet, you said that we do not have the resources to safely do so," President Scott reminded the admiral.

"As notification of a resource issue, not as opposition to the idea. On the contrary, Mister President, it is my belief that we should continue to remove Jung forces from every system within the Sol sector, while we still have the advantage. Eventually, the Jung *will* get a jump drive of their own, either by stealing it or figuring it out for themselves. It might take months, it might take years, but they will get one. Best we create as strong a position as possible, while we still can."

"If we continue to liberate systems, how will the Alliance be able to protect them?" the Pylian representative wondered.

"By installing secondary jump systems in our ships, we are extending our immediate response zone to thirty light years," Admiral Dumar replied. "Once all ships have been outfitted, we should be able to counter anything the Jung are likely to throw at us, barring a full-scale invasion."

"And if they send such an invasion force?" the Pylian representative inquired.

"The more worlds we liberate, the more unlikely that becomes," the admiral explained. "Assuming that there are no battle groups in transit that we have missed, it would be at least three months before any of your worlds could be reached by the Jung. By then, we will have three jump-capable warships with which to respond. By four months, we will have five, not to mention a few dozen gunships, and plenty of KKVs, both jump capable *and* conventional." Admiral Dumar looked at the tired faces sitting at the table with him, knowing that the decisions made at this table today would influence multiple worlds, and billions of people. Every person at the table was equally aware, and it weighed just as heavily on their minds as it did on the admiral's. "Gentlemen, we can do this. We just need the commitment of people and resources, particularly your industrial capacities, in order to do so. We can provide you all with Takaran fabrication technology. Within weeks, you will have several of them. Within months you will have dozens. A year from now, your industrial and technological capabilities will have increased one hundred fold."

"Assuming we all survive," the minister from Weldon commented dryly.

"I will not lie to you," Admiral Dumar said. "The risk is great. But inaction carries the same risk, perhaps even more so. Granted, the Alliance liberated your worlds without consent. I truly wish that had not been necessary, but necessary it was... and *still is.* However, I will not drag you further into war *without* your consent. So, I ask each of you, here and now, to support us as full members of this Alliance, complete with all the risks *and* rewards that such an alliance brings, and help us bring the same freedom to the rest of the core." Admiral Dumar looked at the men at the table. "How say you?"

Admiral Dumar watched as one by one, five hands went up. He looked at the sixth man, President Scott, at the far end of the table. "Mister President?"

"There is a famous quote from old Earth," President Scott recalled, "one that my son taught me. It was from long before the great plague. 'All that is needed for evil to triumph is for good men to do nothing.' The Earth and the people of the Pentaurus cluster formed this Alliance for the purpose of protecting all our freedoms. More importantly, we did so to ensure our very survival. We shall not give up."

President Scott raised his hand.

Admiral Dumar smiled. "Gentlemen, I thank you. Return to your worlds, and put out the call. Soldiers, technicians, specialists, engineers, general laborers...everyone is needed. We are going to war."

* * *

Captain Nash walked across the hangar bay of the old Jung fighter base on the small asteroid orbiting Tanna. Crews scurried about, busy with the ongoing task of converting the base into an operational support facility for the new gunships currently being produced on the surface of Tanna. On the far side of the hangar bay stood twenty-two men, clustered around the entrances to the first four boarding tunnels that had been added to the base to allow the new gunships a place to berth when not in operation.

"Fall in!" Lieutenant Commander Rano barked as he noticed his commanding officer approaching.

Captain Nash walked up and stood next to the lieutenant commander as his men quickly got into formation. He paused a moment to look them over.

He had spent the last seven days putting them, and many others, through simulator hell in preparation for this day. He only hoped it was enough.

Once the men had gathered, Captain Nash began. "Gentlemen, welcome to Cobra Base. Those of you gathered here today have consistently scored the highest in both your practical and written assessments. Because of that, you will be the first to receive your ships. For most of you, your ride up from the surface this morning was your first time in space. So, for those of you who left your breakfast on the floor of the shuttle, or worse, on your neighbor's lap, don't feel too bad. You'll get used to it. For the last week, you have all trained separately. Flight crews have trained in the cockpit simulators, engineers and sensor operators on computer simulations, and gunners in the quad-gun simulators. Now, you're going to train together, in the real thing."

Captain Nash glanced at the expressions on the men's faces, none of which looked terribly confident. "Yeah, I know, a terrifying thought. In a perfect world, you'd all spend a couple months in full-ship simulators before you'd go anywhere near the real thing. Unfortunately, this isn't a perfect world. The fact is, we need these ships manned and ready for action as soon as humanly possible. Good idea or bad, it is what it is. All of you were chosen because you were the best of your class, and therefore, have the highest probability of being able to operate your gunships safely, without flying them into one another, or shooting the ship next to you."

Captain Nash paused, noticing a raised hand. "Mister Sennott, is it?" he asked, pointing to the young man.

"Yes, sir. Gunnery Specialist Sennott. I thought our guns couldn't fire on friendlies?"

"It was a joke, Specialist."

"Ah, of course, sir. My apologies," the young man replied, appearing somewhat embarrassed.

"But since we're on the topic, try not to put too much faith in the auto-fire interrupt systems. Nothing built by humans is ever perfect, and the comrade who inadvertently wanders into your field of fire will appreciate your diligence."

Captain Nash raised his data pad to read the names. "I will be in command of Cobra One, also known as Cobra Leader. Lieutenant Commander Rano will be my XO. Annatah and Jahansir, you'll be CO and XO of Cobra Two. Harral and Lucco, you'll be CO and XO of Cobra Three. Orel and Keupek, you'll be CO and XO of Cobra Four. You six will report to me for your pre-assignment briefings. The rest of you report to Lieutenant Commander Rano for your ship assignments. Once you've received your ship assignment, you may board your ships and settle in. But please, do not touch anything. Just take a look around, get familiar with your ships, and wait for your COs to arrive. Your first flight will be at fourteen hundred, Tannan Mean Time, or three hours from now. Welcome aboard, gentlemen."

Captain Nash watched and waited, as the men broke apart into two separate groups. Six of them forming up on him, while the others swarmed around his XO, Lieutenant Commander Rano. His attention turned to the six young men now standing in front of him, their expressions a mixture of pride, excitement, and anxiety. "Gentlemen, I'd like to congratulate you all on your promotions," he began, as he passed out rank insignias and data pads to each of them. "Your job will be the hardest. Not only will you have to learn to fly your ships with the least amount of simulator training time ever, but you'll have to manage your crews at the same time. To make things even more difficult, your instructor, myself, has less than one hundred flight hours in this type of ship. Granted, they handle a lot like the Scout-class on which they were based, but they are very different, believe me. They are faster, more maneuverable, and have much bigger teeth. Luckily, as you know, they are also far more automated. So if you get overwhelmed, better you fall back on your auto-flight systems rather than put your crew, and your ship, in danger. Just remember, always fly your ship first, worry about your crew second, and the enemy third. It is almost always better to bug out and survive to fight another day."

"Sir?" Captain Annatah asked, "You said *almost* always. How do you know when it *isn't* a good idea to bug out?"

Captain Nash offered a half smile. "Trust me, you'll know."

* * *

"My name is Captain Gilbert Roselle, and I am the commanding officer of the Jar-Benakh. I am an arrogant, egotistical, loud-mouthed, hard-ass son of a bitch of a captain, if ever there was one. I will tolerate nothing short of your absolute best effort, as I will always give you mine. I will never ask you to risk your lives unless I am willing to risk my own as well, and I will never put you in harm's way without due consideration. But make no mistake, you have all volunteered to serve on a combat vessel, at a time of war. For that, each of you has already proven that you are worthy of my respect. Just try to keep it that way."

Captain Roselle glanced at his XO, who could barely control the smirk at the corner of his mouth. He turned his attention back to the one hundred men gathered in the middle of hangar deck four. "You men will be trained in the basic operation of this ship. You will be relentlessly drilled, over and over, until you can perform your jobs in your sleep. It will seem excessive to the point of frustration, but believe me, your first time under fire, you'll thank me for it. You, in turn, will help train the next one hundred, and the hundred after them, and so on. Eventually, a few months from now, this ship will be properly staffed, and ready for anything."

Captain Roselle paused for a moment, his expression turning even more serious. "Some of us will die. That is a foregone conclusion on a combat vessel in a time of war. Try as we will to prevent it, it will come. The best advice I can give you is to not fear death. Only fear failure, and me, of course." Roselle snickered as he turned to his XO. "How's that for a pep talk, huh?" he said as he stepped down from the podium.

Commander Ellison stepped up to the podium to take over. "Gentlemen, your duty assignments are posted on the data displays on the wall to your right. You will find your berthing assignments there as well. Once dismissed, find your bunks and stow your gear. Review your procedures and restrictions. I caution you not to wander into areas of the ship which you are not authorized to enter. The Ghatazhak take security very seriously. Neither they, the captain, nor myself tolerate stupidity very easily. Your first meal call will be at twelve hundred, ship time. You will report to your duty assignments at fourteen hundred for orientations. Your training officers will give you your training schedules at that time. See that you adhere to them."

Commander Ellison allowed the slightest smile to form on the corner of his mouth. "Welcome aboard the Jar-Benakh."

Captain Roselle watched the men as they crowded around the data displays on the wall, each of them eager to see where they would be serving.

"What do you think?" Commander Ellison asked as he approached.

"I think we're fucked," the captain grumbled.

"I don't know, Gil. They seem like a good group of able-bodied young men."

"Not one of which has any military training, let alone combat experience."

"Everyone's got to start somewhere, Gil."

"Hell, half of them don't even speak English."

"Give them time," the commander replied. "Meanwhile, we've got plenty of translators. At least most of them have technical backgrounds."

"Yeah, as long as all they have to do is push buttons, they'll be fine," Captain Roselle grumbled as he turned and headed toward the exit.

"The first hundred are the most qualified of all the volunteers that have come forth so far," Commander Ellison reminded him. "That's why we are starting with them. These guys will probably end up as department heads."

"Yeah, I know," Roselle replied, still uneasy about the situation. "How are the mark fives doing?" he asked as they entered the corridor.

"Fourth one is going in today. They should be

ready to start calibration and testing by the end of the week."

"Good," the captain replied. "I'll feel better once they're up and running."

"The hull repairs will be wrapped up by tomorrow afternoon."

"What about the broadside cannons?"

"The mark threes arrived from Karuzara last night...all twelve of them. It'll take another two days to finish installing the tracks, so we should be able to start installation three days from now," the commander explained.

"I wish I could see the face of the first captain to be on the receiving end of them," Roselle said with a devious grin. "Gonna surprise the hell out of him, that's for sure."

"I'm sure it will."

"Any word on the jump missile program?" the captain asked as he came to a stop outside the elevator door.

"Only that they are conducting the first test firing tomorrow."

"Let's not waste any training time on the missile systems until we know for sure what we're going to be firing, Commander. It's bad enough we don't have adequate training time to begin with, let alone having to waste time retraining them."

"Already planned on it, sir. They'll be concentrating on launcher maintenance for now."

"Great," Captain Roselle said as the elevator doors opened and he stepped inside. "I'll be in command."

* * *

"Heavy One Four reports target drone is deployed," Mister Bryant announced.

Admiral Dumar glanced up at the tactical display

in the Karuzara Command center as the flashing red icon representing the target drone separated from the steady blue icon of the cargo jump shuttle.

"Target drone is on course and speed," the tactical officer reported. "Missile targeting system has a lock on the drone. We have a good targeting data link with the weapon. We are ready to launch."

"Board is clear," the sensor operator reported. "No other ships in the area."

"Launch the jump missile," the admiral ordered. The admiral turned his attention to one of the many view screens on the far wall. The missile launcher tilted upward slightly, then pivoted to the right a few degrees. The launcher's rails lit up as electromagnetic energy surged down them, propelling the missile off the rails and into space. On the next screen to the right, the admiral could see the tail of the missile come to life, bright yellow thrust blasting out the back of the missile as it accelerated away. Then, only a few seconds later, the entire missile disappeared in a blue-white flash of light.

The admiral glanced at the tactical display, where the icon for the missile also disappeared. He then turned his attention to the view screen displaying the feed from the targeting drone. There was another blue-white flash of light. For a few seconds after, he could see a faint white dot of the missile coming toward the camera, growing in size as it drew closer. The screen flashed yellow, filled with scrambled image fragments, then went black, the words 'Loss of Signal' displayed in its center.

"We have missile impact," the tactical officer announced. "Waiting for confirmation."

"Targeting drone is gone, jump missile is gone," the sensor officer reported. "I'm picking up debris in the area of the target drone's last position. Type matches the drone, spread matches the trajectory of the weapon. We have a confirmed kill."

Admiral Dumar turned to look at Lieutenant Tillardi, who was standing at the back of the room, looking like a proud father. "Nice work, Lieutenant."

"Thank you, sir."

"Now, make us two hundred more."

Tillardi smiled. "Yes, sir."

* * *

"Turn two, complete," Captain Nash reported as he powered back his gunship's main propulsion system.

"Return jump in ten seconds," Lieutenant Commander Rano replied. "Think they'll get it right this time?"

"I hope so," the captain replied, "but I'm keeping my hands on the controls, just in case."

"Jumping."

The cockpit windows turned opaque for a brief moment.

"Contacts!" Ensign Doray announced from the tactical console directly behind the pilot's station. "Cobra Two! Fifty meters to port and closing!"

"Two, Leader!" Captain Nash called over the comms as he pulled the nose of his ship up and brought his engines to full power. "Pitch down and break left! Three! Down and right! Four, up and right!" Nash glanced out his window as Cobra Two slid in under him, then fell away and back left as Nash guided his gunship up and away from the approaching ship, narrowly avoiding a collision.

"Two is falling away and left," the ensign reported. "Three falling away to the right. Four is climbing with us and fading right as well."

"Damn it," Captain Nash cursed. He took a deep breath, then lowered his nose level with the system's ecliptic and reduced his main engines to zero thrust once again. "Cobra Leader to all ships. Form up on me. Standard diamond. One high, Four low. Be ready to transmit your flight logs to me."

"*Four copies.*"

"*Three copies.*"

"*Two copies... Sorry, sir.*"

Nash looked at his XO. "It's a simple maneuver. Everybody comes back around on nineties from one another, arriving at one hundred meter spacings."

"Maybe we should start with thousand meter spacings?" his XO wondered.

"So that we're spread out over four kilometers? We won't be able to concentrate our fire power that way."

"All these maneuvers are programmed into the auto-flight systems, you know. That's how they're going to do it in battle...with the auto-flight."

"I know," Captain Nash agreed. "But they have to be able to do it manually first, and that's going to require practice."

"And if they should have to defend this system in the meantime, shouldn't they have *some* experience executing such maneuvers using the auto-flight systems?"

"Of course, but if those systems fail..."

"Perhaps we should mix it up? Sometimes let them use the auto-flight to execute the maneuver. It might help them see where they went wrong during manual execution."

Captain Nash thought for a moment, as he adjusted his gunship's course heading. "Good point." He sighed. "Okay, we'll do the next one with auto-flight." He keyed his comms. "Cobra Flight, Cobra Leader. Rendezvous at Echo four seven and prepare for another mock attack run." Captain Nash looked at the lieutenant commander. "We're going to keep doing this until we get it right."

"Give them time," Lieutenant Commander Rano said. "They'll get the hang of it."

"They'd better," Nash replied wearily. "Their lives may depend on it."

* * *

Master Sergeant Jahal scanned his data pad, then looked back at his commander. "All twenty of them met the thirty-second deployment maximum. Total time from jump-in to jump-out was less than two minutes across the board. The average was ninety seconds."

"How long does it take for a chaser to travel from the launcher to its target?" Commander Telles asked.

Jahal raised his brow skeptically. "I'll tell them to get it under one minute."

"At least." The intercom on the commander's desk beeped. "Yes?"

"Sir, Admiral Dumar's shuttle just landed."

Telles looked at his master sergeant in silent accusation. "Were you aware that Dumar was coming?"

"Negative," the master sergeant replied.

The commander pressed his intercom button again. "The admiral's destination?"

"Word from the ground crew is that he is headed to see you, sir."

"Very well."

"Surprise inspection?"

"If he were a Ghatazhak general, I suspect that

would be the case. Besides, such inspections are not in the admiral's nature."

"He does seem more of a 'big picture' kind of leader," Jahal reasoned.

"See that those times are improved," the commander insisted.

"Yes, sir," the master sergeant replied.

"Once you do, run the same insertion drills during the night, and in varying terrain and weather conditions, as well," the commander added. "I want under a minute in *all* conditions, not just favorable ones."

"Of course." The master sergeant turned and exited the commander's office.

Commander Telles placed his data pad on his desktop, then stood as he heard one of his office staff announce that the admiral was 'on deck.' The admiral entered his office seconds later, followed by one of his security detail personnel, who closed the office door behind him and waited outside.

"Commander," the admiral greeted. "I apologize for the unannounced visit."

"No apologies necessary, admiral," the commander assured him. "To what do I owe the honor?"

Admiral Dumar sighed as he took a seat. "Please," he said, gesturing for the commander to also sit. "I'm afraid this Alliance has asked quite a lot of you and your men."

"Nothing we cannot handle, sir," the commander replied as he took his seat. "It is what we Ghatazhak are for, is it not?"

"It may have been, but it cannot continue to be, as there are too few of you remaining, and there are no more coming."

98

Commander Telles did not reply, anticipating that the admiral had more to say.

After a brief pause, the Admiral continued. "Tell me, Commander. What is your assessment of the Jung ground forces?"

"Well trained, well equipped, and willing to sacrifice themselves when so ordered."

Admiral Dumar's eyebrow went up in surprise. "Interesting."

Commander Telles looked puzzled. "How so?"

"Your choice of words. 'When so ordered.' I would have expected something more along the lines of, 'for what they believe in,' or 'for their people.' The words you chose reflect a certain lack of respect on your part."

"Hardly. I am merely stating what I know to be facts."

"How so?" the admiral wondered, turning the phrase back on the commander.

"I judge the quality of their training by their level of confidence under fire, and the skilled manner in which they move. Both reflect many hours of repetitive skills training to create muscle memory. The reason I chose the words 'when so ordered' is because I have no way of knowing *why* they are willing to die. I have, however, seen them charge into certain death…*on command*. Thus, I can use the words 'when so ordered' with reasonable accuracy."

Admiral Dumar chuckled. "The Ghatazhak are nothing if not logical and precise in their thought processes."

"Logic and accuracy are critical to our success," the commander explained. "The human mind has a tendency to play tricks, leading us to believe that

99

something is true, simply because we wish it to be so. Such inaccuracies can be deadly."

"But you still follow your 'gut' at times, do you not?" the admiral asked.

"Admiral, the only thing my gut tells *me* is when it is time to eat, and when it is time to evacuate my bowels."

"I think you know what I mean, Commander."

"If you are referring to making a decision when the facts could lead to more than one opposing conclusion, then yes, sometimes we do 'follow our gut.' I believe the people of Earth call it a 'hunch.'"

"Indeed. So, with that in mind, I ask for your assessment of the Jung ground troops once more... and I would appreciate it if you offered more than just *facts*, as such things I could easily discern from your combat action reports."

Commander Telles took a deep breath, thinking for a moment before responding. "As I said, their training is of higher than average quality. I believe them to be on par with the Corinari. Their morale and overall health appears to be good, which indicates that they are properly supported, logistically. However, although they *are* willing to fight and die on command, I do not believe their hearts are in it."

"How did you come to that conclusion?"

"When a Ghatazhak fights, he does so with every fiber of his being...to the point that it takes considerable restraint for us to *not* kill our opponents. When the Jung fight, they are trying to accomplish their goal while still surviving. When the Ghatazhak fight, survival is not on their agenda, only the goal is on their minds. You can see it in our eyes, *if* you know what to look for."

"What is it that one would look for?"

"Fear," the commander replied without hesitation. "There is fear in the eyes of the Jung foot soldier. Not all, but most."

"You're saying that the Ghatazhak do not feel fear?"

"No, sir, I am not. The Ghatazhak feel fear, just like any other man. We simply choose not to let it interfere with what we *know* must be done."

Admiral Dumar looked confused. "I don't see how that can be done."

Commander Telles looked down at his desk for a moment, recalling the words of one of his instructors from his days as a young Ghatazhak cadet. "Suppose you and I are running to escape a charging *garatahk*, bent on our destruction. Ahead of us is a deep, yawning chasm, one wide enough that we are unsure whether or not we can jump over it safely. You will experience fear. Fear based on your own doubt in your abilities. That fear creates indecision. That moment of indecision, as brief as it may be, could cause the power in your stride to falter slightly. One, maybe two strides that are not as strong as they could have been. Will it be enough to ruin your chances of jumping the chasm? Or worse yet, will you stop running, and turn and face the charging *garatahk*, and likely die? I, on the other hand, being a Ghatazhak, will continue running at full speed as I judge the width of the chasm, the prevailing winds, and then weigh the odds of clearing the chasm versus turning to defeat the beast. Once done, I will simply choose the best course of action and follow through with it to the best of my ability."

"And survival is not a factor?"

"No, it is not. The *goal* is what dictates my

101

decision. Of course, the goal *could* simply be to survive."

"That's a very fine line, Commander."

"Yes, it is," the commander agreed. "It is also an important distinction, especially for a Ghatazhak. Training alone is only half of what makes the Ghatazhak what we are. The other half is mental. It is knowledge. It is understanding. It is the ability to see the entire picture. To analyze it, and all the possible actions and outcomes...all in a single instant."

"And the Jung do not have that?"

"No, they do not. Nor do the Corinari. As far as I know, the Ghatazhak are the only ones who approach combat in such a way."

"And that time when you ordered the massacre of civilians threatening to breach the fence around the evacuation port? Or when you decided to engage that man in a knife duel?"

"The Ghatazhak never do anything without a reason," the commander explained, "and a well thought out reason, to be sure. As was the case in both of the incidents to which you refer. I can explain my thought processes in both incidents, if you would like?"

"No thank you, Commander," the admiral said with a wave of his hand. "It was not my intent to question your decision-making processes, but rather to take advantage of them. You see, I lack the emotional self-control of a Ghatazhak, and at times, my judgment becomes clouded by my own emotions and bias."

"You seek advice, Admiral?"

"I do."

"About?"

"How would you handle the current situation with the Jung?" Admiral Dumar asked.

"Admiral, that is not for me to..."

"You are as qualified as anyone, Commander," the admiral reassured him. "Perhaps even more so."

"But, there may be intel that I am not..."

"I assure you, Commander, you know everything that I know, and then some. Please, I will not hold it against you, should your views differ from my own."

Commander Telles took a deep breath and sighed, considering his words carefully before he spoke. "I agree with your plan to expand the Jung-free zone around Sol as far as possible. Every light year that is added to its radius is time that the Alliance has to build its forces and prepare a defense. However, it is imperative that you remove not only their space forces, but also their ground forces."

"And how would you propose we do that, considering the fact that your own forces are limited?"

"Orbital bombardment, then air strikes, then follow up with boots on the ground for clean-up. Simple as that."

"And what of collateral damage?" Dumar asked.

"It is not a factor," the commander replied without hesitation or remorse.

"Even if they are innocent civilians? Women, children, elderly..."

"You've read the teachings of Lord Evatay, have you not?"

"I have."

"Do you agree that the citizens share in the responsibility of a corrupt government, if they have done nothing to correct the problem?"

"Overall, yes. However, many of these people do not have the ability to take action."

"True, but again, it is not a factor in my decision as to whether or not to risk collateral damage. Our goal is to neutralize the enemy forces, and to do so with minimum casualties to our *own* forces. In order to do that, I cannot be concerned with the welfare of nearby non-combatants."

"But there are ramifications to the loss of lives deemed to be innocent by their fellow citizens."

"When our ships target their ships, they target the entire ship, not just the members of the crew that operate her weapons. The engineers, the medical staff, the galley staff, the barber...everyone on board that ship dies. Are they fair game simply because they agreed to enlist? Did they agree to enlist? Or was their service an inescapable requirement of their society?"

"We don't know..."

"Which is why we cannot be concerned with that fact."

"Your analogy is flawed, Commander," the admiral argued. "We cannot defeat the ship without killing the non-combatant members of her crew. The Jung do not surrender."

"Nor can we afford to take out the enemy's ground forces without loss of indigenous non-combatants... not if you wish the Ghatazhak to survive long enough to liberate all the worlds in this sector, Admiral. *That* is a fact that must be considered when formulating a plan."

"Which is why I am here, speaking with you," Dumar pleaded. "I need a way to eliminate those ground forces without significant loss of indigenous non-combatants."

"Why do you care about these people?" Commander Telles wondered.

"Because I need them to join us," the admiral replied. "Not because they fear us, but because they believe in us. We need people...thousands of them. Hundreds of thousands, in fact. We need them to fight. We need them to build. We need them to farm. More importantly than all of that, we need them to believe. To believe that, together, we can defeat the Jung."

"That is the problem, Admiral," the commander said, shaking his head. "You cannot defeat the Jung."

Admiral Dumar looked surprised.

"It is simple math. When you look at the number of ships, the time required for interstellar communications, and the time required to move ships into position for coordinated attacks, then compare them to even the most optimistic build schedules—even if you had every system in this sector on your side, and every one of them had a shipyard like the Cetians—the best you could ever hope for would be a stalemate. *That*, Admiral, is an irrefutable fact."

"Then why do you and your men fight?" the admiral wondered.

"The logical answer would be because we were programmed to be loyal to the Alliance, and in my case, to Captain Scott. But it goes deeper than that. We fight for the Alliance because we believe it is the right thing to do."

"An odd statement, coming from a man who was trained to kill without remorse."

"You make that statement because, just like everyone else, you do not understand the Ghatazhak."

"Then enlighten me, Commander," the admiral requested, leaning back in his chair and crossing his arms across his chest.

"You believe that the Ghatazhak *enjoy* fighting, that we *enjoy* killing. Nothing could be further from the truth. We take great pride in our abilities, and we take great satisfaction in carrying out our missions with efficiency and success. However, the ultimate success for a Ghatazhak would be for our efforts to lead to a universe where such violence would no longer be necessary...that the mere threat of it would be enough to prevent it from ever occurring." The commander sighed. "Unfortunately, such is not the nature of the human animal, and I suspect that it never shall be."

"A sad statement."

"On the contrary," the commander disagreed, "it is our violent nature that ensures the very survival of our species. It enables us to survive under the harshest of conditions. It enables us to endure the worst hardships. And it even causes us to 'cull the herd' when it gets out of control and threatens to collapse us under our own weight. You see, the flaws that so plague humanity are also the very same ones that lead to our successes. Without them, we would be like herds of *gorato*, grazing and shitting, waiting to die, accomplishing nothing more than the creation of fertilizer through our excrements and our rotting corpses, destined to eventual extinction at the hands of our predators."

This time, it was Admiral Dumar who let out a heavy sigh. "You have an unusual view of the universe, Lucius."

"I would argue that it is a realistic one."

"Perhaps." The admiral sighed again.

"It is obvious this decision weighs heavily on your mind, Admiral," the commander commented.

"Indeed it does," Dumar admitted. "I must find a way to defeat the ground forces without losing one of my most valuable resources. Namely, you and your men."

"Do not worry about the Ghatazhak, Admiral," Commander Telles said. "We will gladly fight to the last man. You only have to ask."

"I have what I hope is a better idea," the admiral said. "If I were to give you a thousand able-bodied young men, each of them willing to fight and die for our cause, could you turn them into an effective fighting force?"

"Of course," the commander replied with confidence. "We have trained over ten thousand security officers for the Earth Security Force."

"And how long was their training?"

"The basic training consisted of eight weeks. Then the top ten percent went on for an additional eight weeks of training."

"And would you take them into combat against the Jung?" the admiral asked.

"If the odds were overwhelmingly in our favor, yes," the commander replied, realizing where the admiral was heading. "How many men have you acquired?"

"So far, only a few hundred from each member world. In total, about a thousand. But it has only been a few days since we called for volunteers. We are hoping for numbers in the tens of thousands."

"You bring them to us, and we will train them," the commander promised. "They will not be as well trained as the Jung, and they certainly will not be anything like the Ghatazhak, but they will be an effective fighting force."

"One that you can take into combat against entrenched Jung ground forces, and win?"

"Depending on the situation and the force strengths, it is possible."

"I was hoping you would say that, Commander," the admiral said as he stood. "The first thousand volunteers will be arriving in three days. If the current rate of enlistment across all member worlds continues to hold, you will have a new batch of one thousand men every week. Can you handle that?"

"Yes, sir," Commander Telles said, as he also stood. "How soon do you need the first group to be ready for action, sir?"

"Thirty days, Commander."

Commander Telles looked concerned. "A challenging task. May I ask why you need them so quickly?"

"Because in thirty days, both the Aurora and the Celestia will be ready for action, and we will start kicking ass, Commander."

* * *

"Seems kind of tight, doesn't it?" Nathan commented as the elevator pad slowed and he got his first view of the Celestia's new fighter launch deck.

"The idea was to dedicate as much space as possible to the launch tubes," the master chief explained.

"There's barely enough room for ships to maneuver in here. A lot of those Eagle pilots are going to be low-timers. *Really* low-timers, in fact."

"The movement system will be automated," Cameron said. "Ground crews will only have to input where they want a ship to be parked, and the ship will move there automatically. The pilots will only be in the cockpits from launch to landing."

"Throughout the entire ship, or just on this deck?" Nathan wondered.

"The entire ship," the master chief chimed in. "If it rolls on our decks, it does so by control of the auto-movement system."

"It's going to be that way on the Aurora as well," Cameron added.

"I can think of a few pilots who might object," Nathan replied as they stepped off the port elevator pad and headed forward.

"Four tubes per side, so, eight ships will always stand ready in the tubes, and eight more lined up to enter," Master Chief Montrose explained as they walked. "We'll be able to get sixteen Eagles off in just a few minutes of an alert. Another sixteen within the following ten minutes."

"Ten minutes?" Nathan replied, unimpressed. "Surely we can do better than that?"

"Can't be helped," Cameron insisted. "It takes time to get additional ships up from the hangar deck, and we can only fit two Eagles per elevator pad. There just isn't enough space here."

"I still think we should have put the launch tubes on the primary cargo deck," Nathan said.

"That would have taken months," Cameron reminded him. "We would've had to remove propellant tanks, maneuvering thrusters—and the hull is twice as thick there. Besides, if we need to get more ships off faster, we can always launch them from the main catapults on the main flight deck. Three at a time, per side. All in all, it's still a more efficient system than the original design."

Nathan looked into one of the port launch tube airlocks. "Wow, that is really tight."

"I said the same thing when I first saw it," Cameron agreed. "Since they'll never launch anything but Eagles, they made the airlocks really snug, so as to save time repressurizing them between launch cycles. The tubes themselves are slightly bigger, but not by much."

Nathan stopped and looked around, taking notice of all the work still in progress. "How long until everything is complete?"

"It's mostly just touch-up work and adjustments right now," Master Chief Montrose said.

"The first Super Eagles won't start rolling off the production line for a couple more weeks," Cameron added. "This deck will be fully operational long before then."

"How long until you get your first birds?" Nathan asked.

"According to the admiral's office, the first sixteen ships should be delivered to us in forty-nine days."

"Sixteen fighters in less than two months," Nathan commented in awe.

"Fabricator technology is a wonderful asset," Cameron said, equally amazed. "Plasma weapons and shields aside, they've got to be the best thing the Pentaurus cluster gave us." Cameron looked at Nathan. "We wouldn't have them if you hadn't chosen to stay and defend Corinair."

"Despite your objections," Nathan added, a wry smile on his face.

"Despite my objections," Cameron admitted.

Nathan paused again as they reached the center of the compartment, slowly turning a full circle as he took the entire scene in. "Makes me wish I had become a fighter pilot instead."

"You're not cocky enough," Cameron said. "Arrogant, yes."

* * *

"Most of our intelligence comes from the gathering of emissions from the worlds within the system," Commander Saray said. "In addition, we are also able to glean some details from the business transactions between Darvano and Takara, and Savoy and Takara. It is by no means complete, however. And from what we've pieced together thus far, it does not appear that the nobles of Takara are doing anything other than minding their interstellar business interests. In fact, several houses have traded their interstellar assets for interplanetary, or even domestic concerns."

"No doubt, they are trying to reduce their financial risks in uncertain times," Captain Navarro stated.

"A wise move," Commander Golan commented.

"There are a few who are buying up those interstellar interests with considerable enthusiasm," Commander Saray continued.

"They will be worthy of monitoring," the captain cautioned. "As they are taking the greatest financial risks, they will be more concerned with the stability of the cluster than others."

"Or the *instability*," Commander Saray added. "Great profits can be pulled from such conditions, if one is clever enough."

"True," Captain Navarro agreed.

"What we *need* are operatives on the ground," Commander Saray said.

"Have you none?" Commander Golan wondered. "You are the chief of intelligence, after all."

"I have many operatives," Commander Saray defended. "Unfortunately, most of them are *not* positioned within the Takaran system. We had neither warning nor time..."

"Gentlemen, please," Captain Navarro interrupted, "None of us could have foreseen the abrupt changes this sector has experienced in the last year. All we can do is adapt to the changes as best we can."

"I can get operatives onto the Takaran worlds," Commander Saray promised, "but it will take time."

"How much time?" Captain Navarro asked.

"Weeks, maybe even months."

Captain Navarro sighed, a pensive look on his face. "And then it will take additional time for them to position themselves."

"Without raising suspicion, yes," Commander Saray agreed.

"Do what you can, Commander."

"Yes, sir."

Captain Navarro turned to Commander Golan, sitting on the opposite side of the table from Commander Saray. "How are our sensor nets?"

"As instructed, we have deployed reprogrammed sensor drones along all major shipping lanes leading to and from the Takaran system. They are using only passive systems, so they will be difficult to detect, should anyone be looking for them. We have tasked a comm-drone to jump from sensor to sensor, once a day, to collect recorded readings."

"And if an outbound warship should pass one of the sensor drones?" Commander Saray wondered. "If it is a jump ship, the drone will never see it."

"Obviously, it will only detect conventional FTL traffic, in which case the daily collection of data will be more than sufficient. Even if it could detect a jump ship, it would be of no value as the ship in question would reach its destination long before warning could be received, even if the sensor was programmed to abandon its position and jump back to warn us."

"Seems rather pointless."

"The nobles have three ships in total," Captain Navarro pointed out. "And only one of them is currently jump capable."

"*Currently*, being the operative term," Commander Saray emphasized. "Intelligence indicates they are putting every effort into making their remaining ships jump capable, as well."

"A cruiser and two frigates are hardly a concern," Commander Golan said.

"No, they are not," Captain Navarro agreed. "As long as we know where they are. I am more concerned about that battleship."

"The Inman?" Commander Golan wondered, seeming somewhat surprised by his captain's concerns. "She is at least two years from completion, *if* the nobles are able to maintain her build schedule, which I seriously doubt. Besides, did you not warn them not to attempt to increase their fleet strength?"

"We have no indications that construction has resumed on the Inman, Captain," Commander Saray assured the group. "In fact, we have unconfirmed reports of resources and equipment being taken *away* from the Inman in favor of their operational vessels."

"The nobles *will* resume construction of the Inman," Captain Navarro insisted. "House Kalisch has too much invested in her to simply walk away. Furthermore, they know that until the Darvano and

Savoy systems are able to build their own warships, we are stuck here, defending them."

"Perhaps we should strike now," Commander Golan speculated. "The Inman's assembly facility has no significant defenses. A flight of combat jump shuttles, and a handful of jump fighters could easily set the Inman's completion back several years, if not destroy her completely."

"Too aggressive," Captain Navarro replied. "Such an overt act would almost require an armed response by the nobles—to save face, if nothing more."

"Captain, rumor has it that the houses holding ownership of Takara's three warships are demanding compensation from the other houses in exchange for protection," Commander Saray explained. "If this is true, and if the other noble houses agree to such compensation, it will greatly restrict the movements of those ships."

"Especially if the Avendahl continues to be seen as a direct threat," Commander Golan observed.

Captain Navarro leaned back in his chair, folding his arms across his chest pensively. He uncrossed them to rub his chin, pondering the situation. "Commander Golan, should one or two of your sensor drones inadvertently release detectable emissions, I shall not be angry."

"An occasional probe of the outskirts of Takara might be in order as well," Commander Saray suggested.

"A gunship or two, perhaps?" Commander Golan added.

"A single ship should suffice," Captain Navarro insisted. "Let's not make it too obvious."

"Yes, sir." Commander Golan replied.

"You know, Captain, it *is* possible that Lord

Ganna was speaking in earnest. After all, any attempt to expand the Takaran Empire at this time would be extremely risky, and would offer little reward. Furthermore, the Takaran economy is far too fragile at the moment."

"I have considered that," Captain Navarro admitted. "However, I do not trust Ganna, or any of the other major houses of Takara. Such men crave wealth—sometimes at the sacrifice of all else. Let us not forget how profitable the times of expansion were for us all, under the reign of Caius. Our job, gentlemen, is to see that it does not happen again."

* * *

Commander Telles walked briskly across the tarmac toward the assembly of men, Master Sergeant Jahal at his side. "I assume that they have all met minimum physical requirements?"

"Of course," Master Sergeant Jahal replied. "Every one of them was screened at the Karuzara's medical center before being transferred down to us. They are healthy and fit for duty, and there is not a Jung nanite in any of them."

Commander Telles looked at the master sergeant. "That's surprising, considering they all came from worlds that were recently occupied by the Jung."

"That's why there are only a thousand volunteers, at the moment," the master sergeant explained. "More than twice that number volunteered, but only these men were nanite-free."

Commander Telles stepped up onto the podium, turning to face the men assembled before him. Ghatazhak sergeants moved up and down their lines, chewing out volunteers whose stance they did not deem proper. He listened to their voices, remembering those of his own drill instructors many years ago, when he was only a teenager. Those men had scared the crap out of him at first. He had hated each and every one of them. However, over time, he had learned to use that hatred to fuel his own desire to excel, so that those men would have no reason to yell at him.

The commander turned his head slightly, looking at his master sergeant.

"Company, ah-ten-HUT!" the master sergeant barked, his voice loud and sharp enough to be heard over even the distant whine of lift turbines and the *zing* of shuttles disappearing in jump flashes only a few hundred meters above them.

The group of men snapped to attention, their bodies rigid, their hands at their sides, and their eyes straight ahead. The commander paused again as his sergeants went into even greater fury, chastising anyone who was not standing tall in their eyes. After nearly a minute, the last sergeant fell to the side of the line, until the entire company was standing tall and proud.

Commander Telles touched his comm-set, tying it into the loudspeaker built into the podium. "Gentlemen, my name is Commander Lucius Telles. I am the leader of the Ghatazhak, and the commanding officer of all Alliance ground forces. Our number currently stands at four hundred seventy-eight. In thirty days, those of you who pass this course will be added to that number. The men training you are seasoned Ghatazhak, all of whom have survived the bloodiest combat you can possibly imagine...more than once. Each of them trained for more than a decade before they were ever put into harm's way. You will not find better trained warriors anywhere in the galaxy. Make no mistake, when you

116

finish your training, you will not be as them. You will never be as them. However, you *will* be ready to fight. Ready, able, and equipped. You *will* fight, and many of you *will* die. For that is the nature of war. Train hard, as if your life, and the lives of the men standing beside you, depend on it...for they do. As of this moment, you should all be considered brave men. For each of you has volunteered to give your life in the service of something much greater than yourself. There is no braver act, and there is no greater pride. Give me your best effort, and I will always give you mine." Commander Telles turned to his master sergeant. "Master Sergeant Jahal. Get these men into uniforms."

CHAPTER FOUR

"*Admiral Galiardi, you claim that Captain Scott did not have the authority to form the Sol-Pentaurus Alliance, and that the Earth Defense Force should still exist. Can you elaborate on that for our viewers?*"

"This should be good," Jessica said.

Nathan watched the view screen on the wall of his ready room, as the camera switched from the interviewer to Admiral Galiardi.

"*I'd be glad to, Meredith. First of all, although* then *Lieutenant Scott was in fact handed command by the legal commander of the Aurora prior to succumbing to his injuries, according to EDF regulations, the acting captain did not have the same authority as the legal captain, which means Lieutenant Scott did not have the authority to enter into agreements on behalf of the EDF and Earth itself. As the acting commanding officer of the Aurora, he only had the authority to make decisions to ensure the safe return of the ship and her crew back to EDF control, at which time a new legal commanding officer would have been appointed.*"

"That's a crock!" Jessica snorted.

"Ssh! I'm trying to listen," Nathan scolded.

"*But when the Aurora arrived back in the Sol system, the Jung had already seized control of Earth, and the EDF had surrendered,*" the interviewer said.

"*That's irrelevant to the question of whether or not the Alliance is binding upon the people of Earth,*" the admiral insisted. "*The question is whether or not the formation of this alliance was reasonably necessary in order to ensure the Aurora's safe return to EDF control. When you look at the performance logs of the Aurora's jump drive while she was still in the Pentaurus cluster, it becomes apparent that she probably could have made it home unaided, possibly even before the Jung invaded."*

"Now that *is* a crock!" Jessica blurted out.

"Jess..."

"You know damn well we wouldn't have made it home in time, even if we had headed back immediately."

"We can't know that for sure," Nathan reminded her.

"Even if we had, we would have been in no shape to take on the Jung fleet that invaded Earth," Jessica argued. "And we wouldn't have any of the weapons or technology that we have now..."

"Jess, please," Nathan begged.

"But he is *so* full of shit."

"The EDF did not cease to exist after we surrendered to the Jung. The fact is, a highly trained force went underground—myself included—all according to a plan devised years prior," Admiral Galiardi told the reporter.

"So, you're saying that the surrender was all part of some elaborate plan?" the interviewer asked for clarification.

"Precisely," the admiral replied. *"We determined a long time ago that if the Jung came at us with more than a dozen or so ships, Earth would likely fall. Surrender was our backup plan. We had been stockpiling arms and munitions for years. We even laid traps out among the asteroids in hopes of luring Jung ships in and destroying them. When we surrendered, everyone who knew of the plan went into hiding, including all of our scout ships. The idea*

was to wait in hiding, and attack when opportunities presented themselves."

"But you were captured by the Jung, tortured by them..."

"I wasn't exactly tortured," the admiral corrected.

"You spent the better part of a year in the hospital because of capture..."

"Not because of torture," the admiral corrected. *"Most of my injuries were the result of my attempts to evade capture."*

"And the neurological injuries that you sustained?" the interviewer asked.

"Those were the result of the more aggressive nanite protocols the Jung used to extract information from me."

"Wouldn't that be called torture?"

"Perhaps, but not in the traditional sense. But we are wandering from the point, here, Meredith. The fact of the matter is, the EDF did not technically surrender. Therefore, it should still exist as a military entity. An entity governed by the duly elected leaders of Earth, and not by people from halfway across the galaxy."

"But Admiral, haven't those people volunteered to help us? Haven't they been sacrificing themselves to help protect Earth?"

"Yes, and we should be forever grateful," the admiral agreed. *"I just don't think we should be allowing them to have control over our people and our ships."*

"I can't watch this crap any longer," Jessica said, picking up the remote and turning off the view screen in disgust.

"Maybe I wanted to watch it?" Nathan said, displeased.

"He's just trying to make waves," she insisted. "He's just trying to call attention to himself."

"To what end?" Nathan questioned.

"I don't know. Maybe he wants to run for president, or something?"

"Strange way of going about it. From what I've seen on the Earth nets, most Terrans support the Alliance and are damn glad that we created it."

"That's just because of Takaran fabrication technology," Jessica insisted. "Without it, most of us would still be living in makeshift camps."

"Plenty of us still are, Jess," Nathan pointed out.

"There are more than a thousand fabricators chugging away on the surface," Jessica replied, "and they're making more of them every day. Because of them, we're recovering faster than anyone could have dreamed. In a few years, it will be like it never happened."

"I seriously doubt that," Nathan muttered.

"Not as long as there are people like Galiardi out there, spouting his mouth off and stirring up dissent."

"Did it ever occur to you that he might actually believe what he is saying?" Nathan asked. "I mean, we *are* spread a little thin, after all. Sure, all of the worlds that we've liberated thus far will be within our maximum double-jump range, but if we keep expanding, that won't be the case. There is a logical argument to be made for concentrating on our own safety, before going out and liberating everyone else."

"It didn't stop you from liberating Tanna," Jessica argued, "and they're *way* outside our double-jump range."

"Yes, but we desperately needed propellant at the time."

"That's my point. It was a calculated risk, just like attacking the battle group at Alpha Centauri B, and Tau Ceti, and all the others. That's the way wars work. Risk versus reward. Galiardi should know that. Which is why I'm crying foul here, Nathan. If that old fart was still in command, he'd have us obliterating everything with a Jung logo on it throughout the sector. He's just bitching because he's *not* in command, and he desperately *wants* to be."

"Perhaps," Nathan admitted, "but it won't happen anytime soon, that's for sure. Not as long as my father is in office."

* * *

Commander Telles stood at the rail of the watchtower, looking out across the training grounds. In the distance, he could see a group of men making their way through the obstacle course. Directly opposite, he could see another group on the rifle range, and a third group on the handgun range. In front of him, several groups were receiving instruction in hand-to-hand combat from Ghatazhak sergeants. He watched as, one by one, the trainees failed to disarm their Ghatazhak instructors. He sighed.

"It's only been four days, Commander," Master Sergeant Jahal reminded him, noticing his frustration. "I doubt I could disarm Sergeant Toomey myself."

"They have determination, but they have no skills." The commander looked at the master sergeant. "They will be easy fodder for the Jung."

"They may yet surprise you," Master Sergeant

Jahal said. "A few of them do have some natural skills." Both men winced as one of the trainees hit the ground hard after being thrown by his instructor. "Not *that* one, obviously," the master sergeant said, holding back a laugh. "Perhaps he will do well on the range?"

"How is the body armor coming along?" the commander asked.

"The engineers have come up with a modified system that combines the EDF tactical protective gear with our own tactical helmet, comms, and power packs. They will not have the full capabilities of our combat gear, but it will provide considerable protection, and more importantly, it will link up with our own tactical data systems."

"An odd combination, is it not?"

"There was already plenty of EDF gear available, and the additional Ghatazhak elements can be fabricated easily enough."

"But the EDF gear was designed to defend against projectile weapons," the commander said.

"Yes, but they create a decent substructure to which we can easily attach our own elements. Trust that the men will be adequately protected."

"It would be better if we could put them all in full level-two Ghatazhak combat gear."

"The assistive undergarment is more complex to fabricate, especially if it must be done so for different sizes. And without the undergarment, our combat gear is rather heavy."

"Yes, I remember," the commander said, recalling the days spent training without functioning assistive undergarments.

"They are also working on various modifications, such as more heavily armored versions for the front lines, and even combat shields that can be carried for additional protection."

"Sounds rather cumbersome."

"Perhaps," the master sergeant admitted, "but these men will not be trained to fight in the same style as the Ghatazhak. Therefore, they will require different gear."

"A wise observation, my friend," the commander said, as he watched one of the trainees below finally manage to perform the disarming move correctly. He looked at his master sergeant. "Well, that's one."

* * *

"You want to send them our fighter pilots?" Commander Montague asked in disbelief. "Excuse me, sir, but whose brilliant idea was that?"

"Mine, actually," Captain Navarro replied.

"I see," the Avendahl's wing commander said.

"We are not likely to see significant action in the near future, Commander. Even if we did, it would likely be ship-to-ship, not fighter engagements. And we are surely not engaging in any ground assaults requiring close air support in the months to come. In fact, it is quite likely that we will remain here, in the Darvano system, for the next few years."

"But, Captain..."

"It would only be a loan," Captain Navarro explained, "until they can train new pilots from Alliance worlds in the Sol sector."

Commander Montague sighed. "I wasn't aware that they even *had* any fighters."

"They do not. But they soon will. The first Super Eagle will roll off their new production line in about a week's time. Within a few months, they will have two full squadrons. Your men would not only be helping to train their new pilots, but they would be gaining valuable combat experience."

"Assuming they don't get killed," the commander protested. "If I remember correctly, their Eagles were no match for the Jung fighters."

"The *old* Eagles, yes. The Super Eagles will be much more formidable," Captain Navarro explained, trying to sell the commander on the idea. "Maybe even more formidable than our own."

"In the hands of my men, perhaps."

"Exactly my point. Meanwhile, we can begin training replacement pilots here, using Corinairans and Ancotans."

"Why?"

"As you said, some of our pilots might not return. In addition, the demand for pilots in the Sol sector will always be high, just as it will be here. We might as well be prepared."

Commander Montague sighed again, resigning himself to the inevitable. "How many?"

"Thirty-two," the captain replied. "In four groups of eight."

"That's a third of our pilots, Captain."

"I was going to ask for half," Captain Navarro confessed.

"Fine, thirty-two it is. How soon will they be leaving?"

"Thirty days, at the most. I have already received the specifications on the Super Eagles for your men to study, so they can be prepared to get to work as soon as they arrive."

"Will there even be enough ships for them to fly when they arrive?" the commander asked.

"No, but they can take turns until more ships are built. The remaining groups will not be sent until

125

their ships are ready. That will give our first eight pilots plenty of time to get to know their ships, and be able to pass their expertise on to the rest of their fellow pilots when they arrive."

* * *

Captain Nash watched the monitors as crew inside the simulator went about the business of crashing their ship into an asteroid. "Cause?" he asked the simulation controller.

"I gave them a failure in the port bow thrusters," the technician replied. "They were on final approach to perform a slingshot maneuver around the asteroid when I initiated the failure."

"At what range?"

"A few hundred meters."

"A little close, don't you think?"

"It should have been enough time for them to compensate with the docking thrusters instead," the tech insisted.

"Yeah, but this crew has what, ten hours of sim time? Maybe you should throw it at them at a distance of at least a kilometer to start with."

"You said to be tough on them, sir."

"Yeah, I know," the captain admitted. "But ease them into the hard stuff. We can't afford to shake their confidence too much in the beginning. If they have too many failures early on, they'll be second-guessing themselves forever."

"As you wish, Captain," the technician replied.

"Give it to them again, from further out."

"The same problem?"

"Yes, the same problem. Let them realize that they *are* able to work the problem."

"Yes, sir."

Robert leaned back in his chair and ran his hands over his face and up through his hair.

"How long since you've slept?" Lieutenant Commander Rano asked.

Robert turned in surprise, having not heard his XO enter the simulator control room. "I don't know." He glanced at the time display on the wall. "Twenty hours, maybe? How did the flight go?"

"It went well. Room for improvement, of course, but overall I think Captain Annatah and his crew are ready to start their service tour."

"Great," Robert replied. "Let's get them out on a standard perimeter patrol. It'll be boring as all hell, but it'll be good for them to get some time in space without anyone looking over their shoulders or yelling at them over the comms."

"I'll send them out first thing tomorrow."

"What about Cobra Three?"

"Rescheduled," the lieutenant commander replied. "Problem with a power coupling. I'm going to take out Cobra Four instead."

"Are they ready?"

"We will see. How is the next group doing in the simulators?"

Captain Nash groaned in frustration. "Not as well as the last bunch, that's for sure. I'm having Tori ease up on them a bit, try and build their confidence before we start slamming them with impossible scenarios."

"Are you sure that is wise?"

"You too?"

"I am only asking," the lieutenant commander said. "The second pair of simulators will be operational in a few days. That should help."

"We can only hope," Captain Nash said.

Lieutenant Commander Rano paused a moment, unsure if he should say what was on his mind. "May I offer a suggestion, Captain?" he asked, sheepishly.

"Sure, Izzu."

"Before simulator two was officially online, I spent several hours in her by myself, just flying her around the system. Nothing fancy, just practicing whatever maneuvers I wished. At times, I would just coast, and fiddle with the systems, just to become more at ease with everything. I believe it made me much more relaxed in the cockpit, as I had the time to become familiar with my surroundings, all without any pressure. Perhaps, that is what this crew needs?"

"I'm not sure we have the time to let crews just play around in the sims, Izzu."

"Maybe try it with just this crew. Give them an hour or two by themselves. You and Tori can get something to eat. See what happens."

"I could use a break, I suppose." Captain Nash turned to the technician. "What about you, Tori? You hungry?"

"I could eat."

"Very well." Captain Nash tapped his comm-set. "Ensign Poray, Ensign Ullweir, the ship is yours for the next two hours. Do whatever you'd like."

"*Sir?*" Ensign Poray replied in confusion over the comms.

"You heard me, Ensign. Do whatever you want. Fly her into an asteroid. Fly her into the sun. Fly her into an ocean. Do loops and rolls for two hours if you'd like. Hell, you can even put her on auto-pilot and take a nap, if that's what you think you need to practice. Specialist Tori and I are going to get a bite to eat, and watch a movie or something. When we get back, we'll get back to it."

"*But sir, what if we crash? Who is going to reset the simulation?*"

Captain Nash smiled. "See that you don't, Ensign. Otherwise, it's going to be a long, boring two hours." Captain Nash stood up. "Come on, Tori, let's go." He looked at Lieutenant Commander Rano. "You comin' with, Izzu?"

"Of course."

* * *

"It is an impressive ship, indeed," Admiral Dumar said as they made their way across the Celestia's port flight deck. "Your people have done well, Captain. You have gotten your ship fully operational more than a week ahead of schedule."

"Thank you, sir, but there are still a few bugs to work out," Cameron replied.

"As expected. I assume that you have prepared a training schedule for the Aurora's crew?"

"Of course," Cameron replied, handing her data pad to the admiral.

Admiral Dumar looked over the schedule on the data pad, before passing it to Nathan. "Have you had a chance to look at this?"

"No, sir, but I'm sure it will be fine," Nathan replied as he took the pad from the admiral.

"Very well." Admiral Dumar turned back toward Cameron. "I thank you for indulging me, Captain. The tour was quite enjoyable. She's a fine ship, and I'm sure you'll do us proud."

"We won't let you down, sir."

"Captain," the admiral said, bidding farewell to Captain Scott as he turned and headed toward his shuttle.

Nathan looked over the training schedule on the data pad as the admiral walked away. "Pretty aggressive schedule."

"Don't blame me," Cameron defended. "Kovacic made the schedule."

"*You* let someone else make a schedule?" Nathan teased.

Cameron flashed a half-hearted smile. "Would you like to watch the launch?"

"Sure."

"This way," Cameron said, turning and heading toward the hatch on the other side of the new forward elevator pad.

"I notice A-shift is putting in the most hours," Nathan commented as they walked.

"They are your primary shift, and they'll be the ones on duty during general quarters," Cameron explained. "The commander figured they needed to have the most training in the beginning. The other shifts pick up the pace later, after A-shift is good to go. Besides, you don't even have the personnel to complete all four shifts yet."

"That's because I gave half my crew to you, remember?"

Cameron pulled the hatch open and entered the corridor. Nathan followed her in, pulling the hatch closed behind him, causing the noise from the flight deck to all but disappear. He followed her through the next hatch to the right, stepping into the port launch tube control room. Two men sat on either side of the room, watching their consoles. A third man, the launch controller, sat between them, his chair standing a bit taller so he could see over his console and out into the port launch tube through the large window in front of him.

"A direct window into the launch tube?" Nathan commented, seeming surprised.

"Some sort of alloy the Takarans invented. As clear as glass and as strong as steel. I don't remember the name."

"Corobal," the launch tube controller provided.

"We decided to eschew the cameras in place of this window," Cameron told him. "Less complicated."

"What if it's damaged?" Nathan wondered.

"This compartment can be sealed, and the corridor can be used as a transfer airlock," Cameron explained. "All the controls can be operated while wearing pressure suits. During general quarters, they'd all be wearing them, just in case. There's also a pressure door that will automatically drop, sealing this compartment off from the launch tube, in case of sudden decompression."

"My personal favorite feature," the launch controller added.

Nathan nodded as he watched the admiral's shuttle pull into the launch bay on the other side of the window. "Why the center catapult?" he asked, noticing that the shuttle was pulling up to the center track.

"Standard shuttles can launch on any of the three tracks, as can Falcons and Eagles," Cameron told him. "Anything larger, like cargo shuttles, must launch on the center catapult track."

"We use the center track for personnel shuttles whenever possible, sir," the launch controller explained. "It's thirty percent longer, so we can get them up to minimum launch speed a little more gently. It's easier on the passengers."

"Makes sense." Nathan continued watching as ground crew wearing helmets, comm-gear, and specialized vests walked alongside the shuttle. A man in a pressure suit stood a few meters forward of the beginning of the center catapult, straddling the track. He watched carefully as the shuttle came to a stop, and the catapult's grappling arm rose up from the carriage and magnetically attached itself to the underside of the shuttle.

"Main door, coming down," the tech on the right announced.

The man in the pressure suit pointed at each of the other two men on either side, waiting for them to indicate that their respective sides of the ship were ready for launch. After returning the okay sign to the man in the pressure suit, they both headed quickly aft, ducking under the main door. The man in the pressure suit moved out of the way toward the far bulkhead.

"*Shuttle Three Two, ready for launch,*" the copilot's voice called over the launch control room's speakers.

"Green light on ground. Crews are clear," the tech on the right reported. "Main door is sealed."

"Depress," the launch controller ordered.

"Depress, aye," the tech on the right replied.

"Shuttle Three Two, Port Cat-Con. Launch in thirty."

"*Shuttle Three Two, aye.*"

"*Port Lead, secure,*" the voice of the man in the pressure suit reported as he stepped behind his protective barrier.

"Depress complete," the tech on the right reported.

"Open inner doors," the launch controller ordered.

"Opening inner doors."

"Echo check is good. Tube is clear," the tech on the left reported. "Cat two is charged and ready."

"Open outer doors," the launch controller ordered as he glanced up at the launch clock.

Nathan also glanced at the clock. It read fifteen seconds and was counting down.

"Outer doors are open. Tunnel is clear. Cat is green. We're good to launch on cat two."

"Flight ops, Port Cat-Con, Launching Shuttle Three Two in ten," the launch controller announced.

"Green light from flight ops," the tech on the left reported.

"Shuttle Three Two, Port Cat-Con. Launch check."

"*Shuttle Three Two, ready to launch.*"

"Drop the grav," the launch controller ordered.

"Gravity dropping to ten percent," the tech on the left replied.

"Launching Three Two in three......two...... one......"

Nathan watched as the admiral's shuttle suddenly accelerated down the launch tube. He turned his head to the left, straining to see the ship as it disappeared from his view. He looked up at the overhead view screen displaying the launch tube camera, just in time to see the shuttle shoot out of the end of the tube and pull away from the Celestia's bow.

"*Shuttle Three Two, away,*" the copilot's voice reported.

"Close her up," the launch controller ordered his men.

Nathan turned to Cameron. "Nice."

"Speeds up launch operations quite a bit," she replied.

"A little unnerving for the passengers, I bet."

"You'll find out in a few minutes," Cameron replied. "Your shuttle is launching next."

Nathan smiled. "You forget, I qualified in Eagles. I've been shot out of a launch tube before."

* * *

Captain Roselle sat in the command chair at the center of the Jar-Benakh's command center, watching the status displays lined up on the overhead just forward of his command platform.

"We're clear of the platform," his helmsman announced.

"Departure reports we are free and clear to maneuver," the communications officer reported.

"Tactical?" Commander Ellison queried as he paced the lower command level, directly in front of his captain. "The threat board is clear, Commander," the tactical officer replied. "The only traffic in the area is what's coming and going between the shipyard and the surface."

Commander Ellison turned around to face the captain. "This ship is ready to maneuver, sir."

"Helm, steer course one four five, up ten relative," Captain Roselle ordered. "Give us a one-minute burn at twenty percent forward thrust."

"Course one four five, up ten. One minute at twenty percent on the mains, aye," the helmsman answered.

Captain Roselle continued to watch the status screens as the ship changed course. He glanced at the larger screen on the forward bulkhead that displayed the forward camera view, as the two distant dots of light that were Kohara and Stennis slid to the right of the screen and down into its lower corner.

"Mains burning at twenty percent," the helmsman reported.

"Stand by on the pre-jump recon drone," the captain ordered.

"PJRD is loaded and ready for launch," the tactical officer reported.

"Engineering reports perfect burn on the mains, Captain," the systems officer announced from behind the captain and to his right.

"Very well."

"Thirty seconds to end of burn," the helmsman reported.

Commander Ellison stepped up onto the main command platform, coming to stand to the captain's right.

"Please tell me it's not always going to be this complicated," the captain said under his breath.

"I expect we'll get the hang of it after a while, sir."

"End of burn," the helmsman reported. "Standard departure speed attained."

"Launch the PJRD," Captain Roselle ordered.

"Launching drone."

Captain Roselle watched the forward view screen as the recon drone sped away from the ship and disappeared in a flash of blue-white light.

"PJRD is away," the tactical officer announced.

"Mas, alert Tau Ceti system control that we will be jumping out of the system in approximately one minute."

"Aye, sir," the Jar-Benakh's communications officer replied.

"Jump Control, XO," Commander Ellison called over his comm-set. "Final check."

"*All jump systems show charged and ready, Commander. We are ready to jump.*"

Ryk Brown

"Navigator?" the commander called.

"Jump to waypoint Alpha Seven, plotted and locked," the navigator reported.

"Sensor contact," Ensign Marka reported from the sensor station. "Jump flash. It's the recon drone. Receiving data stream now."

"Recover the drone," Commander Ellison ordered.

"PJRD data shows the arrival area to be clear," the sensor operator reported.

"Drone is coming in now," the tactical officer reported. "Secure in ten seconds."

Commander Ellison looked at his captain again.

Captain Roselle took a deep breath. "Ensign Noray, jump us to waypoint Alpha Seven."

"Jumping to waypoint Alpha Seven, in five..."

"All hands, prepare to jump," the communications officer announced over the ship's intercoms.

"Three..."

"Here we go, Marty," the captain muttered.

"Two......one..."

On the main view screen, pale blue light began to spill out from the emitters, engulfing the Jar-Benakh's hull like a runaway flood.

"Jumping..."

Once completely covered, the coating of pale blue light quickly intensified, turning a brilliant white that flashed and filled the screen, gently illuminating the interior of the command center for a split second before disappearing.

"Jump complete," the navigator announced.

"Verifying position," the sensor operator added.

The seconds ticked by. Captain Roselle realized he was holding his breath.

"Position verified," Ensign Marka reported triumphantly. "We are at waypoint Alpha Seven."

Cheers broke out amongst the skeleton crew manning the Jar-Benakh's command center.

Commander Ellison reached out to shake his captain's hand. "Looks like the Alliance finally has a third, jump-capable warship in her fleet."

"Let's not get ahead of ourselves, Commander," Captain Roselle warned. "We may be able to jump, and we may have a few weapons working, but we're a long way from being ready to jump into battle."

"Yeah, but at least now we're no longer sitting ducks."

"You got that right," the captain agreed. "Mister Sahbu, put us on course for the next test-jump waypoint."

"Aye, sir," the helmsman replied.

* * *

"*The doors are opening now,*" the reporter announced.

Nathan and Vladimir watched the view screen on the wall as the hangar doors parted, revealing the first ship to roll off line one at the Super Eagle production facility on Earth.

"I can't believe it only takes them two weeks to build one of those things," Nathan exclaimed as the door buzzer sounded.

"They started fabricating parts months ago," Vladimir said. "They had enough to build at least thirty ships before the plant even opened."

"But the first test flight was only a month ago," Nathan said as he opened the door. "Hey, Jess."

"Did it roll out yet?" she asked as she walked past Nathan and headed for the couch.

"The doors are just opening," he replied, closing the door behind her and returning to his chair.

"I like the new tail," Jessica commented as she sat down next to Vladimir. "Makes it look meaner."

"I don't think that was the intent," Nathan commented.

"Where's the food?" Jessica asked.

Vladimir passed her a bowl of chips.

"Are they going to fly it?" she asked.

"They're supposed to."

"Even in the rain?"

"It's a fighter, Jess," Nathan replied. "It can handle a little rain. Hell, I used to fly my grandfather's old biplane in worse than that."

"Your grandfather had a biplane?" Jessica wondered, surprised.

"Yeah, that's where I first learned to fly. He started teaching me as soon as I could see over the console. Hell of a lot different than flying an Eagle, though. Real stick and rudder flying. No automation. Not even an auto-leveler."

"I heard the Super Eagles are highly automated," Vladimir commented. "They even have combat maneuvers preprogrammed into them. Auto-chase, auto-land... I heard you can just get in, push a few buttons, and wait for it to take you to the engagement area. You might even be able to fly an entire mission without ever having to touch the flight control stick."

"It'll never happen," Nathan said doubtfully.

"Why not?" Jessica asked.

"No pilot is going to turn his fate over to an auto-flight system," Nathan explained. "I don't care how good it is."

"Even if it's better than the actual pilot?" Vladimir asked.

"If it's better than the actual pilot, then that pilot doesn't belong in the cockpit."

"What if the pilot is injured?" Jessica wondered. "Wouldn't you let the auto-flight take over for you then?"

"Okay, that's the exception."

"I don't get it," Vladimir said, shaking his head. "I would think a pilot would appreciate the speed at which the computers could perform the maneuvers. If used in combination with the pilot's instincts, it seems like…"

"If you were a pilot, you'd understand."

"Are you saying you never used the auto-flight systems during your Eagle training?" Jessica challenged.

"Oh, I used it all the time," Nathan said. "Just never in combat situations."

"You never flew in combat," Vladimir sneered.

"I meant combat simulations."

"I don't know, I think I'm with Vlad on this one. It seems like just another tool in the pilot's arsenal, if you ask me."

"Perhaps," Nathan agreed. "Maybe someday it will become more accepted and commonplace."

"Josh is climbing into the cockpit," Vladimir said, pointing at the view screen.

"The Super Eagle represents hope," the reporter said. *"Hope for the recovery of Earth, hope for our very survival. At a production rate of one Super Eagle every three days, this plant, and the other two currently under construction, will turn out thousands of fighters over the next few years. The Super Eagles will operate from ground bases on Earth and other Alliance worlds, as well as on Alliance ships and the Karuzara asteroid base in orbit around our world. Combined with the Cobra gunships being assembled*

on Tanna, they will provide a fast, agile, and potent defensive shield for Alliance worlds."

"He's starting up," Nathan said as he watched the canopy close on the Super Eagle.

"The test pilot, Ensign Joshua Hayes, appears to have started his engine. Any minute now, he will be rolling out across the tarmac to the runway for the first flight of Super Eagle Zero One."

"Must be a slow news day," Nathan commented. "She's really trying to make this as dramatic as possible."

The camera followed the fighter as it pulled out onto the runway. It paused briefly, wiggling its control surfaces and running up its engine for a few seconds before taking off. Finally, its engine spun up to takeoff power, and the Super Eagle rolled down the runway, accelerating at an incredible rate. Within seconds, its nose pitched up ever so slightly, and the fighter lifted off the runway. After its landing gear swung upward into its body, the fighter pitched straight up as its engine went to full power. It rode a tail of bright, yellow-orange thrust as it climbed, then it disappeared in a flash of blue-white light.

"Super Falcon Zero One has just successfully taken off and jumped away. Right now, it is well beyond Earth's orbit, and is turning around to jump back to us." There was a flash of blue-white light that lit up the airfield, followed by a deafening crack of thunder and a triple sonic boom as the Super Falcon reappeared and streaked over the airfield at three times the speed of sound. The reporter cringed, ducking instinctively to avoid the passing fighter. Her lips were moving as if she were talking to the camera, but the roar of the Super Falcon's

engine, as it went vertical again, made it impossible for them to hear her.

"I guess Josh is putting on a show, huh?" Jessica commented, smiling.

"I'm sure Prechitt will have something to say about his theatrics," Nathan said with a grin.

* * *

Lieutenant Tillardi entered the newly created jump missile conversion facility, within the Karuzara asteroid base, for the first time since his jump missile prototype had been successfully tested. Excavation of the cavern itself had been completed long ago, in anticipation of future needed space for base expansion. They had only recently prepared the chamber for its first task.

Before him were four assembly lines, each with six stations. Technicians all stood at the ready, waiting for his arrival and inspection before beginning the conversion process. Behind them, along the far wall of the cavern, were rows of Jung missiles, two hundred of them from what he understood, all taken from the Jar-Benakh only days ago.

"What's wrong?" the shift supervisor, Mister Daviore asked, noticing the lieutenant's pale skin color as he approached.

"They removed the warheads first, right?" he asked, his voice barely audible.

"Yes, sir," Mister Daviore assured him. "They're stored in one of the munitions bays, on the far side of the asteroid."

Lieutenant Tillardi swallowed hard, a wave of relief washing over him. "Of course, I should have known that, shouldn't I?"

"It's quite alright, Lieutenant. I know the admiral has you spread over several projects these days."

"You can say that again," Tillardi replied. "Jump KKVs, jump missiles, orbital jump comm-drones..."

"Orbital what?" Mister Daviore wondered, unfamiliar with the term.

"A new type of jump comm-drone," Lieutenant Tillardi explained. "A variant of the mini-jump comm-drones our ships have been using for long-range communications. They fly a set course, jumping between two set worlds, doing a half orbit to turn around and jump back."

"I thought we were using the old converted Takaran comm-drones for interstellar communications?"

"We were, but the admiral wanted them replaced. Something about them being too bulky and complex, needing a lot of service, and using a lot of propellant. I guess he wanted something more efficient."

"What is he going to do with the old ones?" Mister Daviore wondered.

"I have no idea," the lieutenant admitted. "Nor do I care. It's one less thing for me to deal with, as far as I'm concerned. Are we ready to get started?"

"Yes, sir," Mister Daviore replied energetically.

"Great."

"No disrespect intended, sir, but we *can* handle this without you. Your team already figured out how to do the conversions. We're just going to be copying what your guys did, and I know how busy you are."

"I know you can, Markum," the lieutenant replied. "I think the admiral just wanted me here for the first day, just to make sure things get off to a good start. The two most important things for the Alliance right now *are* these jump missiles, and the JKKVs. Trust me, as soon as I see things are going smoothly here, I'll be out of your hair."

"Understood."

Lieutenant Tillardi patted Markum Daviore on his shoulder as they headed for the lines. "Shall we get started?"

* * *

"You wanted to see me, Commander?" Jessica asked from the doorway.

"Lieutenant Commander Nash," Commander Telles said, rising from his office chair. "Yes, but it was not necessary for you to come all the way down to Porto Santo."

"It was a good excuse to see my parents," Jessica said, taking a seat across the desk from him, and putting her feet up. "What's up?"

Commander Telles squinted, irritated by both her casual demeanor and the expression. "I would like to ask for your help."

"Really?" Jessica giggled. "I can't wait to hear this."

"Indeed," the commander replied stiffly, sitting back down. He was the first to admit that he did not understand the female mind, and the lieutenant commander was even more perplexing than most. "I was hoping that you could help train our men."

"On what? How to be insubordinate?"

"Hardly. Hand-to-hand combat."

"I thought you guys were such badasses. What could I teach them?"

"The Ghatazhak methods take considerable time to master. We have attempted to give the men a... how do you say it? A 'crash course', but it does not seem to be working. The Ghatazhak methods are very efficient, and they require considerable mental discipline. This is something that cannot easily be taught."

"So, you think it's easy to teach someone to fight like me?" Jessica appeared insulted.

"I didn't mean..."

"Relax, Telles, I'm just playing with you. But in all seriousness, it did take a while to learn to fight the way I fight, as well."

"Of course. What I meant was, the EDF spec-ops style has a certain... *abandon*. It is very aggressive."

"That's probably more *me* than it is spec-ops training," Jessica admitted.

"Nevertheless, I believe it would be a more effective method, given the allotted time. In addition, you are more familiar with the EDF weapons, which we will be using to arm these men."

"So, what you're saying, is that *I'm* more qualified to teach them than *you* are." Jessica smiled, appearing quite pleased with herself. "Damn. How could I say no? I get to yell at a thousand marines and tell them what to do...call them names. Sounds like fun. And on top of that, I get out of most of Captain Taylor's screwy drills. Sign me up, Chief."

"Thank you."

"By the way," Jessica said as she took her feet off the commander's desk. "How much time do we have?"

"Two weeks."

Jessica's eyes widened. "Shit. I guess we'd better get started." She stood up to leave. "First thing in the morning?"

"That would do nicely," the commander replied.

"You got it, Chief."

"I have another favor to ask," Commander Telles said. "Please don't call me 'chief'. I am a commander, not a chief."

"Right." Jessica turned to leave.

"Lieutenant Commander Nash?" the commander called after her.

Jessica turned back around, feigning irritation. "Yes?"

"You are dismissed."

Jessica straightened up and offered a half-hearted salute.

Commander Telles returned her salute, and waited for her to depart before returning to his reports. "A difficult case, that one. Difficult indeed."

* * *

"God, this is fun," Loki exclaimed, as he chased Super Eagle Zero One through the skies over the gulf.

"*What did you say?*" Josh called over the comms.

"I said this is fun!" Loki replied.

"*Set your jump range to one thousand meters and follow me,*" Josh instructed as he pointed his fighter straight up and went to full power.

Loki rolled the dial on the side of his flight control stick until the jump range indicator on his flight status display read one thousand meters. He pitched up and went to full power as well, coming to vertical just as Super Eagle Zero One disappeared in a blue-white flash of light. He could feel the acceleration pushing him back into his seat, far more so than he had ever felt in the Falcons. He had originally been opposed to the idea of giving up some of the inertial dampening capabilities, but he was enjoying the sensation of power. He felt as if he were sitting at the tip of a ballistic missile, its massive thrust driving it through mach after mach. He pushed the select switch on the top of his flight control stick forward into the jump position, then pressed the trigger. His canopy instantly turned opaque, and

145

when it cleared a second later, Super Eagle Zero One was again in front of him, still climbing straight up.

"*You still with me?*" Josh wondered aloud.

"You bet," Loki replied, knowing full well that Josh's Super Eagle was linked to his own through a tactical data stream.

Josh's fighter flashed again and disappeared. Loki initiated another jump to follow him, instantly moving another thousand feet higher toward space. He followed Josh, guiding his fighter over to an inverted position, reducing his throttle as his nose came over, eventually settling into an inverted forty-five-degree dive toward the turquoise waters ten kilometers below them. He rolled back upright as he continued his dive, chasing Josh from only thirty meters away and slightly to his starboard side.

"*Let's try a tandem jump,*" Josh suggested. "*Dialing up five kilometers.*"

"Don't you think we should try the first tandem jump in level flight?" Loki argued.

"*Screw that,*" Josh replied. "*Designating Zero One as lead.*"

"Link confirmed," Loki replied. For a moment, he wondered why he was agreeing to partake in Josh's antics. He looked at his altitude tape on his flight status display. It read six thousand meters. "Oh, shit," he exclaimed, his eyes widening. "Josh!"

"*Just be ready to pull up, Lok.*"

Loki glanced at his jump system readouts, noting that his drive was active and ready, and set to five thousand meters.

"*Jumping.*"

Loki's canopy turned opaque again. As it did so, Loki immediately pulled back on his flight control stick, pulling his nose well above the horizon line on his flight status display, as he slammed his throttle forward to full power. When his canopy cleared, he could see Super Eagle Zero One, also at full power, and also struggling to decrease its rate of descent and avoid slamming into the Gulf of Mexico.

For a few tense moments, neither of them spoke. Loki watched as his altitude tape went down to five hundred meters, then four hundred, and finally three hundred, before he finally managed to level off.

"*Guns, guns, guns,*" Josh said in a near giggle. He snap-rolled into a tight left turn, which Loki instinctively followed. As he rolled out of the turn and back to level, he noticed that his jump drive was still linked to Josh's, and that the jump range was changing back to one thousand meters.

"*Jumping,*" Josh announced without warning.

Again, Loki's canopy turned opaque. When it went clear, Josh's fighter was executing a hard right turn, right across Loki's flight path. Loki pushed his nose down slightly to dive under him, and then rolled into a hard right turn to follow.

"*Climbing on one four five, at fifty meters per second,*" Josh reported.

Loki rolled out onto the same course heading and pulled his nose up while he added power to hold the same rate of climb.

"*Selecting range of two kilometers,*" Josh continued. "*After the jump, turn to three four zero, ten degrees down, at one thousand KPH.*"

"Fuck," Loki mumbled, as his canopy turned opaque momentarily. He executed the next maneuver as instructed, changing course and diving toward the surface at a ten-degree angle at one thousand kilometers per hour. Then he pressed the link override button.

"*What are you doing?*" Josh asked.

"We're not here to play games, Josh. We're here to perform a series of two-element tactical tests."

"*That's what I was doing.*"

"You know what I mean," Loki said, as he leveled off and turned to a new course.

"*Where are you going, Loki?*"

"I'm headed for the test range, like we were supposed to do when we first took off. If you don't want to get another ass chewing from Prechitt, you'll do the same."

"*All right, all right,*" Josh relented as his ship pulled up to Loki's left and flew alongside him. "*Killjoy.*"

Loki sighed.

* * *

"Skipper!" Jessica called from down the corridor, as she jogged up to Nathan.

"Lieutenant Commander."

"I was wondering if I could skip the staff meeting today?" she asked as she fell into step beside him.

"Again?"

"It's not like I have anything to contribute," Jessica complained. "All you guys ever talk about these days is repairs and upgrades."

"That's not true."

"Oh, really? What's on the agenda today?" she asked.

"Uh...repairs and upgrades."

"That's what I thought."

"You going down to Porto Santo again?"

"That's what I was hoping."

"You've been spending a lot of time down there,

lately. Cameron says you've missed two training days on the Celestia."

"Cameron is *way* too big on training."

"Are you going to be able to handle the new tactical console?"

"It's a piece of cake," Jessica said. "Delaveaga took me through it in less than an hour. In fact, it's a hell of a lot easier than the old layout."

"Yeah, he used to complain about it a lot," Nathan said. "He came up with the new design, you know."

"Yeah, I know," Jessica replied. "And like I said, it's a lot easier to use, so, no I won't have any problem with it."

Nathan sighed in resignation as he reached the door to the command briefing room. "What's got you so busy down there, anyway?" he wondered. "I thought you were just going to train a few guys how to fight, and then let them train the others?"

"That was the plan. It's just taking more effort than I expected. I don't have a lot of time, remember?"

"I know."

"Once we leave dry dock and get back on the liberation campaign, I'll barely have time to check in on them once in a while."

"Then I suppose I don't have any choice, do I?"

"Not really," she said with a smile.

Nathan looked her in the eyes. "Just be sure you know how to use that console by the time we leave dry dock," he insisted, "or I'll be looking for a new tactical officer."

"No problem, Skipper," she said, turning to depart. "Thanks."

"My pleasure," he replied, turning to enter the command briefing room. "As you were," he said, before the guard at the door could call 'captain on deck'. He despised the formality of having everyone stand when he entered the room, especially since the few people in attendance were all either close friends, or subordinates who he worked with on a regular basis.

Nathan made his way around the table, heading for his usual spot at the end. "You're up, Vlad," he said as he took his seat.

"All thirty-two mark one mini-quad plasma turrets are installed," Vladimir began. "We now have twice the point-defense capabilities as before, without having to worry about running out of slugs."

"Hardly seems worth it, since we usually jump away from incoming ordnance," Mister Navashee commented.

"True, but if we ever lose our jump drive again, you'll be glad we have the extra firepower," Nathan replied.

"Speaking of jump drives, installation of the second set of field generators should be completed by tomorrow," Vladimir said. "After that, all we have to do is wire up the second set of energy banks, and we should be in business."

"Any word on reducing the recharge time?" Lieutenant Yosef wondered.

"Black Lab is still working on it," Nathan said. "I talked to Tilly the other day, and they've made progress, but the prototype is still a few weeks away. Even then, it's going to have to undergo a lot of testing before they're going to put them into our ships."

"How are they going to test them?" the lieutenant asked.

"Once we get enough gunships up and running, they're taking Scout One out of service to use as a test vessel," Nathan explained. He turned to Vladimir. "Has the Celestia's cheng reported any issues with the two-stage jump system?"

"Not yet, but they are still waiting a few minutes between max-range jumps," Vladimir replied.

"Still, thirty light years in a few minutes is nothing to complain about."

"If the improved energy banks aren't going to be ready for a while, maybe we should consider installing another set?" Lieutenant Yosef suggested. "Make it a three-stage system."

"We don't have enough room for another set of energy banks," Vladimir protested. "Not to mention the heat exchange issues."

"I think we can make do with a thirty light year max-range for now," Nathan stated, trying to move the meeting along. "How are our shields coming?"

Vladimir glanced at his data pad. "One week."

"The problem routing around the topside exchangers get solved?" Nathan wondered.

"I made them remove the damaged bulkheads and replace them," Vladimir answered, a sly grin on his face. "They were not happy."

"Is that going to set us back?"

"No, I ordered them to make sure it did not. That's why they were not happy."

"What about the super-tubes, Master Chief?" Nathan asked.

"Starboard side is going like clockwork, Captain," Marcus answered. "Port side is being a bit of a bitch." Marcus glanced at Lieutenant Yosef. "Apologies, sir."

"What's the problem?" Nathan wondered.

"It was pretty badly damaged. The heat from the plasma generators fused most of the decking around it into the framework below deck. We had to cut it all out and replace every spar at the start of the inboard tunnel."

"Is it going to be a problem?"

"No, sir," Marcus insisted. "I've got them working double shifts to stay on schedule. Those tubes will be ready by the time we leave dry dock."

"It's okay if they aren't, Master Chief," Nathan told him. "Better it's done right, than quick. We can get by with the starboard tubes for a few days, if we must."

"Don't worry, Captain. They'll be done," Marcus promised.

"How is the training going, Commander?" Nathan asked, turning to Commander Willard, his executive officer.

"Latest reports show that A-shift is fully checked out in the new consoles," Commander Willard reported. "They've scored high nineties in the last few simulations, as well. The emphasis is on B-shift now. Once they're up to speed, we'll be running mixed crew simulations."

"How much longer until our bridge is ready?" Nathan asked.

"Two days," Vladimir said. "They're running final systems checks now."

"I asked them to put the bridge in simulation mode once the checks are completed," Commander Willard added, "so our crews can practice here, as well as on the Celestia."

"Good thinking, Commander." Nathan turned to Lieutenant Yosef. "How are the new long-range sensor arrays working out?"

"The ones on the Celestia are fantastic. Since our new ones are the same design, they should be good as well."

"Are they completely installed?"

"Yes, sir. I just can't try them out because we're deep inside of an asteroid. But I've been spending a lot of time at the Celestia's long-range sensor console, as has Mister Navashee."

"Sorry you have to pull shifts on the bridge again, Lieutenant, but we're going to be shorthanded until we get another shift trained."

"It's not a problem, Captain."

"Very well, people. We've got nine days left to get this ship ready for action. Let's get back to work."

* * *

"*Many would argue that the technological benefits the Alliance has brought—such as Takaran fabricators and Corinairan nanites—are enough of a reason to maintain our relationships with the member worlds from the Pentaurus cluster,*" the reporter stated.

The camera shifted to Admiral Galiardi. "*I would agree that there have been benefits, but that doesn't negate the diverging needs of the worlds in the Sol sector, and the worlds in the Pentaurus cluster. We are facing two completely different enemies. The flow of volunteers and resources from the Pentaurus cluster has significantly slowed, and what is still flowing are resources that we can produce right here on Earth. If the Pentaurus worlds were sending warships, I might be singing a different tune, but they are not. Nor will they be in the near future. Now that the Takarans have withdrawn from the Alliance, the worlds of the Pentaurus cluster have no choice but to concentrate their efforts on their own security.*"

The broadcast was interrupted by the intercom built into Admiral Dumar's desk.

"*You have an incoming call from Doctor Galloway, Admiral,*" the comm officer said.

"Put her through," the admiral replied, as he switched the main view screen from the recording of Admiral Galiardi's most recent interview to the vid-link with Doctor Galloway at the research facility in Geneva. "Doctor Galloway. To what do I owe the pleasure?"

"*I have good news, Admiral,*" the doctor replied. "*We have figured out how to get rid of the Jung nanites without causing any harm to the host.*"

"Really? That is good news. How did you do it?"

"*Actually, we designed an entirely new nanite of our own. Sort of a combination of Corinairan and Jung nanite technologies. The Jung nanites are self-replicating. They use materials found within the human body—more accurately, materials taken into the human body through the process of eating—to create new nanites. Under normal conditions, which we refer to as 'stage one', the Jung nanite hive only reproduces enough nanites to maintain their current capabilities. In stage one, that is simply to record information and transmit it on interrogation by an outside controller. If the nanite hive receives an order to grow to stage two, they begin producing more nanites, primarily for the purpose of keeping the host healthy, and to be able to record and store more data. At stage two, they can also initiate the transmission of data at will—either on a schedule, or when their data buffers are full. When given a stage three order, the hive produces even more nanites in order to provide control over the host body and mind, turning the host into an unknowing agent. I believe Lieutenant Commander Nash referred to it as 'Jungifying' the host.*"

"This is all very interesting, Doctor, but..."

"*By comparison, Corinairan nanites are*

individually programmed. They do act in hive fashion, but only within a limited scope. And they are not adaptive. Their programming must be regularly updated during the healing process for which they are used. The Jung nanites, on the other hand, can make decisions on their own."

"Smart nanites?"

"In a manner of speaking, yes," the doctor continued. *"A certain number of nanites work together as a 'hive brain'. That brain is able to make decisions that control the rest of the hive, based on the protocols for whatever 'stage' the hive is currently in."*

"So, what is the solution, Doctor?" the admiral asked, growing impatient.

"Well, we were unable to break the Jung nanite control codes. However, we were able to reproduce the Jung nanites in the lab. We were able to put an identifier in our Jung nanites that enable them to differentiate between our Jung nanites—which we refer to as 'Terran nanites'—and the original Jung nanites. Furthermore, the Terran nanites have our control codes, not the Jung's."

"I'm still not seeing the solution."

"We simply inject our nanites into the infected host, and let them fight it out. As long as we put in two to three times as many Terran nanites as there are Jung nanites, the Terran nanites will win."

"And this does not cause the host any discomfort?" the admiral asked.

"No, sir. None at all. The interaction between the Terran and Jung nanites does not involve the host's tissues. It merely takes place within the host. Therefore, the host feels nothing. And not only will the Terran nanites prevail, but they will then use the

155

disabled *Jung* nanites as raw materials to replicate more Terran nanites. The overall result is a healthier host."

"Healthier? How is that possible?"

"Since they are based on the Jung nanites, the Terran nanites are also 'smart', as you say. Their 'hive mind' can analyze the host, and make whatever decisions necessary to maintain the host's overall health. We may even be able to program them to aggressively treat traumatic injuries without external commands."

"You mean, like healing the wounded in the field?" the admiral asked, his interest piqued.

"Exactly," the doctor confirmed. *"In fact, if we maintain a high enough concentration, an injury that would have required evacuation to a medical facility may only require the consumption of some raw materials in the form of food, or intravenous therapy, and a few hours of rest, all of which can be done in the field. It's all very exciting."*

"Indeed it is," Admiral Dumar agreed. "How long until this becomes a reality, Doctor?"

"Well, we still have a lot of testing to do, but I would expect that, in a few months, we should be able to start mass-producing Terran nanites. We will need trillions upon trillions of them to rid everyone on Earth of the Jung nanites, but it is doable, given time."

"And what about giving starter doses to individuals who are *not* infested with Jung nanites?"

"Like current members of the Alliance?" Doctor Galloway guessed.

"Indeed. Specifically the Ghatazhak, and the Marines they are training. They are going to be seeing a lot of action over the next few months."

"I'll see to it that special emphasis is given on that area of application testing, Admiral."

"Very well," Admiral Dumar replied. "Good work, Doctor."

"Thank you, sir."

Admiral Dumar ended the vid-link and resumed the playback of Admiral Galiardi's latest interview.

"I simply do not believe that the benefits of this alliance outweigh the risks," Admiral Galiardi said.

"Let's see what you think after news of the Terran nanites gets out," Dumar mused.

CHAPTER FIVE

"Captain on the bridge!" the guard at the port entrance to the Aurora's bridge called out as Nathan passed.

Nathan walked up to the comm station, pausing at the main console. "Good to see you back where you belong, Miss Avakian," Nathan said.

"Thank you, sir," Naralena replied. "It's good to be back."

"I trust you had time to get used to the new consoles?"

"Yes, sir, I did. They are not that different from the old ones. And I can always rearrange them to my liking, if need be."

"Of course."

"Thank you for the additional time off, Captain," she added gratefully.

"I trust your visit went well?"

"Yes, it did," she said, smiling. "It was good to finally see home again. Thank you for arranging that."

"It was Deliza's idea to offer PC residents transportation to visit home. After all, the Mirai wasn't doing anyone any good just sitting in a hangar bay."

"Well, we all appreciated it."

"It was our pleasure," Nathan replied, turning to head forward.

"Captain," Jessica nodded as Nathan passed the tactical station.

"You good to go?" Nathan asked. "You know how to work that thing?"

"Piece of cake," Jessica replied confidently. "I spent a couple of extra hours practicing last night."

Nathan nodded his approval, turning to take his seat in the new command chair. As he sat, the clear panels that protruded at forty-five-degree angles from the forward end of each armrest, came to life. He tapped the comm-panel on the left, choosing engineering. "Cheng, Captain."

"*Go ahead, sir,*" Vladimir's voice replied through the overhead speaker, as well as through his comm-set.

"How are we looking?"

"*Reactors are hot, power levels are normal, and all maneuvering systems show ready. The ship is completely under her own power, Captain.*"

"Very well." Nathan switched off the connection. "Mister Navashee, how's the weather outside?"

"Dry dock is fully depressurized, sir. Main doors are open, and the main chamber is clear of all traffic."

"Karuzara Control reports exit bravo is clear," Naralena added.

"Very well. Notify Karuzara Control that we are ready to leave dry dock."

"Aye, sir."

"Ensign Reese, stand by to release all umbilicals. Mister Riley, stand by to release all moorings," Nathan ordered.

"Ready to release all umbilicals," the systems officer replied.

"Ready on the moorings," Mister Riley added.

"Release the umbilicals," Nathan directed.

"Releasing umbilicals," Ensign Reese replied.

Nathan tapped his right control panel, calling up the ship's primary systems status display on the large glass display screen set to the right of his helmsman. As expected, none of the readings changed as the eight umbilical cables that had provided power, life support, and communications services to the Aurora during her time in port, disconnected from his ship and retracted into the walls of the massive dry dock chamber.

"All umbilicals have cleanly disconnected," the systems officer reported.

"Dry Dock Control reports all umbilicals are secure," Naralena added. "We are clear to release."

Nathan took a deep breath and sighed. Although he had enjoyed the freedom to travel around a bit the last two months—especially enjoyed not having to shoot or be shot at—he was ready to get his ship back into space. It wasn't that he wanted to be back in action, he simply wanted to finish the job and get his own life, as well as the lives of everyone else, back to some semblance of normal. They had all been struggling to survive for nearly two years, and they were finally in a position to really make a difference...to break the cycle of barely hanging on, and finally be able to gain some ground. They would continue their offensive, and create a bigger, stronger Alliance by adding twice as many new members as currently existed. If nothing else, it would be sending a message to the Jung that the worlds of the Sol sector were no longer going to put up with them. They were going to fight back, together.

"Release all moorings," Nathan ordered.

"Releasing all moorings," Mister Riley answered, reaching for the mooring control panel to his left. "All moorings released. The ship is free-floating."

Nathan paused, waiting for the final word. A few seconds later, it came.

"Dry Dock Control reports all mooring arms secured," Naralena reported. "We are free to maneuver."

"Very well. Mister Chiles, if you please. Back us out, slowly," Nathan ordered.

"Back slow, aye," the helmsman replied.

———

The Aurora backed out of the Karuzara dry dock, slowly passing between its two massive, multi-part doors with only twenty meters to spare on either side. Spotters in full pressure suits and maneuvering packs floated alongside, watching, with trained eyes, the ship they had worked on for months. Backing the massive ship out of the confines of dry dock was not only a delicate maneuver, but it was also the first real test of the ship's repaired docking thrusters. If anything went amiss, service tugs hovering nearby would have to move quickly into position to provide the needed corrective thrust.

Finally, after fifteen long minutes, the bow of the Aurora cleared the dry dock doors and fired her aft thrusters to slow her rate of travel to a complete stop. With a few more minutes, as well as a few dozen blasts of her aft docking thrusters, the ship's backward motion finally came to a stop, and she fired her port thrusters to start a slow starboard rotation.

———

Nathan watched the main view screen as the walls of the Karuzara asteroid's main cavern slid slowly to the left. He looked all around the screen—right to left, up and down. It was one of the few times that he really liked the quarter-sphere view screen that encapsulated the forward half of his bridge. At such times, the view was tremendous.

"Applying counterthrust," the helmsman reported as the entrance to bravo tunnel approached the center of the screen. Their rotation began to slow, the entrance eventually coming to a stop directly ahead of them.

"Rotation complete," Mister Chiles reported.

"Karuzara Control advises we are clear for departure via bravo," Naralena announced.

"Take us out, Mister Chiles," Nathan ordered. "Ahead slow."

"Ahead slow, aye," the helmsman acknowledged. "Engaging auto-flight, bravo departure."

"Bravo departure, auto-flight tracking, locked," Mister Riley answered from the navigator's chair. "Bravo internal threshold in two minutes. External in eighteen."

"Twenty minutes just to get out into open space?" Jessica wondered.

"Standard departure is slow and easy," Nathan explained. "Emergency departure gets us out in half that. You'd know that if you'd been at all the training sessions." Nathan smiled, enjoying the jab at his friend.

The entrance to bravo tunnel grew larger on the view screen, stretching nearly from side to side.

"One minute to bravo," the navigator announced.

Jessica raised her brow as she ran additional systems checks on all her weapons systems. "Ten minutes is a long time when you're under attack," she muttered.

"Which is why we try to stay *out* of port as much as possible," Nathan replied.

Jessica flashed a courtesy smile that went unseen by her captain.

"Entering bravo," the navigator announced, as the opening finally engulfed the entire ship. A shadow passed over the bridge as the ship passed the threshold into the Karuzara asteroid's main exit tunnel. Back before the Aurora had left the Pentaurus cluster for Sol, bravo tunnel had barely been large enough for a shuttle to pass through, and was considered only suitable as an emergency escape path if the main entry tunnel became damaged. With the increase in shipping traffic, and warship service, the main cavern had been enlarged, along with bravo tunnel, giving the Karuzara asteroid base both an entrance *and* exit for ships as large as the Aurora and the Celestia.

"Seventeen minutes to the exit," Mister Riley added.

Nathan watched the circumferential lighting panels slide past them, as the Aurora's auto-flight system steered the ship along a preprogrammed flight path that followed the gentle curves of the tunnel with precision. It was, indeed, an agonizingly slow pace. However, at this speed, they would cause minimal damage should they collide with the tunnel wall.

Nathan rose from his seat, slowly strolling around the perimeter of the newly remodeled bridge. Every console had been updated to the sleeker, high performance touch screen panels used by the Takarans. The results were far more user friendly, and gave the operators the information they needed efficiently and clearly. The addition of the upright glass panels along the edges of the tactical console, as well as the helm and navigation stations,

163

enhanced each operator's situational awareness. They also provided displays that Nathan himself could easily read from his command chair, negating the task of asking his staff for information updates. He especially liked the larger clear panels sitting on the floor, forward and to either side of the flight consoles. They were the captain's display screens, and he could put whatever information he wanted on them, instead of asking his tactical officer to put up separate windows of information on the main view screen. The end result was an increase in his own situational awareness, which had become quite apparent to him during the training drills on board the Celestia the past two weeks.

"What are you doing?" Nathan asked Jessica as he strolled up to her station.

"Experimenting with different layouts," she replied. "Trying to figure out which one works best for me."

"You're not going to be running the turrets any longer," he reminded her. "Just designating targets to Fire Control back in Combat Command."

"I know, but I still have to run all of our torpedo cannons, and our broadside cannons, as well as our two forward quad mark twos. If we're dealing with a single target, it's pretty straightforward. If we have several targets, it gets a bit more complex. It will probably take me a few battles to figure out what works best."

"All the more reason to be at the training drills," Nathan mumbled.

Jessica rolled her eyes. "All right, I got it. I missed too many drills. I'll make up for it," she promised. "Besides, if I could kick ass with the old system, and without shields or half as many guns, I'm pretty sure I can kick ass with this package as well."

"I'm just giving you a hard time, Jess," Nathan said under his breath.

"I know," she replied in similar tone, "and it's pissing me off," she added with a smile.

"Two minutes to exit," Mister Riley reported.

"Karuzara Control reports no traffic in the departure area," Naralena announced. "We are clear for straight out departure to ten kilometers, then a course of two one seven, up twenty to leave orbit. After the turn, speed at our discretion."

"Mister Riley?" Nathan called.

"Cleared for straight out to ten, then to two one seven and twenty up at any speed to leave orbit," Mister Riley repeated. "Got it." He looked down at his console. "One minute to exit."

Nathan smiled at Jessica. "Back into the void, we go." He returned to his seat, just as the exit threshold passed over them, and the main view screen filled with the inky black, star-filled scenery to which he was accustomed.

"Clear of bravo," Mister Riley reported.

"Bring the mains up, one percent burn, Mister Chiles," Nathan ordered.

"One percent on the mains, aye," his helmsman answered.

Nathan tapped his right control panel, switching his starboard view screen to the aft cameras just in time to see the Karuzara asteroid fall away, shrinking as the distance between them grew.

"Coming up on ten kilometers," Mister Riley announced.

"Coming to course two one seven, up twenty,"

Mister Chiles reported as he initiated a starboard turn.

"Let's head for the first test waypoint, gentlemen," Nathan ordered. "We've got a lot of systems to shake down."

"Aye, sir," Mister Riley replied.

"Speed?" the helmsman inquired.

Nathan smiled. "Indulge yourself, Mister Chiles."

* * *

"Jump complete," Loki announced.

"Seriously, Lok, you gotta stop saying that," Josh protested.

"Sorry. Old habit."

"I mean, I know the jump is complete. I can see through the windows again."

"I said I'm sorry."

"You're such a geek."

"Contact," Loki reported. "Five kilometers out, ten up and twenty to port. It's the Aurora."

"I should hope so."

"Aurora Flight, Falcon One," Loki called over his comm-set. "Three Super Falcons inbound for landing."

"*Falcon One, Aurora Flight. Sensor contact. Four point five clicks to stern, eighteen to port and nine up. Approach from stern, port side. Land single file, one-minute separation. Intercept auto-flight control beacon at two clicks out, one up.*"

"Intercept ACB at two by one, Falcon One." Loki keyed his secondary comm-channel. "Falcon Flight, Falcon One. Proceed on current heading for two minutes to intercept the Aurora's flight path astern of her. Space out to one-minute intervals. Follow our turn."

"*Falcon Two copies.*"

"*Falcon Three copies.*"

"I fucking hate auto-flight," Josh grumbled.

"It saved our ass, remember?" Loki reminded him. "Besides, they're not going to make you use it every time. They probably just want to test it out with a multi-element flight."

"It's probably just because it's us. Prechitt has it in for me. He's always finding something to bitch at me about."

"It's not like you make it difficult," Loki commented as he finished checking the ship's systems in preparation for landing.

"Ha, ha." Josh fired his thrusters to change the ship's attitude and then fired their main engines to initiate a slight turn to the left. He watched his flight display, as his ship's predicted flight path lined up with the Aurora's port landing approach path. He killed his burn and fired some counterthrust to stop his turn, just as the lines matched and turned green. "On approach."

"You could have just input the turn and let the auto-pilot perform it," Loki told him.

"I need the practice."

"You need to practice flying both hands on, *and* hands off the stick, Josh. There's a time and place for both."

"You sound like Prechitt," Josh said.

"I'll take that as a compliment."

"You would." Josh yawned. "I like flying the old Falcons better. Although I don't miss those helmets. They made my head itch."

"You just have to think of flying the Super Falcon like the Aurora. You have to fly her more like a ship than a fighter."

"Might as well be a shuttle pilot."

"In a lot of ways, it's very similar. It's about the mission."

Josh stopped watching the stern of the Aurora grow larger in their front windows, and turned to look at Loki. "It's always been about the mission, Lok."

"Not for you, it hasn't," Loki disagreed. "For you, it's always been about the *act* of flying, not the *reason* we were flying."

"I don't see why there has to be a difference."

"*That's* why you're always getting chewed out, Josh. You don't *always* have to push your ships to the edge, not in *every* moment of *every* flight."

"But it's more fun, *and* it keeps my skills sharp."

"Then do it in the simulator, Josh, and not on missions."

"Simulators aren't the same."

"*Falcon One, Aurora Flight, ten seconds to intercept. Call the beacon.*"

Loki glanced down at the auto-flight status display, just as the beacon capture light illuminated. "Falcon One has the beacon," he called over the comms. "Auto-flight has control."

"And the computers land the ship," Josh moaned.

"You are the only pilot in the universe that could find something to complain about when flying such a ship, Josh."

Josh turned and grinned at Loki. "I gotta be me."

* * *

Master Chief Taggart smiled and walked up to the first Super Falcon as it rolled off the port forward elevator pad. He watched the ship pull into its parking spot. The topside hatch just aft of the cockpit opened a minute later, and Josh climbed out.

Marcus said nothing, pretending to keep a watchful eye on the ground crew to ensure they were doing their jobs correctly. In reality, he was just happy to see his boy.

Josh climbed down off the Super Falcon's wing and walked up to Marcus. "Master Chief," he said, unable to control the wide smile spreading across his face.

Marcus stiffened up into a stance that somewhat resembled standing at attention, and then offered the young officer a half-hearted salute.

Josh smiled, raising his hand to salute, but instead feigning a light punch to Marcus's gut. "How's it goin', old man?"

"I'll show you who's old, you little shit," Marcus said, feigning a few blows of his own. He put his arms around Josh and gave him a hug. "I missed ya, boy."

"Surprisingly, I missed you too."

"You hungry?"

"When am I not?"

"I got the captain's cook to whip up your favorite."

"Fried molo and dollag steaks?"

"Yup. We didn't have any churubo fat, so they had to use pig fat. Tastes pretty much the same, though."

"Hi, Marcus," Loki greeted as he joined them.

Marcus stood even straighter and offered a salute to Loki as well. "Welcome aboard, Ensign Sheehan," he added, as he reached out to shake Loki's hand.

"Thanks, Marcus. It's good to see you again."

"Hey, Lok, Marcus has fried molo and dollag steaks for us. You want some?"

"We've still got to debrief, you know."

"That's right," Josh said with a frown, realizing

he had forgotten about the briefing. He turned back to Marcus. "Meet you in an hour?"

"I can wait," Marcus said. "I'm just happy to see you."

"I hope Kaylah feels that way," Josh said.

* * *

Biorgi Saladan had been standing in line for nearly an hour. First, it was the line to receive his inoculations, then the line to receive his prophylactic dose of Corinairan nanites. After that, it was to receive his weapons and his tactical helmet. And now, finally, he was waiting for his final inspection before boarding one of the four troop shuttles waiting for them on the far side of the tarmac.

Biorgi looked at his weapon again. It felt identical to his training weapon—same weight and balance, the same controls. It even looked like it, and kicked the same when fired. There were only two things that made it different. First, it had no wear marks on it, as it was fresh from one of the Earth Defense Force's hidden armories. The second was that it fired real bullets. It was not like his training weapon. When a shot from one of them hit you, you felt nothing more than a little sting, just enough to let you know you'd been hit. This one could kill.

His weapon had come with ten additional magazines of ammunition. Combined, he carried five hundred rounds. When one of his fellow marines had asked their instructor if it was enough, the Ghatazhak soldier told them, "If it isn't, then you have bigger problems to worry about." Not exactly reassuring, but then again, the Ghatazhak were not exactly the nurturing type.

"Are you nervous, Saladan?" the Ghatazhak sergeant asked as he stopped in front of Biorgi.

"Sir, no, sir!" Biorgi barked out of habit, while standing straight and stiff.

"Stand at ease, Private," the sergeant insisted. "A simple 'no, sir' is all that is required. You're not a recruit any longer. You're an Alliance Marine."

"A killing machine," Biorgi replied proudly, a smile creeping onto the corner of his mouth.

Sergeant Lazo grinned. "Damn right. Show me your weapon, Private."

Biorgi unslung his weapon from his shoulder, checked that the weapon was unloaded and the chamber was empty, then held it up for the sergeant to inspect.

Sergeant Lazo took the weapon from Biorgi and looked it over.

"Are these weapons going to be enough?" Biorgi asked, his voice low.

Sergeant Lazo glanced up at him curiously.

"I mean, the Jung have energy weapons, like you."

"You put a round in the right spot, and your enemy will die," the sergeant told him flatly. "Projectile or energy weapon...dead is dead, Private."

"Yes, sir."

Sergeant Lazo handed the weapon back to Biorgi. "Remember, the Jung body armor is designed to stop energy weapons, not bullets. Especially not the armor-piercing stuff you're carrying. Face, neck, abdomen, and thighs. Never the chest or back, as they are the most heavily armored areas."

"Where would you aim, Sergeant?" Biorgi asked.

Sergeant Lazo smiled, placing his hand on Biorgi's shoulder. "The neck. Nothing freaks people out like blood gushing from a neck wound, especially from one of your fellow soldiers. Then, while the Jung next to him is staring in disbelief at the amount of blood spurting from his friend's neck, you can kill him as well."

Biorgi nodded. "Yes, sir."

"Is it the real thing, Sergeant?" the marine next in line asked. "Are we really deploying?"

"Hell yes, Marine," Sergeant Lazo replied, "hell yes."

* * *

"Jump flash," Mister Navashee announced from the Aurora's sensor station. "Comm-drone."

"Incoming message," Naralena added. "The Celestia reports all bravo group elements are in position and ready to jump."

"All alpha group elements show ready as well," Jessica reported from the tactical station.

"Mister Riley?"

"Jump plot to low orbit over Niorai, plotted and locked," the navigator replied.

Nathan glanced up at the battle clock. It read one minute to zero hour. "Comms, message to all elements," he began calmly. "Cleared to execute jump at zero, zero, zero, battle time."

"Aye, sir," Naralena replied.

"Comm-drone has jumped back to the Celestia," Mister Navashee reported a few moments later.

Nathan sat patiently as the seconds ticked by. The liberation of 82 Eridani was to be the easiest of the many liberation missions planned over the next few months. The Jung fleet that had once occupied the Eridani system had departed for Earth more than three months ago. That battle group was still nearly nine months away from the Sol system. Meanwhile, 82 Eridani had no Jung space forces to protect them. There was nothing more than a couple airbases, and a handful of troop bases on the surface of Niorai. Intelligence estimates put the Jung troop strength at less than ten thousand, most being housed safely away from Niorain populations.

"Thirty seconds to jump," Mister Riley reported.

Although the Aurora and Celestia's role in the liberation of the 82 Eridani system was low risk, for the Ghatazhak and the new Alliance Marines, it was not. They would be facing well-trained Jung soldiers, who would be fighting desperately for their very lives. Desperation made greater by the knowledge that reinforcements would not be coming any time soon, if at all. Such knowledge would make them either easy, or extremely dangerous, to deal with. Commander Telles expected the latter.

"Ten seconds," Mister Riley reported.

———————

Biorgi Saladan sat alongside his fellow marines on the deck of what had once been the Aurora's main cargo bay. Located directly below the old main hangar deck, the massive bay had been converted into the main hangar bay, allowing the old bay above it to remain open to space at all times, instead of just during combat operations.

All one thousand marines, the entire first graduating class from the Alliance Marine training base on Porto Santo island, had been brought up to the ship more than an hour ago. They sat on the deck in the forward corner of the hangar bay the entire time.

"Listen up!" Sergeant Lazo of the Ghatazhak barked. "First eight rows will now board the troop jumper shuttles on the far side of the hangar. You will board in two columns of twenty-five. Rows one and two to the fourth jumper. Rows three and four

173

to the third, and so on. Once inside, you will buckle in. Do not unbuckle until the jump shuttle is on the ground, and you are ordered to disembark. Double-check your weapons and your ammo. Your weapon should be unloaded, chambers empty, safeties on. Check your tactical helmet and comms before and after you board. Rows nine and beyond, if you haven't taken a leak recently, I suggest you do so now."

An alarm horn squawked loudly, and blue beacons on the wall flashed.

"What's that?" the marine next to Biorgi asked nervously.

"It means the ship is jumping," Biorgi explained. "Where were you during the last jump, the one from Earth to the staging area?"

"I was in the head," the marine admitted, sheepishly. "I wasn't feeling well."

The blue beacons stopped flashing.

"All right! First eight rows! Mount up!" Sergeant Lazo ordered.

"In orbit above Niorai," Mister Riley reported from the Aurora's navigation station.

"Scanning the surface for targets," Jessica announced from the tactical station.

"Multiple contacts," Mister Navashee reported. "Three Jung shuttles, one just leaving orbit, the other two appear to be on approach from elsewhere in the system to Niorai. No weapons."

"I'm picking up three Falcons and ten combat jumpers, average altitudes of four hundred meters," Jessica said. "I've got the first two targets, Captain. An airbase, and what looks like a training base, about two clicks south of the airbase. I'm picking up two more targets as well, but I can't make them out."

"Light up the first two targets," Nathan ordered. "Green deck. Launch the utility shuttles."

"The other two targets are surface-to-orbit missile launchers!" Mister Navashee reported. "They're powering up now!"

"Proximity to civilians?" Nathan asked.

"Embedded, sir," Mister Navashee reported.

"Topside quads locked on primary targets," Jessica announced. "Firing."

"Flight, redirect the Falcons to those two missile launchers," Nathan ordered.

"I've got three more of them to the north and west," Mister Navashee warned.

"Flight?"

"I'm on it, sir."

"Why didn't we know about those launchers?" Nathan demanded.

"Our cold-coasts only pick up emissions, Captain," Jessica explained. "I only spotted them because we're using active scans."

"Utility shuttles have launched," the flight operations officer reported. "We'll have a full CNS-sat deployment in five minutes."

"Missile launches," Mister Navashee reported. "From the surface."

"Point-defenses are charged and ready, Captain," Jessica declared. "No way they're getting anywhere near us."

"Falcon One reports first launcher in twenty seconds," the flight officer reported.

"Twenty seconds to missile impact," Loki reported from the right seat of Falcon One's cockpit. "Locked on to second launcher. Firing... Missile away. Thirty seconds to impact. First missile impact in five."

"*Falcon One, Aurora Flight, new targets. One eight five, five hundred clicks, then one two zero, two-twenty. More launchers. Engage and destroy.*"

"Flight, One. Targets one and two have been destroyed. Receiving data for three and four. Vectoring now."

Josh turned the ship to the left, rolling level on the first course that the flight controller on the Aurora had given them. "How far out you want me, Lok?"

"One hundred clicks."

"You got it," Josh replied, dialing up his jump distance. "Jumping."

The canopy turned opaque for a moment.

"Range to target three, ninety-eight and closing," Loki reported. "I have a lock. Firing... Missile away."

"Turning to one two zero," Josh reported as he started his turn. "Dialing in one hundred for the next jump."

"I've got the fourth one on sensors," Loki reported. "I've also got eight bandits, just off from the airbase."

"Jumping." Josh announced as the canopy turned opaque again. "I thought the Aurora already destroyed that base?"

"Target lock on four. Firing... Missile away."

Josh pulled the nose of the ship up to climb and get a little more altitude under them.

"They did," Loki explained. "Those eight must have been the ready birds. They probably launched the moment the Aurora jumped in. I'm surprised it was only eight of them."

"*Falcon One, Aurora Flight. Eight bandits to the*

southeast. One up, four hundred out. Vectoring Falcon Two to assist."

"Flight, One, three and four destroyed," Loki called over the comms. "Falcon Two, One. ETA to bandits?"

"One, Two... ten seconds," the copilot on Falcon Two replied. *"Jumping in five."*

"Come to one four seven and jump three-fifty," Loki instructed.

Josh immediately made a slight course correction to the right, as he changed his jump range to three hundred and fifty kilometers. "Say when."

Loki watched the data feed from Falcon Two. Once his jump drive indicated it was activated, he shouted, "Now!"

———

Ten flashes of blue-white light appeared in the pre-dawn sky around the cloud of dust and smoke rising from the Jung troop base a few kilometers from the airbase. A few more kilometers beyond, the city of Anders had a rude awakening: the result of the thunderous roar as both Jung bases near their fair city were obliterated in a hail of rail gun fire.

Ten more flashes of blue-white light could be seen in the distance around the airbase. From where the flashes had been, now small, armed shuttles dropped from the sky, riding quickly down to the surface on fiery tails of thrust from their four upturned engines. They came to hover only a meter or two above the fields that surrounded the training base, pausing just long enough for four men dressed in black combat armor to jump from the shuttles' open doors to the ground below.

Once their passengers had landed, the shuttles began to climb into the brightening sky, each of them disappearing seconds later behind more flashes of blue-white light.

"Eight total inbound," Mister Navashee reported. "More contacts downrange! From at least seven more launch sites!"

"The inbounds are damned fast," Jessica said. "I'm going to have to engage them before they even clear the stratosphere."

"I'm starting to understand why the Jung didn't feel the need to send more ships to protect this world any time soon," Nathan commented. "Mister Riley, keep a ten-click escape jump ready, just in case we need to skip ahead a step to avoid the inbounds."

"Aye, sir."

"How long until the CNS-sat network is online?" Nathan asked.

"Three minutes."

"Comms, dispatch a jump comm-drone to make sure the Celestia is on the lookout for those missile launchers," Nathan ordered.

"We now have twenty-seven total inbound missiles!" Ensign Kono warned from the Celestia's sensor station. "Nearest ones will reach us in thirty-seven seconds!"

"I'm already targeting them down in the mesosphere," Luis said. "Recommend having a short escape jump queued and ready."

"Mister Sperry?" Cameron said.

"Already on standby, Captain," the navigator replied.

"Comms, warn the Aurora…"

"Jump flash," Ensign Kono reported. "Comm-drone."

"Inbound message from the Aurora," Ensign Souza announced. "They're warning us, sir!"

"More jump flashes," Ensign Kono reported. "It's the combat jumpers."

"All ten are inbound to reload," Luis reported.

"Picking up bandits near the surface," Ensign Kono reported. "Two hundred kilometers east of the airbase."

"What? There's no facility there, is there?"

"Unknown," Ensign Kono replied.

"Flight is vectoring Falcons Four, Five, and Six toward the bandits."

"What about those missile launchers?" Ensign Kono wondered.

"Helm, take us higher," Cameron ordered. "Make our altitude ten thousand. That'll buy us more time to intercept the incoming missiles." Cameron tapped her comm-panel. "Flight, Captain. We're increasing orbital altitude. Warn all shuttles that we're climbing to ten thousand kilometers."

"*Aye, sir.*"

"That's going to decrease our accuracy on the ground targets," Luis warned.

"All of those launchers are embedded in civilian areas," Ensign Kono warned.

"As soon as our Falcons deal with those fighters that somehow managed to get off the ground unscathed, we'll send them after those missile launchers. They're too fast for the missile launchers to track, and the Super Falcons can take the launchers out with minimal collateral damage," Cameron reasoned. "Meanwhile, pay close attention to our new point-defense systems, Lieutenant. I believe they're about to be put to the test."

———

Alarm sirens sounded in the distance as dust and smoke swirled about. Men in black body armor jumped out of armed shuttles that appeared and disappeared behind brilliant flashes of light. Upon landing, the black-clad soldiers ran toward the cloud of dust and smoke with amazing speed and grace, both their handheld and shoulder-mounted weapons firing at Jung soldiers as they ran out of the cloud in an effort to escape the destruction. Red-orange bolts of plasma energy struck the disoriented Jung soldiers as they fled the chaos, dropping them in their tracks. Few, if any, returned fire at first. Within the first minute of the assault, those who managed to escape the onslaught looked frantically for anything to provide cover. They ducked behind mounds of dirt, chunks of building debris that had landed in the surrounding fields after the initial bombardment had torn the buildings apart, and vehicles that had been tossed clear by the shock wave, strewn across the ground in unnatural locations and orientations.

It was a scene unlike any other. Clouds of dust and smoke flashed with the red-orange reflections of energy weapons fire exchanged by both sides. Flashes of blue-white light joined as the armed shuttles returned, dropping another wave of black-clad soldiers behind the first wave. Then more flashes, only two of them, but bigger and louder than the others. From behind the flashes, two large shuttles appeared, riding even bigger tails of fire down to the surface. They touched down in the fields, well behind the soldiers in black, their wide aft ramps quickly dropping open.

Hordes of soldiers, dressed differently but wearing the same helmets as those in black who came before them, came charging down the ramps.

Fifty or so from each ship. They charged forth to join the black-clad soldiers in the slaughter, splitting up and spreading out to join up with their leaders.

With the addition of more men, the firefight intensified. Ten times more fire blasted into the cloud of dust and smoke than came from it. Men fell on both sides, although the number of fallen defenders far outnumbered those of their attackers.

———

"This ship does *not* handle as well in the atmosphere as it used to," Josh muttered angrily as he pushed the Super Falcon into a spiraling left turn. The Jung fighter in front of him broke his turn, rolling back to the right and diving. Josh continued his roll to the left, then stopped it in an inverted position and pulled his flight control stick back hard as he chopped his throttles. The Super Falcon pulled through a dive and then leveled, and Josh rolled the ship slightly to the right as he pushed his throttles all the way forward again. "Crazy eights!" he shouted.

Loki tapped his control pad, then activated the nose turret. "Crazy eights it is!" Red-orange, needle-like bolts of plasma energy spit forth from beneath their nose, fanning out in eight different directions as if shooting at eight different targets, all within a few degrees of each other. The jinking Jung fighter in front of them, try though he might, could not avoid the spread of plasma energy, and took several hits before finally coming apart in a fiery explosion.

"Splash two!" Josh shouted with glee.

"Two, One," Loki called over the comms, "Break right and dive! You've got three on you... Two to port and one directly astern!"

Falcon Two did not respond. Loki watched his

display, noting that the other Falcon was doing exactly as instructed. Its icon suddenly vanished, then reappeared five kilometers further down range along its pre-jump course and still climbing.

"They're changing course to reacquire you," Loki warned over the comms. "Hold your climb and let them chase you. We'll broadside them!"

"*Make it quick!*" the copilot from Falcon Two said. "*They'll have range in ten seconds!*"

"Josh, right thirty and fifteen up," Loki instructed.

Josh did as Loki suggested, turning and pitching up.

"Two, One. Do an escape jump as soon as you see us jump in. Otherwise, your ass is going to get toasted."

"Two-click jump," Loki added, "in three..."

Josh quickly spun the select dial on his flight control stick and chose a jump range of two kilometers.

"*Two copies!*"

"Be ready on the mark twos..." Loki warned. "One..."

"Always." Josh pushed the selector switch to the jump position and held it there.

"Jump!" Loki ordered.

The canopy turned opaque for a split second.

"Fire!" Loki ordered as they came out of the jump.

Josh let go of the selector switch, allowing it to automatically come back to the 'Mark 2' position, then pressed and held the trigger. Triple-shots of red-orange balls of plasma, a group from each side, shot out from just behind and slightly below their cockpit, joined by another blast of the eight-point firing pattern from their nose turret. At the same time, there was a blue-white flash of light, higher and to their left, as Falcon Two jumped away. Three explosions appeared directly in front of them. Josh ceased fire, pulled up hard, pushed his selector switch forward again, and pressed the trigger once more. Their canopy cycled to opaque and back to clear.

"Splash three more!" Loki yelled.

"Unbelievable!" Josh declared.

"*Nice shooting, One!*" Falcon Two cheered.

There would be no congratulations from Aurora Flight Control. "*Falcon One and Two, Aurora Flight. Join up with Falcon Three and proceed to the far side to assist bravo group.*"

———————

"That's the last one," Jessica announced, relief evident in her voice. "Remind me to kiss the guys who installed our new point-defense system when we get back."

"Flight reports all missile launchers on alpha side have been destroyed," Naralena reported. "The area is clear of all hostile surface aircraft as well. They are sending all three of our Falcons to bravo side. They have twice as many active launchers to deal with, and they've now got over twenty Jung fighters in the air."

"Is the sat-net up?" Nathan asked.

"Yes, sir. It just went live."

"Pass the word to Telles that alpha side is clear of all air defenses," Nathan ordered. "Then notify the alpha-group boxcars to begin operations."

"Aye, sir."

"I'm picking up a Jung mechanized convoy on the surface, headed toward the airbase," Mister Navashee reported.

"Where did *that* come from?" Nathan wondered.

"Maybe they were out on a training exercise?" Jessica suggested.

"Perhaps. Backtrack along the roads they likely drove," Nathan instructed his sensor operator. "Maybe there's another base nearby we don't know about."

"Yes, sir," Mister Navashee acknowledged.

"What's the convoy's ETA to the airbase?"

"Eleven minutes at present speed."

"Lieutenant Commander, I believe our people on the ground would appreciate it if that convoy did *not* arrive."

"My pleasure, Captain," Jessica replied.

———

Four jump flashes appeared only a few kilometers from the destroyed Jung airbase. It was followed by two more, even larger flashes and, finally, one really big flash. Four combat jumpers dropped to a hover a meter off the ground, pausing just long enough for their Ghatazhak passengers to jump down to the surface. As the four combat jumpers climbed and began to circle, the two troop jumpers set down nearby, dropping their ramps so the marines inside could disembark. Finally, the boxcar descended in the middle of them all, gently placing its massive cargo pod on the ground. Its engines still running, the boxcar disconnected its mooring clamps from the cargo pod, then brought its engines back up to full power, climbing effortlessly upward.

Commander Telles and Master Sergeant Jahal strode confidently across the field toward the cargo pod, as the ascending boxcar that had placed it there disappeared in a blinding flash of light. It illuminated the area, adding to the light of what was nearly a full sunrise on the planet Niorai. A sudden, thunderous roar caused them both to stop and turn toward the sound. Explosions went off as glowing rail gun rounds, super-heated by their hypersonic journey down through the atmosphere, tore into a distant target.

Master Sergeant Jahal put his hand to his helmet for a moment, concentrating on an incoming message. He then tapped his commander on the shoulder. "The Aurora detected a mechanized convoy headed our way."

"It looks like they won't be a problem," the commander said, as he turned and continued toward the cargo pod.

The walls on the cargo pod slid outward, as gun towers on each corner extended upward. Men came running out from behind the walls, carrying motion-detector stakes for deployment around the perimeter. The gun towers reached their maximum height, locked into position, and then came to life, panning back and forth in their automated scans for unwelcome visitors.

The commander and the master sergeant walked briskly to the now operational command center and ducked behind the wall to go inside.

A moment later, Commander Telles and Master Sergeant Jahal entered the command center's core.

"Report!" Commander Telles barked as he stepped up to the planning table at the center of the dimly lit room.

"Alpha airbase, and the nearby training base are fully under our control," the comm officer replied immediately. "Our Falcons have been reassigned to bravo side for the time being. However, all airborne Jung assets, and all surface-based air defenses were eliminated prior to their departure."

"Casualties?"

"Twenty-seven marines dead, eighteen wounded. No Ghatazhak casualties, sir."

"And the Jung?"

"As of yet, we have found no survivors."

"At least none that lived to talk about it," Master Sergeant Jahal mused grimly.

"Any word from bravo side?" the commander asked.

"Not yet, sir," the comm officer replied, "but the CNS-sats have only been live for a few minutes."

"There are thirty-two more missiles inbound," Luis reported from the Celestia's tactical station.

Cameron couldn't remember the last time she heard her tactical officer sound nervous. "Recommended safe distance?" she asked her sensor operator.

"Their warheads are all nuclear," Ensign Kono warned. "If they go off within a couple kilometers, we'll lose sensors and comms for a few, but we'll be okay. The radiation won't penetrate our hull."

"Five kilometers, Mister Sperry," Cameron said. "They get inside five, and you jump us, with or without my order."

"Yes, sir."

Luis continued monitoring the point-defenses as the thirty-two, quad-barreled, mark one mini-plasma cannon turrets located around the perimeter of the Celestia, on both her upper and lower sides, worked in unison to destroy the incoming missiles.

"Range to nearest?" Cameron inquired, growing impatient.

"Twenty kilometers and closing fast," Luis

replied. "Four more around thirty. Twelve more around forty... They're coming in waves, Captain."

"Flight, Captain. We need those missile launchers on the surface taken out, now."

"*All six Falcons are engaged with more than twenty fighters, sir,*" the flight operation officer replied. "*Those damned fighters are doing their best to protect those launchers.*"

"How long?"

"*A few minutes before we can start targeting them.*"

Cameron turned to Luis. "Pick the launcher that has the least number of civilian structures around it and take it out."

"From this altitude, anything within five hundred meters is gonna take a hit," Luis warned.

Cameron turned back forward, studying the pattern of incoming missiles.

"Twenty-click wave has been neutralized," Luis reported.

"Captain, I'm getting word from the commander of bravo forces," Ensign Souza said urgently. "They're taking a beating, sir."

"We need to take out those two bases for them," Cameron muttered. "Lieutenant, concentrate all point-defenses to defense quadrant three alpha seven to three alpha twelve."

"Captain..."

"Punch me a whole to the surface, Lieutenant," Cameron ordered. "Mister Hunt, pitch down forty-seven degrees, directly toward defense quadrants three alpha nine and ten. Burn at fifty percent."

"Diving toward three alpha nine and ten, at fifty percent burn," Mister Hunt acknowledged.

"How far is the furthest missile?" Cameron asked.

"Four hundred kilometers," Luis replied.

"And what altitude do you need to give me clean hits on those damned launchers?"

"You mean like clean, clean? Maybe one hundred kilometers."

"On dive now," the helmsman reported.

"Nearest missiles are ten kilometers," Ensign Kono warned. "Captain, we're gonna take a lot of atmospheric friction at that altitude."

"How long?"

"Ninety seconds, tops," Ensign Kono warned. "After that, we'll start losing systems. Jump field emitters will be the first to go."

"You get one minute, Lieutenant. Take out as many as you can."

"Yes, sir!" Luis replied. "Clear path, now!"

"Jump!" Cameron ordered.

The interior of the bridge lit up momentarily as the blue-white light of the jump flash washed over them.

The bridge began to shake violently, as the massive ship found itself plowing through the planet's mesosphere.

"Jump complete!" the navigator reported.

"Level us off!" Cameron directed. "Get us a jump line out of here!"

"At this altitude, it's going to take a full burn!" Ensign Hunt warned.

"Do it!"

"Locking on the launchers!" Luis announced.

"Forty seconds!" Ensign Kono shouted.

"Firing!"

"Detonations!" Ensign Kono announced. "Above us! From four to twenty kilometers!"

"They're detonating anything near us!" Cameron

realized. "Trying to hit us with shock waves while we're in the atmosphere!"

"Four launchers destroyed!" Luis reported. "Retargeting!" Luis struggled to push the correct buttons, as the ship shook so badly he could barely make out his displays.

"Thirty seconds!" Ensign Kono reported.

"Firing again!"

"Have we got a clear jump line?" Cameron asked.

"Working on it!" her helmsman replied.

"Eight destroyed!" Luis announced. "Retargeting!"

"Twenty seconds!"

"Twelve destroyed!"

"Get me that jump line!" Cameron demanded.

"Ten seconds!"

"Sixteen destroyed!"

"Mister Hunt!" Cameron begged.

"Almost there!"

"Five seconds!"

"Twenty destroyed!"

"Three......two......"

"Clear jump line!" Mister Sperry cried.

"Jump! Jump! Jump!"

The jump flash filled the bridge before the captain could finish her orders. Suddenly, the ship was calm again, the violent shaking gone.

Cameron looked around the bridge, trying not to appear shaken. The image of the planet Niorai was once again positioned neatly across the bottom of the main view screen, stretching from side to side. "Altitude?"

"Eight hundred and twenty-four kilometers," Mister Sperry reported. "In stable orbit above Niorai."

Cameron turned around and looked at Lieutenant Delaveaga. "How many?"

"All but three of them, sir," Luis beamed with pride. "That was some move, Captain. I didn't know you had it in you."

"Neither did I," Cameron admitted, sighing. "Collateral damage?" she inquired, turning toward her sensor officer to her right.

"One moment," Ensign Kono requested, "I've got a lot of targets to survey."

"Lock onto those two bases and take them out, Lieutenant," Cameron ordered.

"Aye, sir."

"Comms, tell Bravo Command to pass the word to his men to keep their heads down for the next minute or two."

"Collateral damage around the missile launcher sites appears to be minimal, Captain," Ensign Kono reported happily.

Cameron relaxed back into her chair, relieved. She tapped her comm-set. "Damage Control, Captain. How are we doing, Master Chief?"

"*No damage reported, Captain,*" Master Chief Montrose answered over the comms. "*However, I'd appreciate it if you wouldn't shake us up so much. I spilled coffee all over my clean uniform.*"

* * *

"It seems that the people of Niorai were quite happy to be liberated," Admiral Dumar told President Scott, as he took his seat in the president's office. "Our forces on the ground were greeted with open arms, despite the fact that the liberation did cost a few hundred civilian lives."

"A few hundred?" President Scott asked, surprised at the low number. "Compared to a population of what?"

"About three billion," the admiral replied. "I

know the number seems low by comparison, but it is still rather high, in my opinion. Had the Niorains not been as displeased with the Jung, that number might have had greater importance to them."

"Then they will be willing to join the Alliance?" one of the president's advisors asked.

"It will be at least a few days before any type of provisional government can be put together on Niorai. However, the few local leaders that I have spoken with seem receptive to the idea. It should be noted, Mister President, that the Niorains have nothing to offer in the way of military or industrial capacities."

"It was my understanding that we were selecting systems to liberate based on distance from Sol, not potential contributions to the cause," President Scott said curtly.

"That is true, Mister President," Admiral Dumar admitted. "However, what Admiral Galiardi says is true as well. Every world that we liberate places additional responsibilities upon the Alliance, in that we must protect our members equally, regardless of their contributions to our cause, or lack thereof. Taking on such worlds will only help to fuel the admiral's argument that the Alliance is weakening the security of Earth, rather than increasing it."

"You have a point," President Scott realized, rubbing his chin thoughtfully.

"Especially in light of Admiral Galiardi's most recent announcement," Miri added.

"I apologize. I've been so preoccupied with the liberation of Niorai that I haven't read my morning intelligence briefing."

"Galiardi is now circulating a petition amongst

191

the people of Earth," Miri explained. "He wants to restore the Earth Defense Force."

"To what end?"

"He knows he cannot convince the people to withdraw from the Alliance," one of the president's advisors explained, "not while the Jung threat still looms over us."

"And restoring the EDF would put ultimate control of both the Aurora and the Celestia in the hands of the EDF," Admiral Dumar surmised, "and ultimately, his hands."

"Ultimately, mine, actually," President Scott corrected, "but you are otherwise correct."

"Galiardi, and many others, want those two ships dedicated to protecting Earth, not other systems," Miri said, "even if they are our allies. He wants Earth to concentrate on building up its own military assets, and let other worlds worry about their own destinies."

"I understand his point," Admiral Dumar said. "I suspect I would do the same in his shoes."

"Galiardi has been trying to get uncontrolled buildup for decades," the president explained. "When I was chair of the EDF budget oversight committee, we spent many hours in heated debate over such issues." President Scott shook his head. "The admiral is no stranger to the ways and means of manipulating the hearts and minds of those he wishes to influence. That's how he got his position as commander of the EDF to begin with. By playing to the emotions of the public *after* the catastrophic failures of the first two Defender-class ships."

"What happened to them?" Admiral Dumar asked.

"The Defender was plagued with problems from the start," President Scott remembered. "Structural failures, computer problems, you name it. It was simply too big a leap for us at the time, going from building a handful of scout ships to building massive warships. Those ships were supposed to be FTL capable, by the way."

"I was not aware of that."

"The first ship was eventually scrapped before she completed flight trials. There were just too many problems. It was a massive failure that cost President Baumgarten his career."

"They scrapped an entire starship?" Admiral Dumar asked in surprise.

"They salvaged as much of her as possible to put into the second ship, the Valiant," President Scott continued. "Unfortunately, her antimatter reactors experienced problems during her FTL tests. As a result, her mass-cancelling fields become unstable, and the ship came apart in transit, killing most of her crew."

"And Galiardi used these events to take command of the EDF?"

"He had argued all along that we were wasting time and resources trying to build FTL ships before we were truly ready. He proposed building sub-light ships instead. Bigger, more heavily armored, and with far more firepower. 'Defense before offense' has always been his motto." President Scott took a breath before continuing. "Admiral Jarlmasson was forced to step down as leader of the EDF, and Galiardi took his place. Ten years later, we had four redesigned Defender-class ships patrolling our system, and the people felt 'safe'." President Scott chuckled. "They had no idea."

"But the Explorer-class ships," Dumar wondered. "They came about under Galiardi's watch."

"Galiardi wanted to keep building Defender-class ships, but the anti-military crowd wanted us to reach out to the Jung in peace. We couldn't very well do that by arriving in heavily-armed warships, so the Explorer-class was developed."

"But Galiardi used them both as test ships for the jump drive," Dumar recalled.

"The jump drive came about later," the president explained. "Galiardi had been running concurrent development projects on the STS idea for nearly a decade. After all, before he took over as commander of the EDF, *he* was in charge of special projects. That's why he didn't oppose the Explorer-class idea too strongly, as he didn't want to risk trying the jump drive out on a Defender-class ship. They were far too precious to him."

"And now, he is using the same tactics to get the people to side with him, and his desire for a massive military buildup," Dumar said, putting the pieces together.

"Precisely." President Scott leaned back in his seat. "Honestly, I sometimes wonder if Galiardi didn't know all along what was going to happen. Perhaps he even *wanted* it to play out this way. After all, he's closer to getting what he wants *now* more than ever before. Unrestrained military buildup."

"You can't be serious?" Miri said in disbelief.

"I'm not suggesting that he *planned* it that way," the president said. "Too many variables that you simply cannot predict. What I'm saying is that I wouldn't put it past him." President Scott looked around at everyone gathered. "That never leaves this room, by the way."

Admiral Dumar thought for a moment. "I may

not care for his methods, but if the end result is a bigger, more powerful military..."

"One that he controls..."

"With *your* oversight..."

"With *my* oversight, and that he will eventually use as his stepping stone to greater power."

"You believe he seeks to gain political power as well?" Admiral Dumar asked, surprised.

"It is the nature of such men," President Scott said. "I have seen it my entire life. I have walked the halls, shared the floor, and engaged in debate with such men. Hell, some would say I *am* such a man."

Admiral Dumar paused for a moment, contemplating the situation. "This petition, will it succeed?"

"We believe so," the president said. "It's just a matter of time before he gets enough signatures and submits it to the World Congress."

"How much time?"

"A month or two? It would have taken considerably longer had we not gotten our global networks back online so quickly," he mused. "After that, depending on the level of public support, Congress could act upon the petition in as little as a few days, to a few weeks."

"Recommendations?"

"Liberate as many worlds as possible, before Congress ties our hands."

Dumar sighed. "That may not be possible. I had hoped to wait until upgrades on the Jar-Benakh were completed, before liberating any more worlds."

"You liberated 82 Eridani just fine without the Jar-Benakh," the president reminded him.

"82 Eridani had no Jung ships to defend her."

"What about the jump KKVs?" the president asked.

"We only have nineteen of them at the moment, and it takes at least three to four of them to take down a battle platform alone."

"But we are making more of them."

"Indeed we are," the admiral confirmed, "at a rate of one every other day, in fact. But that still might not be enough to complete the job in such a short time. There are still two more Jung-held systems that lie within twenty light years of Sol, and another nine that lie between twenty and thirty light years. That is why I wanted to wait until the Jar-Benakh was ready for action. As long as a single jump KKV has hit a battle platform and brought down a full fifteen percent of its shields, the Jar-Benakh can defeat her. In addition, with her new armaments and jump systems, she can defeat another Jung battleship without the use of jump KKVs."

"Perhaps Galiardi is right," President Scott mused, frustration in his tone. "Maybe we should be concentrating all our efforts on building self-propelled jump KKVs, and park them all around us for protection."

"Jump KKVs are an offensive weapon," Dumar explained. "They are only of value when used in a surprise attack, when the targets are not taking aggressive evasive actions. Nothing short of a few battleships can take on a Jung battle platform that is on full alert. Such ships would take several years to build, even if the designs were in hand and the factories were tooled and ready for production. The best we can hope to do now is to capture a few more Jung battleships, and convert them in the same manner as the Jar-Benakh."

"How likely is that to happen?" the president wondered.

"Not as likely as one might think. The Jar-Keurog and the Jar-Benakh were both flukes. We were lucky enough to be in the right place at the right time. And in both instances, a lot of good men died securing those assets. It would be unwise to count on our luck continuing in such fashion."

It was President Scott's turn to sigh. "I would never try to tell you how to run your campaigns, Admiral. However, I would strongly suggest that you use whatever means you have at your disposal to liberate as many worlds as possible, while you can."

"You believe *that* strongly that Galiardi will succeed in his efforts?" the Admiral asked.

"I do."

Admiral Dumar looked at the others, then to President Scott. "Might I speak with you alone, Mister President?"

President Scott looked offended, his eyes narrowing. "These people are my trusted..."

"I would not ask, were it not necessary," Dumar replied.

President Scott stared at the admiral for a moment, taking note of the determined look on his face. He had not known the admiral for long, and certainly did not know him well, but he knew that his son, Nathan, trusted the admiral implicitly. "Very well." He looked at his staff. "Everyone, please clear the room."

The president and the admiral sat quietly as the others rose from their seats without saying a word, and departed the room.

Once the door closed, the president spoke. "What's on your mind, Admiral?"

"How secure is this room?"

"We are five hundred meters underground. The walls are solid concrete, and there are no internal listening devices," President Scott explained. "I doubt anywhere on Earth is more secure than this very spot."

Admiral Dumar sighed. "I have lived a long time, Mister President," he began. "I have served three different regimes, four, if you count your new coalition of nations. I have been called upon to do many distasteful things, and I have done them all. Not because I enjoy them, but because they were necessary for the greater good. Furthermore, it is what men such as myself were created to do."

"What are you getting at, Admiral?"

"You have a problem, one that I can make go away, if so ordered."

"You're talking about Admiral Galiardi?"

Admiral Dumar nodded his head.

"What are you suggesting? Assassination?"

"It is a tool, like any other. One used to accomplish a goal."

"And how do we explain that to his followers?"

"He has Corinairan nanites still within him, does he not? It would be relatively easy to command them to cause a heart attack, or a stroke of some sort."

"And start more controversy?"

"There will always be controversy, Mister President."

President Scott sighed, displeased with the idea. "I have been the victim of an assassination attempt, Admiral. I can't say I liked it much. I don't know that I'm ready to take that step just yet."

"I understand."

"Besides, having the Alliance involved in the assassination of a Terran citizen would be too risky."

"Agreed."

"I appreciate your candor, Admiral," the president said. "If—and that is a big 'if'—I decide to use that 'tool', as you put it, I'm sure I can find someone not affiliated with the military to perform the task."

"I would expect so," the admiral agreed.

President Scott stood. "I appreciate your time here today, Admiral, and your advice. I will take all of it to heart, I assure you."

"As will I, yours, Mister President," Admiral Dumar replied as he stood to depart.

CHAPTER SIX

Captain Nash made his way through the nearly completed Cobra Operations Center on the small asteroid moon orbiting Tanna. The caverns themselves had been relatively quick to create, thanks to the engineers provided by the Karuzara asteroid base. The interior structures and equipment had taken a bit longer to fabricate than expected. Due to the demands of the gunship assembly plant, there were few fabricators available.

Luckily, someone in planning had been smart enough to spend the first few weeks making additional fabricators. Eventually, they got enough of them assembled to not only build the new extension to the old Jung fighter base, but they now had the ability to create spare parts for the Cobra gunships.

The facility had everything they needed to support the continuous operation of at least twenty-four gunships. It currently had only twelve docking ports, but construction of another row of twelve was under way. In addition, they were also planning on carving out four caverns to be used as dry docks, in order to perform maintenance and repairs in shirt-sleeve, zero-G environments.

Their hope was to eventually operate a guard fleet of forty-eight ships, using seventy-two crews. This would allow them to maintain an adequate border patrol, while having plenty of ships to defend their system, should the Jung return.

In a few days, the twelfth gunship would be delivered. Captain Nash's first four crews were doing well, and had entered the advanced tactical combat phase of their training. The second group of four gunship crews was just finishing up basic flight, and the third group was still in the sims. However, everything seemed to be progressing smoothly, and his staff had finally developed an easily repeatable process of turning wide-eyed young men into well-trained gunship crews.

Despite his initial disappointment with his assignment, Robert Nash had actually grown to enjoy it. The Tannans were passionate people, willing to study and train hard. They were also polite to a fault, modest, and unassuming. In short, they were a pleasure to be around. More importantly, they believed in what they were doing. The entire planet seemed focused on one goal, to defend their world, and the worlds of the Alliance, against the Jung. Captain Nash had no doubt that if asked, they would fight to the death without hesitation.

One could not help but respect such people.

Although he hated to admit it, Captain Nash was also enjoying the relative calmness of his life as chief instructor. He worked fourteen to sixteen hours a day. But he was sleeping in a very comfortable bed each night, and eating four hot and healthy meals per day. The Tannan food was a bit spicy, but delicious, and they made every meal a celebration of sorts. He even found time on occasion to go back down to the surface and enjoy the outdoors. Tanna had such a stark contrast between its landscapes. Half the planet was barren tundra and desert. But where there was water, it was green and lush, with thick forests filled with all manner of creatures, many of them brought over from Earth a millennium ago when the first settlers had staked their claims on the previously untouched world.

"Captain on deck!" Lieutenant Commander Rano barked as Captain Nash entered the Cobra flight briefing room. The cavern was large enough to hold at least two hundred people, with the seats clustered in groups of six to accommodate the gunship crews. The chairs were comfortable, with small tables that could be folded away if desired. The rows formed wide arcs that faced the front and center of the room, where there was a large view screen, with a lectern off to one side.

"As you were," Captain Nash said as he stepped up to the lectern. He glanced out at his men. There were only four crews, including his own, for a total of twenty-four men, including himself. The room looked empty, considering it was designed to accommodate thirty-six crews at once. "Gentlemen, today you start your training in advanced combat tactics. More specifically, how to hunt as a group. You have performed simple maneuvers as a group in the past, using simple methods of timing, speed, and precision manual flying. Now we're going to get really precise. We're going to use the automated flight control systems, as well as the Relativistic Combat Data Link systems. You all know what the auto-flight systems are. They're the little orange button that none of you were allowed to touch until you proved that you knew how to manually fly your ships. Well, now you get to use them. In fact, you will probably use them ninety percent of the time from this point forward." Captain Nash smiled. "Yeah, I know. Sounds boring. You're right, it is. But it is far more precise than hand-flying, and precision is what we are after when operating in groups."

Captain Nash picked up his remote and activated the main view screen. A flowchart appeared on the screen. "This is the intermittent combat data link system, or ICDLS. You can call it 'ick-dills.' It is designed to share flight and systems status information between linked ships. The intermittent aspect is because it is designed to work in an environment where the time delay between linked ships varies, or is temporarily broken. It uses predictive algorithms to estimate each unlinked ship's status, adjusting as needed whenever a broken link is restored. It is what enables the lead ship, which for purposes of training will be Cobra One, to monitor the status of all other ships in the linked group, and to relay instructions to them. It uses a combination of repeated command broadcasts and command verification receipts, through standard direct comms, and from miniature comm buoys. This system allows a group of linked ships to use auto-flight to precisely perform any number of pre-programmed attack maneuvers, as indicated by the lead ship in the linked group. In other words, I decide what attack pattern we are going to fly, and it sends the orders to the auto-flight systems in your ships so that they fly the attack pattern I assigned."

"What if the auto-flight doesn't receive the command?" Captain Annatah asked.

"No ship will initiate until all ships have verified receipt of the command. Usually, this is accomplished by giving a command during a pass, and then cycling through two or three attack passes, if needed, to get everyone's verification."

"If this is all being done by auto-flight, then what do we do?" Captain Harral wondered.

"The auto-flight will take you through the setup, but you will still have to make final course corrections once on the attack run, in order to line up your cannons on target."

"How is this any better than just flying the patterns manually?" Captain Orel inquired.

"The auto-flight is far more precise than we can ever hope to be," Captain Nash explained. "The attack patterns that we are going to fly are complex, and are designed to maximize our firepower while minimizing risk. They introduce randomization variables that would be difficult for us to implement, in order to prevent the gunners of the ships we attack from predicting which angle we will next attack from. They turn us into a collection of mobile cannons, always on the move, and always firing from different points in space, yet all firing at the same target. Trust me, it will work better than you could possibly imagine. More importantly, it will keep us from jumping into one another," he added with a wry smile. "Now, let's get started. Attack pattern alpha one," he said, advancing to the next frame on the view screen.

* * *

Nathan stood on the Aurora's bridge, casually leaning against the side of the tactical console as he chatted with his tactical officer. "I'm not saying it's not doable," he continued, "nor am I saying that it's unwise. What I'm saying is that it may be playing into Galiardi's cause."

"Feeding it, you mean," Jessica commented as she monitored her console.

"Five minutes to attack zero," Mister Riley announced. "We are now back down to attack speed."

"Kill your burn," Nathan ordered.

"Decel burn is off," Mister Chiles replied. "Holding present course and speed."

"Yes, *feeding* would be a good word," Nathan agreed, turning his attention back to Jessica. "Galiardi complains that we are poking the dragon with a stick. An assault on their assets and subsequent liberation of one of their worlds every five days? Anyone would consider that an act of war."

Jessica looked at him in surprise, as if she couldn't believe it was really Nathan saying the words. "The Jung did attack us first, remember?"

"Of course I remember," Nathan said dismissively. "I wasn't inferring that we are not justified in our actions, you know that."

"Just checking," Jessica said with a shrug, her gaze returning to her console.

"I'm just questioning whether or not it is the most effective overall strategy, and that depends on what our end game actually is. Is it to destroy the Jung, or is it to protect the Earth and the member systems of the Alliance against further Jung hostilities?"

"The two are not mutually exclusive, you know."

"Agreed, but take the timing of this campaign, every five days. The timing was chosen based on our production rate of jump KKVs, and how much time we estimate we have before Galiardi can get his petition in front of Congress and force them to act. Why not stop after Delta Pavonis? Why not hold at twenty light years? We don't know for sure that the Coalition Congress *will* side with Galiardi. They may tell him to go to hell. In the meantime, we could stockpile jump KKVs, jump missiles, Super Eagles... we could even get all three captured ships ready to go."

"Not to mention twenty or thirty gunships," Jessica added.

"And what, ten thousand more marines? That's a lot of force available for liberation campaigns, as well as to defend the member systems we already have."

"You're starting to sound a lot like Galiardi," Jessica commented, one eyebrow raised in suspicion.

"A lot of what he says makes sense."

"Then you agree with him?"

"I didn't say that," Nathan replied. "One side doesn't have to be wrong for the other side to be right."

"You know what I think?" Jessica asked.

Nathan paused a moment, turning to look over his shoulder at her directly.

"I think you think too much."

"It's my *job* to think," Nathan insisted.

"It's our *job* to kill Jung," Jessica countered.

"If so ordered, yes. And I have no problem with that order. But understanding of all possible actions *and* outcomes better prepares us to make decisions on the fly, if required."

"Jump flash," Mister Navashee reported from the sensor station.

"Finally," Jessica sighed, grateful for the interruption.

"It's Scout One."

Nathan turned aft toward the comm station.

"Incoming message from Scout One," Naralena reported. "They confirm there are no changes to any of the targets' courses or speeds."

"Our luck holds," Nathan said.

"Sooner or later, the other Jung-held systems will get word, and they'll start taking combat postures around the clock," Jessica reminded him.

"But not today," Nathan replied confidently as he

turned around and glanced at the mission clock on the starboard display to the right of his helmsman. "Mister Riley," he said as he moved to his command chair. "Jump us to waypoint zero."

"Jumping to waypoint zero, aye."

"Set general quarters," he continued as he took his seat, "and send confirmation to all forces at all staging points. Execute as planned."

"Jump complete," Mister Sperry reported from the Celestia's navigation station. "We are at waypoint zero."

"Sensor contacts," Ensign Kono announced. "And a jump flash. The Aurora just jumped in. I'm also picking up all eight JKKVs, still on designated course and speed."

"Transmit the launch authorization codes for our four weapons," Cameron ordered.

"Transmitting launch authorization codes," Luis acknowledged from the tactical station.

"All departments report general quarters," Ensign Souza reported from the Celestia's comm station.

"I've got four good replies," Luis reported. "Our jump KKVs are armed and will launch in one minute, fifteen seconds."

"Primary attack jump in ninety seconds," Mister Sperry added.

Commander Telles sat quietly in the back of the combat jumper as it coasted silently through the cold, dark void just beyond the Eta Cassiopeiae system. Their course had them on an intercept with a large moon orbiting the system's sixth planet, a massive gas giant called Hartog. The planet had many moons, only one of which was inhabited. In fact, it was the only hospitable world within the entire system, made so a millennium ago through the process the Terrans called terraforming. Its gravity was only half that of Earth, and the commander's forces had spent an entire day, living and training, inside an acclimation facility they had constructed on Porto Santo that could simulate any gravitational and atmospheric environment desired. They would have considerable strength, but the thinner atmosphere would reduce his men's endurance. It would have taken weeks for them to truly acclimate to the extreme differences, and they had been given a single day. At best, his men had learned to detect the early signs of hypoxia. As a precaution, they carried supplemental oxygen, which they would breathe via nasal cannulas during all surface ops on Adlair. Some of his marines did not need the additional oxygen, as the worlds they hailed from also possessed lower atmospheric pressures than that of Earth. His Ghatazhak troops, of course, had extensive training in all imaginable combinations of gravitational and atmospheric conditions.

The commander, his trusted subordinate, Master Sergeant Jahal, three Ghatazhak soldiers, and the three members of the combat jump shuttle's crew, had been sitting in near silence for almost an hour. Even the combat shuttle's talkative crew chief, Sergeant Torwell, had been quiet...at least part of the time.

"I wouldn't mind getting a chance to run around on the surface a little, I can tell you that," the young sergeant spouted over the comms. "Maybe try to see how high I can jump, or something." The sergeant looked down between his legs, trying to look at the face of the Ghatazhak sitting below and around him as he sat in the gunner's seat, suspended from the ceiling. "With those black pajamas of yours, I'll bet you guys could jump fifty meters, straight up. We should have brought a basketball, LT. Played a little three on three against another crew, in half gravity. That would be a blast, wouldn't it?"

Ensign Latfee sat in the combat jump shuttle's copilot seat, leaning against the cool side window of the shuttle's cockpit, as he stared out at the array of combat shuttles, troop shuttles, and boxcars spread out around them. All of them, as well as three other groups at other rally points, had been waiting for the proper time to execute their insertion jumps.

A small flash of light appeared beyond the furthest boxcar, causing the ensign to perk up. "Jump flash, to port," he announced straightening up slightly in his seat. He looked down at his console. "Must be a comm-drone. We've got an incoming message."

"Please, tell me it's a go order," the pilot, Lieutenant Kainan pleaded.

"Message is valid," the copilot reported, adjusting himself upright in his seat again to be ready. "It's a go order. We jump at mission plus two. That's two minutes and twenty seconds from now."

"Update our jump plot, Ensign," the lieutenant ordered, "and power up all weapons. You too, Torwell."

"Already on it, LT," the sergeant replied as the plasma generator behind his shoulders came to life in a subdued whine that sent a shiver down his spine. "Damn, I hate this thing," the sergeant commented. "Feels like ants crawling up my neck every time I fire."

Commander Telles smiled, quite familiar with the sensation of which the sergeant was complaining.

He glanced at the mission clock display in the upper right corner of his visor's tactical display, as the last few seconds counted down to mission time zero. The Aurora and the Celestia would already be jumping.

"Jump complete," Mister Riley reported as the blue-white jump flash faded from the Aurora's bridge.

"Contact!" Mister Navashee reported. "Dead ahead! One hundred kilometers and closing! It's the battle platform, sir! She's still intact!"

Nathan straightened slightly in his seat, concerned. "Did we miss?" he wondered, finding it impossible to believe.

"No, sir! We hit her. She's got heavy damage to her number four arm. That entire arm is without power or shields."

"Tactical..." Nathan began.

"Locking all forward tubes!" Jessica replied, cutting him off. "Triplets on the mark fours and full power singles on the mark fives. Helm..."

"Turning five to starboard and up three to line up the shot," Mister Chiles reported quickly, anticipating the lieutenant commander's request.

"Incoming fire," Mister Navashee added. "She's opening up with her big rail guns."

"Firing all forward tubes," Jessica announced.

The interior of the bridge lit up repeatedly with red-orange light as multiple plasma torpedoes sped away toward the battle platform.

"She's launching missiles as well," Mister Navashee reported. "Wide trajectories, from her opposite arms. I suspect she's lost targeting on the near side."

"Another round, Jess!" Nathan ordered. "Mister

Riley, a sixty kilometer jump, on my order. Helm, change course to dive us under her, close in, a few kilometers at the most."

"Captain, there's a debris field spreading out from her," Mister Navashee warned.

"Firing!" Jessica announced.

"We've got shields," Nathan replied as the bridge flashed red-orange several times in rapid succession.

"Changing course to dive under, three kilometers," the helmsman acknowledged.

"Range?"

"Ninety kilometers and closing," Mister Navashee replied.

"Keep firing!" Nathan urged, calling back over his shoulder toward Jessica at the tactical station. "What about the battleship?" he asked his sensor officer.

"The battleship is destroyed," Mister Navashee replied. "I'm just now picking up the Celestia's jump flash in the battleship's vicinity." Mister Navashee glanced at his other screen. "Two frigates are spinning up their FTLs for action, as well."

"What about the cruisers?" Nathan wondered.

"They're still on the far side of Hartog. The Celestia can see them from her position, though."

"Course established," the helmsman reported.

The bridge again lit up with red-orange flashes as the Aurora continued to fire her main forward torpedo cannons.

"First volley has hit the battle platform," Mister Navashee reported. "Major damage to the unshielded arm."

"Range?"

"Eighty kilometers."

"Pitch us up thirty degrees, Mister Chiles,"

Nathan ordered. "Be ready to fire all forward tubes, single shots, full power, no locks." Nathan glanced at the tactical display on the new transparent view screen to the left of his navigator, watching as the indicated range to the battle platform decreased.

"Rail gun fire," Jessica warned.

Swarms of tiny, pale blue dots appeared and disappeared on the Aurora's main, spherical view screen that encompassed her bridge. It was almost magical, and would have been entertaining had it not been for the fact that it signaled tens of thousands of rail gun slugs, each of them the size of a city bus back on Earth, slamming into their shields and draining them of their ability to protect the ship.

Nathan glanced at the range readout again, then at the ship's attitude display on the screen to the right of the helmsman. "Execute the jump...... Now."

———

"Battleship has been destroyed," Ensign Kono reported. "I've got two cruisers coming over the horizon of Hartog now. Their shields are up, and their weapons are at full power." Ensign Kono turned to look at her captain. "They're ready to fight, Captain."

"I guess they've got comm-sats to relay around that gas giant after all," Cameron said. "Helm, take us to the nearest cruiser and prepare to jump in to attack."

"Turning toward the near cruiser," Ensign Hunt replied.

"Lieutenant Delaveaga," Cameron continued. "We'll jump in, fire two full power rounds on the fours and fives from a range of ten kilometers. Then we'll jump to above her bow and pass over her at five hundred meters, showing her our starboard side. We'll pound her with all guns, including our broadside cannons, as we pass her length. If she tries to quick-shot her missiles at us as we pass, don't wait for my order to snap-jump us out of harm's way, Mister Sperry."

"Understood," Luis replied.

"I won't let them touch us," the navigator, Ensign Sperry, assured his captain.

"On intercept course," Ensign Hunt declared.

"Jump plotted and ready," Ensign Sperry added.

"Execute the jump," Cameron ordered.

———————

"Visors down, weapons loaded!" Sergeant Lazo barked from the front of the troop shuttle. "Check your safeties. Check the pack of the guy in front of you. We jump in two minutes! Boots on the ground in two thirty!"

Biorgi Saladan pulled an ammo magazine from one of the thigh pockets of his combat armor and inserted it into his weapon. After ensuring that his safety was on, he pulled back the lever to load the first round into the chamber.

"Remember," the sergeant continued, "single shots, no auto-fire unless ordered. When you have the shot, take the shot. If you don't have the shot, reposition and get the shot. A round that strikes an enemy has the potential to injure or kill. At the very least, it lets the enemy know that someone is trying to kill him...that a marine is trying to kill him. A round fired in haste that misses its target is a wasted round."

Biorgi pulled his combat visor down, activating the tactical display. He still didn't have the knack for absorbing the constant stream of data it provided without having to stare at the display. After weeks of training and one combat landing, he was starting to wonder if he would ever get the hang of it, despite the fact that his instructors assured him the skill would come in time.

Biorgi turned to the man sitting to his left, checking that his pack was secure, tugging at the straps and checking the gear, as he felt the guy behind him doing the same to his pack.

"Remember your training," Sergeant Lazo reminded them from the front of the troop shuttle, "and remember, you don't fight for anyone other than the men who fight with you. Kill your enemy, and protect your friends. Live or die, you are all heroes of the Alliance, and protectors of your worlds. Mah-REENS!" the Ghatazhak sergeant barked proudly.

"DO OR DIE! DO OR DIE!" the men replied proudly in unison.

Sergeant Lazo smiled as his comm-set crackled. *"One minute to jump."*

"Jump complete," Mister Riley reported as the jump flash faded from the Aurora's bridge.

"Got her in my sights," Jessica reported. "Firing all forward tubes!"

Nathan waited a split second for all eight plasma torpedoes to clear their bow on their way to their target. "Roll us onto our port side and hold this attitude."

"The guns on arms three and five are swinging in toward us!" Mister Navashee warned.

"Jess!" Nathan called while the image of the battle platform that filled their main view screen rotated from left to right as the Aurora rolled onto her port side. "Hit them with our starboard broadside cannons!"

"Already on it!" she replied. "Rail and plasma quads as well!"

"They've got us!" Mister Navashee warned.

The swarms of pale blue dots did not announce the arrival of enemy rail gun slugs as before. This time, the flashes were at least ten times as large, and their color was a brilliant blue, tinged with angry, fiery yellow-orange halos that cast eerie flashes of light across the interior of the bridge as the Jung rail gun slugs slammed into their shields.

"Firing broadside cannons!" Jessica announced as the bridge shook from the impacts against their shields. "Firing quads!"

"All starboard shields are down to fifty percent!" Mister Navashee reported as the bridge continued to shake in the eerie, strobe-like illumination. "Forty percent!"

"I've lost the angle!" Jessica declared as the Aurora passed under the massive battle platform. "We're hitting shields again!"

"Escape jump!" Nathan ordered, the blue-white jump field spilling out over the Aurora's hull on the view screen just as the words left his mouth.

———

The Celestia's bridge flashed red-orange repeatedly as her plasma torpedoes left their tubes.

"Target two is launching missiles!" Ensign Kono reported. "Time to impact: thirty seconds."

Another round of plasma torpedoes lit up the bridge again.

"Time to first wave?" Cameron asked, despite the fact that she had memorized the jump schedules of every phase of the mission.

"One minute," Luis replied from the tactical station.

"Mister Hunt, change course for Adlair. Jump as soon as ready."

"Missiles will impact in fifteen seconds..."

"Turning for Adlair."

"You don't want to use the broadside cannons on the second cruiser, sir?" Luis wondered.

"It was a wasted effort on the last one," Cameron replied. "She was already coming apart. But I would appreciate it if you kept those missiles off us until we finish our turn and jump."

"Already on it, sir," Luis replied.

Cameron glanced at the main view screen as the mark two point-defense plasma turrets around the perimeter of the ship continued firing on the incoming missiles as the ship turned away from its attack run.

"Direct impacts," Ensign Kono reported. "Target two is destroyed."

"On course for Adlair," Ensign Hunt reported.

"Jump us to Adlair and get us into our orbital track for attack on the troop base," Cameron ordered, glancing at the mission clock. "The Falcons are jumping in ten seconds, and the troops in less than a minute."

"Jumping to Adlair in, three......two......one..."

———

"Jump complete," Loki reported from the copilot seat on the right side of the Super Falcon's cockpit. "Five good flashes. Locking weapons on assigned targets. Hold your course and speed."

"No problem," Josh replied as the Super Falcon buffeted lightly in the thin atmosphere of Adlair.

"Picking up twelve bandits, rising from the target area," Loki reported. "Falcon Flight, One. Bandits in the air. Count twelve. Two, take control of my busters. I'll take everyone's chasers and deal with the bandits. The rest of you stay on your primary targets."

"Two copies. Taking your busters."

Loki opened his ship's weapons bay doors as the rest of the Super Falcons confirmed his instructions. He watched his tactical display, as his weapons targeting system took control of all chaser missiles in the weapons bays of the other five Super Falcons in his flight, as well as his own. He quickly traced a circle with his index finger on the screen, selecting all twelve bandits headed their way. Then he pressed the auto-assign button to allow his weapons logic systems to automatically assign targets to the chaser missiles in the belly of each of the Super Falcons in their formation. Icons on his weapons display representing two of his four buster missiles turned red as Falcon Two initiated their launch. Loki initiated his own launch a few seconds later, sending four missiles from each Super Falcon, a total of twenty-four chaser missiles, streaking toward their distant targets at more than six times the speed of sound on Adlair. Another six icons appeared from the target area, indicating more bandits had gotten off the ground. Seconds later, the buster missiles hit their target, no doubt destroying the Jung airbase still more than two hundred kilometers away at their current speed. He did not assign more chasers, however. He simply selected the additional targets and instructed the weapons system to vector any leftover chaser missiles that missed their targets to reassign to the new targets. His plan worked. All twelve icons from the first group disappeared as they were picked out of the sky by fourteen of the chaser missiles launched in the first wave. The remaining ten missiles continued on, finding and destroying the additional six Jung fighters that had managed to get off the ground before the buster missiles had destroyed the airbase.

"Threat board from target alpha is clear," Loki announced. "Falcons Three through Six, vector to target bravo. Two, follow us in to verify the destruction of alpha."

"*On your six, four right, One,*" Falcon Two reported.

"Like shooting fish in a bucket," Loki bragged, feeling pleased with his performance.

"A barrel," Josh corrected. "The expression is 'like shooting fish in a barrel'."

"Are you sure?"

"I'm sure," Josh insisted as he pitched their nose up slightly and reduced power to both climb and slow their ship down to subsonic speeds. "You know, I'm kinda liking this thinner atmosphere. Not as much control authority, but we don't get our teeth rattled as much when we jump in low."

"Are you sure it's a barrel?" Loki challenged. "I mean, that doesn't even make sense. Barrels have a lid on them. They're sealed up, right? How do you shoot the fish if there's no opening?"

"Hey, I didn't make the saying up," Josh defended, "and I sure as hell never said it made sense."

———

"Jump complete," Ensign Latfee reported as the jump flash windows on the combat jump shuttle turned clear again. "Fifty meters up, four clicks out, two-fifty closure. Thirty seconds to insertion point."

"Nothing on my threat board," Sergeant Torwell reported from his gunner's bubble atop the combat jump shuttle.

"Just the way I like it," the lieutenant said.

The sky outside was a brilliant topaz, as the two hundred and thirty hour day was about to begin on Adlair. Light reflecting off the gas giant Hartog provided the primary illumination for the first eleven and a half hours of the Adlairan day, after which the world would be bathed in direct sunlight from their parent star, Eta Cassiopeiae, for an equal amount of time.

"It's beautiful, isn't it?" the sergeant declared in awe as he gazed outside.

"What did you guys do to Torwell?" the lieutenant asked. "Did one of you spike his water bladder?"

Commander Telles smiled as he gazed out the window. The young, talkative sergeant was correct. It was a breathtaking sight to behold. The commander had studied the data on this world in great detail, and he knew that for the next two hundred and thirty hours, this world would cycle between this dreamlike, topaz night sky, and its usual pale blue daytime sky, every eleven hours. It would then return to perpetual darkness for another two hundred and thirty hours, as the moon made its way quickly around the backside of its parent planet, Hartog, plunging the world into frigid temperatures. Were it not for the large moon's constant internal volcanic activity, kept in constant motion by the pull of Hartog's massive gravity well, the moon would be a ball of frozen rock and ice, instead of the rich, lush world that the terraforming engineers of a thousand years ago had created.

It was no surprise, however, that the people of Adlair preferred to live in small villages contained within protective domes built into the sides of the planet's many rolling hills. While it might be warm and lush during the sunny part of their trip around

Hartog, it was less than ideal during the other half of their journey.

"Weapons hot," Master Sergeant Jahal ordered. "If it's armed and it isn't wearing black, kill it."

"Fifteen seconds," Ensign Kainan announced.

"I've got a lock on the target," Lieutenant Delaveaga reported from the Celestia's tactical station. "Ready to fire."

"Troops are in the airspace, ten seconds from deployment," Ensign Kono announced.

"We're late," Cameron realized unhappily. "Comms, tell the Ghatazhak to hold position on the ground and take cover while we blast the target."

"Yes, sir."

"Lieutenant, as soon as those CJs move off to safe range, you're cleared to fire."

"Yes, sir," Luis replied. "Estimate thirty seconds."

"Confirmation from Commander Telles, sir," Ensign Souza reported. "They are taking cover in place."

"Any sign of the Aurora?" Cameron wondered. "She should have handled those frigates by now."

"No, sir," Ensign Kono replied. "And I'm picking up two FTL signatures that I believe are the frigates."

"Are you sure?"

"That they are FTL signatures, yes," the ensign assured her. "But there's no way for me to tell what kind of ships they actually are. I'm just guessing that they're the frigates, since they're too small to be cruisers."

"All combat jumpers are clear of the target area," Luis reported. "Opening fire on the troop base on the surface with our ventral quad rail guns."

"Very well," Cameron replied. Still concerned,

she turned toward the comm station at the aft side of the bridge. "Mister Souza, dispatch a jump comm-drone to the area of the battle platform and auto-hail the Aurora."

"Aye, sir," Ensign Souza acknowledged.

Luis looked at his captain. "You think they ran into trouble?" he asked. "Like, *battle platform* kind of trouble?"

"Doubtful," Cameron admitted. "Just playing it safe, that's all."

"Two contacts!" Mister Navashee reported urgently from the Aurora's sensor station. "Frigates! Just came out of FTL! They're locking missiles on us, sir."

"Continue firing on that battle platform until we jump!" Nathan ordered his tactical officer. "Be ready on the escape jump, Mister Riley. Execute when our port shields reach forty percent, or *any* missiles get within a kilometer of us."

"I've got my finger on the button, Captain," Mister Riley assured him.

"Maintain a clear jump line at all times," Nathan reminded his helmsman. "Jess, try to angle some of your quad shots under their neighboring shields as we pass. Try to take out some of their shield emitters so we can get a clean shot at one of the other arms."

"You got it!"

"Inbound missiles," Mister Navashee reported as the bridge shook from rail gun impacts against their weakening shields. "Eighteen of them. First ten are twenty seconds out!"

"Point-defenses are engaging the incoming missiles," Jessica assured him.

"Jump flash!" Mister Navashee added. "Comm-drone."

"Incoming message," Naralena reported. "From the Celestia. They're asking for our status."

"Message: Engaged with battle platform and frigates. Require immediate assistance. End message."

"Sending."

"Arm four is coming apart!" Mister Navashee declared in excitement.

Nathan turned back toward the main view screen, switching camera views just as the bulk of the heavily damaged number four arm of the Jung battle platform broke off from the platform's central structure and began separating into several pieces, rocked by internal explosions deep within the arm itself.

"Yes!" Nathan declared triumphantly. "That was one of her maneuvering arms, right?"

"Yes, sir," Mister Navashee replied. "She's going to be slow to rotate and keep her good shields toward us as we pass."

"Then at least we've got a fighting chance," he declared. "Mister Chiles, turn us toward the nearest frigate. We can't fight a battle platform with a couple of frigates pestering us, now can we?"

―――――――

"*Telles, Celestia Actual,*" Captain Taylor's voice called over the commander's helmet comms as the bombardment suddenly stopped.

"Celestia Actual, Telles. Go ahead," he replied as he rose to his feet and stared at the settling dust a few hundred meters away.

"*We need to disengage the target. The Aurora is heavily engaged with the battle platform and two frigates, and they need our help. Can you handle the situation on the surface as is?"*

Commander Telles glanced at his tactical display on the inside of his helmet visor, noticing very few red icons, most of which were moving around slowly and in haphazard fashion. He then checked the weapons status displays for the four Super Falcons circling high above them. Each of them still had two busters, and four chaser missiles. "I believe so," the commander replied. "Deploy the CNS-sats, then go and help the Aurora. I believe they need you far more than we do. Return when you can."

"CNS-sats are already on their way out," Cameron assured him. *"The net will be up in two minutes. Celestia Actual, out."*

"On our own, again?" Master Sergeant Jahal wondered, a broad grin on his face.

"It is less complicated this way," Commander Telles replied.

"Holy shit, Lucius! Was that a joke? From Captain Serious?"

"That's *Commander* Serious," Telles replied without missing a beat. "Advance on the target, and confirm with the Super Falcons that we own the skies. Then clear the marines in close behind us, just in case."

"Yes, sir," the master sergeant replied, still grinning.

———

"I've got four more bandits to the northeast," Loki reported with surprise.

"Where the fuck did they come from?" Josh wondered. "There was nothing left of that base when we flew over, that's for damn sure."

"They must have been parked elsewhere," Loki

223

replied. "Maybe they keep some tucked away, or something. Two, One. We're turning northeast to intercept. Targets are low and slow, only four-twenty closure. Range in twenty seconds. You take the two on the right, we'll take the two on the left. Pop two, jump up and then jump back down vertical on them to finish with guns in case they manage to evade."

"Two copies. Selecting two on right. Will pop two, then jump up and take them in a vertical dive with guns as needed."

Loki quickly selected the two targets on the left and assigned one chaser to each target, leaving two more in his weapons bay. "Falcon One, popping two," he announced over the comms as he fired the two chaser missiles.

"Pitching up," Josh said as he pulled the ship into a forty-five-degree climb and added power to maintain airspeed.

"Falcon Two, popping two."

"Chasers have acquired," Loki said. "Ten seconds."

"Jumping," Josh announced as he pushed the selector switch on top of his flight control stick forward and pressed the execute button.

The windows of the Super Falcon's cockpit turned opaque for a brief moment. Josh pulled his throttles back to zero thrust, rolled the ship inverted, and pushed their nose down onto an intercept course with the four Jung fighters passing far below them.

"Five seconds," Loki reported. "They're taking evasive actions."

Josh watched their altitude rapidly decrease, moving the jump range select dial one click at a time to match their decreasing altitude.

"Impact! One down, the second one is breaking to the east and climbing."

Josh rolled slightly right and altered his angle of dive before initiating the next jump. When the cockpit windows cleared, the fleeing Jung fighter was passing right in front of him at a range of less than one hundred meters. Josh squeezed the gun trigger on his flight control stick, sending a pair of plasma blasts from their wing cannons into the target, causing it to explode. "Two down," he said as he rolled right and leveled off, adding power again to maintain airspeed.

"*Falcon Two. Two down.*"

"Two, One," Loki replied. "All four targets are destroyed. Local threat board is clear. Join up on us. We'll make a few wide perimeter sweeps to make sure before joining the others."

"*Two copies. Rejoining.*"

"Now *this* is the kind of liberation I like," Josh declared. "Jump in, blow some shit up, kill a few fighters... Easy as pie."

"I thought it was *easy as cake*?" Loki wondered.

"No. The expression is, 'A piece of cake'."

"Where does the pie fit in?"

Josh shook his head. "You're hopeless."

The rear cargo ramp lowered as the troop shuttle touched down in the open field just south of what was once the Jung troop base on Adlair. The shuttle's engines immediately began to wind down to idle as troops began pouring out the back, spreading out right and left as they left the ramp.

Biorgi followed the man in front of him, turning right once his boots hit the crunchy, tan-colored soil of Adlair. Energy weapons fire could barely be heard in the distance over the sound of the shuttle's four, massive engine pods.

As soon as the last man left the ramp, the shuttle's engines spun back up, lifting the ship into the air. She climbed slowly, accelerating forward as her aft cargo ramp raised up into its fully closed position. A moment after the ramp closed, the troop shuttle disappeared in a blue-white flash of light against the topaz morning sky.

With the shuttle gone, the sound of energy weapons fire was more noticeable. In fact, it was growing louder with every step. Biorgi continued to follow his platoon leader, Ghatazhak Sergeant Lazo, toward the dissipating cloud of dust and smoke that their forces had encircled.

After running for a few minutes, Biorgi saw Sergeant Lazo raise his hand and then drop it, signaling them to hit the ground. Biorgi did as instructed, assuming a prone position, his weapon aimed in the direction of the devastated Jung troop base. He looked at his tactical display. Stretched out from side to side were both blue and red icons... more red ones than blue. They were oriented along the horizon. Biorgi thought the commands, causing his visor to zoom in directly ahead so he could see the targets in greater detail. He could scarcely make out the Ghatazhak, in their menacing, flat-black combat armor, as they attacked the line of Jung soldiers. The enemy was easier to distinguish. They wore the traditional dark gray uniforms and armor, with the red trim that the Jung seemed to favor. Many of them were unarmored, appearing to have been caught by surprise by the orbital bombardment that all but leveled their base.

The enemy soldiers took cover behind fallen

structures and chunks of tan-colored concrete that had been strewn about by the rail gun impacts. They tried to create a coherent defensive line, but the Ghatazhak were too aggressive, too precise. The black-clad soldiers continued to press forward, their line finally merging with that of the enemy.

Biorgi took aim at a Jung soldier with a red icon on him and checked his range... *Too far.*

"Squads One and Two, move left one hundred meters," the sergeant ordered. *"Seven and Eight, move one hundred right. The rest of you fan out evenly between them in groups of two squads."*

Biorgi rose to his knees, his weapon still aimed toward the battle, waiting for those members of his squad to his left to move. Then he got to his feet and followed them, in a running crouch, for one hundred meters, before falling back down onto his stomach.

He looked back toward the engagement zone. Getting up and running had caused his tactical display to zoom back out to zero magnification, so again, Biorgi thought the commands to zoom in. He picked another target and took aim. He was still too far to guarantee a kill, but it was better to be ready.

"First Platoon," Sergeant Lazo's voice called over Biorgi's helmet comms. *"Move forward to optimum firing range and take up firing positions. Move, move, move!"*

Again Biorgi rose, and again his tactical display automatically reverted to normal magnification. He followed his squad leader, as did the rest of his squad, and the second squad behind them. In a crouch, with their weapons still trained on the engagement area toward which they ran, they moved briskly across the uneven, jagged terrain of Adlair. The sound of energy weapons grew louder with each crunch of their boots. Red energy bolts slammed into the tan soil in front of them, sending bits and pieces of the moon spraying into them as they ran. One of the bolts slammed into the man next to him. Biorgi stopped in his tracks, spinning around to look at his fallen comrade. His instinct was to help him, but he realized that he was beyond help. Half his face was gone, along with the side of his head... all of it neatly cauterized by the Jung energy blast that had taken the marine's life.

Biorgi felt someone shove him forward, urging him on, and he complied. Seconds later, that same man who had shoved him forward toward the battle also fell to enemy fire, his right leg and hip melted away and still burning as the man screamed in agony. Biorgi spun around and saw that someone else had dropped to the man's side to help him, followed by another. Biorgi spun around and continued to charge forward into the battle.

Finally, his squad leader fell to the ground, as did the rest of his squad and the squad behind him. Biorgi quickly took aim, checking the range on his tactical display. *We're still too far.* Biorgi looked toward his squad leader. He was lying on his belly, his weapon oddly aimed. He wasn't moving. Biorgi willed his display to zoom in, and he immediately saw smoke rising from his squad leader's unmoving body. The man nearest him reached out and shook the squad leader, but got no response. Biorgi could see the panic on the man's face, unsure of what to do as Jung energy weapons fire, most of it errant shots that had missed the Ghatazhak soldiers, continued to impact into the dirt around them.

Biorgi rose to his feet again. "Squad One! Continue forward!" he ordered, signaling with his left arm toward the battle. Biorgi continued his charge forward, jumping over the body of the dead squad leader and the soldier still shaking him. He maintained his crouched run, his weapon up and held tightly against his shoulder, ready to fire, as he had been trained to do, watching the range readout on his tactical display as it counted down. Red bolts of energy streaked past him, first to his right, then to his left. Others slammed into the dirt in front of him, sending bits of tan soil flying into his face as he charged forward.

Finally, his range display changed from red to orange. A few seconds later, it turned green. Biorgi hit the ground again. He quickly willed his visor to zoom in, and he picked his first target...and fired. His weapon sounded, recoiling sharply against his shoulder. The magnification setting on his visor allowed him to clearly see the blood spraying from the target's armpit, as his first shot grazed the uncovered area just above the Jung soldier's chest armor. He willed his visor to zoom in a bit more, and placed his aiming dot onto the enemy soldier's abdomen, and squeezed his trigger again. The second round easily pierced the Jung soldier's weaker abdominal cover, sending copious amounts of blood and tissue spraying out to either side from under the enemy soldier's armor. The man fell to his knees, after which a blast from a Ghatazhak energy weapon robbed him of his head.

Biorgi paused in shock and disbelief. Today was not his first combat action, and it was not the first time that he had fired his weapon. But the liberation of 82 Eridani had been far easier, as he had been in the second wave, not the first. He had not even fired

229

his weapon in anger that day. Today, he had killed a man.

It was time to kill more.

Biorgi mentally adjusted his visor's magnification, then picked another target and fired. A head shot, passing just under the Jung soldier's visor and striking him in the right cheek. The man fell backward, exposing his unprotected groin as he writhed in pain. Another shot put an end to his suffering.

Biorgi continued to pick targets, dropping them one by one...sometimes with a single shot, sometimes with two. He missed a few, but not many, and within minutes, it was over. The Ghatazhak forward line had broken through, and was engaged in hand-to-hand combat with the few Jung soldiers who remained.

"*First Platoon! Cease fire!*" Sergeant Lazo called over Biorgi's helmet comms. "*Move in to secure the perimeter. No one gets out alive.*"

Biorgi rose to his feet. He took a moment to wipe the sweat from his face. He looked around, noticing that the rest of his squad was waiting for him to move forward before they followed.

Today, he felt like a marine.

———

"Frigate two is destroyed," Mister Navashee announced from the Aurora's sensor station.

"Take us about to reengage that battle platform," Nathan ordered.

"Coming about, aye."

"How are our shields doing?" Nathan asked his systems officer.

"Starboard forward, and all bow shields are back up to sixty-two percent," the systems officer replied.

"If you can keep their big guns off them for a few minutes, they'll get back up to full power."

"On our next run, we'll jump in at ten clicks, fire two salvos into the unshielded side of her core, where arm four used to be," Nathan explained. "Then we'll pitch our nose down relative, say forty-five, and jump in close to pass with our bow shields away from her. We'll start by showing her our port side, where our shields are currently strongest." He turned back toward Jessica. "Hit them with quads and broadside cannons as we pass. Your firing window will be short, twenty seconds at the most, so don't get fancy, just fire away at her and hope for the best."

"Aye, sir," Jessica replied.

Nathan turned forward. "We'll make two passes the same way, but from different angles. That should give our starboard and bow shields a chance to reach full power. Then we can alternate sides with each pass. Left, center, right."

"Coming to jump point now," Mister Riley reported.

"Take us in," Nathan ordered.

"Jumping."

The blue-white jump flash washed over the bridge, and the image of the wounded Jung battle platform again filled the center main view screen. Even from ten kilometers away, she was visible without magnification, bathed in the light of Eta Cassiopeiae.

"Firing all forward tubes," Jessica announced.

The bridge flashed a reddish-orange momentarily as the plasma charges left the Aurora.

"Helm, nose down forty-five, roll ninety to starboard," Nathan ordered.

"Down forty-five and ninety to starboard," Mister Chiles replied.

The image of the distant Jung battle platform began to rotate as it slid from the center of the main view screen, up and to their left, disappearing off the left side of the view screen.

"Maneuver complete," the helmsman replied seconds later.

"Jump us in close," Nathan commanded.

"Jumping."

Again, the blue-white flash of the jump washed over them.

"Contacts!" Mister Navashee warned.

"Firing quads and broadside cannons!" Jessica reported.

"The other two frigates!" Mister Navashee continued.

"Damn it!" Nathan swore.

"They're locking missiles on us!"

"Mister Riley, prepare to escape jump..."

"They're firing missiles! Impact in twenty..."

"Point-defenses!" Nathan ordered.

"All point-defenses are engaging!"

"How many?" Nathan snapped.

"Twenty-four inbound!" Mister Navashee replied. "Make that twenty...eighteen... Ten seconds. They're reloading their launchers. Incoming rail gun fire from the battle... JUMP FLASH! It's the Celestia!"

The bridge shook as more rail gun rounds from the battle platform's massive guns pounded the Aurora's port shields.

"She's firing on the frigates!" Mister Navashee reported in glee.

"I can't get them all!" Jessica warned.

"Snap jump!" Nathan ordered.

The jump flash was building before the order left the captain's mouth.

"Jump complete," Mister Riley announced.

"Bring us back around for another pass," Nathan ordered. "Mister Navashee, what's the status of those other two frigates?"

"One moment, sir," the sensor operator replied. "They're thirty light seconds out, now."

"Damage reports?"

"Port shields down to sixty percent," the system officer replied.

"No reports from damage control," Naralena added.

"Jump flash," Mister Navashee reported. "It's the Celestia, again."

"Incoming transmission from Celestia Actual," Naralena announced.

"Put her on," Nathan replied gladly.

"*Aurora Actual, Celestia Actual,*" Cameron's voice called over the loudspeakers.

Nathan felt a wave of relief wash over him. "Go ahead, Captain," he replied.

"*Sorry it took us so long,*" Cameron said. "*We had a troop base to squash.*"

"No problem. Your timing couldn't have been better."

"*I assume you have a plan to bring down that platform?*"

"Swinging hammer? Say...split twenties, high and low, odds and evens?"

"*Sounds good,*" Cameron replied. "*You want odds or evens to start?*"

"Odds, of course. We'll drop our targeting markers with each pass. Once we bring down another arm,

233

we'll have a big enough gap in her shields to take her out once and for all."

"*Yes, sir.*"

"Just keep your time in the zone short, Captain. Her big guns are a *bitch.*"

"*Understood. Celestia Actual, out.*"

———

Commander Telles walked along the perimeter of the rubble that was once the Jung troop base on Adlair. Bodies of the dead were everywhere. Most of the troops who had been housed in the base had undoubtedly perished in the orbital bombardment that leveled the facility. Those who he saw before him were the ones who escaped the initial attack, only to find themselves fighting for their lives against a Ghatazhak onslaught that took them with equal surprise.

Commander Telles looked to his master sergeant as the man approached, a captive Jung officer following behind him, escorted by two Ghatazhak soldiers. "Casualties?"

"Two Ghatazhak injured, none killed," Master Sergeant Jahal reported. "Fourteen marines dead, twenty-two injured. They fought bravely. Without their supportive fire, our own casualties might have been higher."

"And the enemy body count?"

"Their force strength was estimated at ten thousand. This is the only survivor that we have found. So..."

Commander Telles stepped up to the officer, pausing to study the young man's rank insignia. "You are a major, are you not?"

"I am," the Jung officer replied proudly.

Commander Telles looked him over more

carefully. "You are of command rank. A leader of warriors. Your base lies in ruins, your men dead, and yet, you have nary a scratch on your person. How is that?"

"He was in a secure bunker under the rubble," Master Sergeant Jahal sneered. "Hiding like a coward."

"You have made a grave error," the Jung major warned the commander. "The battle platform will send gunships, troops... You will be outnumbered, and you will not have the element of surprise on your side." The major leaned forward, seething with anger. "You will all die."

"The battle platform?" the commander replied. The cheers of marines, as well as gasps of disbelief of the many locals who had come to see the destruction, caught their attention. Commander Telles and the others turned and looked skyward, like all the rest. Far above them was a massive explosion of a very distant, and very large, object.

"*That* battle platform?" the commander said, a small smile forming on the corner of his mouth. "I think not." He stared at the major for a moment, then turned back to his master sergeant. "Transfer him back to Porto Santo for interrogation."

"Who are you people?" the major asked.

"We, are the Alliance," Commander Telles replied. "And we are the *means* to *your* end."

CHAPTER SEVEN

"Can't they just build more of the damned things?" Josh complained. "I thought we were combat pilots. Now we're flying ordnance retrieval missions?"

"What's the big deal, Josh?" Loki wondered as he studied his sensor console on the right side of the Super Falcon's cockpit. "It isn't that difficult of a mission."

"Excuse me," Josh disagreed. "Those things are designed to blow up after they miss, aren't they?"

"Only if they do not receive an abort signal within twenty-four hours of missing their target."

"Or, someone tries to tamper with them," Josh reminded him. "I was at the briefing too, Lok."

"We won't be within the blast radius until the system has been disarmed."

"We're still trying to dock with a weapon, with an explosive charge inside, at half light..."

"Piece of pie," Loki insisted.

"...using a retrieval system that has yet to be tested," Josh finished. "And for the last time, Loki, it's 'a piece of cake' or 'easy as pie'!"

"Alright, alright. Why are you being so dramatic? Are you afraid you can't do it? Because, I can..."

"Oh, I can do it," Josh scoffed. "Don't you worry about that, my friend."

"Then what is the problem?"

Josh took a breath and let out a sigh. "I just think it's a poor use of our talents, that's all."

"Falcons are the only ships, besides the Aurora and the Celestia, that can catch up to those things. And you're the best Falcon pilot we have."

"Well, since you put it that way..."

Loki shook his head. "Contact. I've got the first JKKV dead ahead."

"What happened to all that 'needle in a haystack' crap you were spouting back in the mission briefing?" Josh wondered. "I've got the course data entered into the auto-flight system."

"It seemed like the right Earth expression at the time."

"Not exactly," Josh said. "I mean, we did have the course and speed data. Just a matter of cruising at the same speed along the same course, and jumping ahead to its calculated location."

"I know. I know. I really thought it was the right expr... Wait, did you say you were entering the data in the auto-flight?"

"I said I was entering the data, not engaging the system," Josh pointed out. "I'm just following procedure."

"Josh Hayes, following procedure?"

"Would you be happier if I did a few barrel rolls on approach?" Josh suggested.

"No, that's quite all right," Loki replied. "We're close enough to transmit the disarm codes. Sending them now."

Josh watched his own sensor display as the Super Falcon closed rapidly on the jump KKV that had been coasting through space since it missed its target the day before. After a few minutes, he flipped on the Super Falcon's landing lights, and looked out the forward window. There, in front of them, was the JKKV still traveling its course at fifty percent the speed of light, just as it had been the moment it left the Aurora's main launch tubes.

Josh let out a low whistling sound. "Man, when

you think of how deadly that thing is, just cruising through space, waiting to strike something."

"This ship has way more mass than that jump KKV," Loki pointed out. "We're just as deadly, if used the same way."

"So is an asteroid," Josh replied. "But it's not designed for that purpose. *That* thing, *is*. And that's *all* it's designed to do. Jump in close and ram its target, transferring all its kinetic energy into whatever it collides with."

"I don't see how it's different from any other weapon."

"There's something simple, something elegant about it. It's way more impressive than the old converted Takaran comm-drones."

"But those were far more destructive."

"Yeah, I know, but..."

"As usual, you're not making any sense, Josh. Let's just retrieve the thing and then go and grab the rest of them so we can go home."

"Why are you in such a hurry?" Josh wondered as he maneuvered the Super Falcon in closer to the JKKV. "Got a hot date?"

"Maybe."

Josh glanced at Loki. "Seriously?"

"Why is that such a surprise?"

"No surprise," Josh said, back peddling. "Who is she?"

"That girl in medical, the one who was originally on Doctor Sorenson's team."

"Cassandra?"

"Yeah, that's her."

"She's hot."

"She's *nice*, Josh, not hot."

"Nice and hot," Josh corrected. "What are you two

love birds going to do? I mean, it's not like there's a lot to do for entertainment on the Aurora."

"It's wacky-cake night in the galley," Loki told him, raising his eyebrows.

"Ohhhh," Josh drooled. "Chocolate. The absolute best thing about Earth. I still can't believe the original settlers of the Pentaurus cluster didn't think to bring a chocolate plant with them."

"I don't think chocolate is a plant," Loki said. "I think they make it from a lot of different ingredients."

"Well, whatever those ingredients are, they should have brought the seeds with them. That's all I'm saying."

* * *

Eight men in well-fitted Takaran officer uniforms stepped out of the passenger jump shuttle and onto the tarmac at the Porto Santo airbase. The men were well groomed and moved with confidence befitting their upbringing.

"Sons of nobles," Master Sergeant Jahal muttered as he watched them approach. "I forget. Do I bow before or after they are introduced?"

"We are Ghatazhak," Commander Telles stated flatly. "We bow for no one."

"I have no love for Takaran nobility, either," Major Prechitt agreed. "Unfortunately, we need pilots. Pilots with experience, and they are in short supply these days."

"You don't really believe these eight men will make a difference?" the master sergeant challenged. "I don't care how good they are."

"Personally, I'd rather have *any* eight Corinari pilots, myself," Major Prechitt said.

"Agreed," Commander Telles added.

"Unfortunately, no more are available," the major

continued. "Hence, the sons of expatriated Takaran nobility. We'll teach them to fly the Super Eagles, and they will help us train pilots from other Alliance worlds...assuming we find any."

Commander Telles turned to look at the major. "None yet?"

"I'm afraid not," the major sighed. "On the bright side, though, we have plenty of volunteers for basic flight school."

Commander Telles did not look amused.

"Thank God for auto-flight," Master Sergeant Jahal joked.

"Gentlemen," the first Takaran officer began as he neared. "Allow me to introduce myself. I am Commander Goodreau of the Avendahl. These are Lieutenants Jarso, Sistone, and Dornahki, as well as Ensigns Giortone, Auklud, Riordan, and Masa. We have been sent by Captain Navarro to act as Super Eagle pilots. I trust we were expected?"

"Indeed, you were, Commander," Major Prechitt replied. "I'm Major Prechitt, air group commander for the Alliance forces in the Sol sector, and CAG for the Aurora."

"Corinari, yes, I have heard of you, Major. It is an honor."

"The honor is mine," the major assured him. "Allow me to introduce Commander Telles, commanding officer of all Ghatazhak forces attached to the Alliance in the Sol sector. And this is his assistant, Master Sergeant Jahal."

Telles and Jahal offered only a polite nod, their hands still folded behind their backs.

"A pleasure, sirs." Lieutenant Commander Goodreau looked past them at the Porto Santo base. "An impressive facility. We were able to get a birds-eye view on approach. It appears to cover the entire island."

"Much of it is housing for civilian support personnel," Major Prechitt explained.

"There was also a city of several thousand in existence prior to our procurement of the island," Commander Telles added. "They have been most helpful."

"Yes, of course. And a beautiful island it is, Commander."

"We have arranged officer's quarters for you and your men here on Porto Santo," Major Prechitt told the leader of the Takaran pilots. "I trust you have all had an opportunity to study the technical data that we forwarded to your captain?"

"Yes, indeed. We have been studying the data for weeks. An interesting design concept, to be sure. Is it true that Deliza Ta'Akar was its designer?"

"In part. It is based on a Terran design that was already in service. Miss Ta'Akar reconceptualized its operational design, with the help of Terran, Corinairan, and Takaran engineers. The concept was hers, however."

"Impressive, indeed. I would love to meet this remarkable young woman."

"I'll see what I can do," the major promised. "If you'll all follow me, I will have my staff see you to your accommodations."

"Thank you, Major," the lieutenant commander replied. "How soon can we get started flying the Super Eagles? I trust you have a few built by now?"

"We have thirteen of them on the line as we speak, and are producing them at a rate of one ship every other day."

"Excellent. I cannot wait to get started."

"You can start using the simulator this afternoon, if you'd like?" the major offered.

"That won't be necessary, Major. Tomorrow will be soon enough. It has been a long journey, after all. Best we get a good night's rest, and start fresh in the morning, I suspect."

"As you wish," the major agreed, pointing the group of pilots toward the waiting transport vehicle.

The group of Takaran pilots walked to the waiting vehicle. After they were beyond earshot, the master sergeant spoke. "I'm so glad my residence isn't in officer's country."

* * *

"*The Adlairans didn't seem to care one way or the other,*" Admiral Dumar said over the vid-link to President Scott's office. "*The Jung showed up about a decade ago and set up an airbase and a troop base. Their only interaction with the locals in all that time has been purchasing of crops and paying for them with basic services such as health care, power generation, sewage treatment... Basic stuff, really.*"

"No propaganda campaigns? No forced rule?" the president wondered.

"*No, Mister President. At least nothing like we've seen on other worlds. To be honest, Adlair is a very simple world. They eschew technology for the most part, and have little interest in expanding or progressing beyond that which they need to continue their simple way of life.*"

"So, they don't have any technology?" the president confirmed.

"*They do, just not much,*" the admiral explained, "*and they don't have any real industrial capacity to speak of, either.*"

"How do they feel about the Alliance?"

"They understand why we are clearing out all Jung forces within reach of Sol, but they have no interest in being part of it. They would prefer to remain neutral."

"Are they asking us to stay away from their world?"

"Not exactly, but neither are they inviting us to come back and visit any time."

"Do they understand what the Jung might do to them, if they return?" the president asked.

"They understand what we believe the Jung may do to them, if they should return. However, they do not believe it will happen. As I said, the Jung have never done anything bad to them. They simply do not care, one way or the other."

"Not exactly the reception we were expecting."

"No, Mister President, it is not," Admiral Dumar agreed. *"In the grand scheme of things, however, it does not matter. There is nothing of value to the Alliance on Adlair."*

"I see," the president replied. "Recommendations, Admiral?"

"I recommend we leave a jump-capable recon drone hidden in the system. It will detect the presence of any Jung ships, and it will provide the means for the Adlairans to contact us, should they change their minds in the future."

President Scott rubbed his chin, somewhat uneasy with the proposed plan. "What's the risk of leaving a jump-capable device behind?"

"Negligible," the admiral assured him, confidently. *"All our jump drives are rigged with self-destruct systems. Especially our drones and jump KKVs."*

"Like the scout ships were?"

"We have made considerable improvements in the self-destruct and tamper protection systems since

the Scout Three incident. I would not be suggesting leaving a recon drone behind if I believed it to be a risk."

"Of course, of course," President Scott replied. "Very well."

"*If there is nothing else, Mister President?*" the Admiral asked.

"Actually, there is one other thing. I was concerned that the battle platform in the Eta Cassiopeiae system was not destroyed by the initial jump KKV strike, putting our forces at greater risk."

"*It was a calculated risk on my part,*" the admiral explained. "*The jump KKVs are not as powerful as the original FTL KKVs. Ideally, we should be launching a spread of eight jump KKVs to ensure a first-strike kill against a battle platform. Unfortunately, the rate at which we are able to convert the old EDF missiles into jump-capable KKVs is limited. It was my call to strike with only four JKKVs, a decision I regret. Luckily, neither ship suffered any damage. However, the Celestia's early departure from her bombardment duties did cost us more lives on the ground than we had hoped, especially considering the distance of the base from the local villages. If the mission had gone as planned, that base would have been completely obliterated, and there would have been little to no resistance on the surface. I take full responsibility for those losses, Mister President.*"

"Thank you for the explanation, Admiral. I wish you and your forces better luck on your next mission."

"*Thank you, Mister President.*"

The image of Admiral Dumar disappeared from the view screen on the wall, replaced by the logo of the North American Union for a moment, before automatically shutting off. The door on the side of the president's office opened without warning, and President Scott's daughter, Miri, entered the room.

"Why didn't you tell him to use more JKKVs in the future?" she asked as she walked into the office.

"It's not my place to tell the admiral *how* to accomplish his missions."

"Since when?" she asked, stopping beside her father's desk. "You're the president of the NAU, as well as the Coalition. If it's not your job, whose is it?"

"My job is to listen to his recommendations, and to accept or reject them, based on the needs of the people of Earth. The same is true of every leader of every member world. Besides, you heard him, Miri. We lack conversion capacity, and thanks to Galiardi's petition, the admiral's operational timetable has been shortened. If he uses too many pre-mission, we may run out of them *before* the job is done."

"I thought they successfully retrieved the ones that missed? If that's the case, then what's the problem? Just fire a bunch of them and recover the ones that missed."

"They've had *one* good recovery mission, Miri. Until we can be sure that we'll *always* be able to recover the JKKVs that miss, I have to agree with the admiral."

"Speaking of admirals, Galiardi is still waiting to see you," Miri reminded him.

President Scott sighed.

"Do you know what you're going to say to him?" she wondered.

"I have some ideas, yes," the president admitted, "but I think I'm going to just listen to what he has to say, and take it from there. The last thing I need to do is to feed the fire."

"I'll send him in, then," Miri said, exiting the room.

President Scott rose from his desk and moved toward the center of the office, in preparation to greet his guest. The door opened, and Miri led Admiral Galiardi into the room.

"Admiral," the president greeted, taking caution to use exactly the right tone and level of courtesy. "A pleasure to see you again," he added as he extended his hand.

"The pleasure is all mine, Mister President," Admiral Galiardi replied politely, shaking the offered hand. "Thank you for agreeing to speak with me. I know how busy you must be."

"Aren't we all." President Scott gestured for the admiral to take a seat in the sitting area to the side of the office.

"Gentlemen, I'll leave you to your discussions," Miri offered politely, backing toward the door to exit.

Admiral Galiardi bowed appreciatively to Miri as she exited, then turned back to the president. "Your youngest daughter, isn't she?"

"Yes, Miranda."

"I almost didn't recognize her," the admiral said as he took his seat.

"The last year has aged us all a decade," President Scott said as he sat.

"Indeed it has."

"How may I be of help to you today, Admiral?"

"Please, Mister President. Call me Michael. I think we've known each other long enough for that. Besides, while I appreciate the respect the title infers, I am no longer an admiral."

"Very well, Michael. How may I help you?"

"I assume you are aware of the petition my people have been circulating?"

"Of course."

"I thought we might discuss its intent."

"I thought its intent was quite clear," President Scott said. "The 'Strength Now' group, of which I assume you are the leader, wants Earth to withdraw from the Sol-Pentaurus Alliance and concentrate its efforts on the *defense* of Earth, and *only* Earth." One of President Scott's eyebrows went up. "Isn't *that* a correct interpretation?"

"Partly," the admiral admitted. "Some of our most vocal members would like nothing less. However, I believe it is the aggressive *expansion* of the Alliance within the Sol sector that we object to, more than the Alliance itself."

"The Alliance's goal is not expansion of the Alliance itself, Mister Galiardi. You know that as well as anyone. Expansion of its member worlds is merely a byproduct of removal of Jung forces from nearby systems."

"Your Alliance is not just *removing* forces, Mister President, they are *liberating worlds*. And with the liberation of worlds comes the responsibility to protect them."

"Agreed, assuming that those worlds are willing to join the Alliance," President Scott replied.

"Mister President, we are barely capable of protecting our own world, let alone dozens of others. One could make an argument that our ability to protect *this* world depends on how many ships the Jung are willing to commit to a single, mass assault."

"I do not disagree with that assessment," the president said. "However, the further from Sol the

247

nearest Jung ship is located, the more time we have to *prepare* our defense. Surely you can see the logic?"

"Of course, but the Alliance is attacking ships that have not taken a threatening posture. The fact that they are parked less than a year's travel from Sol does not justify your actions, at least not in the minds of a military leader. Such leaders can only see your actions as an act of war."

"Which is what it should be," President Scott argued. "The Jung came here. They attacked *our* world, without provocation, with the intent to conquer and enslave our people. We are only responding to that act of aggression, as *any* world would do."

"No, not any world," Galiardi corrected. "Only us. None of the other systems in this sector traveled beyond their boundaries to attack Jung forces elsewhere."

"Only because the Jung had already defeated them during their first strikes." President Scott leaned back in his chair, frustrated. "I don't get it, Michael. I would have expected you, of all people, to be waving the banner and charging into battle, gun in hand."

"No, you are mistaken," Galiardi insisted. "I may be a military man, but I'm not stupid. You don't call out the schoolyard bully unless you're damned sure you can kick his ass, and that's exactly what your Alliance is doing. And it's *our* ass that's going to get kicked...*again*."

"I don't know, I think we've been doing pretty well so far, all things considered."

"Don't kid yourself, Dayton," Galiardi warned. "You've had time on your side. That was the whole reason that I pushed the STS program so hard. But

248

time is running out. Eventually, word will reach the Jung homeworld, wherever it is, and when it does, the Jung will respond."

"And with the time that our forces are buying us by removing all Jung forces from the core, we'll be ready. Our people have done the math as well, Michael."

"Now it's from the entire core? What happened to twenty light years?"

"The core and secondary worlds of Earth, for the most part, have the largest populations, and the greatest industrial and economic capacities."

"Which is exactly why the Jung conquered them to begin with, Dayton," Galiardi countered. "You're not poking them with a stick. You're gutting them with a knife."

"We're sending them a message," President Scott insisted.

"And what exactly is that message?" Admiral Galiardi wondered.

"That we will not bow down to subjugation. That we will not tolerate brutality and injustice. Not against us, nor those we call friends."

"No! The message you are sending is a dare!" Galiardi declared, shaking a pointed finger at the president. "A dare for the Jung to return, in force, to try and finish the job they started. Had you simply liberated Earth, and then taken up a defensive posture followed by a stern warning that we will not tolerate any more incursions into our system, we *might* have had a chance. At the very least, it would have taken several years for the Jung homeworld to learn of the events and take action. Perhaps longer to rally enough ships to cleanly overwhelm us. You could have used the Karuzara facilities to upgrade the Aurora and the Celestia, and maybe even a few more, smaller, ships. But you had to go on a crusade for the good of the entire core!"

"That isn't what this is about, and you know it," President Scott said in a poorly veiled, accusatory tone.

Admiral Galiardi suddenly stopped.

"You didn't need the jump drive program to defend Earth," the president continued. "Over short ranges, you can do the same thing with linear FTL systems. We've already seen the Jung using such tactics, just not as well. You could have fixed the problems with the FTL systems in the second version of the Defender-class ships. Hell, you could have built four more of them for the same time and money that you spent on the STS drive and building the Explorer-class ships. That would have given us eight FTL warships. No other core world had that size of fleet, not even Alpha Centauri. The Jung, who by your own assessment prefer to use overwhelming force, would have needed to amass twice as many ships, which would have taken years, possibly decades longer."

"There was no way to know that at the time, Dayton..." the admiral defended.

"I'm not so sure about that," the president argued. "You're a smart guy, Michael. I'm sure you considered all the angles, yet you still chose *not* to oppose the construction of Explorer-class ships."

"If you remember, Mister President, it was the leaders of Earth who wanted the Explorer-class ships, not I. In fact, I believe I made it clear that abandoning the Defender-class design would make us weaker in the long run."

"Yet your assessments of the time available before

the Jung could be in position to attack Earth in force did not support a long-term approach to Earth's defense. In fact, *you* recruited *me*, to participate in your little stalling tactic, in the hopes of making the Jung operatives on Earth believe that postponing an invasion would be in their best interests."

"Which, if successful, would have given us two completed, Explorer-class ships, fully armed, with working jump drives, along with our existing Defender-class ships. We might even have had enough time to convert them to jump-capable ships, as well! Can you imagine? It would have taken decades for the Jung to gather the forces needed to successfully defeat us!"

"Yes, it was a wonderful plan," President Scott agreed. "Which is why you were given command after Jarlmasson was forced to resign." The president leaned forward. "But it didn't work." He paused and took a breath. "And now, we find ourselves finally getting off the ropes, after millions upon millions of people have died, and our world was nearly annihilated. Given all that has happened, and all that the Jung have done to us and the rest of the worlds of the core, I'm surprised *their* leaders are not calling on the Alliance to launch a spread of KKVs at the Jung homeworld, assuming we can ever find it."

Admiral Galiardi took a moment to compose himself. "Trust me, Dayton, you do not want to incur the *full wrath* of the Jung. We have *seen* what they are capable of. We have *seen* them glass *entire worlds* and simply move on without batting an eye. If you continue to try to expand and grow this Alliance, you will leave the Jung no choice. They will have to attack. Not only us, but every other world that you have unwillingly put into harm's way. You used the word millions. I'm talking *trillions* of lives. Do you understand?"

Dayton Scott stared back at Michael Galiardi, unwavering in his determination. "It's the *right* thing to do, Michael. It's as simple as that."

"*Nothing* is ever *that* simple, Dayton. Are you really willing to risk your *entire world*, just to satisfy your own sense of morality?"

"Some things *are* black and white," the president insisted. "Not many, but some. This is not about *my* sense of right and wrong. This is about the will of the collective. This is about what all of humanity considers just. If you can't see that, then you're not as smart as I have given you credit for all these years."

Admiral Galiardi leaned back in his chair. "You know we will fight you every step of the way."

"I do," President Scott replied confidently.

Admiral Galiardi waited, staring into Dayton Scott's eyes, hoping to find some break in his resolve. Finally, he stood. "I truly hope that I am wrong about this, Dayton...I truly do. But I've never been one to grasp at straws."

Dayton Scott watched without speaking as Admiral Galiardi turned and headed for the door. When the admiral reached the door, he spoke. "Michael, there was something I always wanted to ask you."

Michael Galiardi turned back toward the president, his coat in his hand.

"Why is it that Nathan was transferred to the Aurora, when Eli clearly asked for him to be reassigned to a surface assignment?"

"I wouldn't know," the admiral replied. "I was

the commanding officer of the entire Earth Defense Force, Dayton. I had no direct knowledge of duty assignments."

"And how is it that the Jung knew exactly where the Aurora would come out of her first test jump? Even I didn't know that."

"Maybe you should have asked Eli?" the admiral suggested.

"I'm asking you, Michael."

Galiardi smiled. "Thank you for seeing me, Mister President." He turned back toward the door and reached for the knob. "See you in the trenches."

* * *

"Today's exercises were good," Captain Nash told the gunship crews gathered in the mission briefing room on the asteroid spaceport orbiting Tanna. "Maneuvers were tight, executions were by the numbers, and your transitions between attack patterns were tight." He paused and looked out into the crowd. "Well, most of you, anyway. Hopefully, Captain Annatah will be more awake next time."

"I will make sure of it," Captain Annatah's copilot, Lieutenant Commander Jahansir, promised.

"If that new baby of yours is too much for you, Captain, just say the word, and I'll be happy to restrict you to base for the rest of your training cycle," Captain Nash teased.

"That won't be necessary, sir," Captain Annatah replied.

"See that it isn't."

Lieutenant Commander Rano entered the room and walked up to Captain Nash, whispering in his ear. The captain nodded. "Lieutenant Commander Rano will be taking over the remainder of the briefing. I'll see you all tomorrow morning, at zero six hundred, Tannan Mean Time."

Captain Nash stepped down from the podium and left the briefing room. He moved quickly down the corridor and entered his office, finding Admiral Dumar sitting there waiting for him. "Apologies, Admiral," he said, offering a salute.

"As you were, Captain," Admiral Dumar replied, returning the salute without standing. "No apologies necessary. You had no warning of my visit." The admiral gestured toward the door. "Close the door, Robert. We need to talk."

Captain Nash squinted suspiciously as he closed the door. "Is something wrong?" he asked as he moved behind his desk to sit.

"How is the training going?" the admiral wondered. "Your first eight crews getting the hang of things?"

"As well as can be expected, considering it's only been a few weeks."

"You mean, a few months, don't you?"

"I was speaking of actual flight time...in real ships," the captain explained. "The first four crews have only had their ships for about six weeks. The second four about half that."

"But they have all had extensive simulator time, have they not?"

"Yes, sir, they have, but..."

"Are the simulators not realistic enough?"

"No, they're plenty realistic, but no matter how realistic a simulator is, it's still just a simulator. The knowledge that you cannot *die* in it is what makes the difference."

"True enough, I suppose."

"Why are you asking?"

"I was wondering if you think they are ready for combat."

Captain Nash leaned back in his seat and sighed. "I was afraid you were going to ask that."

"Then you believe they are not ready?"

"I suppose it depends on the mission, sir," Captain Nash responded. "If you want them to do some patrols, or maybe even go up against some Jung fast-attack shuttles, or even some of their gunships, I might be inclined to say yes, they are ready."

"Frigates," the admiral said, getting straight to the point.

Captain Nash sighed again. "You want them to take on a Jung frigate?"

"No, frigates," the admiral corrected, emphasizing the plural.

"How many?"

"Four."

"By themselves, or as part of a battle group?"

"The frigates are part of a standard Jung battle group in the Delta Pavonis system," Admiral Dumar explained. "However, the larger ships in the battle group would already be dealt with by the Aurora and the Celestia."

"Then why not just have the Aurora and the Celestia take out the frigates as well," Captain Nash suggested. "I'm sure they can take out frigates in a single pass, maybe even a single shot with those big mark fives they're carrying now."

"Chiya is the only inhabited world in the Pavonis system," the admiral began. "A little smaller than Earth, not nearly as much water, only her upper and lower middle latitudes are habitable. Problem is, there are more than one hundred thousand Jung

255

troops on that world, spread out over six different bases. They've also got a few dozen surface-to-orbit missile bases, and four airbases. We don't have the air power yet to deal with so many surface bases. Luckily, most of the facilities are well removed from the population. Seems the Chiyans have been less than cooperative, so they kept the bases away from the cities for security reasons. We plan to have the Aurora and the Celestia strike them from orbit. However, to do so, they must jump in and strike quickly, before the airbases can get fighters and fast-attack shuttles in the air. If they do, we won't be able to get boots on the ground, and the chaos that will ensue when the troop bases are destroyed could get quite ugly."

"And if the Aurora and the Celestia have to take time to deal with the frigates..."

"They won't be able to catch those fighters on the ground, and their defense missiles will already be in orbit, waiting to strike. In short, we won't be able to touch the surface assets."

"Might it be better to wait, then?" Captain Nash wondered. "Maybe until we have more assets? How long until the Jar-Benakh goes into service?"

"Less than a week, actually," the admiral replied. "The problem is the Delta Pavonis system is one of four systems, all within twenty light years of Earth, that we've identified as primary staging for forces bound for Earth. We've already dealt with Tau Ceti and 82 Eridani. Delta Pavonis and Beta Hydri are next."

"I still don't see why you can't wait."

"Will waiting a week really make that big of a difference?" the admiral asked. "Will two weeks?"

"It might," Captain Nash replied.

Admiral Dumar leaned back in his seat. "When I was a cadet, so very long ago, there was a ritual called *norey movah*. Loosely translated, I believe its meaning is the same as your expression, 'trial by fire'. This was done early on in a combat pilot's training, in order to determine beyond all doubt, which of us was truly worthy of continuing to the next level of training."

"A test."

"Precisely."

"And what happened if you failed the test?" Captain Nash wondered.

"It was combat," the admiral replied without emotion. "You died."

"They threw you into actual combat, *before* you were properly trained?"

"We were trained. We could fly. We could fight. We knew our ships and weapons. It was our way. Those who survived went on to advanced training. We were given the newest ships, the best weapons, and the highest training."

"Seems rather barbaric."

"I suppose it was, in a sense," Admiral Dumar admitted, "but it *was* effective. Surviving actual combat, when others did not, gave us an edge...a level of confidence that we could not get from mock-combat training. You yourself argued that a simulator is not the same as actual flight in space. *Norey movah* was just an extension of that idea."

Captain Nash sighed again. "So, you want to put my crews to the test...see which ones survive?"

"No, I do not *want* to put anyone into harm's way. However, if they are going to protect their world, and they are going to teach their fellow Tannans to do the same, they *need* to taste actual combat. Better

257

in this fashion, against only four frigates, without threat of reinforcement, than against a sudden surprise attack. Or would you prefer their first taste of combat to be in the defense of their world?"

"It's not that I don't see your point, Admiral."

"You've just never had to send crews into combat," the admiral surmised.

"Yeah, I guess that's a part of it."

"You've never had children, have you, Captain?"

"No, sir. I haven't."

"I have a family, back on Corinair. Originally, it was part of my cover, but over time, I grew to love my wife, as well as my children. A son, and two daughters. When my son was still very young, maybe two, my wife and I took him to the playground. He was fascinated by the swings. Such a simple thing really, a seat on two cables. He was waiting patiently for his turn, standing to one side, when a child got off the swing on the far end. My son set off directly for the vacant swing. It never occurred to him that the kids who were swinging might hit him. My wife jumped from the bench where we were sitting, yelling to warn our son of the danger, but she was too late. I grabbed her hand, and pulled her back down. The first swing missed him, but the second did not. It knocked him several meters, and he started wailing. Again, his mother wanted to run to him, to hold him, but I would not allow it. He needed to learn. He saw that we were not running to his aid, and eventually he realized that he was not truly injured, and he stopped crying and got on the empty swing. From that moment on, he always took a wide path around those swings when there were children using them."

"No offense, Admiral, it was a charming story,"

Captain Nash said, "but we're not talking about getting knocked over by a kid on a swing. We're talking about death in combat."

"I'm afraid you missed the point of the story, Captain, which was that sometimes, *experience* is the best teacher."

"So, you're saying I have to let them go?"

"If you want these men to be able to defend their world, they need to know that they can do so. They need to know that they will not turn away in the face of mortal danger. They need to know that they are capable of putting their lives on the line for what they believe. You were correct when you pointed out that lack of actual risk is what makes a simulator not as good as the real thing. The same can be said for mock combat versus actual."

Captain Nash stared at the admiral, considering his words. "Do I have a choice, Admiral?"

"Of course. This is your command, Captain. I will not order you to send men into battle who you truly feel are not ready. But sooner or later, there will be no choice, and there also may not be any control over when and where their first combat experience is to be had. The Jung may make that decision for you."

Captain Nash took a deep breath, letting it out slowly. "Had you asked me this question a week ago, I would have said no. However, over the last few days, the first two groups have really been starting to click. It might be advantageous to throw them into the deep end of the pool while their confidence is high."

"A wise choice, Captain."

"How soon are we talking?"

Admiral Dumar pulled a data card out of his

pocket and handed it to Captain Nash. "The mission profile is on this data card. Have your men at their jump-off waypoints by fifteen-thirty, Earth Mean Time, tomorrow."

Captain Nash looked at the time display on the wall, quickly doing the math in his head. His eyes suddenly widened. "That's fifteen hours from now, Admiral."

"Indeed it is," the admiral admitted as he rose. "I suggest your men stay on base tonight, Captain, to avoid complications."

"Yes, sir," Captain Nash agreed, standing. "Admiral, can I ask you something?"

"Of course," the admiral replied.

"That *norey movah* thing. Do the Takarans still do that?"

Admiral Dumar smiled. "Why do you think Takaran fighter pilots are so arrogant?"

"Weren't you one?"

"I've mellowed with age." Admiral Dumar turned to depart. "Good luck, Captain."

* * *

Cameron stood behind her command chair, leaning against its back, facing the tactical station directly aft of her. The large, clear, view screens that had been installed during the refit of the Celestia's bridge had greatly increased each operator's situational awareness, and the two-way capability of the tactical station's main screen made it easy for Cameron to see what her tactical officer was explaining to her. The technology was amazing, to say the least. Despite the attempts of the Takaran technicians to explain to her how they worked, she could never quite understand how two sides could be displaying opposed images, yet still seem clear to viewers on opposite sides. She was just enjoying the flexibility it was giving her and her tactical officer, as he showed her some of the attack patterns he had been experimenting with using computer simulations.

"The last one, which I call 'Delta Seven with a flipped reversal,' is the same as the standard Delta Seven attack pattern, but we flip over as we reverse course, keeping our forward tubes on the target throughout the one-eighty."

"I'm not sure our maneuvering thrusters are powerful enough to pull that off," Cameron said.

"*If* we are at the slowest combat maneuvering speeds, and we *roll* the ship as we flip over so that we can use one outboard main in deceleration mode, and the opposite one angled outward in normal mode, it *should* work. At least it does in the simulation."

"Have you run this past Lieutenant Hunt?"

"Yes, sir. He thinks he can pull it off as well."

Cameron studied the simulation as it continued to replay on the clear view screen between them. "That's going to put a lot of torque on the ship, with the outboard engines working in opposition that way."

"I checked with the cheng, and he didn't seem too concerned."

"Well, if Lieutenant Commander Allison isn't worried..." She paused mid-sentence, as the simulation reached the point in the maneuver that concerned her. She shuddered at the sight of it, seeing her ship do something that shouldn't be possible. "It looks like something Nathan would do," she commented with a slight chuckle.

"Maybe," Luis agreed. "I may have even gotten

the idea from him. I did room with him for four years at the academy, and we did go through basic flight together."

"Some of his craziness must have rubbed off on you, Lieutenant," Cameron agreed. "Add it to the training schedule, and we'll give it a whirl during our next exercise. But we'll start at well below combat maneuvering speeds, just in case the cheng is too optimistic in the amount of lateral torque our main frame can withstand."

"Yes, sir," Lieutenant Delaveaga replied, pleased with himself.

"Deceleration burn complete," Ensign Sperry reported from the Celestia's navigation station. "We are now on course and speed for entry into the Delta Pavonis system."

Cameron stood up straight, turning to face forward. "Very well," she replied as she glanced at the time display on the starboard auxiliary view screen. There were still three minutes until zero hour.

"Plot our jump to the launch point and stand by," she ordered.

"Aye, sir."

"How do our weapons look, Ensign Kono?"

"All six jump KKVs are on course and speed for the target area," her sensor operator replied. "Currently eighteen point five million kilometers ahead of us and increasing range rapidly."

"Jump is plotted and is auto-updating as we go," Ensign Sperry reported. "Ready to jump on your command."

"Very well," Cameron replied as she took her seat. She glanced at the time display once more. "We jump to launch point in one minute."

"Two minutes," Lieutenant Commander Rano reported from Cobra One's copilot seat.

Captain Nash glanced at the mission time display on the center console on his right. His eyes dropped to the tactical and navigation display just below it, noting their course and speed. There were four blue icons on the screen. The one indicating his ship was at the center of the display, with the other three icons spreading out behind and to starboard, in a perfect line.

He thought about the other group of four gunships, currently on a similar approach track, but from the opposite side of the Delta Pavonis system. He had considered breaking that group up, and mixing it with two of the ships from his own group. His pilots had several more weeks of experience in their ships, and while Captain Nash was still not certain they were ready for combat, they *were* better prepared than any of the crews in the second group. However, there had not been time. Despite their lack of actual flight time, what time they *did* have was together. Breaking them apart on short notice and without any time to get used to one another would only have created new problems...ones they didn't need going into their first combat action.

He looked at the mission plan on the display screen below the tactical display. Their first attack pass was using attack pattern Alpha Four Five, with the second pass being Alpha Four Five plus twenty, and the third one minus ninety. With any luck, a fourth pass would not be needed. Theoretically, their snub-nosed mark three plasma torpedo cannons could overwhelm and collapse a single section of a Jung frigate's shields with only twelve to eighteen direct, full-power hits. So, by the time they made their third pass, the target's hull would be unprotected, making her easy to destroy.

But that was in theory.

———

"Jump flash," Mister Navashee reported from the Aurora's sensor station. "Comm-drone from Scout One."

"Receiving incoming data stream," Naralena added. "Transferring to tactical."

Jessica examined the latest recon data being sent to them by Scout One's comm-drone. "No change in their positions or patrol patterns. Target packages are still valid."

"Mister Riley, jump us to the launch intercept point," Nathan ordered.

"Aye, sir," the navigator replied. "Jumping to launch intercept point, in three......two......one..."

The main view screen dimmed momentarily as the jump fields built into a flash that briefly illuminated the interior of the bridge with a momentary blue-white light.

"...Jump complete."

"Contacts," Mister Navashee reported. "All six weapons, coming up from behind, passing us to starboard."

"All weapons are on course and speed, and have proper spacing," Jessica reported. "Time to launch point: thirty seconds."

"Transmit launch authorizations." Nathan ordered. "Comms, notify the Celestia and all units at the rally point. Go as scheduled."

"Drones launching now," Naralena replied.

"All launch codes transmitted, all verifications

received. All six jump KKVs are armed and will jump in fifteen seconds," Jessica announced.

"Attack jump one, plotted and ready," Mister Riley reported.

"Weapons are passing us now," Mister Navashee added.

Nathan glanced up at the mission clock, as the countdown changed from minus eight, to minus seven seconds.

"Jump KKVs launching in five seconds," Jessica reported. "Three......two......one......"

Nathan looked to the main view screen, as six small flashes of blue-white light, spread apart evenly, appeared simultaneously far ahead of them and slightly to their right.

"JKKVs away," Jessica reported.

Nathan imagined the weapons coming out of their two-light-year jumps a split second after they had disappeared from his view, only a few kilometers from the Jung battle platform they had been sent to destroy. Some of them would miss their targets, and continue to cold-coast across the Delta Pavonis system, until one of the Super Falcons could be sent to retrieve them. The others, hopefully more than one or two of them, would slam into the shields of their target, overpower them, and cause them to collapse, allowing the following JKKVs to impact the hull of the massive platform. Just once, he wanted to witness that event, instead of seeing it thirty seconds later.

"Coming up on attack jump one," Mister Riley warned.

Another glance at the mission clock. Five seconds.

"Execute," Nathan ordered calmly.

"Attack jump one, aye. In three......two......one..."

Nathan closed his eyes momentarily, taking in a deep breath as the jump flash again washed over them. He remembered the last attack against the battle platform in the Eta Cassiopeiae system. It had not gone well.

"Jump complete," Mister Riley reported.

"Contact," Mister Navashee reported with his usual calm. "Jung battle platform... She's coming apart," he added, with a little extra excitement in his voice.

Nathan could see several distant flashes far ahead of them on the main view screen. He tapped his control pad on the right armrest to magnify the image. Before them, the battle platform, riddled with internal explosions, was breaking apart. Two of her six arms were already gone, sending large debris fields spreading away along the trajectory of the JKKVs that had passed through them. Two more arms were in the process of exploding, as secondary systems came apart inside them and caused their hulls to open up to space. Even the main central column, to which the six arms were connected, was lighting up with internal secondary explosions.

"How many?" Nathan wondered.

"One moment," Mister Navashee replied.

"Incoming message from the Celestia," Naralena reported. "They confirm the Jung battleship has been destroyed. They are changing course to attack cruiser one."

"I'm picking up two of our JKKVs, outbound," Mister Navashee reported. "That makes four direct hits on the platform."

"New course," Nathan ordered as he reset the magnification on the main view screen to normal. "Cruiser two, attack pattern Delta Seven."

"Cruiser two, Delta Seven, aye," Mister Riley reported. "Next jump in twenty seconds."

"Both cruisers are still several light minutes out from the primary attack zones," Mister Navashee confirmed. "They'll never see us coming."

———————

"Jung frigate, dead ahead," Lieutenant Commander Rano reported as the jump flash faded and their forward windows cleared. "Pitch up five."

"Up five," Captain Nash answered.

"Gunners, weapons free," the commander added. "Fire at will."

"Pitch complete, tracking as we pass under," Captain Nash said, as red bolts of plasma energy raced past his windows on either side, headed toward their target, passing only five hundred meters under them.

"Their shields are coming up," Lieutenant Commander Rano warned.

"I've got a firing solution," Captain Nash announced. "Firing all forward tubes."

"First four away," Lieutenant Commander Rano reported, as the red-orange light of their plasma torpedoes lit up their forward windows. "Second four away."

Captain Nash continued pitching his ship up and over, keeping their nose on the target, as they slid under the enemy frigate.

"Third four away."

"Jump flash," his sensor operator reported.

Lieutenant Commander Rano glanced at the tactical display as another blue icon appeared on the screen, behind them and slightly to the right of the track. "Cobra Two is firing."

"Jumping away," Captain Nash reported as

he pressed the jump execute button on his flight control stick. He pitched the nose of their gunship back over forward as they jumped, then brought his power up to execute their next turn.

"Flying the attack manually, I see," Lieutenant Commander Rano commented.

"Just testing how she handles in real combat, my friend."

Lieutenant Commander Rano smiled. "Come to three four seven, up eight, and maintain speed. Next jump waypoint in thirty seconds."

"Jump flash to port," the sensor operator reported. "It's Cobra Two. They've finished their first attack run and are making their turn."

"So far, so good," Captain Nash stated as he continued his turn.

"Firing, triplets and singles, all forward tubes," Lieutenant Delaveaga reported from the Celestia's tactical station.

"Pitching over," Lieutenant Hunt reported from the helm.

"Jumping forward, one click," Ensign Sperry added.

The red-orange light from their departing plasma torpedoes was suddenly replaced by the blue-white light of their jump flash, as the Celestia jumped one kilometer forward, instantly passing under the enemy cruiser as all sixteen plasma torpedoes, twelve mark three and four mark fives, slammed into the cruiser's protective shields.

"Jump complete," Ensign Sperry reported as the jump flash subsided.

"Cascade shield failure!" Ensign Kono declared. "They're all coming down!"

"Ten seconds to firing angle," Lieutenant Hunt reported.

"Target is bringing her main rail guns onto us," Ensign Kono warned.

"Fire when ready," Cameron ordered. "Same pattern, triplets and singles."

"She's firing her guns!"

They watched the main view screen as the ship finished pitching over and the cruiser came to rest in the middle of the main view screen, growing smaller as they moved away from it. Swarms of pale blue flashes appeared all around the view screen as the incoming rail gun rounds impacted the Celestia's shields, robbing them of all their kinetic energy.

"Firing all forward tubes," Luis announced. "Triplets and singles."

The swarms of pale blue flashes faded, overpowered by the red-orange light from their departing plasma torpedoes. Three seconds later, distant reddish-yellow explosions, followed by more intense, yellow-white ones tinged with orange reported the Jung cruiser's fate.

"Direct hits," Ensign Kono reported from the sensor station. "Numerous secondaries. The target is coming apart."

"Message from the Aurora," Ensign Souza reported from the comm station. "Phase one and two are completed, they are moving to phase three."

Cameron spent no time enjoying the victory. There was more work to be done. "Lieutenant Hunt, take us to Chiya."

Captain Nash rolled his gunship onto its starboard side as it came out of its jump, pulling the nose up until his torpedo targeting system gave him a green light. A squeeze of his trigger, and four full-power, mark three plasma torpedoes shot from their tubes, skimming under their bow as they departed and raced toward the Jung frigate passing over them.

Swarms of pale blue flashes lit up their forward shields, the result of rail gun slugs fired from the enemy's point-defense systems impacting the gunship's protective shields. With their kinetic energy stripped away as they passed through the shield barrier, they simply bounced harmlessly off their hull.

Another round of plasma torpedoes, a touch on the jump button, and they were suddenly well beyond the range of the frigate's defenses, but still within reach of her missiles.

"Come to one seven five, down four," Commander Rano instructed.

"Coming to one seven five, down four," Captain Nash replied.

"Two just jumped in behind us, turning away and climbing relative," his sensor operator reported.

"*Cobra One, Cobra Two!*" Captain Annatah called excitedly over the comms.

"Two, go for One," Nash replied.

"*Cobra Three's last shot took down the target's starboard ventral shield! Another pass might do it, sir!*"

"One copies. Stay on plan."

"*Aye, sir!*" Captain Annatah replied. "*Two out.*"

"Jump point in five seconds," Lieutenant Commander Rano warned.

"I got it," Captain Nash replied. "Let's go finish them off, shall we?"

———

"Oh shit," Josh swore as the Super Falcon began

to shake violently. "They said the atmosphere here was thick, but damn! I can't even read my displays!"

"It'll smooth out as we drop out of this cloud layer!" Loki assured him.

Josh glanced out his forward window, seeing nothing but dark, blue-gray fog. "What the hell is this stuff?"

"Thunder storms," Loki replied. "Really common over this world's populated latitudes. They form in the equatorial regions, where most of the water is, and then..."

"I don't need a fucking weather report, Loki!" Josh interrupted impatiently. "Do you have the targets or not?"

"Affirmative," Loki replied. "I've got all eight missile batteries, selected and locked in. Hold her steady while I launch busters."

"Just make it quick, will you? I wanna get out of this crap."

"This *crap* is obscuring their sensors, so they can't see us."

"I'm pretty sure they saw us jump in," Josh insisted.

"Weapons bay open. Launching eight." Loki pressed the launch button on his weapons panel, sending eight buster missiles dropping out of the Super Falcon's oversized weapons bay on their underside. Each missile fired its propulsion system, extended its maneuvering winglets, and raced away from the Super Falcon.

Josh glanced outside, still seeing only the blue-gray fog. "Did they launch? I can't see a fucking thing!"

"Eight busters away, running hot and true, with

target locks. First impact in twenty seconds," Loki assured him.

"Great," Josh replied. "Turning to second target. Please tell me it isn't in this muck again."

"It isn't," Loki promised. "Jump point in five seconds."

———

"Jump complete," Mister Riley reported from the Aurora's navigation station. "Entering orbit over Chiya."

"First firing point in twenty seconds," Jessica announced. "Locking ventral quads on targets one and two."

"Detecting multiple explosions on the surface, directly under, and aft of us, to either side," Mister Navashee reported.

"Looks like our Super Falcons are doing their job," Nathan said.

"Five seconds," Jessica added.

"Fire when ready," Nathan instructed.

Jessica waited until they reached their optimal firing position, then activated the first firing sequences. "Firing on targets one and two."

"More explosions on the surface," Mister Navashee reported. "Super Falcons are pressing the attack aft of us in the opposite direction, as planned. I'm counting twenty-four targets destroyed so far."

"Firing sequence complete," Jessica reported.

"Scanning target areas," Mister Navashee said. "Both targets are destroyed."

"Decelerating," the helmsman reported.

"Jump point to secondary target area in twenty seconds," Mister Riley announced.

"Comms, notify flight ops to launch the CNS shuttles after the next jump," Nathan instructed.

"Aye, sir."

"Starting to pick up a little heat on our ventral shields, Captain," the systems officer reported.

"Five seconds left in the decel burn," Mister Chiles promised.

"Ready to jump," Mister Riley added.

"Killing the decel drive," the helmsman said.

"Jumping."

Nathan sat calmly as the blue-white jump flash washed over them, and the Aurora jumped forward from its new, lower orbital altitude. It followed a straight line, to its new position along the same orbital track, only back at their original altitude and a quarter of the way around the planet from their last location.

"Jump complete."

"Targets three through twelve coming up," Jessica reported. "Roll us onto our starboard side, perpendicular to our track, Mister Chiles."

"Changing orbital attitude, aye," the helmsman reported.

Nathan rotated slowly in his chair until he could see Jessica through the clear view screen, standing behind the tactical station.

"I can get all four quads, dorsal and ventral, firing at the same time. I can pound half of the targets as they fall behind us, the other half as they come towards us," she explained with a fiendish smile. "Kills more of them, more quickly."

"By all means, let's be efficient," Nathan replied.

———

"Holy shit!" Sergeant Torwell exclaimed as his gun turret bubble cleared after the jump. "Are you guys seeing this?"

"My God," Lieutenant Kainan muttered, as he

273

stared out the windows, scanning the area from side to side. Four streams of red-hot slugs rained down from orbit, terminating in massive clouds of dust, debris, and explosions as they pummeled their targets on the surface. Less than ten kilometers ahead of them and slightly left was the closest target, and even from that distance, the rising cloud looked ominous.

"I'm pretty sure there's going to be no one left to fight down there," Ensign Latfee muttered from the copilot seat.

"Doubtful," Commander Telles commented from the back of the combat jump shuttle.

"Yeah, there are always a few lucky bastards who survive the death from above and are blessed with the honor of fighting us," Master Sergeant Jahal mused.

———————

"What do we do if we can't see their damned guns?" Specialist Taji Sennott asked as he peered out through his turret canopy on the port side of Cobra Two, as the Jung frigate approached.

"*Then just shoot at anything,*" his counterpart in the starboard gun turret, Specialist Turchin, suggested.

"*Don't worry about their guns,*" Captain Annatah told them. "*They won't get through our shields anyway.*"

Four mark three plasma torpedoes streaked away from the gunship, their red-orange light nearly blinding Taji for a moment. "Damn, those torpedoes are bright!"

"*Stop complaining and open fire,*" Rom instructed, yelling over the sound of his quad-barreled plasma cannon as he opened fire at the passing ship.

Taji moved his control yoke to his right and twisted over, bringing his turret around to face forward and slightly to port, while rotating it on its longitudinal axis to get a better angle. He squeezed his trigger and held it, causing his weapon to fire continuously. His quad barrels fired, one at a time, half a second apart each. He moved his control yoke carefully, in small increments, attempting to keep his targeting point on the same part of the now unshielded Jung frigate until it passed under them.

Another salvo of plasma torpedoes lit up his gun turret. Squinting, he picked a new point on the frigate's hull and fired. Several explosions erupted across the ship, first on the surface of the hull in the area he was targeting, growing deeper and larger.

"*Jumping,*" his captain warned over the comms.

Taji's gun bubble suddenly went opaque as the ship jumped. He spun his weapon around aft, twisting it over at the same time, in order to fire aft as they came out of what he expected to be only a two-hundred-meter jump to get clear before Cobra Three opened fire. As he came to point aft, his gun bubble cleared, and he was greeted with a massive explosion. "Oh, my God!" he exclaimed. "I think I got her!" Taji let go of his control yoke and turned to look back into the tunnel that led into the ship. He could barely see his cohort, Rom, sitting in his turret at the other end of the tunnel on the far side of the gunship. His turret lit up with the yellow-white explosions of the dying frigate. "Did you see that?"

"*I'm pretty sure it was the plasma torpedoes,*" Rom insisted.

"*We've got the first Cobra kill!*" he heard his captain exclaim over the comms.

"I don't care what it was," Taji grinned. "That was incredible!"

"*Jumping in thirty seconds,*" the copilot's voice announced over the comms.

"One minute!" Sergeant Lazo yelled from the front of the troop shuttle's cargo compartment, warning his men to be ready to disembark. "Visors down, weapons loaded, safeties on! Check your buddy's gear! It will be late afternoon on the surface, so set your visors to auto-tint. Don't be fooled by Chiya's dark cloud cover! It's full of holes, and when that big-ass sun of theirs pokes through, it will blind you for several seconds. The Jung know this, and they will use it to their advantage."

"If any of them survive the orbital bombardment," the private next to Biorgi joked.

"Enough of them will," Biorgi said sternly, admonishing the young private. "Better you expect it, and be pleasantly surprised."

"Come on, Biorgi," the young man argued. "There can't be that many of them who survive. Besides, the Ghatazhak are going in first. We're just here to maintain order until the locals can take over."

Biorgi nodded. "I'll be sure to remind you of that when I'm dragging you back to the aid station with half your body scorched by a Jung energy weapon."

"Never going to happen," the young man insisted. "I'm just going to follow your lead, Corporal."

"Don't follow Biorgi," another man said, "Haven't you heard? Biorgi charges the enemy head on."

"*Jump complete,*" the copilot announced over the comms.

"Twenty seconds!" Sergeant Lazo warned. "Marines! Stand ready!"

Biorgi rose to his feet and turned to face the aft door as it began to swing down and away from the aft end of the compartment. He could feel the thick, musky Chiyan air rushing in to greet them. It was humid, and smelled of strange plants and animals, both of which the planet was renowned for possessing in great abundance. It also smelled of death. Burning human flesh, melted body armor, the bitter taste of smoke and dust as it swirled into the compartment.

The roar of the troop shuttle's engines was deafening as the door opened fully, all four of the massive, rotating, engine pods at full power as the ship settled to the ground. The ship bounced slightly, settling in as the door fell the last half meter to the ground forming a ramp down to the surface. The first squad charged out the back of the shuttle, running down the ramp and heading to the left. Biorgi was next, leading his squad of twelve down the ramp after them, but instead, he turned to the right.

The surface of Chiya was much different than the crunchy, tan soil of Adlair. And the thick atmosphere was difficult to suck into his lungs as he ran in a low crouch toward the Ghatazhak element they were to reinforce.

The soil of Chiya was thick, with an almost muddy feel to it, even though it was not excessively moist. It was dark and pungent, full of old, rotted vegetation. The grasses were tall, nearly waist high, and had an odd lavender color, with yellow tips that seemed to release a fine powder when disturbed. There were lots of shrubs, as well. Thick, dense ones, with barbed branches that could tear your flesh from your bones if you fell into them.

Biorgi led his men across the clearing and into

the thick woods at the perimeter. He did not stop, continuing to run, weaving between the tall, wide trunks of the majestic trees. At times, the trunks were so close together they almost formed a wall. He had heard that the roots of the trees were all intertwined, and that some believed the entire forest was actually one big underground plant, with massive stalks that broke through the ground and reached up through the low lying clouds that blocked the sun half of the Chiyan day.

Biorgi paused briefly, checking his visor to make sure they were getting closer to the Ghatazhak element they were assigned to reinforce. But his tactical display wasn't behaving properly, and the blue icons that represented the Ghatazhak squad kept fading in and out.

"Come on, Biorgi!" the young private who had expected an easy day yelled. "What are you waiting for?"

"My visor, something is interfering with it..."

"It's the trees. They warned us about that. Let's move. They're over there. I can hear their weapons fire."

"No, the sound could be bouncing off the trees, mis..."

The private took off, heading deeper into the forest.

"Dukette!" Biorgi yelled. "Damn it." Biorgi motioned for the rest of the squad to move out, then ran around the tree in pursuit of the eager, but stupid, young marine. The Ghatazhak drill instructors were supposed to weed out men exhibiting such behavior, but apparently a few of them had slipped past.

Energy weapons fire sounded from Biorgi's left, followed by a muffled scream of pain a few meters

278

ahead of him. Biorgi fell to one knee, turning to his left and bringing up his weapon while he raised his right hand to signal the rest of his squad to take cover. Several gunshots sounded from just ahead of him, followed by more energy weapons blasts.

Biorgi motioned for his men to spread out. "Tobin, Ramsa, Moray...swing wide left. Bellotta, Arroya, and Yorrel...wide right. The rest follow me." Biorgi waited for several seconds, watching his tactical display as his men fanned out. He then rose and advanced between the trees. Energy weapons fire streaked past him from the left, and was instantly answered by gunfire from the men he had sent to the left. He dropped to one knee again, but the weapons fire stopped. "Report."

"*Clear right.*"

"*Three kills, clear left.*"

Biorgi's tactical display suddenly came back to life, resuming normal operation and clearly displaying the Ghatazhak element they were attempting to locate. He looked in the upper right corner of his visor, noticing a new icon had appeared. "The CNS-sats are up," he announced over the comms. "Our tactical displays should be okay now."

Biorgi heard a noise nearby. A rustling of grass, and gasping sounds. He looked around, then spotted movement in the grass next to one of the massive tree trunks. He signaled the two men next to him to spread out to either side of the tree, then got up and advanced toward the sound. His weapon up and ready to fire, he moved quickly around the tree, then stopped dead in his tracks. "Dukette."

The young man was lying on the ground, his hand shaking badly as his injured muscles twitched. His chest armor was a heap of melted composite, and half his head was flash-burned away, leaving a gaping hole in the side of his neck that bubbled with blood as he tried in vain to breathe. The look in the young man's eyes was terrified and desperate. He knew he was dying.

The other two men came around as well, stopping to stare in shock at their dying comrade.

Dukette's remaining eye looked up at Biorgi, pleading to him. Biorgi reached into his thigh pouch, and pulled out a pneumo-ject filled with a powerful analgesic. He knelt down, wiped the blood away from the uninjured side of the young marine's neck, and emptied the entire contents of the pneumo-ject into the dying man. Private Dukette's eye glassed over and slowly closed.

"You want me to call for a medevac?" one of the men asked.

"Don't bother," Biorgi said. "I gave him the whole load."

"Jesus, Biorgi," the other man said, astonished. "That'll kill him for sure."

"He was already dead," Biorgi said, rising to his feet. "His brain just didn't know it yet."

The other two men stared at Private Dukette as the young man's respirations became less and less pronounced, finally fading away completely.

"Move out!" Biorgi shouted back as he continued into the forest.

"That's the last one," Jessica reported from the Aurora's tactical console.

"Flight reports we own the skies of Chiya," Naralena announced from the comm station.

"Any word on the frigates?" Nathan asked.

"Frigates one, three, and four are destroyed,"

Jessica replied. "Captain Nash's pack is finishing up frigate two now."

"I am picking up a few unarmed shuttles making a run for orbit," Mister Navashee reported.

"Have flight vector the Falcons to intercept any ships fleeing the surface until the gunships can take up orbital cover," Nathan instructed. "And let Commander Telles know he can start the second wave."

"Aye, sir," Naralena replied.

"Once the surface is under control, we can release the gunships to return to Tanna." Nathan rose from his seat and headed toward his ready room. "Stand down from general quarters, but maintain a high state of readiness in all sections," he instructed as he passed Jessica. "I'll be in my ready room, Lieutenant Commander. You have the conn."

"I have the conn, aye," Jessica replied. She waited until Nathan left the room, then smiled. "This shit's getting easier with each liberation."

* * *

Captain Nash and his crew exited the docking tunnel into the boarding area at the Cobra asteroid base. Captain Annatah and his crew were already being lifted into the air by the hordes of technicians and support staff who had gathered to welcome the newest heroes of Tanna.

Captain Nash paused to watch the festivities as his crew ran into the welcoming crowd. He looked at his XO, Lieutenant Commander Rano, noticing the grin on his face. "What are you smiling about?" he wondered. "*We* didn't score a kill."

"Yes, we did," Lieutenant Commander Rano insisted. "We all did. Look at them," he added, gesturing toward the festivities that were growing in size as more Cobra crews disembarked and joined the cheering crowd. "Today, all of Tanna has seen that we *can* fight back."

"That was only one victory, in a huge war, my friend."

"But it was a *Tannan* victory. *Our* victory. We have been living under the boot of the Jung for so long, we had almost forgotten who we once were."

"And who was that?" Captain Nash wondered.

"This world was settled by people who refused to adhere to the standards and expectations of the larger core and secondary worlds. We survived the plague, with fewer deaths than many. We rebuilt our world, regrew our population, only to be knocked back down by Jung oppression. It nearly robbed us of our very souls." Lieutenant Commander Rano looked back at the celebration, his smile growing again. "They now remember what it feels like to fight for something they believe in. What it feels like to be free...*truly* free."

"This is what, a hundred people maybe?"

"But they will tell others of this day," the lieutenant commander said. "Friends and family. Strangers at the local tavern as they share drinks. Anyone who will stop and listen to their pride-filled tale of the day that Tannan crews, flying Tannan-built ships of war, attacked and defeated Jung ships much bigger and more powerful than our own."

"I think you're making more out of it than it really is, Izzu."

"You do not see it, because you are not Tannan. But this day...this day will be remembered for as long as a single Tannan breathes air. Those who insisted that we are powerless against the Jung will be without words, and the recruitment stations will be overwhelmed with volunteers." Lieutenant Commander Rano turned to face his captain. "We could not have done this without you, Robert. For that, I will always be in your debt."

"I didn't do this," Robert insisted. "*We* did this. You, and I, and all of them. Every one of them. Don't ever forget that."

"I shall not, my friend."

"Now go," Robert insisted. "Go and celebrate with your countrymen."

"You are not joining us in celebration?" the lieutenant commander wondered.

"Not today. I'm exhausted. I'm getting too old for this fly-boy stuff." Captain Nash watched as Lieutenant Commander Rano left to join the celebration. By now, the last of the eight Cobra crews had disembarked, and people were opening bottles of Tannan celebratory wine.

Robert Nash thought about that day in the hospital, when his baby sister had told him of his new assignment. He had loathed the idea of becoming an instructor. Now, he realized how wrong he had been. He was doing more than training young men to go into combat. He was giving hope to a world.

CHAPTER EIGHT

"Gentlemen," Major Prechitt said, as he led the Avendahl pilots into one of the Eagle hangars at the Porto Santo airbase, "these are your Super Eagles, fresh off the line. Each of them has been through their basic shakedown flight to verify that all systems are working properly."

Commander Goodreau and his men walked past the major toward the row of eight Super Eagles lined up across the hangar abreast, their wings retracted to save space.

"I'd like to introduce Ensign Joshua Hayes, and Ensign Loki Sheehan. They served as the primary test pilots for the Super Eagle prototypes. I've asked them here today to share their observations about the handling characteristics of the Super Eagle, and the differences they've noticed between the Super Eagle simulator, and the actual ship."

"I don't think that will be necessary," Commander Goodreau said. He paused for a moment, turning to Josh and Loki. "No disrespect intended to the young ensigns, of course. We have read all your reports."

Major Prechitt looked confused. "I thought that you might find their..."

"We are quite well versed in the technical and performance data of the spacecraft," the commander interrupted. "I believe we shall do fine without wasting the valuable time of Ensign Hayes or Ensign Sheehan."

"Commander..."

Commander Goodreau took a deep breath and turned back toward Major Prechitt. "Major, I have just over a month to get thirty-two of my pilots ready to fight in these cobbled-together ships, and the remaining twenty-four of those pilots won't be here for two more weeks. In addition, I am expected to train another thirty-two pilots, most of whom have little to no flight training, shortly thereafter. That *is* assuming, of course, that the good people of Earth can continue the ludicrous, breakneck pace at which they are slapping these ships together."

"Commander, these ships are hardly *cobbled together...*"

"Terran airframes and flight control systems. Old Corinairan propulsion systems, picked up from the junkyards on Palee, no less. Takaran weapons systems and avionics. My dear major, the Super Eagle is the very definition of *cobbled together*. My God, the only thing that makes this ship remotely interesting is her jump drive's control system. A remarkable idea, really." He turned back to look at the Super Eagles he and his men were about to fly. "However, I suppose that shouldn't be too surprising, since the idea was conceived by the daughter of a nobleman." He turned back to the major. "I hear she is quite a remarkable young woman."

"Indeed she is," Major Prechitt agreed, realizing that there was no changing the commander's mind. "Very well, Commander," he added with a nod. "I'll leave you and your men to your task." Major Prechitt looked at Josh and Loki, gesturing to the side with a slight nod of his head for them to follow him.

Josh and Loki looked at one another as the major turned and walked toward the exit, then back at Commander Goodreau and his men as they headed toward their ships to prepare for their first flights.

Loki turned and followed Major Prechitt out of

285

the hangar, with Josh following close behind. Once outside, they both jogged a few steps to catch up to Major Prechitt.

"Is that guy serious?" Josh wondered out loud.

"I'm afraid he is," Major Prechitt replied.

"I heard that Takaran fighter pilots were arrogant, but..."

"You heard right," the major said bitterly.

"So, you're just handing them eight Super Eagles, and they've got, what, maybe twenty hours in the sim, each?"

"You had less than that, Josh," Loki reminded him.

Major Prechitt stopped in his tracks, turning to look at Josh and Loki. "Look, the deal was that Commander Goodreau is in charge of his own pilots. If that means he wants to see to their orientation and training, that's his decision."

"But they've never even *seen* a Terran Eagle before," Josh protested.

"Neither had you," the major retorted.

"That's different."

"Why, because you're Josh Hayes?" the major asked.

"No, I just..."

"Takaran fighter pilots are arrogant bastards, yes. But they are also the best trained pilots in the Pentaurus sector..."

"I don't know," Josh said doubtfully. "I've shot a few of them down, you know."

"And *these* aren't *Takaran* fighters," Loki added.

"No, but the Eagle airframe is very similar to the old Takaran trainers that a lot of those men trained in when they first started basic flight. They'll be fine. Now, if you'll excuse me, I have work to do."

Josh and Loki stood there, dumbfounded, as the major walked away.

Loki sighed. "So much for the orientation lecture I stayed up late preparing."

Josh looked back toward the hangar, narrowing his eyes, then turned back at Loki. "Those guys are a bunch of dicks."

* * *

"Jump flash," Mister Navashee reported from the Aurora's sensor station. "A big one. It's the Jar-Benakh."

Nathan glanced at the battle clock. "Right on time."

"Incoming link from the Jar-Benakh, Captain Roselle," Naralena announced.

"Put him on."

"*Aurora Actual, Jar-Benakh Actual,*" Roselle's voice called over the comm speakers.

"Captain Roselle," Nathan replied. "Glad you could make it to the party. How's your ship doing?"

"*We're good to go. Truth be told, I've been dying to take her into action since we finished her last trials a few days ago. Wish I could have been there for you at Eta Cassiopeiae.*"

"Well, you're here now, Captain. That big ship of yours is going to make these missions a lot easier."

"*I assume the plan still stands?*"

"We'll jump in and ambush the cruisers, the Cobra packs will handle the frigates. You finish off anything that survives our jump KKVs."

"*Not much of a challenge,*" Roselle said, "*but I guess we have to get our feet wet somehow.*"

"Well, we're trying four and four again this time, so there's hope." Nathan glanced at the mission clock again. "We're off to launch our jump KKVs,

Captain. We'll see you in Beta Hydri after the dance. Aurora Actual, out."

"*Benakh Actual, out.*"

"That guy is pretty happy for someone taking six hundred people into battle." Jessica commented.

"Well, he has been in port for the better part of three months now," Nathan said. "Hell, I was getting restless after the first three weeks. Besides, if I had that many guns, I'd be dying to use them as well."

"I suppose so."

"Mister Riley?" Nathan called.

"Ready to jump to launch initiation point, sir," the navigator replied. "Jump point in ten seconds."

"Jump on the mark," Nathan ordered.

"Tell me again why we're going in first this time?" Josh wondered as he scanned his flight displays.

"We're not going in *first*," Loki corrected. "We're going in at the *same time.*"

"Fine. Why?"

"Most of the Jung fleet is in orbit over Nifelm," Loki explained. "And there are about twenty surface-to-orbit missile launchers that need to be taken out *before* our ships can safely engage the fleet."

"I thought it takes three or four minutes for a STO missile to reach a target in orbit."

"Nifelm is about a quarter the size of Earth. The Jung STO missiles can probably reach a target in orbit in less than a minute."

"I still don't think it would matter," Josh argued, "not with the Aurora's new point-defenses."

"What are you worried about? There aren't even any fighters on Nifelm."

"No, just a lot of air defenses, that's all."

"Well, whatever you do, don't get us shot down.

We wouldn't survive ten minutes on that frozen rock," Loki warned. "Attack jump coming up in ten seconds."

Josh checked his displays again, then tugged at his restraint harness. He didn't want to be tossed around like the last mission.

"Jumping in three......two......one......jump."

Josh pressed the jump button on his flight control stick. The windows on the Super Falcon instantly turned opaque, clearing up a moment later, revealing a clear, pale blue sky.

The Super Falcon shook slightly, bouncing from side to side, then settled down into smooth flight.

"Hell, that wasn't bad," Josh declared. He pulled at his flight control stick, but the ship was slow to respond. "She's flying more like a harvester, though."

"The atmosphere is really thin here," Loki explained. "I'm picking up the first four targets. Locking busters."

Josh leaned to his left, peering down at the icy, snow-covered, mountainous terrain rushing under them. "Damn, you weren't kidding..."

"Launching four busters," Loki announced.

"...This place *is* a frozen hunk of rock."

"Missiles have acquired and are running hot and true," Loki added. "Twenty seconds to first impact. Come right sixty and pitch down four degrees for our jump to the next target group."

"Damn," Josh exclaimed as he rolled the ship to starboard, initiating a slow turn as he peered out the window on Loki's side of the cockpit, "have you ever seen this much snow in your life?"

"First target destroyed," Loki reported. "No, I haven't."

"Sure as hell looks cold down there, I'll tell you that."

"Second target destroyed."

"You know, I've never actually touched snow."

"Third target destroyed. Picking up sensor signals. Air defenses are trying to acquire us."

"I've flown over it plenty of times, back on Earth, that is. But I've never been *in* the snow. Have you?"

"Can't say that I have," Loki replied. "Fourth target destroyed. Jump us to the next target group."

"We should try skiing someday," Josh said. "Kaylah says it's not that hard to learn how, you know."

"Are you going to jump us to the next target group, or just keep yapping until they shoot us down?"

"Just making conversation," Josh said as he pressed the jump button on his flight control stick.

"Jumping," Ensign Noray, the Jar-Benakh's navigator announced.

There was no jump flash translated through the Jar-Benakh's many view screens, as the system was designed to 'blink out' during the jump.

"Jump complete," the navigator added.

"Multiple contacts, multiple jump flashes," Ensign Marka reported from the sensor station.

"I guess the party's started," Captain Roselle commented, barely containing his eagerness to put his ship to good use.

"Debris field, off our port bow," the sensor operator reported. "One million kilometers, three hundred up... Wait, I'm picking up another contact. A big one. Debris as well."

"Where?"

"Starboard side, six million kilometers, one-fifty down relative. It's the battle platform."

"Has she been destroyed?"

"No sir, not enough debris. Sensors are a bit scrambled in that direction, though. Lots of radioactivity, fluctuating energy readings, EM... My guess is she's still in the game."

Roselle smiled. "Our first dance," he muttered. "Lieutenant Sahbu, change course to intercept that battle platform. Ensign Noray, plot a jump to take us within fifty kilometers of the target."

"Changing course to intercept," the helmsman acknowledged.

"Plotting jump to fifty clicks," the navigator followed.

"Sugar, spin up your big guns. You're up first," Roselle ordered.

"Yes, sir," Sergeant Shugart replied from the Jar-Benakh's starboard weapons station.

Captain Roselle waited patiently for his ship to complete its turn. The Jar-Benakh was big, and she was heavily armed and shielded, but she wasn't fast by any stretch of the imagination. She was slow to maneuver, and slow to accelerate. She simply wasn't designed to be fast. She *was*, however, designed to slug it out at close range. She couldn't take down a battle platform by herself, but against a *damaged* battle platform, their odds looked pretty good to Gil Roselle.

Then again, he was always a bit of a gambler.

———

"Cruiser is destroyed," Mister Navashee reported from the Aurora's sensor station.

"Any word from the Jar-Benakh?" Nathan asked.

"No, sir," Naralena replied from the comm station.

291

"Mister Chiles, take us to high orbit over Nifelm," Nathan instructed.

"Aye, sir," Mister Chiles replied.

"I've got the battle platform's debris field, Captain," Mister Navashee reported. "I don't believe she's destroyed though. The field is similar in shape and mass as the one in Eta Cassiopeiae, when only a single arm was destroyed...maybe a bit larger."

"Any sign of the Jar-Benakh?"

"No, sir. Not yet," Mister Navashee answered. "But, the light we're detecting is only... Wait. I've got her jump flash now. She just jumped in."

"And the battleship?"

"She's closer to us. Nothing left of her. She must've taken at least two direct hits."

"Orbital insertion in two minutes," Mister Chiles reported from the helm.

"Jar-Benakh is turning toward the battle platform," Mister Navashee said.

"He's going to take her on," Jessica surmised.

"He wanted to get his ship into action," Nathan commented.

"Even if that platform is half gone, I still don't see a single battleship as a match for a battle platform," Jessica insisted.

"Comms," Nathan said. "Let the Jar-Benakh know we are available to assist them if needed."

"Aye, sir," Naralena replied.

"If needed?" Jessica said in disbelief. "Are you kidding?"

"We have our job to do, and the Jar-Benakh has theirs," Nathan reminded her. "That platform isn't going anywhere soon. If Roselle feels he can't take her down alone, he'll stand off until we can join him. He knows the mission plan."

"Roselle... Stand off?" Jessica muttered doubtfully.

"Entering high orbit over Nifelm," Mister Riley reported.

"Launch the CNS shuttles," Nathan ordered.

"I've got the Celestia," Naralena reported. "They've destroyed the cruiser on the far side and are moving into high orbit. They also report the Cobra packs have destroyed all four frigates."

"Captain, the Jar-Benakh finished her turn. She's... She just jumped away."

"Toward the battle platform?"

"I believe so. Stand by."

"CNS shuttles are away," Naralena reported.

"Comms. Relay the Jar-Benakh's movements to the Celestia, and tell them to be prepared to engage the battle platform if needed."

"Aye, sir."

"I've got the Jar-Benakh again, Captain," Mister Navashee said. "She's in close to the platform. About fifty meters and closing."

––––––––––

"Firing all starboard weapons," Sergeant Shugart announced from the Jar-Benakh's starboard weapons console.

"The platform is trying to hail us," Ensign Jullen reported from the comm station.

"What do they want?" Commander Ellison asked.

"I don't know, sir," Ensign Jullen replied, smiling. "I don't speak Jung."

"They're probably wondering why we're shooting at them," Captain Roselle commented, also smiling. "Man, I'd love to see the look on their faces right now."

"Target is bringing their big guns around to fire on us," Ensign Marka warned.

"What about their missile launchers?" Commander Ellison wondered.

"The ones on the near side are damaged," Ensign Marka answered. "And the ones on her other arms don't have a clean shot."

"They can still fire them and vector them around onto us," Commander Ellison warned.

"Their missiles are pretty fast off their rails, so they'll have to turn wide," Captain Roselle surmised. "Jobu, take us in closer, say, twenty-five kilometers."

"Moving in to twenty-five kilometers, aye," Lieutenant Sahbu acknowledged.

"If they can rotate around and get those active batteries pointed directly at us, we're going to have less than a minute to shoot those missiles down."

"Any sign of them trying to rotate the ship?" Roselle asked his sensor officer.

"No, sir," Ensign Marka replied. "I don't think they have any maneuvering at all."

"You let me know if they do, Weedge," Captain Roselle instructed.

"We're taking heavy rail gun fire," Lieutenant Commander Kessel reported from the tactical station. "Starboard shields are already down five percent."

"If they get below fifty, jump us out," Roselle instructed his helmsman.

"Aye, sir," Lieutenant Sahbu answered.

"Target just lost one of her shields that was extending to cover her damaged arm, Captain!" Ensign Marka announced.

"Sugar!" Roselle called to his trusted sergeant at the starboard weapons station.

"Concentrating our midship guns on the platform's unshielded area," Sergeant Shugart replied.

Captain Roselle looked up at the view screens above his flight team's heads, watching as dozens of bolts of red-orange plasma energy streaked away from his ship toward the distant target.

"Range to target is now twenty-five kilometers," Lieutenant Sahbu reported.

"Jesus," Lieutenant Commander Kessel muttered, staring up at the screen from the tactical station. "Twenty-five clicks away, and she still fills the view screen."

"Damn thing is twenty clicks wide herself," Captain Roselle said.

"Incredible," the lieutenant commander exclaimed.

"Just keep pounding her with everything we've got," the captain said.

"I've got thirteen of them on her now, Captain," Ensign Shugart replied.

"Are we even making a dent?" Commander Ellison wondered.

"The first few shots tore the rest of her number two arm up," Ensign Marka answered from the sensor station. "Arms two and three are both gone, and she's taken some damage to her core as well. But she managed to extend other shield sections to protect herself, sir." Ensign Marka turned to look at the captain. "And she's launching missiles... Lots of them."

"Be ready with those point-defenses, Flash," Captain Roselle warned.

"I'm on it," Sergeant Garza replied.

"Maybe we'd better take the Aurora up on her

offer," Commander Ellison suggested to his captain in a hushed voice.

"Not yet, Marty," Captain Roselle insisted. "I want to see what this ship can really do."

———

"CNS-sats are up," Naralena reported. "We've got global coverage."

"I'm getting data links," Jessica reported from the Aurora's tactical station.

"Here too," Mister Navashee added. "I can see the entire surface, Captain."

"All the Jung data-sats are gone?" Nathan asked.

"Yes, sir," Jessica replied. "The Falcons took them out after they finished with the STO missile launchers."

"Comms, transmit the warning broadcast globally. Set to repeat every minute."

"What about the Jar-Benakh?" Jessica wondered. "Are we going to just sit here and wait for a response?"

"Mister Navashee?" Nathan called.

"The Jar-Benakh appears to be holding her own for now," the sensor officer replied. "She's pounding the platform with all her starboard guns, and fending off a wrap-around missile attack with her port side point-defenses."

"Are they making headway?"

"It looks like two of the platform's arms are gone, and she's not showing any signs of maneuvering, so I'd say yes. She has managed to extend her shields over her damaged areas to protect herself, but those extended sections won't hold as long, not while they're trying to cover that much area."

"We can let the comm-sats repeat the message to the people of Nifelm," Jessica suggested.

"Someone's gotta be here to receive a response," Nathan reminded her.

"The message gave them twenty-four hours to respond before we start obliterating those Jung bases on the surface. Are we going to just sit here and wait for an answer while the Jar-Benakh is slugging it out with that platform?"

"Yes, we are," Nathan replied sternly, "*unless*, Captain Roselle requests assistance. Those *are* our orders, Lieutenant Commander."

"Aren't they just going to abandon their bases and take cover?" Josh wondered as they circled the city of Toray, one of the six domed cities of Nifelm.

"To where, the snow?" Loki replied.

"Or into the city...duh!"

"I'm sure command has thought this through, Josh."

"Doesn't sound like it to me."

"I'm pretty sure the message is more of a warning to the locals than to the Jung," Loki explained. "To give them a chance to seek shelter before the attack. Those bases are awfully close to those domes, after all."

"Still doesn't make any sense," Josh insisted.

"Maybe the locals can keep the Jung soldiers from entering the domes?"

"If they could, there wouldn't be any Jung bases down there at all, Loki."

"Probably right about that."

"Why don't they just send the Ghatazhak down there to attack the bases directly?"

"Even the Ghatazhak don't want to go into that frozen wasteland," Loki replied.

"Loki, the Ghatazhak cold-coasted across the

system to that asteroid base over Tanna, remember? What was that, like twenty hours or something? In space? I'm sure a little ice and snow is nothing to them."

"Perhaps, but the marines don't have that kind of gear, and there aren't enough Ghatazhak to take on all the Jung forces on Nifelm."

"But, if the Jung go into the cities and mix in with the locals, how will the Ghatazhak tell them apart?"

"I have no idea," Loki replied.

"Starboard shields are down to an average of forty-seven percent," the Jar-Benakh's tactical officer warned. "I don't think our shields will hold longer than theirs, Captain."

"Damn it," Roselle cursed under his breath. "Can you reroute power from our other shields?"

"Yes, sir," Lieutenant Commander Kessel replied. "But if one of those missiles gets past our point-defenses..."

"Lieutenant Sahbu, swing our nose into the target and bring our mark fives to bear. I'm tired of this slug-fest."

"Yawing to starboard, bringing tubes onto the target, aye," the helmsman answered.

"As we turn, drop our other shields, starting with those aft and to port, and channel all power into our starboard shields, and then into our bow shields. We'll give her a smaller target to shoot at."

"Or a single shield to concentrate their firepower onto," Lieutenant Commander Kessel warned. "That's also going to leave the rest of the ship exposed to missile attacks, sir."

"Keep our forward guns on the platform, and

task the rest to target those inbound missiles, if you have to."

"Our big guns weren't designed to defend against missile attacks, sir. They don't track that fast."

"They don't have to," Commander Ellison chimed in, moving over to the tactical station to assist the lieutenant commander. "They'll be coming straight on, not laterally."

"Tubes are coming to bear," Lieutenant Sahbu announced. "You should have a firing solution in fifteen seconds."

"Transferring all shield power to bow shields," Commander Ellison reported.

"Targeting incoming missiles with port guns," Sergeant Garza announced.

"Same to starboard," Sergeant Shugart added.

"I have a firing solution," the tactical officer reported.

"All tubes, full power singles," Captain Roselle ordered, "and keep firing."

"All tubes, full power singles... Firing!"

"Target is launching more missiles!" Ensign Marka announced from the sensor station. "Holy crap, sir. They're firing everything!"

"Time to impact?" Captain Roselle asked.

"First wave in seventy seconds!" the senor operator warned. "After that..."

"Fire everything you've got at those inbounds, boys," Commander Ellison told his two weapons officers.

Neither sergeant replied, their attention focused on the task of preventing any of the enemy missiles from breaching their defenses.

"Target's shields are down to thirty-four percent!" Ensign Marka reported urgently.

"Forward shields are at eighty-five," Commander Ellison added. "They're pounding our shields with every rail gun they've got left, Gil."

"Move in closer," the captain ordered.

Lieutenant Sahbu turned, looking back over his shoulder at his captain in disbelief. "How close?"

"Just start toward her, Jobu!"

"Aye, sir," the lieutenant replied.

"Add some upward drift as well, and enough pitch to keep our tubes on them."

"Yes, sir."

"Ray-ray, can you pull off a five-hundred-meter jump?"

"That's at the bottom end of our jump range, sir," Ensign Noray warned.

"Can you do it?"

"I can sure as hell try," the navigator replied.

"What happens if it doesn't work?" the captain asked.

"Worst case, we jump a little further."

"Hopefully not right into a wave of inbound missiles," Lieutenant Commander Kessel commented.

Captain Roselle turned to look at his executive officer helping out at the tactical station.

"I see where you're going with this, Gil," Commander Ellison said, noticing his captain's look.

"Target's shields are at thirty-five percent," Ensign Marka reported. "They're channeling all their power into them, dropping their shields on their far side."

"How fast?" Captain Roselle asked.

"Sir?"

"How quickly are they able to raise and lower their shields that way?"

Ensign Marka looked confused. "Uh, I'm not sure, Captain."

"Take a guess, Weedge," Roselle urged.

"Thirty seconds, maybe?"

"Add a little port drift as well," Captain Roselle ordered his helmsman. "Not too much. Make it look like sloppy piloting or something."

"Yes, sir."

"Forward shields down to seventy percent," Commander Ellison reported.

"Five-hundred-meter jump, plotted and ready," the navigator announced.

"Helm, increase your rate of pitch change. Execute the jump," Captain Roselle ordered.

"Jumping."

Captain Roselle paused a moment.

"Jump complete."

"How long until we have a firing angle?"

"Five seconds," the helmsman replied.

"We're no longer taking rail gun fire..."

"...Missiles high to port, fifteen seconds..."

"...I'm on them..."

"...I have a solution..."

"Fire and repeat!" the captain ordered.

"Firing all tubes!"

"Keep your rate of pitch change," Roselle added. "Ray-ray, as soon as we lose the firing solution, jump us again."

"I got it, Captain," the navigator replied, realizing his captain's plan, as he glanced at the helmsman, who had the same look of comprehension on his face.

"Taking fire again," Commander Ellison warned. "Their guns have reacquired us."

"Stop firing whenever we jump, then resume as soon as we come out," Roselle added.

"We can't keep that rate of fire up for long," Commander Ellison warned.

"Target's shields are down to twenty percent!" the sensor officer reported.

"Flash, yours is the hardest job," Roselle warned. "Every time we jump..."

"Understood."

"We're losing the solution," the tactical officer warned.

"Jump us again, Ray-Ray."

"Jumping."

"Bow shields down to fifty percent," Commander Ellison warned.

"Jump complete," Ensign Noray reported.

"Five seconds to solution," the tactical officer reported.

"Their shields?" Roselle asked. "Are the rest of them down?"

"Firing all tubes again," Lieutenant Commander Kessel announced as he resumed firing the Jar-Benakh's massive, mark five plasma torpedo cannons.

––––––––

The Jar-Benakh drifted slowly upward and to port, relative to the massive Jung battle platform now only ten kilometers away from them. Bolts of plasma energy streamed outward in all directions from more than one hundred point-defense turrets, while much larger balls of plasma targeted missiles further out as they raced around the battle platform and toward the Jar-Benakh. The battleship's bow shields shimmered as swarms of pale blue flashes reported the impacts of hundreds, if not thousands, of rail gun slugs, some of them as large as a Cobra gunship.

The battle platform's only active shield, the one protecting her already damaged areas, as well as the still intact arms within reach of the Jar-Benakh's weapons, flashed reddish-orange with the impact of each mark five plasma torpedo. Massive rail gun muzzles of turrets located on the arms of the battle platform repeatedly flashed blue-green as slugs left their rails, streaking toward their attacker.

Then, without warning, the attacking battleship disappeared behind a flash of blue-white light, reappearing five hundred meters away from their last position, moving up and left relative to the battle platform in the blink of an eye.

The exchange of weapons fire by either ship ceased for a moment, starting up again a few seconds later. First, the battleship's point-defenses fired, then her main guns, and finally her forward torpedo tubes. Seconds later, the battle platform's massive rail guns reacquired the attacking battleship, and resumed firing.

———

"Target's shields are holding at twelve percent!" Ensign Marka exclaimed. "They're pumping everything they've got into those shields, Captain! They're launching gunships as well! Out of the number five arm!"

"Our bow shields are down to twenty percent!" Commander Ellison warned. "We can't take much more of this!"

"Jobu! Translate hard to port! Full thrust!" Captain Roselle ordered. "Give me a one-click snap jump!"

"Translating to port, full thrust..."

"One-click snap jump...in five..."

"Kessel, cease fire!"

"Four..."

"Holding fire on the mark fives," the tactical officer answered.

"Three..."

"Eighteen percent and falling!"

"Stand by to pitch down and starboard, hard as you can!"

"Two..."

"Stand by to fire all mark fives, full power!"

"One..."

"And don't stop!" the captain added.

"Jumping!"

"Down and starboard! Now! Now! Now!" Captain Roselle ordered.

"Jump complete!"

"Pitching down and starboard hard as I can," the helmsman replied.

"Holy crap!" Ensign Marka exclaimed with excitement. "We've got a clear firing line! No shields between us and the target!"

"How long, Jobu?" Captain Roselle asked his helmsman.

"Fifteen seconds, sir."

"The platform has dropped their last shield. They're powering up the shields between us and them, Captain!" the sensor officer warned.

"How long?"

"Unknown!" Ensign Marka replied. "I'm reading massive power transfers from all over the ship!"

"They're bring their guns around," Commander Ellison warned. "They're reacquiring."

"Missile launches!" Ensign Marka warned.

"Number five arm! Directly ahead! Impacts in twenty seconds!"

"We don't have enough guns forward to stop those missiles, Gil!" Commander Ellison warned.

Captain Roselle stood motionless, waiting for the last few seconds of his plan to unfold.

"Firing solution in three..."

"Fire all tubes..."

"Two..."

"Fifteen seconds to impact!"

"One..."

"Incoming rail gun fire!" Commander Ellison warned.

"Firing all tubes!" the tactical officer announced.

"Target's raising shields!" the sensor officer reported. "Ten seconds to missile impact!"

"We can't reach them!" Sergeant Garza realized in a panicked voice.

"Stand by with another five-hundred-meter snap jump," Roselle ordered.

"Firing again!"

"DIRECT HITS!" Ensign Marka exclaimed triumphantly.

"Cease fire!" Captain Roselle ordered. "Snap jump!"

"Ceasing fire..."

"Snap jump, aye..."

"Keep pitching down and starboard to keep our tubes on her, Jobu," Roselle instructed.

"Jump complete," Ensign Noray reported.

"I'm on it," the helmsman assured his captain.

"They missed!" Ensign Marka exclaimed. "The missiles slid right under us!"

"I have another firing solution," Lieutenant Commander Kessel reported. "Firing all tubes!"

"Number five arm is heavily damaged!" Ensign Marka announced. "The core has taken several direct hits as well!"

"Keep firing!" Roselle instructed.

———————

Massive, red-orange balls of plasma leapt from the underside of the Jar-Benakh's bow, streaking toward the Jung battle platform, and slamming into her core structures. Within the platform, secondary explosions sent debris spewing out in all directions. Rail guns stopped firing. Missile launchers stopped launching. More importantly, there were no shields active.

———————

"She's lost main power!" Ensign Marka reported. "No shields anywhere!"

"Can she still fire?" Roselle asked.

"No, sir! She's dead in space! She is launching every gunship and every shuttle she's still got inside!"

"Lieutenant Sahbu. Circling course from five clicks out. Keep our starboard broadside cannons on her," Captain Roselle instructed. "Sergeant Shugart, pound her with everything you've got. Sergeant Garza, keep our far side protected, in case any of those fleeing gunships try to be heroes for their stinkin' empire." Captain Roselle stood tall, breathing in deep, savoring his victory. "Gentlemen, let's finish this bitch off for good, shall we?"

———————

"Incoming transmission from the surface," Naralena reported from the Aurora's comm station.

"Is it Jung?" Nathan asked.

"No, sir. I believe it's civilian."

"Put it up."

"They're sending video as well, sir."

"Fine. Put it on the main view screen."

The screen switched images, revealing an adult male, in his forties, with perfect features. Standing behind him and to his left were two more men who looked exactly like him. Behind and to his right were three women, each of whom appeared to be exact replicas of one another.

"What the hell?" Jessica exclaimed.

"This is Captain Nathan Scott, of the Alliance ship, Aurora," Nathan greeted. "To whom am I speaking?"

"*I am Emel number twelve-twenty, seventy-five, Chief of Security for Nifelm,*" the man replied quickly, as if panicked.

"I take it you received our..."

"*Yes, yes,*" the man replied, interrupting the captain. "*We received your message, Captain. Please, attack without haste, I beg of you!*"

"Sir, you do understand, that attacking the Jung assets on your world will result in significant collateral..."

"*We are aware,*" the man replied impatiently. "*We can rebuild. Please...*"

"Lives will be lost," Nathan warned. He turned to Jessica.

"Thousands, at least," she clarified.

"Thousands, possibly tens of thousands," Nathan said to the man on the view screen.

"*Physical bodies can be replaced,*" the man insisted. "*Souls can be transferred. Please, Captain. The Jung are already entering our cities in an attempt to evade destruction. If you do not attack now, the destruction will be much worse, believe me.*"

I'm begging you, Captain. Destroy the Jung bases, immediately!"

"Very well," Nathan replied. "Tell your people to take cover. We will attack in five..."

"*You must attack now!*" Emel begged. "*Please! You must trust me!*"

Nathan took a deep breath. "As you wish." He turned to Naralena, signaling for her to end the link. "Fire when ready, Lieutenant Commander."

"Yes, sir," Jessica replied.

"Miss Avakian, relay the order to begin immediate bombardment of all Jung surface assets to the Celestia."

"Yes, sir," Naralena replied.

"Weapons locked on first target," Jessica announced. "Initiating firing sequence." She pressed the firing button, then looked at Nathan. "Clones?"

"I'm guessing, yes," Nathan replied.

"That would explain why the admiral didn't seem concerned with the Jung trying to hide among the locals."

"Yes, it would."

"Captain," Mister Navashee interrupted. "I'm picking up energy spikes, explosions, and a lot of radiation from the battle platform's last position."

"What about the Jar-Benakh?" Nathan wondered.

"She's still there, sir."

Nathan smiled. "Nice to have a battleship on our side again."

"Sure as hell is," Jessica agreed. "First target destroyed. Second target will be in range in fifteen seconds."

"Comms, dispatch a jump comm-drone to Sol," Nathan instructed. "Let Commander Telles know that he will be cleared to begin cleanup of Nifelm within the hour."

* * *

Every afternoon, Captain Dubnyk had gotten into the habit of taking his afternoon tea and *pabva* cakes in the gazebo at the far corner of his back garden. Built by one of his students in exchange for teachings, it was just big enough for two or three people. However, today, as was the case on most days, he took his tea alone.

It was a ritual he quite enjoyed, actually, as it gave him time to reflect on the teachings of the morning while his midday meal settled. The process left him energized, and ready for the afternoon lessons.

Fayla stepped out of the kitchen door and down the steps into the back garden, weaving her way through the vegetable garden to join her employer. "How was your tea?" she asked as she approached.

"Lovely, as usual, my dear," the captain replied. "In fact, I could be convinced to partake in a second cup, if a lovely young lady were to insist."

Fayla smiled as she bent over to pick up the captain's empty cup and saucer. She spied the empty plate that had contained two *pabva* cakes. "Your appetite improves," she said, relieved. "You rarely ask for a second cup, let alone finish both cakes."

"I believe the treatments are working," Captain Dubnyk told her, "much to my surprise, I must admit."

"I told you," Fayla said as she sat across from him. "Do not question the healing powers of Tannan herbs and teas. Without them, our people would not have survived the dark ages that followed the great plague."

"How did you know of such things?" he asked. "You are far too young to know anything of the dark ages."

"Stories handed down by the elder women of my tribe," she explained.

"Ah, yes, the tribes of Tanna."

"I know you must find the notion of tribes somewhat antiquated in this day and age. But to many, our past is more of who we are than our present."

"On the contrary, tribes were quite common after the plague," the captain said. "It was the only way to survive. Strength in numbers, and all that. They existed on Earth, as well as many of the core worlds that I visited before fleeing the sector."

She scrutinized him closely, looking into the whites of his eyes, and examining the color and texture of the wrinkled skin on his face. "You do look better," she admitted. "Your eyes are much clearer, and your skin color has improved." She grinned. "You may even have fewer wrinkles than before."

"One can dream," the old captain replied.

"Another cup, then," she said, rising from her seat. "And maybe another *pabva* cake as well?"

"Yes, I think," he replied, smiling.

She bent over and placed his teacup and saucer on top of the empty *pabva* plate. She stood up straight again and turned back toward the house. "Oh, I almost forgot," she said, reaching into her apron pocket. "Brill's younger brother, Tylor, delivered this for you a few minutes ago," she said as she handed the captain a small envelope.

"Will you?" he asked. "My fingers are still not what they once were."

Fayla carefully opened the elaborately folded

envelope until it was no longer an envelope, but a note. She attempted to hand it to him again.

"Nor are my eyes, I'm afraid," the captain said.

"It is from Brill. He has been accepted into the Alliance Marines. He leaves this evening for Earth."

"How wonderful for young Mister Daymon," Captain Dubnyk said happily.

Fayla looked at the old man, a puzzled look on her face. "I thought you did not approve of the Alliance?"

"I neither approve nor disapprove of them," he explained. "I am, however, happy for Brill. He will learn much, see much. And someday, he will return and share what he has learned with all of us. He will add his knowledge and experiences to our own, and we shall all be the richer for it."

"If he survives," Fayla reminded him. "There is a war being fought, do not forget."

"Of course, of course," Captain Dubnyk agreed. "We shall send him our positive thoughts."

Fayla handed the paper to her employer and departed.

Captain Dubnyk folded the paper in half, then half again, and then held it in the candle's flame. The paper quickly caught fire, and he held it in front of him for as long as he could. Finally, he set it next to the candle and allowed it to burn into ashes, which were carried away by the afternoon breeze.

He smiled at his good fortune.

* * *

"He *is* always ragging on me," Josh complained as they walked across what had once been the Aurora's main cargo bay, and was now her main hangar deck.

"It just seems that way because you avoid talking to him," Loki insisted.

"Because he's always ragging on me."

"Well, maybe if you weren't always breaking procedure..."

"I wouldn't always be breaking procedure, if so many of the procedures weren't stupid."

"Just because you don't like them doesn't mean they are stupid, Josh."

"Yeah, it pretty much does, Lok," Josh argued, "at least in my eyes, it does."

"You'd make a terrible transport pilot."

"Please, those guys aren't even pilots," Josh scoffed, stopping to watch the final converted Super Falcon pull off the elevator pad and roll toward its parking spot in one of the starboard alcoves. "All they do is push buttons all day. Auto-flight take me here, auto-flight take me there. Oh, and don't forget the seatbelt sign. That's a tricky one."

Loki tuned his partner out, as usual, instead choosing to watch the crew of the eighth and final Super Falcon open their side canopy windows and climb out of their ship and down to the deck. "Come on," he told his friend as he headed toward the Super Falcon.

Loki walked up to the Super Falcon crew. "Hi, I'm Loki Sheehan," he greeted offering his hand. "This is my partner, Josh Hayes."

"Dorrel Lasan," the first man replied, shaking Loki's hand. "This is Gannon Parkin."

"A pleasure," the second man greeted in a thick brogue.

"You're Corinairan?" Josh asked.

"What gave it away?" Gannon asked with a smile. "Me dashin' good looks, was it?"

"Something like that," Josh replied, shaking the man's hand.

"You're not Corinairan," Loki said to the first man.

"Palean," he replied.

"Really?" Loki said, shocked. "I think you're the first Palean we've had on board."

"No, there's a guy in environmental... Yarik something," Josh said.

"Are you two our welcoming committee, then?" Gannon wondered.

"Flight ops asked us to show you guys around, help you find your quarters, the mess...you know. All the important stuff."

"Shouldn't we check in first?" Dorrel asked.

"CAG's in a meeting right now. He said to have you report to his office after dinner."

Gannon looked sidelong at Loki, eyeing him suspiciously. "You wouldn't be trying to pull a fast one on us, now would ya? Trying to get us in the dutch with the boss on our first day?"

"In the dutch," Josh laughed. "You're definitely Corinairan."

"If it was Josh offering, then yes, I'd be suspicious," Loki admitted. "I can take you to the CAG, if you'd prefer?"

Gannon looked Josh up and down, then looked at Loki. "I see your point. He does look a might untrustworthy."

"What? Me?" Josh said innocently.

"You, on the other hand, have a face like a choir boy," Gannon joked. "I suppose I can trust you." He turned to Dorrel. "Whattaya think, Lasan?"

Dorrel nodded his approval. "Lead the way, gentlemen."

* * *

Admiral Dumar entered the mission briefing room on Karuzara and headed straight for the podium.

"Admiral on deck!" the guard at the door barked.

Everyone in the room rose to their feet and came to attention.

"As you were," the admiral instructed as he stepped up to the podium. The large view screen on the wall behind him came to life, displaying the chart of a star system. "Tomorrow's mission will be Mu Cassiopeiae, both A and B elements."

Nathan quickly glanced at Jessica, checking to see if she was as shocked as well. A turn of his head to the left revealed that Cameron had the same reaction.

"With the success of the attack on Beta Hydri, and the way the Jar-Benakh was able to handle the damaged battle platform, we expect this mission to be one of our easiest to date. First, there are no local inhabitants in either system, other than the Jung."

"Why are the Jung even there?" Commander Kovacic asked.

"Mu Cassiopeiae is a stepping stone of sorts. It serves as a communication hub for that area of the Sol sector, as well as a convenient refueling point for ships traveling between Eta Cassiopeiae and the fringe worlds of Iota and Theta Persei, as well as Iota Pegasi, HR 51, and Capella."

"Then it has a propellant depot?" Cameron surmised.

"Yes, but that's not why we're taking it out. In fact, we don't plan on trying to capture the processing facilities intact, as they are fairly well protected against landing parties. If we are able to capture the system with the propellant storage fields intact, so be it, but I do not intend to put anyone at undue risk to that end."

"So, we're just hitting it because of the Jung ships that are stationed there?" Commander Willard commented skeptically.

"Partly, yes," Admiral Dumar admitted. "At twenty-four point seven light years from Sol, the presence of those ships is a significant threat to Earth. More importantly, however, is the fact that it is a centrally located, major distribution hub. Intelligence indicates numerous visits from supply and troop ships, with more ships arriving full than departing."

"Then it's a logistics staging point," Commander Kovacic realized.

"That is our conclusion as well," the admiral concurred. "One that is very well situated, with at least three worlds less than fifteen light years away, and five more less than twenty-five...including Earth. From Mu Cassiopeiae, the Jung can bring a sizable force to any of those worlds in less than, or a little over one year."

The admiral paused for a moment, letting the strategic value of the next day's target sink into the minds of his officers. "We will initiate the attack as usual, taking out the platform and battleship first with jump KKVs. However, this time, we will not be jumping in to verify their destruction before pressing the attack to other ships. Experience has shown us that with our current spread of twelve to sixteen jump KKVs, the odds of completely missing either target is extremely slim. So, at the very least, the targets will be damaged, and therefore will be unlikely to interfere with our attack on the remaining assets in the system. We will press the attack, with

315

the Jar-Benakh taking out the two cruisers, and the Cobra gunships taking out the frigates. Meanwhile, the Aurora will target the supply base on Pallendale, and the Celestia will take care of the troop base on Darmath."

"What about the fuel plant?" Nathan asked.

"Super Falcons should be able to handle both the processing plant and the propellant depot defenses."

"You indicated that there would be an attack on both systems," Nathan reminded the admiral.

"Indeed," the admiral replied. "Mu Cassiopeiae B has no planets, but it does have a rather large asteroid field. One of them, an asteroid about twice the size of this base, is believed to have a spaceport inside of it. On one of Scout One's flybys, long-range passive sensors detected several ships that appeared to approach the asteroid, but did not depart. We sent a Super Falcon with an advanced sensor package on it, and were able to verify entrances into the asteroid, as well as detect several ships arriving and departing."

"What size ships?" Nathan wondered.

"So far, we've seen nothing bigger than a frigate enter the base, but considering the asteroid's size, I suspect it could accommodate larger ships as well."

"How are we going to capture that thing?" Captain Roselle wondered. "They've got to have an awful lot of defenses, and maybe even a few cruisers in there... Or worse."

"Which is why we aren't going to bother trying to capture it," Admiral Dumar said, surprising everyone in the room.

"Admiral," Nathan started to question.

"The plan is to hit it with jump KKVs at the same time. The asteroid's orbit is quite predictable, so it should be easy to hit. We calculate that at least four JKKVs should do the trick. The Aurora will launch the B group first, then the A group. A jump shuttle will initiate launch of the B group, at zero hour like all the rest."

"If that is a shipyard, it's a hell of an asset to just throw away," Captain Roselle objected.

"Perhaps," Admiral Dumar replied, "but the potential cost of capturing that asset is too great. It would require significant human resources in the form of boarding parties. Furthermore, we have no data on her internal defenses. The only option would be the use of the Ghatazhak, and Commander Telles agrees that without further intelligence about their internal defenses, we cannot even guess at a probability of success. It is just too risky."

"Could we wait?" Cameron wondered. "Pass it by for now, and come back later in the hopes of having additional manpower?"

"Not an option," the admiral said, shaking his head. "We don't know how long we can continue to expand our Jung-free zone around Sol. Because of that, we must work outward, evenly, all the way around us. Leaving a logistical strong point like Mu Cassiopeiae untouched is too much of a risk. It must be destroyed."

"Then that's what we're going to do," Captain Roselle agreed confidently.

* * *

Captain Poc entered the admiral's office, pausing at the doorway. "You wanted to see me, sir?"

"Captain, yes," Admiral Dumar greeted him, gesturing to an empty chair. "Please, come in. Have a seat."

Captain Poc entered the admiral's office and sat down.

"When did you get in?" the admiral asked, more out of courtesy than genuine interest.

"About half an hour ago," the captain replied.

"It must be nice to get out and stretch your legs a bit. I know we've been keeping you and your ship pretty busy these past few months."

"Completely understandable, Admiral."

"Well, the intelligence that your ship has provided has been invaluable. You and your men should be proud of that fact."

"Thank you, sir. I'll pass that on to my crew." Captain Poc cocked his head to one side. "Sir, if I might ask a question?"

"Of course."

"Usually, when we come into port for turn around, we already have an idea of what our next mission will be. However, this time, we were simply instructed to make port, and for me to report to your office."

"More of a statement than a question," the admiral observed. "I speak with most of my ship captains on a regular basis. However, due to the constant demands on your ship, I rarely get to speak with you."

Captain Poc looked confused, his brows knit together. "What would you like to speak about?"

"How do you think things are going?"

"Things are going fine for us."

"No, I meant overall, for the Alliance, for Earth... that sort of thing."

Captain Poc thought for a moment. "Well, from a campaign perspective, I guess things are going fairly well. The liberations of Mu Cassiopeiae, Chi Draconis, and Lamda Serpentis, were all executed flawlessly, with very few casualties, and almost no damage to our ships. Even the collateral damage to those systems was minimal."

"Yes, we have been quite fortunate as of late."

"For the Alliance as a whole, or at least for the forces in the Sol sector, we seem to be picking up quite a bit of support from our new member worlds. At least in manpower, that is."

"Yes, that is true."

"I am concerned about the popularity of Admiral Galiardi and his Strength Now party," Captain Poc admitted. "If they gain influence on the new Coalition Congress, our ability to conduct operations could become problematic."

"Which is exactly why we have been so aggressive with our timetable," the admiral replied.

"Understandable."

Admiral Dumar paused to take a breath, letting it out in a long sigh. "How do you feel about your ship?"

"It's a good ship. A little old, perhaps, but still in good working order. She could use better sensors, though. I've heard of the stuff they're putting into the recon module for the new Super Falcons. I wouldn't mind getting a few of them installed in my ship."

"You will, sort of."

"Sort of?" Captain Poc echoed in confusion.

"We're taking your ship down for a month or so," the admiral explained. "Putting her in dry dock. She'll get new defensive weapons, new shields, and a completely new sensor package. We're even going to increase her crew by four specialists in order to monitor those new sensors. We're turning her into a dedicated recon ship."

"Interesting," Captain Poc replied thoughtfully.

"Where are you going to put the extra crew, Admiral? We barely have enough room for eight as it is, let alone twelve."

"We're gutting her interior spaces and redesigning. Her missions will be limited to eighteen hours, maximum, and she'll be on constant duty cycles, standing down a few days for refit every few weeks. She'll have rotating crews, so each crew will be flying a mission every other day, on average, with a few days off every ten days."

"That will take some getting used to," Captain Poc observed. "We've been living in that ship for several years now."

"Actually, you'll have a lot more to get used to than you think," Admiral Dumar told him. "You're all getting reassigned."

"To where?"

"Congratulations, Captain," Admiral Dumar said, standing and offering his hand. "You're taking command of the Kent."

Captain Poc stared at the admiral, so shocked that he forgot to shake his hand. "The *Kent*, sir?"

"The Jung frigates in the Tau Ceti shipyards. The first one will be ready to begin service in three weeks' time."

"I thought it was bad luck to rename a ship?"

"It seems the Jung don't assign a name to a ship until the day it is launched," Admiral Dumar explained. "Therefore, we decided to name her the Kent."

"A good choice," Captain Poc agreed.

"Then you'll take her?"

"Of course, sir, thank you," Captain Poc replied, finally standing and shaking the admiral's hand. "But, what about a crew?"

"Like I said, you'll be taking your crew with you."

"But surely they are not enough to run a frigate?"

"No, they're not," the admiral agreed. "It actually takes one hundred and twenty to crew a frigate. I just figured you'd like to take your crew with you. You can assign them roles as you see fit, Captain."

"And the rest of her crew?"

"You'll start with one full shift of forty," the admiral explained, "and you'll have three weeks to get them trained and ready. Captain Roselle has agreed to give you his third shifters to use as your first shift, as many of the systems are similar between both ships. So you should be able to get your first shift ready for action in short order."

Captain Poc felt a smile forming on his face. "Thank you, sir. We won't let you down."

"Of that I am certain," Admiral Dumar replied.

* * *

Commander Telles stood on the observation platform, watching the newest batch of recruits going through advanced hand-to-hand combat training. "Which class is this?" he asked Master Sergeant Jahal.

"Class eight. They have reached the halfway point of their training."

The commander continued to watch, paying particular attention to a rather aggressive, dark haired young man. "That one," he said, pointing to the man. "I believe he has yet to be beaten." He watched as the recruit used the methods taught to him by his instructors, and brought down a much larger man by using his opponent's momentum against him. "He uses motion and energy well." The commander turned to the master sergeant. "Are we teaching them combat kinetics?"

"Just basic leverage and momentum," the master sergeant replied. "No time to get into physics and kinesiology with them."

"This one has natural instincts," Commander Telles commented as he continued to watch. "They will serve him well. How did he score on the range?"

Master Sergeant Jahal leaned against the rail. "Sergeant!" he yelled toward the Ghatazhak sergeant below on the training line. The sergeant turned to look at his superior, who signaled him to join them.

"Yes, Master Sergeant," the sergeant said as he stepped onto the observation deck, saluting both the master sergeant and the commander.

"The young man with the black hair," Master Sergeant Jahal said. "He seems to have a knack for hand-to-hand."

Sergeant Lazo turned to look at the men below, spotting the one the master sergeant was referring to. "Recruit Daymon. Yes, he has been doing well."

"Are his scores on the range equally impressive?" Commander Telles inquired.

"He scored ninety-eight on static targets, both sidearms and auto-rifles. However, his scores on the course were lower. Ninety-two, I believe."

"Why the lower score on the combat course?" the commander wondered.

"He's a bit too aggressive," Sergeant Lazo explained. "He took out a lot of civilians by accident."

"And how many enemies escaped him?" Master Sergeant Jahal asked.

"None, sir."

"How is he at improvising?" Commander Telles asked.

"Better than most," Sergeant Lazo admitted.

"Are you thinking of bumping him to advanced

training?" Master Sergeant Jahal asked the commander.

"He hasn't finished basic yet, sirs," Sergeant Lazo warned.

"He can fight, he can shoot, and he can improvise."

"He hasn't even seen a tactical display system yet," the sergeant told them.

"When does the next advanced class begin?" Commander Telles inquired.

"Day after tomorrow," Master Sergeant Jahal replied.

"Assign one of your men to teach him to use the tactical gear, then transfer him to the advanced class," Commander Telles instructed.

"He'll miss out on some of the group maneuvers," Master Sergeant Jahal cautioned.

"If he ends up on an aggressor team, he'll have to unlearn it all anyway," Commander Telles said. "Make it happen, Sergeant."

"Yes, sir," Sergeant Lazo replied. He snapped a salute, then turned and departed, returning to the training line.

"An unusual call," Master Sergeant Jahal commented.

"Perhaps," Commander Telles admitted. "But we need more aggressor teams, and sooner rather than later."

CHAPTER NINE

Nathan stood on the aft end of the starboard catwalk, leaning on the railing and looking down at the first Super Eagle coming off the elevator pad below him.

"Nice-looking ship," Vladimir said as he came out of the fighter deck control room.

"Yes, it is," Nathan agreed. "I trained in the original version, you know."

"How did you like it?" Vladimir asked as he joined his friend at the railing.

"It was an easy ship to fly. Lots of automation, faster than hell to orbit. Maneuverable as well. She could out-turn *and* out-accelerate a standard Jung fighter. At least that's what we were told at the time. I'm not sure anyone had actually seen a Jung fighter in combat back then."

"Then it was fun to fly?"

"*Fun* wouldn't really be the right word," Nathan said. "It was a good ship, well suited for its task... But fun to fly? No. *Fun* would be my grandfather's old Carson Twelve-B. Little two-seat aerobatic job. He taught me to fly in it when I was about twelve. Now *that* was a fun plane to fly. Real stick and rudder stuff. Not a single bit of automation aboard. Heck, it barely has any instruments. Just airspeed, altitude, and a few engine gauges. *That* was real flying."

"You should take me for a ride sometime," Vladimir suggested, as he watched the second Super Eagle roll off the elevator pad on the opposite side of the bay from them.

Nathan looked at him, thinking. "You know, I'm

not even sure if that plane still exists. I mean, it did before the Jung attacked. It was in a hangar on my grandfather's property outside of Vancouver."

"Call him and ask."

"He died when I was in college. Our family kept the property and the plane. My father had someone living there as a caretaker for the estate. I think he imagined that I would live there someday... Raise a family, and all that."

"Maybe your father knows if the plane is still intact?"

"Maybe," Nathan said. "I'll ask him about it next time we speak." Nathan smiled, remembering his flying adventures in the old plane. "I wouldn't mind flying her again, that's for sure."

Nathan and Vladimir watched as the third Super Eagle rolled off the elevator below them. The spacecraft rolled forward, then turned ninety degrees to its right and pulled into the second starboard launch tube airlock.

"Have you seen the fighter deck control room?" Vladimir wondered, pointing to the large windows along the back wall just to his left. "It's a lot bigger than I expected."

"Yeah, they decided to keep the aft observation window, so they could take over as approach control if flight ops goes down," Nathan explained. "Of course, we lost our observation deck."

"Like anyone ever had time to use it," Vladimir commented. He looked across the bay as another Super Eagle rolled off the port aft elevator platform. "How many of them are we getting today?" he wondered.

"Twelve are coming here, and the other twelve are going to the Celestia."

"That's it? Twelve fighters?"

"They can only make them so fast," Nathan replied. "Two squadrons of twelve is all they could get built and get pilots for so quickly. That number will double in a couple months. Within six months, we'll have forty-eight fighters each. Within a year, we should have another forty-eight stationed at Karuzara."

"Six months," Vladimir said. "It is sometimes hard for me to believe that we have been at this for nearly two years now."

"We'd both be up for rotation next month," Nathan commented, as another Super Eagle rolled off the elevator beneath them.

Vladimir sighed. "This is where we belong, you and I."

Nathan looked at his friend. "You don't buy into all the destiny crap, do you?"

"Not really. What I meant was that you and I are doing what we were *born* to do. What we are *good* at doing. We each could be doing many different things than this, but *this* is what we are best suited for. *You* are a natural leader, and *I* am good at fixing things."

"So, that's all we're good for?"

"Of course not. I am good at *many* things. Fixing things, computer programming, I am an excellent shot, a wonderful cook..."

"I don't know about that last one," Nathan teased. "Speaking of cooking, did you have plans for lunch?"

"Why do you think I am here? To watch your Super Eagles roll around on the deck?"

* * *

Captain Nash stepped up to the podium and looked out at the group of new trainees gathered at the Cobra training center on Tanna. "Welcome, ladies and gentlemen, to the next phase of your training. Each of you has completed the didactic portion of your training, and are ready to enter the simulators. We now have three types of simulators. Flight simulators, which are a complete mock up of the flight deck of a Cobra gunship; station simulators, which are mock-ups of each individual station on board the ship, including the quad turrets; and now the ship simulator, which provides a simulated working environment of the entire interior of the ship. This last addition will allow full crews to run mission simulations together, as a team, to better refine your ability to work together."

"To date, there are eighteen gunships in service, with the nineteenth gunship launching later today. Twelve of those gunships have seen combat, and no gunships have yet been lost, or even taken serious damage due to hostile enemy fire. I added that last clarification due to a few docking incidents that we won't talk about today."

Captain Nash looked at his first eight crews gathered along the back of the room, noting a few guilty faces. He smiled.

"Thus far, Tannan gunships have destroyed twenty Jung frigates, thirteen gunships, and twenty-seven fast-attack shuttles. Not a bad tally for only five combat missions. She may not be big, but the Cobra gunship packs a hell of a punch, and when used in well-coordinated group attacks, she can be even more deadly than a ship ten times her size. Just ask the captains of those Jung frigates," he added with a grin. "The last two battles at Chi Draconis and Gliese 793 proved that as few as two Cobra gunships could bring down a frigate, under the right conditions. In those simulators is where you will learn how to do just that. You will spend countless hours executing the same maneuvers time and time again, until you can do them in your sleep. That way, by the time *your* gunships are ready, your transition into actual spaceflight will be seamless."

Captain Nash looked to his right, spotting his second in command. "Today marks an important milestone in the Cobra gunship program. While it has been an honor to personally train the crews who came before you, it is time that I started delegating more of that responsibility to others. After all, while the Cobra gunship may be a combination of Terran, Takaran, and Corinairan technologies, they are built and flown by Tannans. It is high time that Tannans started teaching their own. To that end, my role in your training will become more administrative, and the task of teaching Tannans how to operate the Cobra gunship will now fall on the crews standing behind you. Each of these men and women have proven themselves in combat, and have learned through trial and error exactly what their ships are capable of. It was a journey of discovery that we took together, as I had precious little time in this design, prior to the start of this program."

Captain Nash looked at his executive officer. "Lieutenant Commander Rano, class three is yours to instruct."

Everyone in attendance began to applaud, as Lieutenant Commander Rano walked to the podium. He shook hands with Captain Nash, and took to the podium with ease, going right into his opening briefing.

Captain Nash stepped back and moved off to the side of the room. He stood and listened to the lieutenant commander as he scanned the faces of the men and women of Tanna who had been selected as the third group to enter the final phase of training. He remembered what his friend had told him a month ago, when his people had scored their first kill in the battle to liberate Delta Pavonis. He had been correct; the volunteers had started pouring in. They now had more volunteers than they had positions to fill. There was even talk of creating another gunship production facility. This world now believed that they could fight the Jung, and that they could win.

* * *

"Jump to Alula Australis in one minute," the Jar-Benakh's navigator announced.

"All weapons show ready," Lieutenant Commander Kessel reported from the tactical station. "All guns are pre-aimed and charged, forward torpedoes are ready, as are our broadside cannons. Shield generators are on standby."

"Final go order?" Commander Ellison inquired.

"Coming in now," Ensign Marka replied. "We are go for attack as scheduled."

Commander Ellison looked to his captain.

"Initiate attack as planned," Captain Roselle ordered. "You have the conn, Commander."

"Aye, sir," the commander replied. "Ensign Noray?"

"Fifteen seconds to jump, sir."

"You are cleared to jump. All hands, prepare to execute attack," Commander Ellison instructed.

"Five seconds," the navigator warned. "Three...... two......one......jumping."

The jump indicator lights they had recently added to the ceiling of the Jar-Benakh's command

329

center turned blue, as a severely subdued jump flash appeared on several of the ship's view screens. Two seconds later, the blue lights went out.

"Jump complete..."

"Shields coming up," the tactical officer reported.

"Two Jung cruisers, dead ahead," Ensign Marka announced from the sensor station. "Five hundred meters and closing fast..."

"Nicely done, Mister Noray," Commander Ellison commented.

"...We're on course to pass between them, five clicks to port, and seven to starboard."

"Plasma cannons to port and starboard targets," Commander Ellison instructed. "Lock on and fire when ready."

"Target lock to port," Sergeant Garza reported. "Firing."

"Lock to starboard," Sergeant Shugart added. "Firing."

"Ready on the broadside cannons."

"We'll have a solution in five seconds," Lieutenant Commander Kessel replied.

"Broadsides when ready..."

"Both targets are trying to raise shields and bring their guns on us," the sensor operator warned. "They're deploying missile launchers as well..."

"I have a solution," the tactical officer reported. "Firing port broadside cannons."

Captain Roselle watched the port camera view screen as red-orange balls of plasma energy streaked away from his ship.

"Massive energy signature in the estimated location of the Jung battleship, sir," Ensign Marka reported from the sensor station.

"Firing starboard broadside cannons," the tactical officer reported.

"...Detecting debris consistent with a Jung battleship... Believe the target is destroyed, sir," Ensign Marka continued. "Direct hits on the port target. She's lost her starboard shields, all of them aft of midship."

"Flash, target her back half," Commander Ellison instructed his port weapons controller. "Continue firing, Lieutenant Commander."

"Starboard target is bringing her missile launchers onto us. Her shields are... Oh! Direct hits! Midship, walking forward! She didn't get her shields up fast enough, Commander! Starboard target is breaking apart!"

"Helm, wide circle to port to keep our broadside cannons on the port target," Commander Ellison ordered.

"Incoming message from the Celestia," Ensign Jullen reported from the Jar-Benakh's comm station. "Relay from Cobra One. All Jung frigates destroyed."

"That was fast," Captain Roselle commented, as he sat in his command chair and watched his crew continue the attack. "I guess Nash trained them well."

"Direct hits to port target's main propulsion!" Ensign Marka reported. "Her mains are down, and she's venting propellant. She's trying to bring her aft missile launcher onto us..."

"I don't think so," Sergeant Garza muttered as he retargeted two of his thirteen guns onto the enemy cruiser's aft missile launcher and pressed the firing button.

"Nice shot, Flash!" Ensign Marka reported

from the sensor station. "Aft missile launcher is destroyed."

"What about her forward launcher?" Commander Ellison inquired.

"I think it's damaged, sir," Ensign Marka replied. "It's half deployed and it doesn't appear to... Wait... Port target's last shields are down! She's taking all incoming dir... She's coming apart as well!" Ensign Marka leaned back in his seat, turning to look at his commander, a big grin on his face. "Port target is destroyed, sir."

"Any word on the battle platform?" Commander Ellison asked his communications officer.

"No, sir," Ensign Jullen replied, "not yet."

_____

"Jump in, fire missiles, jump out. Repeat," Josh said in a disinterested tone.

"So?"

"I think I'd rather be dogfighting."

"Not me," Loki replied. "This is far less risky."

"And far less exciting." Josh sighed. "What exciting mission did you fly today, Ensign Hayes?" he began in mocking fashion. "Well, I pressed a button that caused my ship to automatically jump into the atmosphere of an enemy-held planet. Then my partner pressed some more buttons, which destroyed four surface-to-orbit missile sites about a hundred kilometers away. Oh, but I did get to see the Aurora blow the crap out of a few bases from orbit," he added, pointing ahead and to their right, as two columns of yellow-orange super-heated rail gun rounds streamed down from the sky, slamming into their targets on the surface and sending columns of smoke and dust rising into the air. "Yup, all very exciting."

Loki sighed. "Stop complaining and jump us to the next group of targets."

"Confirmation from Jumper Three," Naralena reported. "The battle platform has been destroyed."

"First two surface targets have been destroyed," Jessica announced from the Aurora's tactical station.

"Multiple jump flashes at low altitude over the surface of Lindera," Mister Navashee reported from the sensor station. "Combat Jumpers have started the Ghatazhak insertion."

"That's everyone," Jessica surmised.

"Time to CNS completion?" Nathan inquired.

"Two minutes," Naralena replied.

"Very well," Nathan said. "Report the destruction of all Jung space borne assets to Commander Telles on Combat One, and let him know when the CNS-sats will be online."

"Aye, sir." Naralena replied.

"Next target in two minutes," Jessica reported.

"Picking up Jung fighters in the area of the next target group. Flight of six," Mister Navashee reported.

"Relay the tracks to flight ops and launch fighters."

"Aye, sir," Mister Navashee replied.

"Eagle One, ready in starboard one." Commander Goodreau reported over his helmet comms.

"*Eagle Two, ready in starboard two,*" the commander's wingman reported.

Commander Goodreau scanned his displays one last time as the rest of his flight of four Super Eagles reported their ready status to the fighter launch controller.

"Eagles One through Four, stand by to launch in sequence, starboard tubes," the fighter launch controller replied.

Commander Goodreau armed his maneuvering systems. The doors in front of his Super Eagle split down the middle and swung open away from the nose of his ship.

"In five..." the launch controller began.

The lights inside the launch tube that stretched out before him began to glow softly, increasing slowly in their intensity.

"...Four..."

He selected a jump range of four hundred kilometers.

"...Three..."

The commander then pushed the jump range to the other three fighters in his group, so that they would select the same altitude at which to come out of their jump down to the atmosphere of Lindera.

"...Two..."

Finally, the commander armed his main propulsion system...

"...One..."

...and tugged at his restraint harness.

"...Launch."

The commander's Super Eagle shot out of the launch airlock and down the launch tube toward the exit, pushing the commander against his seat. The lights inside the tunnel slid past him in a blur, and two seconds later his fighter was clear of the tube. "Eagle One, away," he reported as he pushed his flight control stick to the left and fired his main drive.

"Eagle Two, away," the voice of his wingman, Ensign Giortone announced as his ship shot out the number two starboard launch tube.

"Eagle Three, away," the commander heard as he angled his ship downward toward the gray and brown moon below them.

"Eagle Four, away."

"Tango flight, departing," the commander announced over the comm-channel. The announcement signified that the group of four fighters was now operating as a single element, under the command of Commander Goodreau. "Join up."

"Two up."

"Three up."

"Four up."

Commander Goodreau checked his approach. His auto-flight system had locked onto the descent path for their intercept jump. He pressed the auto-flight button and released his grip on the flight control stick. After glancing at his tactical data link display to verify his formation, he keyed his mic. "Auto-flight engaged. First jump in three."

Seconds later, his canopy turned opaque. One second after that, his ship began to buffet mildly from the sudden impact with the relatively thin atmosphere of Lindera.

The commander paid no attention to the view outside his canopy as it cleared, his attention focused on his displays. His auto-flight had already zeroed his throttle and was pulling him level. "Six targets. One thousand kilometers. Four two closure," he announced as his speed brakes engaged. "Odds target left, evens right." He rolled his jump range selector. "High-low breaks, alternating. Eight-hundred-click jump to intercept in three," he said as he pressed the jump button to engage the group auto-jump sequencer.

Three seconds later, all four Super Eagles disappeared in four blue-white flashes of light.

When the commander's canopy cleared a second later, he was still too far away to see his approaching targets. "Tango flight, engage," he ordered as he took control of his Super Eagle and banked slightly left. He pressed the firing button on his flight control stick, sending two bolts of red-orange plasma streaking forward from either side of his fighter's nose. He fired two more times, sending a total of six plasma bolts toward the first target. Shots from his wingman streaked past him from behind and below him to his right. As he turned his ship further left to engage the third target, his first few shots struck the approaching Jung fighter more than fifty kilometers ahead of him, engulfing the enemy craft in plasma energy that caused it to break apart and explode.

He never saw it. All the commander saw was two of the three icons on his threat display disappear. "One, splash one," he reported.

"Three, splash one."

"I've got the third," the commander announced, as Eagles Two and Four reported their kills over the comms. Two seconds later, he fired again...three times, and the third icon disappeared from his threat display. "One, splash two," he reported as he pulled back on his flight control stick to start climbing. "One and Three, disengaging and climbing."

"Two and four, disengaging and climbing," the leader of the second element, Lieutenant Jarso reported.

"One, turning to one four seven, climbing to ten five. Tango flight join up on me."

"Three, on your wing."

"Two and four, on our way."

A few seconds later, Eagles Two and Four appeared to the commander's left in a pair of blue-white jump flashes. The commander keyed his mic again to report to flight control on the Aurora, high above them in orbit over Lindera. "Aurora Flight, Tango Leader. Splash six. Requesting new targets."

"Tango Leader, Aurora Flight. No more contacts in your operating area. Climb to two zero and assume perimeter patrol. Provide air support as needed. Ghatazhak are on the ground and marines are inbound."

"Aurora Flight, Tango Leader. Climbing to two zero and assuming overhead cover patrol until advised." The commander unkeyed his mic so that he could talk on the ship-to-ship intercom to the rest of his flight. "Well, that wasn't much of a challenge, was it?"

"It was sort of fun, though," Lieutenant Jarso commented. *"I must admit, these ships are rather nice."*

"Please, don't tell Major Prechitt that," Commander Goodreau said. "We'll never hear the end of it."

* * *

"With each mission, we gain new insights into our own abilities," Admiral Dumar explained to President Scott on the view screen on the admiral's office wall. "At Beta Hydri, we learned that a battleship can take down a damaged battle platform. At Alula Australis, we learned that it can simultaneously engage *and* destroy two Jung cruisers, and by Captain Roselle's

337

accounts, perhaps more. In fact, he believes that his ship would prevail in a slug-out with another battleship. We have tested the Super Falcons, our new marines, our Super Eagles, even our use of boxcars to quickly insert Kalibri gunships into the atmosphere of the target world. On Logan, those gunships were indispensable."

"Congratulations on 61 Virginis," President Scott said. *"Logan's industrial and labor base is going to be a great asset to the Alliance."*

"Then they have petitioned to join?"

"We received their request less than an hour ago."

"I will arrange for a regular jump-comm link between Earth and Sol, as soon as the next drone is completed."

"Thank you," the president replied. *"Speaking of petitions, I'm afraid I have bad news."*

"Galiardi?"

"Indeed. It seems his Strength Now party is growing at a much faster rate than expected. People are easily buying into the fear and distrust that Galiardi is spreading."

"Even after all that we have accomplished, and in such a short time," the admiral commented with disappointment.

"Things are still pretty rough down here, Admiral. Galiardi is feeding their anger and molding it into a call for action, a call for strength."

"I believe our campaigns have demonstrated strength beyond reasonable doubt," Admiral Dumar insisted.

"But people are dying in the process," President Scott reminded him. *"Certainly not in the numbers experienced previously, but Galiardi has convinced*

them that no one needs to die while we build up a strong defense."

Admiral Dumar shook his head in disbelief. "I cannot believe that a man with as much military training and experience as Mister Galiardi could possibly disagree with what we are doing. Does he not realize that in order to build a strong defense, he needs time? We are giving him that time."

"*He knows damn well,*" President Scott insisted. "*I still believe he is using this as a stepping stone to something. Exactly what, I have yet to determine.*"

Admiral Dumar sighed. "How long do we have?"

"*I'm afraid his people submitted the petition this morning. Verification and review should take no more than a week, after which the merits of the petition will be debated in the Coalition Congress.*"

"And how long will *that* take?"

"*Days, weeks, months... There's no way to know for sure,*" President Scott admitted. "*A lot depends on the arguments raised. My staff has done some back channel checking, and we believe Congress is evenly split.*"

"Your best guess?"

"*I think this one will go quickly, ten days to a few weeks at the most. It is a hot topic, one that no one will want left undecided for long.*"

Dumar thought for a moment. "It takes two years to build a Jung frigate in the Tau Ceti shipyards. That would require a forty-light-year Jung-free buffer zone, just to get four *frigates*. Battleships would take twice as long. Even if we doubled up our labor force and were able to produce them in half the time, that's still only eight frigates, along with the five ships we have. *Thirteen ships*, against a fleet of possibly hundreds."

"I am aware."

"Not to mention that the Jung could be working on their own jump drive as we speak."

"I will argue your points in Congress when the time comes, Admiral," the president promised. *"Of that you can be certain."*

"Thank you, Mister President."

"How many more systems are left before you reach your next goal of thirty light years?"

"41 Arae and Kappa Ceti," the admiral replied.

"I'm familiar with Kappa Ceti," the president said. *"Another big industrial base with a large and highly skilled population who are less than pleased with Jung occupation. However, I am not familiar with 41 Arae."*

"A binary system twenty-eight and a half light years from Sol. No planets, just a lot of asteroids. One rather large one has some Jung facilities on it. It's basically another logistical point, much like Mu Cassiopeiae. We plan to strike in similar fashion, taking out the entire asteroid with jump KKVs. Kappa Ceti will be a different story, however. There are a few more ships, and a significant Jung presence on the surface of Terravine."

"Well, good luck to you, Admiral," the president said.

"To you as well, sir," the Admiral replied. "I believe you will need it more than I."

* * *

"Current marine force strength is at six thousand seven hundred and fifty-two," Master Sergeant Jahal told his commander.

Commander Telles sat in his office chair, looking across the desk at his master sergeant. "I thought class eight was graduating in two days?"

"They are, at which point their force strength will be seven thousand seven hundred and forty-five."

"Only seven washouts?"

"Six and a failure."

"Who?" the commander wondered.

"Recruit Daymon," Master Sergeant Jahal replied. "The one you promoted to advanced training."

Commander Telles raised an eyebrow, noting his friend's jab. "What did he fail?"

"Both written and psych press."

"Did you offer him a retest?" the commander asked.

"Of course. He passed the psych test the second time, but he still failed the written."

"How is that possible?" the commander wondered. "He passed the entrance exam, did he not?"

"I can only assume so. However, we do not administer them. The local recruiters on their homeworlds do."

"You think he cheated?"

"Or a recruiter changed the score for him," the master sergeant said. "It wouldn't be the first time."

Commander Telles picked up his data pad and called up Recruit Daymon's test scores. "Did you look at his test answers?"

"Failing is failing," the master sergeant insisted. "I don't care which answers he got wrong. All I care about is that he's not smart enough for the job."

"You're probably correct about that," the commander agreed. "After all, he wasn't smart enough to answer incorrectly on the same questions on both tests."

"What do you mean?"

Commander Telles handed him the data pad.

"Either he is incredibly stupid, or he wanted to wash out."

"Why?" the master sergeant wondered. "He was two days from graduating."

"Maybe he lost his nerve," the commander suggested.

Master Sergeant Jahal thought for a moment. "He was one of the recruits helping to unload the wounded from Logan. You think that spooked him?"

"Possibly," the commander said. "It does not matter. He was a volunteer. If he no longer wishes to be a marine, that is his choice. Better his change of heart was discovered now, than in the middle of battle. See to it that he is provided transport back to his world."

"It will take a few days to cycle him out. Meanwhile, he will be moved to off-base barracks for civilian personnel."

"Very well," Commander Telles said. "A shame, really. He had a natural ability."

"Would you like to speak with him?" the master sergeant wondered. "Maybe try to convince him to remain?"

"No," the commander insisted. "I do not wish to command anyone who does not believe in what they are doing. Mister Daymon has made his choice. He can live with the consequences."

* * *

Captain Poc exited his office and headed down the short corridor to the Kent's command center. He had only been in command of her for three weeks, but it had already become his home.

He had expected it to feel far more foreign, being that it was a nearly completed, captured Jung frigate. However, the Cetian technicians had done their best to make it feel less like a Jung ship and more like the Alliance ship it now was. The interior color and lighting scheme matched that of the Explorer-class ships, and all of the labeling throughout the vessel had been replaced with English translations. Even her exterior seemed more Alliance than Jung, as they had decided not to apply the black and red color scheme to her hull, instead leaving her exterior with only the gray primer coat that was given to each hull component before it was added to the ship. The result was not pretty, but it did not *look* like a Jung ship, which was an important distinction in Captain Poc's mind.

It was a small ship, only two thirds the size of the Explorer-class ships, and a large portion of that space was taken up by missile storage. The actual, pressurized, crew-accessible areas of the ship took up less than a sixth of her overall mass. In fact, so much of the ship was automated, it only took thirty people to fill out a standard, operational shift.

Still, a crew of one hundred and twenty was much larger than anything he had ever commanded, and he was still getting used to using the standard, operational command structure. He had spent the last two decades running a crew of eight, including himself, and had gotten quite set in his ways.

Luckily, he had been able to bring his entire crew from Scout One along with him to his new assignment. Having the familiar faces on his senior staff and in his command center made the transition easier, without a doubt. They had only pulled out of the shipyard above Sorenson a week ago, but they were already feeling quite comfortable in their new roles.

"Good morning, Captain," Commander Jento

greeted as the captain stepped through the hatch into the Kent's command center. The commander was standing at the planning table at the aft end of the command center, reviewing the details of the upcoming mission using the table's 3D projection system.

"Commander," Captain Poc replied, stepping up next to him at the planning table. "How are we looking?"

"We've received the go order from the Aurora. Targets are as expected. We execute on schedule." The commander looked up at one of the overhead view screens, checking the mission clock. "We jump in three minutes."

"I trust all systems are operating properly?" the captain asked as he turned to move forward.

"Yes, sir."

"Very well. Sound general quarters," the captain instructed as he headed forward.

"General quarters, aye," the commander replied.

Captain Poc moved forward, walking between the elevated tactical station and the deck-level stations to his right. The Kent's command center was tight, despite the fact that ten to twelve people at a time were expected to work in the compartment.

The captain stepped up onto the elevated platform to his left, tucked in behind the center helm console that divided the navigator from the helmsman. He took his seat in the command chair, reached forward, and pulled his console toward him, locking it in place just within his reach. Unlike the command chairs on the Explorer-class ships, or the Jar-Benakh, his chair did not rotate. His chair also had interface consoles and data displays on both arms, as well as on a console that he could pull in tight in front of him. It wasn't much, but it was better than sitting there without anything to do with his hands, a skill, that by his own admission, even Gil Roselle had not yet mastered.

The other skill he was finding difficult was the art of letting someone else fly his ship. He had been a pilot for nearly thirty years, the last twenty-three of which had been in the same ship. He may have spent much of that time in stasis, but he was still *his* ship's pilot. Now, he was a decision maker. A giver of orders.

Captain Poc looked to his left, forward, and to his right. Because of his chair's fixed, forward-facing position, he could only see four of the seven people he would normally talk to while in his command chair. His sensor officer, navigator, helmsman, and communications officer. His tactical officer, weapons officer, and electronic countermeasures officer were all behind him and out of his line of sight. This, however, he was accustomed to, as most of the crew on his previous ship had been out of his sight from that ship's cockpit. And just like every other Alliance ship, everyone wore comm-sets that automatically linked with the others in the compartment.

The main display for the Kent's command center was composed of three large view screens that spanned the forward bulkhead of the compartment, just above the flight control consoles at her forward end. The center screen was primarily used for exterior camera views, while the angled side screens were set to display tactical data relevant to the ship's current task.

The captain glanced at the mission clock in the upper left corner of the starboard view screen. They were one minute from their jump time.

"All compartments report general quarters," the comm officer announced.

"Insertion jump in Kappa Ceti is plotted and ready," Ensign Vitko reported. "Jumps to second and third launch points are in the queue."

"Thirty seconds to insertion jump," Commander Jento announced as he turned away from the planning table at the back of the command center. He climbed the two steps onto the tactical platform, and took his seat at the console directly behind and one step above his captain. He checked his own displays, and then looked at the three main displays at the front of the compartment, verifying that the proper data was being displayed.

Captain Poc checked the time again. "All right people, let's see what our ship can do. Make ready all missile launchers."

"Deploying all missile launchers, aye," Ensign Cafasso acknowledged from the weapons station.

"ECM and jamming systems ready," Ensign Wilday announced.

"All systems are running normal."

"On course and speed for insertion jump," the helmsman, Lieutenant Serra reported.

"Ten seconds to jump," the navigator warned.

"Execute insertion jump as scheduled," the captain instructed.

"Jumping in three..."

"Missile launchers deployed and ready..."

"Two..."

"Missiles show ready for launch..."

"One..."

Captain Poc stared straight ahead at the center view screen.

"Jumping."

The center view screen flashed a subdued blue-white, then returned to normal. The stars had changed, but the difference was almost imperceptible. The only noticeable difference was the sudden appearance of a distant, reddish-orange, gas giant to the left of center.

"Jump complete," the navigator reported.

"Multiple contacts," Lieutenant Todson reported from the sensor station. "Transferring to tactical."

"I've got them," Commander Jento said. "One battle platform, a battleship, four cruisers, and six frigates... All of them right where they're supposed to be. Same courses and speeds, as well."

"Stand by to jump to second launch position," Captain Poc instructed. "Commander, launch the first wave."

"Jump to second launch position, plotted and ready," the navigator replied.

"Launching first wave of missiles," Commander Jento reported from the tactical station.

Captain Poc watched the tactical display on the left view screen, as multiple missile tracks appeared on one side of center and began tracing outward in several different directions.

"Six missiles away," Commander Jento reported.

"Execute your turn, Lieutenant Serra," Captain Poc ordered.

"Turning to second launch point," the helmsman acknowledged.

"Jump us when ready."

"Jumping in three..."

"First wave of missiles will jump in one minute." Commander Jento reported.

"Two..."

Captain Poc glanced at the system-wide tactical

display on the right view screen. The frigates they had just attacked were more than five light minutes away and were not yet aware that an enemy ship was in their system. Their first sign of danger would be the arrival flashes of the incoming missiles, only seconds before they found their targets.

"One..."

It was the ultimate standoff weapon, and in thirty seconds, he would add six more missiles to the attack, but from the opposite direction.

"Jumping."

"Hey, Lok, do you ever think about what you're going to do after this is all over?" Josh wondered.

"I imagine we'll be doing pretty much the same thing," Loki replied as he double-checked his displays one last time before they jumped. "I suspect we won't be getting shot at as often, however, which is a good thing."

"So, you see us staying in the Alliance?"

"Yup."

"Here in the Sol sector?"

"Wherever they assign us, I suppose."

"I don't know. From what I hear, there may not *be* an Alliance in the Sol Sector," Josh said, "at least not forever."

"Don't believe everything you see on the net," Loki warned. "One minute to insertion jump."

"That guy Galiardi has got a lot of people backing him now, and they don't like the Alliance that much."

"And what are they going to do without it?" Loki asked. "Half the crews on both the Aurora and the Celestia are from the Pentaurus sector."

"They've got two ships," Josh argued. "Five, if you

count the ones from Tau Ceti. And they're pumping out a Super Eagle every few days now."

"And most of the weapons are being either manufactured or converted for use on the Karuzara," Loki added. "Without that base, Earth doesn't stand a chance."

"*Now*, maybe, but what about a few years from now? The Earth has thousands of Takaran fabricators. They can build whatever they want. Hell, they can make their own asteroid base. It's not like they've got a shortage of big-ass rocks to hollow out."

"Still don't see it happening," Loki insisted, "at least not in the next ten years."

"Well, suppose it does. Then what?"

"Someone will offer us a position," Loki said.

"Someone will offer *you* a position," Josh corrected. "I'm a pain in the ass, remember?"

"What are you getting at, Josh?" Loki asked, turning to look at his partner.

"Just thinking about the future, weighing my options, and all that."

"You'd have more options if you weren't always pissing off Prechitt," Loki told him.

"Yeah, like that's ever going to happen."

"It can if you *want* it to happen."

"Maybe I don't?"

"What?"

"Maybe I don't want to play by the rules. Maybe I'd be more happy somewhere else."

"Like where?" Loki wondered. "You want to go back to Haven and fly harvesters?"

"I was thinking of something a little more exciting," Josh replied, "like being an interstellar smuggler or something."

"You've been watching too many of those old Terran, science fiction movies again," Loki told him. "Besides, you need a ship to be a smuggler."

"I could steal this ship," Josh said.

Loki just looked at him.

"I'm kidding, Lok."

"This ship does have a black box, you know."

"I was kidding!" Josh yelled, as if to an invisible listener. "I'm sure I could find a ship somewhere. Go back to the PC, find a flying gig, save some money."

"You're dreaming again."

"Okay, then maybe as a mercenary pilot, for some pirate band or something."

"A space pirate." Loki rolled his eyes. "That's a *really* good career choice."

"I dunno," Josh replied. "It could be fun."

"Can we get serious, Josh? We're jumping in and attacking enemy targets in ten seconds."

"Fine, we'll talk later," Josh said.

"I can't wait," Loki replied sarcastically. "Jumping in three..."

———

"Two minutes to insertion jump," Mister Riley reported from the Aurora's navigation station.

Nathan turned back toward Jessica, leaning against the side of her console as they continued their conversation. "If Galiardi's group gains enough support, it could very well lead to a fracturing of the Alliance into two or more elements," Nathan insisted.

"Come on, Nathan," Jessica argued, "there's no way that's going to happen."

"You really believe that?"

Jessica looked at Nathan as he stood leaning against her console, staring at her. "Okay, maybe it's possible. Maybe the Alliance splits in two, but there's no way it happens quickly. The Earth *needs* the Karuzara to survive. Until they build something to replace her, seceding from the Alliance would be suicide."

"Not if they managed to get the other members in the Sol sector to side with them," Nathan said.

"Split the Alliance in two... Sol and Pentaurus?"

"Exactly. Tau Ceti has a shipyard more capable than the Karuzara's, and they've got the industrial capacity and work force to support it. *And*, Tau Ceti and Sol are within single jump range of one another. In fact, all of the core worlds are within one-minute jump range of Sol, and *they* all have significant industrial capacity as well."

Jessica stared back at him, contemplating his words.

"Imagine it happens," Nathan said. "Who are you going to side with?"

"There's no way I'm working for Galiardi," Jessica answered without hesitation.

"But your family is here."

"It's not like we'd be banned from ever returning if we decided to work for Dumar instead of Galiardi, or whoever they put in command."

"Who knows?"

"One minute to insertion jump," Mister Riley reported.

"You know what your problem is?" Jessica said. "You think too much."

"It's my job," Nathan said, standing up straight to return to his command chair. "I've got no buttons to push."

"You're the only dork I know who would talk

about interstellar politics while waiting to launch an attack," Jessica added.

"Hey, show some respect, Lieutenant Commander," Nathan joked as he took his seat.

"Six jump flashes," Mister Navashee reported. "The KKVs have jumped away."

"A lot of Jung are about to have a really bad day," Jessica muttered.

"Jump point in ten seconds," Mister Riley warned.

"Execute insertion jump on schedule," Nathan ordered.

"Aye, sir," Mister Riley replied. "Jumping in three..."

———

"Launching second wave," Commander Jento reported from the Kent's tactical station. "Six missiles away."

"Execute your next turn, Lieutenant," Captain Poc ordered.

"Changing course toward third launch point," the helmsman replied.

"Reloading missiles," Commander Jento said. "Ready to launch again in one minute."

Captain Poc glanced at the mission clock again. In ten seconds, their first and second wave of missiles would jump to their targets, likely destroying all six Jung frigates. However, their next group of targets, the cruisers orbiting the system's only gas giant, were too far away from the frigates or the Kent to be aware of what was happening. But that would only last three and a half more minutes. In thirty seconds, the jump KKVs launched by the Aurora and the Celestia would strike the battle platform and the battleship, destroying them both. The Kent's job was to attack the frigates and the cruisers, destroying as many as possible in the first few minutes of battle. After that, she was to stand off at a safe distance and await further orders, while the Jar-Benakh and the Cobra gunships finished off anything that managed to survive.

"On course and speed to third launch point," Lieutenant Serra announced from the helm.

"Missiles are jumping," the sensor officer reported.

"Jump point in ten seconds," the navigator added.

"Reload complete," Commander Jento reported from the tactical station. "Eight missiles ready to launch."

Everything was running like clockwork. Their first two rounds of missiles were already slamming into their targets on the other side of the Kappa Ceti system. In a few seconds, they would jump to their third launch point and unleash eight more jump missiles on the still unsuspecting Jung cruisers. Meanwhile, the Aurora and the Celestia would jump into orbit on opposite sides of Terravine and begin their orbital attacks.

"Execute your jump," Captain Poc instructed calmly.

"Jumping in three..."

"Jump complete," Mister Riley reported from the Aurora's navigation console. "We're in high orbit over Terravine."

"Green deck," Nathan ordered.

"Green deck, aye," Naralena replied, as she passed the order on to the Aurora's flight operations center.

"Multiple contacts at Terravine's first gravity point." Mister Navashee reported. "Jump flashes as well...twelve of them. Multiple impacts." Mister Navashee shook his head. "They didn't stand a chance. All six frigates are destroyed, sir."

"I guess the jump missiles worked," Nathan commented.

"Coming up on first three surface targets," Jessica announced from the tactical station.

"Flight ops is reporting the Super Falcons have destroyed all STO sites and are moving to patrol orbits for escape intercepts," Naralena reported.

"I've got locks on the first two targets," Jessica announced.

"Fire at will," Nathan ordered.

"Firing ventral quads."

"More jump flashes," Mister Navashee reported. "Cobra gunships."

"Incoming message from Cobra One," Naralena said. "Captain Nash is asking for new orders, since there's nothing left of the frigates for them to clean up."

"Have them split up," Nathan said. "Four to the area of the battle platform, and four to the area of the battleship. Verify their destruction and make sure no shuttles get away."

"Aye, sir."

"First two targets destroyed," Jessica reported. "Targeting third site."

"Flight ops reports all fighters and CNS shuttles are away," Naralena said.

"Prepare to jump ahead to the next group of surface targets, Mister Riley," Nathan instructed.

"Aye, sir."

"Jump flashes in the atmosphere," Mister Navashee reported. "Combat and troop jumpers."

"Incoming message from the Jar-Benakh,"

Naralena added. "Two of the four cruisers have been destroyed by the Kent's missiles. The other two are damaged. They are finishing them off now."

Jessica shook her head. "This is getting too easy. I almost feel guilty."

Nathan turned slowly in his chair, coming around to look at her with one eyebrow raised.

"I said, *almost*," she reminded him.

* * *

Captain Dubnyk stood in the middle of his vegetable garden, admiring the various plants around him. It was a healthy garden, and it provided more than half of the daily sustenance for himself, Fayla, and the six young men who had come to him for shelter when their families had turned their backs on them for whatever reason. He had never understood the Tannan tendency to shun family members who had brought shame upon them. To Alan Dubnyk, family was everything. It was also the one thing, in all his thousand years of existence, he had never obtained. He had always meant to, but like most young men on Earth back in the day, he yearned for excitement and adventure. Family was something that came later. So he had pursued his career, and he had found his excitement and adventure. But by the time he had gotten his fill, it was too late. All that he had seen and experienced had left him jaded and bitter. He had tried more than once to retire, but it had never stuck. There was always another adventure to be had. So he had returned to work, eventually finding his way to the ill-fated mission to BD+25 3252.

Things were different now. Fate had given him another chance. He had his family, or at least something akin to it. They may not be his biological children, but they depended on his guidance, nonetheless. They needed one another, trusted one another. In his mind, that *made* them family.

"How long have you been standing out here?" Fayla asked as she stepped out of the kitchen door.

"An hour, perhaps," he replied.

"That long?"

"The sun feels good on my face," he said, looking up at the Tannan sky. He looked back down at the garden. "And this garden, with all its healthy plants...it makes me feel alive."

"You should sit, you must be tired," Fayla insisted. "I will get you some tea."

"I am fine."

"Do as I say, and sit in the gazebo. The midday sun is bad for you." She turned back to the house, only to find Brill coming out to join them. "Brill!" she exclaimed with joy. She ran the few steps to Brill and threw her arms around him to welcome him home. "When did you return?"

"Less than an hour ago," he replied. "I haven't even been home yet."

"It is good to see you again," she told him. "I am getting the captain some tea. Please, make him get out of the sun, while I get tea for you both."

Brill nodded in agreement as Fayla went inside, then walked over to Captain Dubnyk in the middle of the garden.

"I was beginning to worry about you," Captain Dubnyk said. "It has been nearly forty days since you left for Earth."

"I apologize," Brill replied. "It took some time for them to provide transport back to Tanna."

"Yes, of course. I suppose that is to be expected."

The captain turned and began to walk slowly toward the gazebo at the far end of the yard.

"You look remarkably well," Brill said, noticing not only the steadiness of his mentor's stride, but also the improved color and tone of his skin. "The treatments must be working."

"To a point, yes," the captain agreed. "But they will not fix the problem. They are only a crutch, a delaying of the inevitable, I'm afraid."

"Do not speak in such ways," Brill insisted. "Our plans will succeed." He followed the captain up into the gazebo, sitting down across the table from him. "I have good news," he said, barely able to contain his excitement. "I was accepted into their advanced training. I learned everything I could, so much more than I would have if I had stayed in basic."

"That *is* good news," Captain Dubnyk insisted.

"I learned about all sorts of weapons, combat techniques, tactics, entries... I even learned the basics of flight. I spent considerable time studying *that* part of my training."

"That is very good, Brill. Then you must teach the others. You must teach them everything you learned."

"I will," Brill promised.

"But not today, I think. Go home to your family, spend some time with them. A few days, perhaps."

"But they will be ashamed of me."

"Tell them you were given a three-day pass, and permission to visit your family before beginning your service. Tell them it was a reward for doing so well in your training."

"But I do not wear the uniform. They will become suspicious."

"No matter. In three days' time, bid them farewell

and return to me. Tell no one of your deception, not even your brother." Captain Dubnyk looked the young man in the eyes. "Do you understand?"

"Yes, sir. I understand. I will return in three days."

Captain Dubnyk leaned back in his chair and sighed. "You have made me very proud, Mister Daymon. More importantly, you have given me hope."

Brill smiled, a feeling of genuine prided washing over him.

"Now, go," the captain insisted. "We will see each other soon enough."

Brill rose from his seat, nodding respectfully before he turned and left.

Captain Dubnyk watched his most loyal student as he made his way through the garden and disappeared into the kitchen. He looked up at the sky above the house and closed his eyes, taking in a deep breath and letting it out in a long sigh.

Fate had indeed given him yet another chance.

* * *

"We believe our next targets should be the Zeta Doradus and the Zeta Reticuli systems," Admiral Dumar announced to his officers gathered in the mission briefing room deep inside the Karuzara asteroid base.

"Those are both nearly forty light years away," Nathan commented. "I thought the idea was to expand the Jung-free zone around Sol?"

"The further away from Sol we get, the greater the number of potential targets," Gerard explained. "Also, by this time, we have to assume that any Jung-held system that we have not yet attacked has been warned of our liberation efforts. The element of surprise *may* be gone."

"And the risk will be higher," Admiral Dumar added. "Therefore, we must choose to attack where it will do the most good."

"Why Zeta Doradus?" Cameron asked.

"During my time on Kohara, I learned that much of the equipment, supplies, and personnel used by the Jung came to Kohara by way of 82 Eridani. After Captain Poc discovered the additional flow of Jung forces through that system, we began to watch it more closely. Prior to the liberation of 82 Eridani, our recon efforts revealed that Jung shipping traffic was coming to that system primarily from Zeta Doradus *and* Zeta Reticuli."

"You think the supplies are coming *from* those worlds?" Nathan wondered.

"We do not know," Gerard admitted. "We *have* seen cargo ships, as well as military vessels passing through both systems from places unknown. Places outside of the Sol sector."

"How far outside?" Jessica asked.

"Again, we do not know. We have not had the recon resources available to commit to missions beyond fifty light years from Sol, as we had been forced to keep an eye on all Jung ships within the danger zone of thirty light years."

"Now that we've cleared that zone, can we start looking further out?" Nathan asked.

"Again, we run into the problem of the number of systems that must be investigated," Admiral Dumar reminded them. "However, we are in the process of refitting Scout One for long-range recon missions. We think it's only prudent that we start by following known shipping routes and see where that leads us.

Scout One, or 'Recon One', as it will be called, will be able to conduct long-range scans, thus enabling her to detect Jung ships within a system without having to penetrate that system. With luck, it may lead us to higher value targets."

The door to the mission briefing room opened, and an officer entered. He walked up to Admiral Dumar and handed him a data pad.

The admiral looked at the data pad as the officer departed. A disappointed look came over his face as he read. Finally, he set the data pad down and sighed.

Nathan looked at Jessica sitting next to him, as he noticed the expression on the admiral's face.

"I've just received word from President Scott. In response to Admiral Galiardi's petition, the Coalition Congress has called for a meeting of all Alliance member worlds, in order to decide how best to proceed. In the meantime, we have been ordered to stand down and discontinue all offensive operations. We are authorized to take whatever steps are necessary to protect the member worlds of the Alliance, and to conduct reconnaissance, but nothing more. We are not to fire on any Jung ship unless fired upon."

The room fell quiet.

"Return to your ships," Admiral Dumar instructed. "I will keep you updated as the situation changes. Meanwhile, I expect you all to maintain a constant state of readiness."

"That's it?" Jessica asked.

"Jess," Nathan scolded.

"I mean, we're not going to patrol or anything?" she added. "Don't we need to let the Jung know that we're keeping an eye on them, or something?"

"I will speak to President Scott directly," Admiral Dumar assured her. "Until then, you all have your orders. Dismissed."

Everyone in the room stood as the admiral departed.

Nathan turned to Cameron. "Well, it's not like we didn't see this coming."

"That doesn't make it suck any less," Jessica grumbled as she turned to follow the others out.

* * *

General Bacca opened his eyes, slowly at first. His eyelids felt heavy, and his body felt weak and listless. The room was dimly lit, making it easier on his eyes. He could see a man hovering over him. The man was speaking.

"General Bacca?" the man said to him. "Are you awake, sir?"

"How long?" the general asked. His voice was harsh, his mouth dry.

"Two hundred and forty-five days, sir," the man replied.

General Bacca recognized the man. He was the shuttle's communications officer. The general reached his hand out. "Help me up."

The communications officer took the general's hand and helped him sit up, repositioning the general's legs to hang over the side of the open stasis bed. He handed the general a bottle of water, giving him a moment to regain his senses before speaking further.

"Two hundred..." the general began, unsure of himself.

"And forty-five, yes."

"Are we still..."

"Yes," another voice said.

General Bacca looked at the other man. It was his pilot.

"We are still in position just over a light year outside of the Sol system," the pilot confirmed.

"Why have you awakened me?" the general wondered.

"We received a message from a passing comm-drone," the communications officer explained.

"It triggered our stasis pods to wake us," the pilot added.

"A message for us?" the general asked, seeming surprised.

"Indirectly, yes," the communications officer explained. "The drone was on its way to Earth, with a message from the Jung homeworld."

"A message? What kind of message?"

"They wish to discuss a cease-fire."

"Absurd," the general responded.

"That is the message they are sending to the leaders of Earth," the communications officer explained. "However, there was another message. One intended for any Jung officers possessing regional command authority."

"And what did it say?"

"The message contains orders," the communications officer explained. "Orders for the nearest RCA officer to head for Earth to negotiate on behalf of the Jung."

General Bacca's brow furrowed, his mind racing. "The communications drone?"

"It is still in sub-light," the communications officer replied, "awaiting our response."

"Recall the drone and store it in our cargo bay," the general ordered.

"Yes, sir," the communications officer replied, turning to exit.

"Captain," the general continued, "how long to reach Earth?"

"At maximum FTL, about twenty-one days," the pilot replied.

"Set course for Earth, maximum FTL," the general ordered.

"Yes, sir."

"Have we been collecting signals intelligence all this time?" the general asked.

"Of course," the pilot confirmed.

"Good, I wish to review all of it, as soon as I get cleaned up and get some food and water into me."

"Are you sure you don't wish to remain in stasis until we get closer?"

"Not a chance," the general insisted. "I want to know everything that has happened while we've been in stasis, and I've got two hundred and forty-five days' worth of signals intelligence from which to learn exactly that."

CHAPTER TEN

Jessica leaned back in her chair and sighed in frustration. Her head fell back against the headrest, her eyes closed. "We've been at this for weeks, and we're still no closer to finding the Jung homeworld than we were when we started."

"I wouldn't say that," Gerard disagreed. He continued staring at the view screens above the three-dimensional map hovering over the planning table in the Aurora's intelligence office. When he realized that Jessica had not responded, he turned to look at her. She was staring back at him, a look of disapproval on her face. "Okay, maybe you're right." He finally conceded.

"I think we need more data," Jessica suggested.

"Are you kidding? We've got tons of data."

"What you need is a programmer," Vladimir said.

"Jesus," Jessica exclaimed with a start. "Where the hell did you come from?"

"Why is it so dark in here?" Vladimir wondered, moving from the doorway deeper into the room.

"We thought it might help us focus on the map and the data," Gerard explained, gesturing to the view screens.

"What are you doing here?" Jessica asked.

"Nathan told me you needed a programmer," Vladimir replied.

"And he sent *you*?"

"Thanks."

"Jesus, I made that request hours ago," she complained.

"Sorry," Vladimir said, "but I do have a day job, you know."

"You're telling me you're the only programmer on this ship?"

"The only one available right now. What is all this?" Vladimir asked, pointing at the same view screens.

"Arrivals and departures from about thirty different systems within the Sol sector," Gerard explained.

"What are all the little lines?" Vladimir asked.

"Projected course on arrival, based on course after coming out of FTL," Gerard explained.

"Fat lot of good it does us," Jessica muttered.

"We're trying to figure out the location of the Jung homeworld by studying shipping patterns. The problem is that the Jung rarely go directly to a system. Usually, they fly a course that skirts the destination system, then turn toward the system just prior to arrival."

Vladimir looked confused.

"They do it to mask their point of origin," Jessica added.

Vladimir nodded. *"Da, konyeshna."* He studied the three-dimensional map for a moment. "Is that the only data you have?"

"It was," Gerard said. "We recently managed to get shipping manifests from some of the systems we liberated. We thought if some of the ships were carrying the same equipment or supplies, and that stuff came from the same place..."

"Then it might reveal the point of origin," Vladimir surmised. "Very clever. Of course, the number of combinations will be astronomical. You will need some sort of algorithm to do the work; otherwise, it will take you years."

"Hence, the request for a programmer," Jessica said. "So can you do it?"

Vladimir shrugged. "No problem."

"Really?" Jessica sat up, suddenly interested. "How long will it take you?"

"Not long." Vladimir pointed to a computer terminal on the side of the room. "I can use this terminal?"

"Sure," Gerard said.

"How long is not long?" Jessica asked again.

"I will need more light."

"How long?" Jessica pressed, growing more irritated, as Gerard turned the lights back up.

"Is this data already in the computer?" Vladimir asked.

"Yes." Jessica replied irately. "How long?"

"A few minutes."

"Are you serious?" Jessica yelled, her patience almost gone.

"Do you want to yell at me, or do you want me to write the algorithm?" Vladimir asked calmly.

"Please, do your stuff," Gerard told him, gesturing at Jessica to back off.

Vladimir turned back to the computer terminal and started typing furiously. He mumbled to himself in Russian as he typed, making several different sounds of approval as he worked. "There are over seven hundred billion possible combinations, based on item, arrival point, and potential departure point. However, if you look at some of the items on these manifests, you will notice that they require not only certain materials, but certain conditions required by the manufacturing process."

"What kind of conditions?" Gerard wondered.

"Microgravity, extreme temperatures, extreme temperature swings..."

"All of which can be created anywhere," Jessica pointed out.

"True," Vladimir agreed, "but only with great effort. Why not go where the conditions already exist?"

"And knowing that helps?" Gerard asked.

"Possibly," Vladimir said as he continued to type. "You see," he said, pointing at the screen, "we have already cut the number of combinations by half."

"Great," Jessica retorted, "only three hundred and fifty billion combinations to choose from."

"What about the course changes?" Gerard wondered.

"We can reasonably assume that the Jung would not double back on their course, as that would require considerable propellant," Vladimir explained. "Of course, they could perform a gravity-assist maneuver, but that adds time to what is likely an already long voyage. So, if we limit the course change to forty-five degrees, we can reduce the number of combinations to less than one billion."

"We managed to get some of the propellant requests as well," Gerard realized, sitting down at the terminal next to Vladimir to search for the data.

"Do we know the amount of propellant and the thrust performance parameters of those vessels?" Vladimir asked.

"A few," Gerard said. "Uh, five of them."

"It is better than nothing," Vladimir said, reading the data off Gerard's terminal as he continued typing. "Ah, see? Those ships could not have made

367

it from their most likely points of origin with any more than a twenty-degree turn."

"Is this actually going to work?" Jessica demanded.

"Maybe yes, maybe no," Vladimir admitted. "There are still so many variables to consider. For example, when did the ships turn? If you turn sooner rather than later, your course correction will be less..."

"But an earlier turn would not be as effective at hiding your point of origin," Gerard surmised.

"Correct," Vladimir replied. "So that helps us a bit in our assumptions, as a ship captain would want to make it appear that they were coming from a different world. A secondary course track that was achieved by an early turn would severely limit the number of worlds that the ship *could* have come from."

"God, I'm dying over here," Jessica complained.

Vladimir turned to look at her.

"What?" she snapped.

"It is done," Vladimir said.

Jessica looked at the three-dimensional display, seeing nothing different. She looked back at Vladimir. "Well?"

"Turn down the lights," Vladimir said. He waited for the room to darken again, and then pressed a single key.

The three of them watched as lines started appearing and disappearing at random all over the three-dimensional map.

"What the hell is it doing?" Jessica wondered.

"Calculating," Vladimir said. A line appeared and stayed. It led from Tau Ceti to a point off the bottom of the map. "There," Vladimir exclaimed. Another line appeared. "Another."

Jessica slowly rose from her seat, entranced by the shifting lines as they rapidly appeared and disappeared. Gerard also moved closer to the display, unable to look away as more lines began to materialize. Vladimir just sat in his chair, arms crossed, smiling.

"There's another," Gerard exclaimed. "That's six of them so far."

"They're all going off the map," Jessica noted.

"We figured the Jung homeworld was not in the Sol sector, right?" Gerard said.

"I thought that was just an excuse, to be honest," Jessica admitted. Another line appeared. "That's seven."

"Eight!"

"How long will this take?" Jessica asked Vladimir.

Vladimir looked at the computer terminal. "Fifteen minutes, I think. But I believe you already have your answer," he said, pointing at the map.

Jessica reached up with both hands, placing them against the edges of the hovering three-dimensional map display, then simultaneously slid her hands upward. The map followed her movements, revealing more of the stars below. She repeated the gesture two more times, until she could see the point where the lines, of which there were now eleven of them, converged. She put both hands together at the point of convergence, and then spread them apart, causing the map to zoom in on the convergence point. "CP-60 424?"

"In the constellation Dorado," Vladimir added. "Also known as GI 204.1..."

"I don't care what names it goes by," Jessica interrupted. "How far is it?"

"Sixty-three point eight light years from Sol," Vladimir replied.

"So that's it?" Jessica asked, pointing at the star on the three-dimensional map. "That's the Jung homeworld?"

Vladimir glanced at his screen. "Currently a probability of eighty-seven percent." Another line appeared on the map. "Make that eighty-nine percent, and climbing."

"Oh, my God, Vlad, I could kiss you!" Jessica exclaimed, throwing up her arms in glee.

"Feel free," he replied.

* * *

Jessica and Gerard sat patiently in Admiral Dumar's office in the Karuzara asteroid base, while he studied their findings.

"How did you figure this out, again?" the admiral asked.

"We compared similar items on shipping manifests that we received from worlds the Alliance has liberated," Gerard explained. "Then we analyzed the items based on where they might be manufactured..."

"Don't forget about the propellant levels, and the turns..." Jessica interrupted.

Admiral Dumar looked confused.

"Once we put it through a computer algorithm, it started spitting out course projections," Gerard continued. "Then it was just a matter of looking for the one point of origin that was most common among all places."

"So, why did it take you three weeks?" Admiral Dumar wondered.

"We only recently got the shipping manifests," Jessica told him. "We had been trying to analyze the arrival courses when the Jung came out of FTL, but they always make a turn before they..."

"I get it," the admiral said, cutting her off. He took in a breath, letting it out in a sigh. "How sure are you of your analysis?"

"The algorithm says ninety-seven point four percent," Gerard replied.

"And Lieutenant Commander Kamenetskiy created the computer algorithm?"

"Yeah, that made me a little doubtful as well," Jessica admitted.

The admiral glanced at Jessica again, as he continued analyzing the data on the pad. Finally, he put the data pad down on his desk. "Obviously, we have to confirm this, and that involves no small amount of risk." Admiral Dumar looked at Nathan, who was sitting in the corner of the office. "You've been suspiciously quiet through all of this, Captain. Do you doubt their conclusions?"

"Not at all," Nathan answered. "Their conclusions make sense, and I trust Lieutenant Commander Kamenetskiy's computer expertise."

"Then the question is, *how* do we confirm this?" the admiral asked. "If indeed it *is* the Jung homeworld, there will be a lot of traffic in the area. Most likely there will also be a sensor net of some sort. So, we can't exactly send a Super Falcon on a cold-coast. It would be suicide."

"Could we send a sensor drone?"

"Yes, but it would probably be intercepted and destroyed," the admiral said. "Also, we'd prefer that the Jung do *not* know that they've been reconnoitered. If they find out that we know the location of their homeworld, they'll be on constant alert."

371

"Then, you're thinking of attacking the Jung homeworld?" Nathan wondered, surprised.

"I'm thinking I'd like to keep that option open, if possible," the admiral explained, "and alerting them to the fact that we have discovered them would pretty much kill that idea."

"Could we send the Jar-Benakh?" Gerard suggested. "We fooled them once. Maybe it would work again?"

"You fooled a bunch of soldiers on the surface, who had limited sensor capabilities, and their only other option was to stay on the surface and face annihilation," the admiral clarified. "Besides, we can't risk such an important asset."

"What about using one of their fast-attack shuttles?" Nathan suggested. "They have FTL capabilities."

"The Jung homeworld is sixty-four light years away," Jessica reminded him.

"We could shuttle them closer, then they could FTL it into the Jung system," Nathan explained.

"Even if it's one of their own shuttles, they're going to be suspicious," Admiral Dumar insisted.

"They'll probably recognize what ship the shuttle belongs to by its transponder code," Gerard said.

"They'd only need a few minutes near the Jung world," Nathan said. "Just get some quick sensor sweeps, then FTL it out again. We can pick them up on the far side."

Admiral Dumar thought for a moment. "The less time they spend in the system, the better their chances."

"If they can keep it under a few minutes, they might go unnoticed," Nathan continued.

372

"Or the Jung might think it's an error, or a sensor echo of some sort," Gerard added.

"If we added a bunch of fixed array sensors, they could look in all directions at once, instead of making sweeps," Nathan said. "That would get them out quicker."

Admiral Dumar was intrigued, but unconvinced. "We can't send the Aurora, or any other warship, though. First, it would take a day and a half just to get there. Second, I can't afford to have an asset that far away from Alliance space, and that deep into enemy territory. It's just too risky."

"Use a boxcar," Nathan suggested.

Admiral Dumar looked at Nathan and nodded with approval, considering the plan. "But who would we get to fly such a mission. It's still incredibly risky, so it will have to be flown by volunteers."

"Someone crazy," Jessica muttered.

"I can think of a couple of pilots crazy enough to do it," Nathan said with a wry smile.

"I'd like to go as well, Admiral," Gerard said. "I speak fluent Jung, and I know their communications procedures and syntax. If they get into trouble, I may be able to buy them some time to get out alive."

"It will take a few days to equip the shuttle with the additional sensors," Admiral Dumar said. "I'll get that started right away. In the meantime, Captain, why don't you see how your two pilots feel about the idea."

* * *

"You want us to do what?" Loki asked in disbelief.

"Count me in," Josh said without hesitation.

"Hold on," Loki insisted. "He's talking about jumping into the middle of the Jung's home system."

Loki looked at Nathan. "That is what you're talking about, right?"

"It is," Nathan replied.

Loki leaned back on his bunk. "I knew we were in trouble when you showed up at our quarters," he said, shaking his head.

"I'm not ordering you," Nathan reminded him.

"I'm in," Josh repeated.

"Shut up, Josh!" Loki exclaimed. He looked at Nathan. "Why us?"

"You guys already know how to fly a Jung shuttle," Nathan said.

"I'm sure there are a few other Alliance pilots who have flown Jung shuttles by now," Loki protested.

"Come on, Lok," Josh begged.

"Shut up, Josh."

"Other pilots? Yes, but not ones whom we can trust to pull it off and come home with the recon data," Nathan explained.

"Oh, jeez," Loki moaned. "You had to go and say it that way, didn't you, sir."

Nathan looked Loki in the eyes, his voice dropping. "Look, Loki, nobody knows I'm here. Nobody knows I'm asking this of you. So nobody will know if you turn me down."

Loki looked at the ceiling, then back at the captain. "*I'll* know, sir."

"Come on, Loki," Josh begged again. "It'll be fun. We'll be heroes. Everyone will want to buy us a drink and hear how we pulled it off."

"That's assuming we make it back," Loki reminded him.

"Pffft!" Josh dismissed. "Piece of cake, easy as pie, a walk in the park."

Nathan looked at Josh, his brow furrowed in confusion.

"Don't ask," Loki told the captain.

* * *

Josh and Loki stared out the forward windows of the Jung fast-attack shuttle as the main cargo pod ramp slowly opened, revealing the dark void of space.

"Holy crap," Loki muttered. "I can't believe we're doing this."

"Neither can I," Gerard said, as he stood behind Loki, peering over his shoulder.

"Doesn't look any different than any other chunk of space," Josh commented, unimpressed, as he checked his flight systems display. "You ready to go?"

"No," Loki replied emphatically.

"All right, then," Josh said. "Rolling forward." Josh pushed the taxi control stick on the center console forward, causing the shuttle to roll toward the open end of the massive cargo pod. The shuttle continued out onto the ramp, and Josh moved his hand to the throttles. He pushed the lever on his control yoke upward with his left thumb. "Translating up."

The Jung fast-attack shuttle lifted gently off the cargo pod's loading ramp as it drifted away from the pod.

Josh fired the forward thrusters. "Thrusting forward."

"Nothing on sensors," Loki reported nervously. "Just a few chunks of ice and rock in the area."

"How's our course look?"

"Looks like it's clear all the way to our arrival point."

Josh glanced at the sensor display in the middle of the center console. "Are we clear yet?"

A blue-white flash of light from behind them cast a brief, eerie light into their cockpit.

Loki looked at Josh. "I guess they didn't want to hang around any longer than they had to."

"Firing the mains," Josh announced, pressing the burn button on the throttle. A dull rumble emanated from the back of the shuttle. "Throttling up to full power," Josh said as he pushed the throttle forward to the stops.

"We've got a good burn," Loki reported.

"How long until we go to FTL?" Josh asked.

"We burn for fifteen minutes," Loki replied. "Then we shut down and transition to FTL for two days."

"Two whole days coasting through the Jung home system," Josh commented in amazement. "Damn, we're a long way from Haven, aren't we, Lok?"

"You know something," Loki said, "I really miss Haven right about now."

Gerard patted Loki on the shoulder. "I'll be in the back," he said, as he turned aft. "Might as well collect as much signals intelligence as I can before we go to FTL."

* * *

Jessica walked down the corridors of the Cobra base on the asteroid orbiting Tanna, looking for her older brother's office. The place was full of technicians and Cobra crews going about their daily business. It reminded her of the inside of the Karuzara asteroid base, which wasn't too surprising since the Karuzara crews had excavated most of the facility.

"Excuse me," Jessica said, stopping a passing technician. "Captain Nash's office?"

"Around the corner to the right, sir," the young man directed, in an obvious Tannan accent.

"Thank you," she replied. She made her way to the corner and turned right as instructed, finding her brother's office a few more meters down the hall. She pressed the buzzer.

"*Enter!*" Robert's voice called from inside.

Jessica pushed the door open and found her brother sitting behind his desk, studying a data pad.

"Jess!" Robert said in surprise. "What are you doing here?" he asked, rising from his seat to greet her.

"The Aurora is picking up a load of propellant to bring back to the Karuzara," she explained. "They carved out some more storage caverns and wanted to stock up while things are quiet." She hugged him after he came out from behind his desk. "So, I thought I'd drop by and say hi."

"It's great to see you," he said. "How long are you going to be here?"

"Takes a while to transfer all that propellant. I was told five or six hours, minimum. I thought I'd go down to the surface and see Synda while I was here as well."

"Well, it is great to see you," Robert repeated, moving back to his seat. "Please, sit. How is everyone back home?"

"They're good," Jessica said, taking a chair opposite his desk. "Everyone's working at the base. Mom is watching all the grandkids during the day, and cooking up a storm at night, like usual."

"I can't wait to get back home and see them," Robert said wistfully as he sat down.

"Well, that's part of the reason I'm here," Jessica

said, alluding to an ulterior motive for her visit hesitantly.

Robert looked suspicious. "What's up?"

"You're being reassigned," she told him.

Robert's suspicion turned to shock.

"You don't look happy," she said, noticing his change in expression. "By the way you reacted when you first got handed *this* assignment, I figured you'd be overjoyed to get a new assignment."

"Uh... I guess you just caught me by surprise."

"Are you sure that's all?"

"I don't know. I guess I've grown to like this assignment. Things have been going pretty well here. The Tannans are great people. A little set in their traditions, but... It's been a really good experience overall, I guess."

"And from what I've seen, you've done a hell of a job getting the Tannans trained. They've racked up more than two dozen kills without a single ship lost."

"Yeah, like I said, they're a great bunch of guys to lead." Robert sighed. "To be honest, I'm going to miss them."

"Well, pack your bags, Bobert," she said, handing him a data chip. "You've got new orders."

"How much time do I have?"

"A shuttle will be here in three days to take you to your new command," she told him, smiling.

"Command?"

"Yup. Dumar is giving you a frigate."

"No shit?" Robert laughed.

"No shit."

* * *

"If it makes you feel any better, we've already collected a ton of really good intel," Gerard told Loki.

"The ship movements and patrol patterns within the system alone are worth the risk."

"I'd feel a whole lot safer if we had a jump drive installed in this thing," Loki said.

"This thing is as fast as any ship they've got," Josh chimed in from the other side of the makeshift crew cabin. "So as long as we go to FTL before they shoot us, we're golden, right?"

Loki looked at Gerard, who said nothing. "Right?"

"Well...yes and no," Gerard admitted. "Yes, any ship they might send after us would likely not be able to catch us. No, as in they might have FTL intercept weapons...something that goes *faster* than their ships...like their comm-drones."

Loki looked concerned. "Wait, we've never *seen* any such weapons, so why would you think they would have something like that?"

"Makes sense to save something like that for defense of your most valuable asset. Better not to advertise such capabilities, lest your enemy knows what to expect."

"And why didn't you bring this up earlier?" Loki asked accusingly.

"Honestly, I didn't think about it until just now," Gerard admitted.

"Relax, Loki," Josh said, getting up from his bunk. "We're already deep inside their system. If they haven't spotted us yet, they probably aren't going to."

"Until we come out of FTL, you mean," Loki reminded him.

"Actually, I'm pretty sure they've spotted us by now," Gerard said.

Both Josh and Loki looked at Gerard in surprise.

"Come on, guys. Surely you assumed they have

some sort of passive FTL detection network? Sensors scattered throughout the outer edges of the system? Maybe linked to mini-FTL comm-drones to alert command of incoming threats?"

"Uh...then why haven't they attacked us?" Josh wondered.

"We're in one of *their* shuttles," Gerard reminded them.

"Squawking a transponder code from a battleship that *should* be in the Tau Ceti system," Loki exclaimed, "fifty-eight light years away!"

"Relax, I sabotaged the transponder," Gerard said. "It only transmits an ID code at random, and at varying strengths and frequencies. Even then, only at random. To the Jung, it will look like the transponder is malfunctioning. Besides, we're a single shuttle. We're no threat. If they have detected us, I'm sure they'll hail us after we come out of FTL."

"And then what?" Loki wondered.

"I lie to them."

"Solid plan, there, Gerard," Josh commented, his tone dripping with sarcasm. "It's almost time, Lok," he added, heading forward.

"Is that seriously your plan?" Loki asked Gerard.

"Pretty much."

"So, we come out of FTL, they ask us who we are and what we are doing. You lie, while we collect sensor data, then we go back into FTL, and hope they don't chase us and blow us all to hell. That's your plan?"

"Did you guys seriously *not* think about any of this *before* you volunteered for this mission?" Gerard asked.

Loki sighed. "Yeah, that's how we usually make decisions." Loki rose and headed forward to join

Josh, moving through the hatch into the shuttle's cockpit.

"We've got about a minute before we drop out of FTL," Josh warned as Loki took his seat.

"And we become visible to every ship in the system," Josh said as he donned his comm-set. "How many of them did you say you had already detected?" he called back to Gerard over his comm-set.

"*Eighty or ninety...so far,*" Gerard replied.

"Great."

"Thirty seconds," Josh warned.

"I can see that, Josh," Loki replied.

"Just let us know if we need to do anything while we're at sub-light," Josh reminded Gerard. "Like, go back to FTL."

"My finger will be on the button and ready, that's for sure," Loki added.

"*Understood,*" Gerard replied.

"Five seconds to dropout," Loki announced.

"Please, Loki..." Josh said.

"Three..."

"Enough with the countdowns."

"Two......one..."

The shuttle's mass-canceling fields shut down, and the ship reverted to its normal sub-light speed.

"FTL fields have shut down," Loki reported. "We're now traveling at twenty percent light."

"*Passive sensors are online,*" Gerard announced from the cabin over their comm-sets. "*Whoa. I'm getting tons of detail about their homeworld. Holy crap! Look at that moon! It's got some sort of man-made ring encircling it.*"

"Encircling the moon?" Loki wondered, finding it hard to believe.

"*The whole damn thing,*" Gerard affirmed. "*It's*

some sort of space port, or shipyard... I don't know what it is, but it's huge. How are we looking up there?"

"I've got at least fifty ships on the traffic display," Loki replied. "So far, nothing is turning toward us."

"*Jesus,*" Gerard continued to exclaim. "*Their world is very heavily populated. I'm seeing very little open space. About forty-percent of the surface is covered with water, most of it deep oceans. But their continents are literally covered with cities. There's got to be at least a hundred billion people on that world.*"

"Ships, Gerard," Loki reminded. "All we care about are ships."

"*Wait, we're being hailed,*" Gerard warned.

Loki suddenly felt his mouth go dry.

Gerard said something in Jung over the comms, which neither Josh nor Loki could understand. There was a pause, then Gerard spoke in Jung again, this time saying a lot more than before.

"What the hell's going on?" Josh asked.

"*They asked who we are, and why our transponder wasn't working properly,*" Gerard explained.

"What did you tell them?" Loki wondered, his finger hovering over the button to engage the FTL fields.

Gerard again spoke in Jung over the comms. The exchange lasted more than a minute, with several pauses as he listened to the incoming messages. Gerard's voice began to sound tense, his tone becoming more adamant, as if he were arguing with someone.

Josh and Loki stared at each other, too afraid to speak. Loki looked at the time display on the center console. "We've been out of FTL for one minute, now," he warned. "Talk to me, Gerard."

"*Stand by!*" Gerard said quickly, immediately returning to his conversation in Jung over the comms.

"Fuck," Josh swore. Even his nerves were starting to frazzle.

Loki kept his eyes on the traffic display, watching for any sign that one of the many ships on the screen was turning to intercept them.

"*Okay!*" Gerard exclaimed. "*Go to FTL!*"

Loki quickly scanned his display, checking that they had a clear line out of the system before pressing the button to activate the mass-canceling fields. A few seconds later, the shuttle slipped back into FTL, but Loki kept his eyes on the traffic display, just in case.

"What the hell just happened?" Josh demanded.

Gerard came through the hatch, coming to stand behind Loki. "I told them we were on a scientific survey mission of the Oort cloud, comparing the composition of objects from varying locations. When they asked about our transponder, I told them we were having problems with our comm-stack. I even started messing with the voice transmission to make it garbled."

"What the hell was all that arguing?" Loki wondered.

"They wanted us to return to port for repairs, but I told them that if we didn't finish the survey now, all of our results would be skewed and we would have to start over. I told him that we couldn't afford that type of financial setback. He wasn't buying it at first, so I made up a bunch of stuff about how I wouldn't graduate, and my family would disown me... Blah, blah, blah. I promised we would return in four days, after the last leg was completed."

"And he bought all that crap?" Josh asked, amazed.

"I don't know. That's when I had you go to FTL." Gerard said. "I guess we'll find out soon enough."

Loki shook his head. "Next time the captain offers us a mission, Josh, just shut the hell up, will you?"

* * *

Jessica's mouth dropped when the door opened. Standing before her was Synda, baby in hand. "Oh, my God!"

"Jessica!" Synda greeted. She switched to a more hushed tone, suddenly remembering she had a baby in her arms. "It's about time."

"I'm sorry I couldn't get away for the birth," Jessica apologized. "Work."

"That's okay," Synda assured her, stepping aside to let her in. "We are a bit out of your way, and all."

"Naw, only forty-seven light years," Jessica joked. "I thought you were having twins?" she said as she closed the heavy wooden door behind her.

"Esma is sleeping," Synda said. "This, is Ania."

"Well, hello there, Ania," Jessica said, greeting the child in hushed, cooing tones.

"This is your auntie Jessica," Synda told her child. "You want to hold her?"

Jessica was suddenly nervous. "Uh... I don't know."

"Come on," Synda teased. "What are you afraid of? You're spec-ops."

"They did *not* teach baby-holding in spec-ops," Jessica said. She stared at the infant in her mother's arms. "Oh, what the hell. She is adorable, after all."

"Yes, she is," Synda said, carefully handing the

child to Jessica. Ania began to cry as her mother transferred her to Jessica's arms. "That's right, support her head with your hand, just like that," Synda instructed.

Jessica cradled the infant carefully, pulling her in close to her body, being very careful not to squeeze her too hard.

"You see, it just comes naturally to you," Synda said encouragingly.

"I don't know about that," Jessica replied. She gently bounced the infant up and down. "It's okay, Ania. I'm your mommy's friend, Jessica." After a few moments, the infant stopped crying.

"You see? She likes you," Synda said.

"Kid's got good taste," Jessica replied. She looked down at baby Ania, who was staring back up at her with big green eyes. "What pretty green eyes, you have," Jessica cooed. "Yes, you do." Jessica looked at Synda. "How long ago did you deliver?"

"Three weeks," Synda replied, taking a seat on the couch. "Right on the due date. The Tannans have this stuff down to a science. Apparently, everyone here delivers right on time."

Jessica could feel the trust in the infant's eyes as she looked up at her, the child's green eyes wide with curiosity at the stranger holding her. "She's amazing," Jessica whispered, as she took a seat on the couch next to Synda. "She's so quiet."

"And she's the noisy one," Synda commented.

"Are they identical?"

"Similar, but not identical. Esma's hair is a little darker, and her eyes are more gray than green. I think Esma's face is a little wider as well, but apparently no one else does. Would you like to see her?"

"Isn't she sleeping?"

"It's time to feed her anyway," Synda said as she rose. "I'll be right back."

"Uh..." Jessica's eyes widened as Synda left the room, leaving her alone with baby Ania in her arms. "Okay. I've got this, I suppose." She looked down at Ania. Her eyes were starting to close. Jessica hummed a lullaby. Ania closed her eyes, and drifted off to sleep in Jessica's arms. For the first time in her life, Jessica had an inkling of what the maternal instinct felt like.

A minute later, Synda returned carrying baby Esma. "This is Esma." Synda placed the baby down in her lap as she sat, uncovering her breast to feed the infant.

"You weren't kidding," Jessica said. "She is quiet."

"Very," Synda said as she started to breastfeed Esma. "To be honest, I think I got lucky with these two. I've heard stories from some of the Tannan mothers."

"I just can't believe you have *two* babies," Jessica exclaimed in disbelief. "One seems like it would be a lot of work...but two?"

"It's tiring, yes," Synda agreed, "but it isn't work. At least, it doesn't feel like it. Work is something that you don't want to do, but must do. This... This is love. You do it because you *want* to do it, because nothing is more important to you than being with your children, and taking care of them. It is simply *what* you do. *Who* you are. I don't know how else to describe it."

Jessica looked down at the sleeping infant in her arms. She was so peaceful and content, wrapped in her little blanket, safe in the arms of another. "I think I understand," Jessica admitted.

* * *

"This has been the longest four days of my life," Loki groaned as their shuttle came out of FTL.

"It's not over, yet," Josh warned. "Not until the fat lady sings."

"Would you stop with the old Earth idioms already?" Loki demanded. "What the hell does that mean, anyway? 'Until the fat lady sings?' Really?"

"It is getting kind of irritating, Josh," Gerard agreed, as he stared out the front windows of the shuttle.

"Where are they?" Loki wondered. "They're supposed to already be here, waiting for us."

"Anything on the sensors?" Josh asked.

"Nothing."

"Shut down everything," Gerard instructed. "Go completely cold. A single passive sensor only."

"How are they going to find us?" Josh wondered.

"Just do as he says, Josh," Loki insisted, as he started shutting down systems.

"We'll see them when they jump in," Gerard explained.

"They were supposed to have *already* jumped in," Loki repeated.

"That's what's got me worried," Gerard said. "There's got to be a reason they're not here."

Loki turned and looked at Gerard. "You think there might be a Jung ship in the area?"

"It's possible."

"Unbelievable," Loki mumbled as he continued shutting down systems. "We fly all the way through the Jung system without a problem, only to get picked off on the far side on our way out."

An alert beep sounded.

Loki glanced at the sensor display on the center console. "We're picking up something."

"A jump flash?"

"Nope. No flash."

"Is it a Jung ship?"

"I don't know," Loki admitted. "Seems kind of small. I suppose it could be a patrol ship of some kind. It didn't come out of FTL, though. It just *appeared*, as if it came out of nowhere. Wait... It's gone again."

"Steer toward it," Gerard instructed.

Josh turned to look at him. "What?"

"It's got to be the boxcar."

"How do you know?"

"You said it wasn't big enough to be a Jung ship..."

"A Jung ship that we know of," Loki corrected.

"Anyone out here would *see* us come out of FTL."

"There it is again," Loki said as the sensor display beeped a second time. "Ten degrees to port, five down relative. About two kilometers. Damn, it's gone again."

"I'm telling you, it's the boxcar," Gerard insisted. "Steer toward it."

"And if it's not?" Josh wondered.

"If it was a Jung patrol ship, it would be hailing us, or firing on us," Gerard insisted. "It wouldn't be flashing in and out as if trying to hide."

"There it is again," Loki said. "It is on the same course as us, a little slower."

"You see? They've been out here waiting for us, running cold. They saw us come out of FTL on passive, so they're signaling us by turning something on and off."

Josh sighed. "Works for me," he said as he initiated a turn to port.

Loki continued watching the monitor as Josh adjusted the shuttle's course to intercept the unknown object. "There it is again. And it's gone. Wait... It's back...and gone. Back, gone..."

"Three flashes," Gerard realized. "They flashed us three times, after they saw us turn toward them."

"I don't like this," Loki said. "We're closing on them, and we can't see them."

"We're too far from any source of light."

"How far are we?" Josh asked.

"Based on the object's last position, course, and speed, about three hundred meters, and closing fast," Loki warned.

"Well, whatever it is, we'll know shortly."

"Wait until you're within one hundred meters, then turn on your forward floodlights," Gerard suggested.

"That's barely going to give us room to decelerate," Loki protested.

"I can do it," Josh insisted.

Loki took a deep breath and sighed, resigning himself to whatever fate had in store for them. "Two hundred meters."

Josh continued staring out the front windows, into the black void.

"One-fifty."

"I'm right, you'll see," Gerard assured them.

"One hundred," Loki announced. "Forward floods coming on."

"Firing deceleration thrusters," Josh said. He looked out the windows again, still seeing nothing but blackness. "I'm not seeing them."

"They're still too far out," Loki warned. "Fifty

meters. Oh, shit! I've got their directional approach beacon! Two degrees down, one more left! Twenty-five meters!"

"Eyes on!" Josh announced as their forward floodlights finally reached the massive boxcar ahead of them.

"Fifteen, still a little fast!" Loki warned. "Ten meters to threshold! Dropping our gear."

Josh's eyes were glued to the view ahead of them, as the gaping rectangular opening into the boxcar's cargo pod rushed toward them, and then passed overhead.

"Four green on the gear! Threshold!" Loki announced. "Translate down!"

Josh didn't answer, instead he pushed the translation switch on his flight control stick. A hissing sound came from above them, as their topside thrusters fired, pushing them down onto the cargo pod's deck.

"We're not going to stop in time!" Loki realized.

"Brace for impact!" Josh warned as he brought their deceleration thrusters up to full power, ignoring any damage they might cause to the interior of the cargo pod.

All three of them suddenly felt incredibly heavy.

"Their gravity has got us!" Loki exclaimed.

"Oh, shit!" Josh shouted as the back wall of the cargo pod rushed toward them.

The nose of the shuttle struck the back wall of the cargo pod. The nose crumpled and the window in front of Josh cracked, but did not shatter. All three of them felt themselves being thrown forward, but the sudden deceleration was not as intense as they had feared.

Alarms sounded, and they heard hissing.

Josh looked about frantically, slightly dazed by the impact. "We're venting atmosphere!" he exclaimed.

"Get in the back!" Loki yelled as he climbed out of his seat.

"I'm right behind you!" Josh climbed out of his seat and followed Gerard and Loki into the makeshift cabin, closing and locking the hatch to the cockpit behind him.

"Damn!" Josh said as he collapsed onto his bunk. He laughed. "Any landing you can walk away from, right?"

"We can't walk away from this one, Josh," Loki reminded him. "The cargo bay isn't pressurized, remember?"

"No problem," Josh insisted. "They'll jump us back to Earth and land at Porto Santo. That'll take what, an hour, tops? We've got plenty of air to last until then."

"He's right," Gerard said. "We made it, Loki." Gerard smiled.

Loki let his head fall back against the bulkhead. "Yup... The longest four days of my life."

* * *

Robert Nash stood in his office at the Cobra gunship base on the asteroid orbiting Tanna. He had spent the last six months training the Tannans to operate their new gunships, and he had enjoyed every moment of it. Soon, the office would belong to his executive officer, Lieutenant Commander Rano, as would the responsibility to both train and command the Cobra gunship wing.

Robert found it odd that he felt such an attachment to this office, since he had actually spent very little time in it. Most of his time had been split between the training facility at the Cobra production plant on the surface of Tanna, or in the cockpit of a gunship as he led his crews through countless training flights. Still, the office was a symbol of his command, and he had grown an unexpected pride for it.

A knock sounded at the open door. Robert looked up and saw Lieutenant Commander Rano. "Izzu."

"Robert. Are you all packed?"

"Just picking up the last of my things here." Robert noticed the new rank insignia on his friend's collar. "Well, now. I see it's *Commander* Rano now. Congratulations, my friend." Robert stepped out from behind his desk to shake the commander's hand. "You deserve it, Iz."

"Thank you," the commander replied. "And thank you for recommending me for promotion."

"Like I said, you deserve it," Robert said, patting his friend on the shoulder. Robert leaned back onto his desk. "So, you ready to take over?"

"I'm not sure. It is a big responsibility, you know."

"Believe me, I know," Robert assured him. "But you'll do fine. Of that I have zero doubt."

"Your faith in me is reassuring, Robert." Commander Rano sat down in the chair against the wall. "So, are you looking forward to your new command?"

"Yes, and no," Robert admitted. "I'm going to miss this place, and all you people. Tanna kind of grows on you, you know?"

"Is it not every officer's dream?" Izzu wondered, "to command a great ship?"

"It's only a frigate, Iz."

"Still, it is much bigger than a gunship, is it not?"

"Indeed it is."

"Well, I am certain that you will..."

Alarm klaxons sounded in the corridor, and the alert lamps turned from standard white to red.

"*Attention. Attention,*" a Tannan voice announced over the loudspeakers. "*General quarters. General quarters. All crews to your stations. Prepare to launch gunships. This is not a drill.*"

Robert tapped his comm-set. "Nash. Status?"

"*Sensor contact, on the edge of the system,*" the comm officer replied over Robert's comm-set. "*No identification yet, but there is no transponder signal being broadcast. Profiles suggest Jung scout ships. Two of them.*"

"How likely is it for a pair of Jung scout ships to show up by themselves?" Robert asked Commander Rano.

"Unlikely," the commander replied. "We are too far out on the fringe. This system was taken by the Jung to act as a refueling and resupply outpost before heading out of the sector. When traveling this far out, fleet commanders like to send scouts ahead *before* arriving, just to be safe. If they are Jung scout ships, it is likely bigger ships will follow."

"How many gunships do we have in port?" Robert asked.

"Sixteen, including ours," Commander Rano replied. "Five more are down for service, and the other eight are on patrol. Cobra Three Zero just rolled off the line yesterday, and is still on the surface."

Robert tapped his comm-set again. "Scramble eight gunships. Tell them to take the scouts by surprise and destroy with maximum force. No one escapes. Put the other eight on ready alert. Send mini-jump comm-drones to all ships on patrol, and vector them to hunt for more incoming ships. If

393

there are more of them coming, I want to know how many and when."

"*Right away, sir.*"

"And dispatch a jump comm-drone to Sol. Notify Alliance command of the situation, and tell them we'll update as the situation changes."

"*Yes, sir.*"

"Izzu, recall all crews from the surface, and bring up any of the trainees who have at least twenty hours in the sims, just in case. Tell your mechanics to get those five ships ready for action, pronto. And tell the production plant to get Cobra Three Zero into orbit as soon as possible. Captain Annatah and his crew are down there teaching basic flight right now. They can fly Cobra Three Zero up."

"Then you believe more ships are coming?"

"I hope not," Robert replied, "but if they are, we need to be ready. We can handle scouts. We can handle frigates. Hell, we can probably even handle a cruiser or two. But if they send anything bigger…" Robert and Commander Rano exchange concerned, knowing looks. "Help is a long way away, I'm afraid."

CHAPTER ELEVEN

Admiral Dumar sat at the conference table, examining the images as Lieutenant Commander Bowden described them.

"Our biggest concern should be that moon," the lieutenant commander said. "The thing is big enough to hold at least one hundred ships, easily. We counted at least twenty mooring stations, and at least ten bays large enough to hold a battleship... And that's just on the side that we could see."

"So, what's your total estimated force strength?" Admiral Dumar asked.

"Based solely on what we could directly observe, there were six battle platforms, twelve battleships, thirty-eight cruisers—eleven of which were of a larger type that we have not seen before—and more than sixty frigates."

Admiral Dumar sighed. "To be honest, that's a lot more than I thought."

"Me, too," Gerard agreed. "And that's just what we could see. For all we know, there are even more ships *inside* that ring. Frankly, I'm starting to wonder if the reports that Jung ships were built in many different locations throughout the Jung Empire are just rumors. I mean, why would you have *that many* ships in one system, unless you were building them there." Gerard changed images. "Look at how some of these ships are just lined up next to each other in orbit. We can't tell from these images, of course, but I'd bet they're all joined together."

"Like a standby fleet?"

"Maybe. Or it could be something else. Something much worse. Like an invasion force."

"Don't you think you're reaching a bit, Lieutenant Commander?"

"Am I? Other than us, the Jung have no legitimate challengers to their power. And they sure as hell didn't build all those ships just to control this sector. Hell, they could do it with half that number, even as slow as twenty times light. I think those ships were built to control much more than just the Sol sector."

"*You* think they're planning on pushing further out into the galaxy."

"For all we know, they already have. Other than the route between the Sol and Pentaurus sectors, we haven't reconnoitered anything further out than fifty light years, *except* the Jung system. We've just assumed that their efforts were concentrated on this sector. We could just be one of several neighboring sectors that the Jung have either conquered, or are planning on conquering."

Admiral Dumar turned to Jessica, who had been quiet the entire time. "What is your assessment, Lieutenant Commander?"

"I agree with Lieutenant Commander Bowden. I don't believe the forces in the Jung system were built solely for conquering the Sol sector. I believe this is solid evidence that the Jung have a much bigger agenda."

"How far do you think they have spread?" the admiral wondered.

"Given the amount of time it takes to build such facilities, and to build ships, as well as their top speed of twenty times light, they couldn't have gotten too far, at least not yet," Jessica insisted. "The problem is, we don't know enough about *where* the populated systems are. The Jung could have expanded in an even sphere, or in branches stretching out from one inhabited system to another. I'm betting the latter, since we've already seen that pattern in the Sol sector."

An alert tone sounded through the intercom.

"*Admiral, Comms. Priority traffic.*"

Dumar tapped his comm-set. "This is Dumar."

"*Message from Tanna, sir,*" the comm officer began. "*Two Jung scouts have entered the 72 Herculis system. Captain Nash has dispatched gunships to intercept and destroy, but he suspects they are advance scouts for a larger incoming force.*"

"Did he indicate an estimated time of arrival for the additional forces?"

"*Negative, sir. They are sending gunships to search the expected arrival route, based on the general direction that the scouts arrived from. They have promised to update us as the situation changes.*"

"Mister Bryant, are you on the line?"

"*Yes, Admiral, I'm here,*" Mister Bryant replied.

"Position of our ships?"

"*Aurora and Celestia are already breaking orbit in anticipation of your order to reinforce Tanna. The Jar-Benakh and the Kent are in the Tau Ceti system.*"

"Clear the Aurora and Celestia for Tanna, and have the Jar-Benakh and the Kent return to Sol. We'll wait for an update from Captain Nash before moving them to Tanna as well."

"*Yes, sir,*" Mister Bryant acknowledged.

"Also, order all Super Falcons to jump ahead to Tanna. It's not much, but it is a few more guns, just in case."

"*Yes, Admiral.*"

Admiral Dumar turned to Jessica. "Take the

Ryk Brown

Mirai to Tanna. See to the safety of Doctor Sorenson. Bring her and her family back here, if you think it's necessary. We cannot allow harm to come to her, or worse yet, allow her to fall into enemy hands."

"Yes, sir," Jessica replied, rising from her seat to depart.

"What would you like me to do, Admiral?" Gerard asked.

"Keep studying that data," Admiral Dumar instructed. "I want you to squeeze every bit of knowledge you can from what you have collected."

"You're thinking about attacking the Jung homeworld, aren't you, sir?"

"I'm just looking for options, Lieutenant Commander, and it's your job to find them for me."

* * *

"Message from Karuzara," Naralena said as Nathan entered the Aurora's bridge from his ready room. "They are requesting that we send our Super Falcons ahead to Tanna... The Celestia's as well."

"Notify flight ops. They can launch once we reach the layover point," Nathan replied. "Any word from Lieutenant Commander Nash?"

"Yes, sir. She's been ordered to take the Mirai to Tanna and evacuate Doctor Sorenson and her family back to Porto Santo. She will join us at the layover point after she completes her assignment."

"Very well." Nathan continued forward, passing the tactical station. "Looks like you're primary TO for now, Mister Sorro."

"Yes, sir," the young lieutenant replied nervously.

"Jump one is plotted," Mister Riley reported. "Ship is on course and speed for the jump."

"Comms, notify the Celestia we are jumping,"

Nathan instructed. "Mister Riley, execute your first jump."

"Aye, sir," the navigator replied. "Jump one, in five seconds."

Nathan tapped his comm-set as he took his seat. "Cheng, Captain," he called over his comm-set.

"Three..."

"*Go ahead, sir,*" Vladimir replied.

"Two..."

"After the jump, I want to shut down all nonessential systems..."

"One..."

"...so that we can charge both jump drives simultaneously."

"Jumping."

"We can do that, right?" Nathan asked, as the jump flash briefly illuminated the interior of the bridge.

"Jump complete," Mister Riley reported. "Calculating next jump."

"*Yes,*" Vladimir replied, "*but you will not be able to conduct normal flight operations, and you will not have active sensors. We will basically be cold-coasting.*"

"But that will get both drives recharged in eight hours, correct?"

"*Seven and a half, actually,*" Vladimir corrected.

"Can we interrupt the process to restore flight operations temporarily, if need be?" Nathan asked.

"*It will delay the recharge, but it is not a problem.*"

"Great. We'll go cold as soon as we launch the Falcons. Be ready."

"*I will.*"

"Jump two is plotted and ready," Mister Riley reported.

"Contact," Mister Navashee reported. "The Celestia just arrived. Fifty kilometers to starboard, a few kilometers below. Same course and speed."

"Captain," Mister Riley interrupted, "jump protocols only require seven percent energy remaining upon arrival..."

"In case we have to do battle. I know, Mister Riley, I wrote them," Nathan finished.

"That's about a light year's worth of jumps, sir. When is the last time we used that much jump energy in a *single* battle? From the recharge layover point, we'll only be *nineteen* light years from Tanna. We won't need a full charge to get there."

"How much will we need?" Nathan asked.

"By my calculations, five and a half hours."

"Are you sure?"

"I haven't run the numbers yet, to be sure, sir," Mister Riley admitted, "but we'll have plenty of time to do so at the layover point."

Nathan turned toward Naralena. "Comms, relay our plans to cold-coast to speed up the recharge to the Celestia," Nathan ordered. "And let them know that we expect to jump to Tanna in five and a half hours."

"Yes, sir," Naralena replied.

Nathan turned back to face the front of the ship. "You may have just saved us two hours, Mister Riley. Well done."

"Thank you, sir."

"Celestia has received the message," Naralena confirmed.

"Very well. Take us to the recharge layover point, Mister Riley."

* * *

Jessica stood in the middle of the Mirai's cockpit as she completed the last jump.

"We are now in the 72 Herculis system," Ensign Nambianno announced.

"I'm picking up a lot of traffic in orbit over Tanna," Sergeant Liamo reported from the sensor station. "Mostly cargo jump ships and jump shuttles..."

"Get Cobra operations on comms," Jessica ordered.

"One moment," Sergeant Isan replied.

"More jump flashes," the sensor operator reported. "Eight of them. Super Falcons."

"Comms, belay last. Open hail." Jessica paused a moment to let the sergeant set up her comm-set. "Falcon One, Mirai. Do you copy?"

"Mirai, Falcon One. Is that you, Lieutenant Commander?" Loki replied over the comms.

"Yes, it's Nash. What are your orders?"

"We're here to reinforce the Tannans as best we can until the Aurora and the Celestia get here."

"What's their ETA?"

"Roughly seven hours. They're running cold, on backup fusion reactors only, so they can recharge both drives simultaneously."

"I've got Cobra operations, Captain Nash, on the comms, sir," Sergeant Isan told Jessica.

"Stand by one, Loki," Jessica instructed. She signaled the sergeant to switch her to the other channel. "Cobra Ops, Mirai, Lieutenant Commander Nash. What's your situation?"

"Mirai, Cobra Ops, Captain Nash. We took out the scouts without any problem. We're currently searching for other Jung ships."

"Bowden says those scouts are short range, so

401

the ships they came from cannot be far away...a few hours at the most," Jessica told him.

"*That's pretty much what we were thinking as well. We just received word from Alliance Command that the Aurora and the Celestia are at least seven to eight hours out.*"

"Yeah, we heard the same. Any idea what's going on with those cargo ships?"

"*We couldn't keep it a secret, I'm afraid. Ground-based sensor stations picked up the scouts, and when we destroyed them, and that put the entire planet in a state of panic. Everyone is either trying to find a way off the planet, or looking for shelter. It's a mess. Tannan security is trying their best to maintain control, but...*"

"Send another message to command," Jessica suggested. "Let them know what's going on down on Tanna. Maybe they can send troops to help keep things under control."

"*Good idea,*" Robert agreed. "*By the way, why are you on the Mirai?*"

"Sorry, Robert. Need to know, and all that," Jessica said. "I'll check back with you later. Mirai out." Jessica glanced at the sergeant again. "Switch me back to Falcon One."

"Yes, sir."

"Falcon One, Mirai. You still there?"

"*We're here,*" Loki replied. "*Sir, you should know that Captain Scott ordered us to fly cover for you while you complete your assignment.*"

"Did he brief you on my assignment?"

"*Yes, sir, he did,*" Loki replied. "*We're vectoring to you now. We'll stay by your side until you're clear of the area.*"

"Good to know," Jessica replied. "Mirai out."

Jessica turned to the pilot. "Jump us in as close as you can to the Cobra production plant."

"Yes, sir," Lieutenant Chandler replied.

* * *

Brill Daymon burst into the main room of Captain Dubnyk's home. He was sweaty and out of breath, and the exhausted and terrified expression on his face told of the chaos in the streets outside. "It is true," he exclaimed in between breaths. "There are ships coming to take people away."

"Which people?" Captain Dubnyk wondered.

"I do not know for sure, but I heard people can buy their way off Tanna if they have the means. My friend told me there are shuttles landing in the square, at the spaceport, at the Cobra plant... Many places."

"Jump shuttles?" Captain Dubnyk asked.

"Some, like at the Cobra plant, and a few at the spaceport. Most are just orbital shuttles, taking those who can pay to cargo ships in orbit."

Captain Dubnyk shook his head in disappointment. "Even in times of global crisis, there are those whose only concern is profit."

"What are we to do?" Fayla asked.

Captain Dubnyk looked at his young assistant. The fear in her eyes was even stronger than when he had first taken her off the streets and into his home. He looked in the eyes of the other young men gathered with him, and saw the same terror. His *family* was looking to him for salvation.

Captain Dubnyk turned back to Brill. "Are they ready?"

Brill looked confused, then his eyes widened when he realized what Dubnyk meant. "I do not know. We thought there would be more time to prepare them."

403

Captain Dubnyk stood and walked over to Brill, putting his hand on the young man's shoulder. "Now is the time, Brill. Such an opportunity may never come again." He looked into Brill's eyes. "Can *you* kill?"

Brill thought for a moment, his eyes darting back and forth. "Yes. Yes I can."

"Can *they*?"

Brill looked at the other young men in the room. He had spent the last month teaching them everything he had learned while at Porto Santo.

Brill looked back at Captain Dubnyk. "Yes, I believe they can as well."

"Good." Captain Dubnyk stepped back from Brill to address the others. "There are two types of men. Those who modestly accept what fate hands them, and those who boldly *take* all that life has to offer... by force if necessary. Luck occurs when opportunity, resources, and action all come together. The panic and chaos is our opportunity. You are the resources. Now, we must act. We must leave this world."

"But, this is our home," Fayla said, her lip quivering. "This is our world. Those are our people. Where...where would we go?"

"This is but one world among many," Captain Dubnyk told her. "Our ancestors fled this sector to escape the bio-digital plague a millennium ago. Hundreds of thousands of them spread out far and wide, settling worlds beyond the reach of the plague and the civilization that spawned it. *That* is where we must go. *That* is where opportunity and fortune await the bold. Out among the stars."

"How are we to get there?" one of the young men asked. "They are so far away."

"They are not," Brill corrected. "It took me less than an hour to get to Earth."

"We must get aboard one of those shuttles," Captain Dubnyk insisted. He took a breath, summoning all the strength left in his tired old body. "Brill, take Tahri and secure a vehicle. Bring it here. Kino and Elaz, gather up all our weapons. Ranin, Oray, and Toma, gather food and water. Fill several packs. Nothing perishable. Fayla, gather all our credits."

"All of them?" Fayla asked.

"Yes, all of them. Put them all in a heavy leather satchel, but fill the bottom with a blanket, first, to make it appear to be more. Everyone, move quickly. We must get off this world, no matter what the cost."

The young men left, heading for their respective tasks. Captain Dubnyk turned to Fayla, who was still standing there, trembling. "Do not be afraid, Fayla," he consoled. "You have seven strong young men to protect you." Captain Dubnyk smiled. "And one wise old one."

Fayla nodded in agreement.

"Now, go and put on something flattering. A pretty young woman serving as a distraction is a very powerful negotiating tactic."

* * *

Jessica climbed into the ground vehicle sitting in the Mirai's cargo hold as the ship's aft cargo doors opened and her loading ramp deployed.

"This is the power," Sergeant Annakeros explained, pointing at the vehicle's console. "Forward, reverse. Pull this card, and the system locks out so no one can steal it. Got it?"

"I got it," Jessica assured him.

"Sergeant!" Ensign Nambianno called from the

port catwalk landing. He tossed a rolled-up gun belt down to the sergeant.

Sergeant Annakeros caught the gun and handed it to Jessica. "You might need this," he said. "Things are getting pretty crazy out there."

"We're on a secure installation," Jessica reminded him as she donned the gun belt and checked the weapon.

"A secure installation full of panicked workers."

"Good point," Jessica replied.

"I thought you were a security officer."

Jessica sneered at him, then activated the vehicle's power and drove out of the bay and down the ramp.

"*I've reached Doctor Sorenson's assistant,*" Sergeant Isan said over Jessica's comm-set. "*Her family is already here. They are loading them, and about twenty of their top engineers and family members, into several vehicles.*"

"How many?" Jessica asked.

"*About seventy people, give or take.*"

"Can we carry that many?" Jessica asked as she raced across the tarmac.

"*The lieutenant says the weight is not an issue. However, space may be a problem.*"

"It's a short trip back to Sol," Jessica said, "and we can leave this vehicle behind and stuff some of them in the cargo bay, if necessary. Where the hell am I going?"

"*Building seven, at the far end of the complex,*" the sergeant replied. "*I am sending directions to your navigation system.*"

Jessica glanced down at her console, just as a map of the complex appeared, complete with a blue line indicating the recommended route. "I've got it."

"Lieutenant Commander," the Mirai's copilot interrupted over the comms. *"Message from Falcon One. The Jung have arrived. Edge of the system, about seventy light hours out. One battleship, four cruisers, and six frigates."*

"How long until they get here?" Jessica asked, as she swerved to avoid another vehicle headed toward one of the many shuttles that were loading personnel for evacuation.

"At current speed, several days, but once they have assessed the situation, they will undoubtedly go back into FTL in order to transit the system more quickly."

"I meant how long at FTL, Ensign," Jessica chastised.

"Sorry, sir. One moment."

Another vehicle, loaded with evacuees, pulled out from behind a building without warning. Jessica slammed on the brakes, bringing her vehicle to an abrupt stop less than a meter from the other vehicle, barely avoiding a collision. "Watch where you're going, asshole!"

"By FTL, best speed would put them within striking range of Tanna in just under four hours."

"Damn it!" Jessica swore. "Let's hope they're not in a hurry."

"Sir, I should point out that from their current position, they have not yet witnessed the fate of their scout ships. However, based on the location where those ships were intercepted and destroyed by Tannan gunships, they will know soon enough. When they do..."

"They'll hightail it to Tanna and start an all-out attack," Jessica finished for him. "Yeah, that's what I figured." She started her vehicle moving again, accelerating quickly as she passed between the rows of buildings. "I'm almost there. I'll let you know when we are headed back."

* * *

"Why must we go so far?" Tahri asked as they continued walking down the street. "There were plenty of vehicles closer to home."

"Better that we do this further from home," Brill explained. "It will take time to get home, load everyone, and get out of the area. We cannot risk someone tracking us back to the captain's residence before we make our escape." Brill stopped at the intersection. Vehicles were moving in every direction as people rushed about, trying to prepare themselves for the impending attack. "Look at them; they are all fools," Brill said disdainfully. He pointed at a man and his son trying to load an antique chair into the back of their vehicle. "Look at those two. They are loading furniture. *Furniture*, of all things!" Brill scanned the chaos and made up his mind. "That is the one we shall take."

"Brill, wait," Tahri begged. "I am not sure about this. Maybe we should look for one that is not already in use?"

"That one is large enough for all of us," Brill insisted. "That is the one," he repeated, heading off across the street.

"Brill, wait!" Tahri begged, following him.

Brill continued walking toward the vehicle. "Step away from the vehicle!" he instructed as he approached.

The man loading the vehicle looked at him, confused. He noticed the look of determination on Brill's face, and his confusion turned to suspicion. "Go inside," he told his son. "Get my gun."

Brill continued toward the vehicle, with Tahri running to catch up to him.

"What did you say?" the man asked Brill, pretending not to have understood him.

"I am taking this vehicle."

"What?"

"You heard me," Brill replied as he approached.

"Look, I don't know who you are, or what you think you're doing..."

Brill walked up and punched the man in the face without warning. The man fell backwards onto the ground, clutching his nose. Brill was on top of him in seconds, digging into his pockets for the vehicle's activation chip. The man struggled, trying to fend him off, but Brill struck him again.

"Get away from him!" a young voice shouted from the doorway to the home.

Brill looked up and spotted the boy, standing in the doorway, pointing his father's gun at Brill. Brill let go of the man and rolled to his right, ducking behind the door of the vehicle as the child fired. A needle-like beam of energy struck the ground near them, barely missing the boy's father. A moment later, Brill had his own weapon drawn. He stood up from behind the vehicle's door and fired, his own energy beam striking the child in his leg and dropping him to the ground.

The boy's father scrambled to his feet and charged Brill, but to no avail. Brill shot him in the chest, point blank, killing him instantly. He pushed the man's body away from him, letting it fall back to the ground.

He heard a woman's scream. By the fallen boy's side was the boy's mother. She had seen her husband's death at the hands of Brill, and she was taking the gun from her son's hand. Brill shot several times around her, trying to force her back inside. He did not wish to kill anyone if it was not required.

A shot rang out from behind Brill. He turned his head, and saw Tahri standing at the back of the vehicle, his weapon raised in front of him, a horrified look on his face. Brill turned back toward the house and noticed the woman lying in the doorway. She was not moving.

Brill turned back to Tahri. "Get in the vehicle!" he ordered as he pulled the old chair out of the side door and tossed it onto the ground next to the dead man's body. "Quickly!" he added, noticing neighbors coming out of their houses to investigate.

Tahri quickly got into the front passenger seat, as Brill inserted the activation chip and started the vehicle. As they backed out of the driveway and sped off down the street, Tahri looked behind them. The dead man's neighbors were running out of their houses. Some of them were running to aid the victims, while others were running toward the fleeing vehicle, guns in hand. "They have guns!" he warned. "You must turn!"

Brill turned the steering wheel hard, sending the vehicle careening around the next corner, as several energy weapon blasts struck the pavement behind them.

"Oh, my God!" Tahri exclaimed, panicking. "What have we done, Brill? What have we done?"

"We did what we had to do to survive!" Brill insisted as he drove the vehicle down the street as fast as it would travel.

"We will be arrested, and executed!" Tahri exclaimed.

"We will not!" Brill insisted. "Do you really think Tannan security has time to hunt us down? To execute us? They will be getting on those shuttles as well!"

"We just killed two people! Maybe three!"

"They would have died anyway!" Brill yelled back. "They were loading furniture, Tahri! They weren't going to try to get on a shuttle, they were going to hide in the mountains with the rest of the fools!"

"But we killed innocent people!" Tahri reminded Brill. "That is a sin against our people!"

"Our people are waiting for us back at the captain's residence!" Brill insisted.

"I don't think I'm cut out for this, Brill," Tahri realized, his voice growing quiet.

Brill slammed on the brakes, bringing the vehicle to an abrupt stop.

"What are you doing?" Tahri said in confusion, glancing back to see if anyone was following them.

Brill looked at Tahri. "Decide now, Tahri."

"Decide what?"

"If you are not strong enough, better you get out now. I do not want to have to kill you later."

Tahri stared at Brill. The young man's eyes were steely and confident, and he had no doubt that Brill could kill him if the situation required. "Drive," Tahri finally replied.

"Are you sure?"

Tahri quickly raised his weapon, putting its muzzle to his friend's head. "I don't want to kill you either, Brill...so drive."

Brill smiled, then pressed the accelerator again.

* * *

Captain Nash stood in the Cobra command center, his arms crossed.

"They are still too far out to know what has happened to their scout ships," Commander Rano reminded him.

"They already know that this system is no longer under Jung control," Captain Nash insisted.

"We do not know that. It could just be another Jung fleet stopping for propellant on their way out of the sector. We are long overdue for such a visit."

"They would have scanned the system from at least a light year out," Captain Nash replied. "That's what I would do. Besides, if our gunships can detect them, then they can detect us. They know we are here, and they know we are armed."

"Then they also know that they have the advantage," the commander added.

"Not necessarily," Captain Nash disagreed. "They do *not* know how many gunships we have, and they do *not* know if we have any other ships... Larger ships."

"It matters not to them," Commander Rano said. "They will attack, of that we can be sure."

"Agreed. The question is, when?"

"We must press the attack now, before they get close. Once they are within striking range, they will destroy our world."

"They didn't last time," Captain Nash pointed out. "Perhaps this system and its propellant refineries are too important to them?"

"They can build new ones, even in the radioactive desolation that remains *after* destroying everything on the surface," Commander Rano said emphatically. "They do not care, one way or the other."

Captain Nash sighed. "Thirty gunships, against eleven warships."

"We have killed Jung ships before," Commander

Rano reminded him. "The frigates will not be difficult..."

"We had surprise on our side, Commander," Captain Nash pointed out. "Those ships will be at full alert. Shields up and weapons hot. And those frigates that you believe to be so easy to kill? They will not hold a steady course and allow you to pick them off, one by one. They will go to FTL, launch missiles, then go to FTL again. They will continue to do so until the fighters from that battleship have lessened our numbers. We may destroy the frigates, eventually. We may even kill a few of the cruisers. But make no mistake, our losses will be heavy. We may even lose all our ships. And that battleship will still be there."

"What else are we to do, Robert?"

Captain Nash looked at his friend. "Nothing," he finally replied. "There is nothing we can do, but fight, and die. If we're lucky, we might be able to hold them at bay until help arrives. At the very least, Tanna won't roll over and die without putting up a fight."

* * *

Nathan sat in his dimly lit ready room, pretending to read reports. He had never experienced time passing so slowly. The Aurora and the Celestia had been sitting at the recharge layover point for half an hour, but it felt like much longer.

It had been enough time to verify his navigator's calculations. But five hours was still an incredibly long time to wait, considering what was going on in the 72 Herculis system at the moment.

"*Captain, Comms,*" Naralena called over the desk intercom.

Nathan pressed the intercom button. "Go ahead."

413

"*Message from Cobra command. Jung fleet detected at thirteen thirty-four, Tannan mean time, approximately seventy light hours out. One battleship, four cruisers, and six frigates. Earliest estimated arrival is seventeen fifteen, Tannan mean time. Captain Nash intends to attack immediately, although he expects that the Jung will go back to FTL for the rest of the journey to Tanna.*"

"That's just under four hours," Nathan realized. "We're not going to make it in time."

There was a long silence.

"*Orders, sir?*"

"None," Nathan replied. "Just pass the message on to the Celestia."

"*Aye, sir.*"

Nathan sighed, then pressed his intercom button again. "Cheng, Captain."

"*Go ahead, Captain,*" Vladimir replied over the intercom.

"I don't suppose there is any way we can speed up the recharge even further, is there?"

"*If there was, I would already be doing it.*"

"What about running the reactors at more than one hundred percent? We did it before...took them to one-twenty, remember?"

"*That was to escape certain death,*" Vladimir said. "*Antimatter reactors are not something to be pushed beyond safe limits whenever you feel like it, Nathan.*"

"Even when the fate of an entire world depends on it?"

"*The Jung fleet arrived,*" Vladimir realized.

"Yeah. They'll be within striking distance of Tanna in just under four hours."

"*And the gunships cannot handle them?*"

"A battleship, four cruisers, six frigates...so, doubtful."

"*Even if I did push the reactors higher, it would not matter,*" Vladimir explained. "*You can only charge the jump drive's energy banks so fast. Exceed that rate, and you risk losing cells, and that would only delay us further.*" Vladimir was silent for a moment. "*I'm sorry, Nathan. I wish there was something I could do.*"

Nathan sighed again. "I know. Thanks, Vlad."

* * *

Jessica brought her vehicle to an abrupt stop outside of building seven at the Cobra production plant on Tanna. She quickly shut down the vehicle, pulled the control chip, and jumped out. She ran around the corner of the building and found several large, flatbed transport vehicles, loaded with Tannan engineers and their families.

"Where is Doctor Sorenson?" Jessica yelled. Several people pointed to the doors leading into the building, answering her in Tannan. Jessica ran inside, where she found more people preparing to leave the building and board the vehicles. "Doctor Sorenson?"

More pointing, this time, down the corridor.

"Abby!" Jessica yelled as she made her way down the corridor. A familiar face peaked out of a doorway. "Abby!"

"Jessica!" Abby exclaimed with relief. "Oh, thank God you're here. Everyone is going crazy..."

"I know, I know," Jessica replied, cutting her short. "We've got to move. I've got a vehicle outside." Two children and a man came out of the office behind Abby. "Is this your family?"

"Yes... This is..."

"No time..." Jessica replied, interrupting her. "Stay together, and stay on my ass... Got it?"

"I got it," Abby replied, nodding.

Jessica turned and headed back down the corridor toward the exit, moving at a brisk pace. "Who are these people?" she asked as she walked. "The ones getting on the vehicles outside."

"Lead engineers, technical specialists, and their families."

"How important are they?"

"If we are going to keep the Cobra project alive, or restart it elsewhere, they are very important," Abby insisted.

"How many are we talking?"

"With their families, a couple hundred, maybe? We can take them with us, can't we?"

"We can take seventy or eighty right now, but that's it. The rest will have to wait for another ride."

"Are more shuttles coming?" Abby asked as they approached the doors.

Jessica stopped at the doorway and looked back at Abby. "I really don't know."

"Jessica, those people..."

"Look, I know. I get it. But my orders are to get you and your family back to Sol, at any cost. *That* is my highest priority right now." Jessica glanced through the window. Outside, she could see that the panicked workers from the production lines had noticed the assembly of people climbing onto the vehicles, and had decided to try and join them. Men on the vehicles were fighting to keep those who didn't belong from climbing on board, and forcing women and children off the flatbed vehicles.

"Pick them up and carry them," Jessica instructed sternly, pointing at Abby's two children. She pulled her weapon from its holster. "Tell them to close their eyes tight, and don't open them until you tell them to."

Abby began to give instructions to her children in Danish, as she picked up their daughter, while her husband picked up their son.

Jessica glanced outside again. The scene was getting even more violent. She turned back to Abby. "Our vehicle is around the corner to the left. When you hear me fire, you run to it and get in." Jessica handed her the control chip. "Put this chip in the slot under the power switch. Wait one minute. If I don't come, drive as fast as you can to pad fourteen. Got it?"

Abby nodded, clutching her daughter close to her body, the child's face buried in her mother's neck.

Jessica pressed the power button on her energy weapon and flipped the safety off. She charged out the door and immediately fired three shots into the ground less than a meter from the men trying to force their way onto the truck. The men ducked, and she fired three more times, as Abby and her husband came through the doors carrying their children and headed to their left.

"Everyone get the fuck back!" Jessica ordered, pointing her weapon at the men in front of her.

The men moved back, a meter at first, then another. Jessica sidestepped over to the cab of the nearest vehicle, glancing at the driver. "Pad one four," she said, holding up one finger, then four fingers, in case he didn't understand. "Just follow me, and drive fast."

Jessica stepped back to her left, keeping her weapon trained on the desperate men standing in front of her. Their eyes were blazing with fear and determination. They were men fighting to survive, and Jessica knew what that meant. They would do anything.

"Look, I know you all want to get off this planet before the Jung arrive," Jessica began calmly. "I get that. But this, what you're doing, the way you're behaving, it isn't going to work."

One of the men began to step forward, rage and desperation boiling in his dark eyes.

"Eh, eh, eh," she warned, pointing her gun directly at his face. "You're not listening." Jessica's eyes widened, staring at the man with an unblinking, deadly gaze. "Step the fuck back, or I *will* drop you."

The man studied her for a moment, unsure whether or not she was bluffing. Then he noticed her finger moving back to the trigger, and decided that he was not yet ready to die, and stepped back. The other men around him followed suit, all of them backing away from the vehicles.

Jessica glanced at the men on the truck who were trying to help the women who had gotten pulled down. "Help your people onto the truck," she instructed calmly. "Quickly." She looked at the driver again, as the men on the truck helped their families on board. "Start 'em up, boys."

As the vehicles' engines started, Jessica heard the sound of another electric vehicle coming around the corner. She glanced over her shoulder. It was Abby, driving the vehicle from the Mirai, her husband in the back clutching both of their children, their faces still buried in their father's chest.

Jessica walked backward to the vehicle. Abby slid over to the right as Jessica climbed into the driver's seat. "More ships will come for you!" Jessica told the men she had threatened. "But if you act like

assholes, they will shoot you dead. Just a warning."
Jessica looked at the driver of the nearest vehicle.
"Follow me, boys," she instructed.

Jessica gunned the electric engine, turning the
vehicle sharply left. "Are the trucks following us?"
she asked Abby as they accelerated between the
rows of buildings.

"Yes, they are."

"And the others?"

"They are just standing there."

"Mirai, Nash!" Jessica called over her comm-set.

"*Go ahead, Lieutenant Commander!*" Sergeant
Isan answered.

"We're on our way! ETA five! I got two trucks full
of people coming with..."

"Three..." Abby corrected.

"Make that three trucks," Jessica updated. "Have
your boys break out the big guns, the people here
are freaked out and liable to do anything."

"*We already have, sir,*" the sergeant assured her.
"*We saw trouble on pad eleven already. They had to
shoot some people. We've already set up a perimeter
around the ship.*"

"Good job!" Jessica replied. "We'll get the
primaries on board first. Put them in the master
stateroom and lock the doors. After they're secure,
we'll load the rest of them. I want to be wheels up
and jumping as soon as possible, understood?"

"*Engines are still running, sir.*"

"Any luck on that call?" Jessica asked.

"*No, sir, I haven't been able to get through to her.
Tanna's public comms are all jammed up right now.
I'm sorry.*"

"Copy that. See you shortly."

"Synda?" Abby asked, having overheard the conversation.

"Yeah. I had the ship's comm-tech try calling her so I could arrange to get her out of here, maybe on another ship or something, but he can't get through. Circuits are all jammed up."

"I'm sorry."

"I haven't given up yet. The Jung are still a little over three hours out, so there's still time."

"What are you going to do?" Abby wondered.

"I'm coming back for her," Jessica insisted. "Just as soon as I get you and yours back to Sol."

* * *

"Cobra Leader to all gunships," Captain Nash called over the comms. "You have your targets. Follow your flight leaders. We'll start with their frigates, then their cruisers. Flight leaders, if your primary target goes to FTL, switch to your secondary target. Do not repeat the same attack pattern with a single ship, especially the bigger ships. Their guns will knock your shields out with only a few rounds, then they'll open you up and tear you apart. Strike fast, single round, then jump away. Keep your time in the kill zone as low as possible. If we lose too many gunships, we lose the planet, plain and simple. So, no heroes today. Just do your jobs the way you were trained. Cobra Leader, out."

"Very inspiring," Commander Rano commented from Cobra One's copilot seat.

"I wasn't going for *inspiring.*"

"I never would have guessed."

Captain Nash looked at his friend with a pained expression. "*Now,* Izzu? *Now* you decide to be funny?"

"One minute to intercept jump," the commander

announced. "On course and speed. Jumping in three..."

Captain Nash took a deep breath.

"Two..."

"Here we go," the captain said.

"One......jumping."

The windows turned opaque, then cleared a second later. A Jung frigate was suddenly in front of them, filling up both windows.

"Pitching up," Robert announced. "Fire away, boys."

"Target lock," Commander Rano reported as streaks of red-orange plasma traced from their side gun turrets toward the rapidly approaching frigate.

"Her shields are already up!" Ensign Doray warned.

"Firing forward tubes!" Captain Nash announced.

"Target's point-defense turrets are coming online," Ensign Doray added. "Direct hits on target's midship ventral shields. Down twenty percent! Jump flash behind us!" the ensign added. "Cobra Two is lining up for a shot!"

"Jumping out," Commander Rano reported as their forward windows turned opaque.

Robert called up the next maneuver and activated the auto-flight system. The gunship immediately responded, firing its maneuvering thrusters to change its flight attitude, and then firing its main engines to initiate its first turn. As much as Robert preferred to fly the maneuvers manually, he knew damn well that the auto-flight systems could do it more precisely. Today, of all days, there was no room for error.

———————

"*Target is firing point-defenses,*" Ensign Saari reported over Captain Annatah's comm-set.

Cobra Two's copilot, Lieutenant Commander Jahansir, glanced at the threat board on the center pedestal between them, taking note of the direction of fire. "Suggest left translation, Captain."

"I'm on it," Captain Annatah replied, pushing his flight control stick to the left so his gunship would slide to port, away from the enemy frigate's point-defense turret directly to their starboard side.

"Target lock."

"Firing forward tubes," the captain announced.

Four red-orange plasma torpedoes shot out from under their bow, streaking toward the enemy frigate and slamming into her shields, causing them to glow a bright yellow.

"Direct hits," Cobra Two's tactical officer reported. "Her shields are down to sixty percent."

"Jumping," the copilot reported.

Captain Annatah smiled. "First one might be ours, Vann."

"Either us or Cobra Three," his XO said as they came out of the jump.

"No way," Captain Annatah said as he activated their next maneuvering sequence. "Twenty percent each means Cobra One drops their shields, and *we* get a clean shot for the kill."

Lieutenant Commander Jahansir smiled.

"I'm telling you, Vann, the number two spot *is* the kill slot."

"At least when it comes to frigates," the lieutenant commander replied.

———

"They should be down to twenty percent by our next shot," Commander Rano said.

422

"If this was any other mission, I'd double-tap and finish her off myself," Captain Nash commented.

"Jumping in five..."

"But, I can't very well do what I told them *not* to do, now can I?"

"...Two......one......jumping."

Captain Nash waited one second for the windows to clear after the jump, but when they did, there was nothing but empty space and distant stars in front of them. "What the hell?" the captain wondered, looking around. "Doray?"

"I got nothing, sir."

"They must have gone to FTL," Commander Rano concluded.

"Doray, where's our secondary target?" Captain Nash asked.

"There is nothing, Captain," the ensign replied. "No ships anywhere...except Cobra Two, who just jumped in behind us."

"Falcon One, Cobra One," Captain Nash called over the comms. "You got eyes on?"

"*Cobra One, Falcon One,*" Loki replied. "*All targets went to FTL about twenty seconds ago.*"

"Did we get any of them?" Captain Nash wondered.

"*No, sir,*" Loki replied over the comms. "*Not that we saw. Counted eleven FTL transition signatures.*"

"Damn it!" Captain Nash swore. "I was hoping we'd at least get one or two of them before they went back into FTL." Captain Nash sighed. "We'll wait for everyone else to finish their maneuvers and jump back. Then we'll form up and return to base." Captain Nash keyed his comms again. "Falcon One, Cobra One. Keep a track on them, and let us know if anything changes."

"*Falcon One, copies.*"

"I'm sorry, Robert."

"This is going to get ugly, Izzu," Captain Nash said. "Nothing is worse than fighting with your back against the wall."

* * *

Commander Telles and Master Sergeant Jahal stood to the side of the Mirai's cargo ramp as the Tannan engineers and their families were escorted from the ship by Alliance marines. After nearly ten minutes, the last of the evacuees walked down the ramp and onto the tarmac.

Jessica was next, followed by Abby, her husband, and their two children.

"Doctor Sorenson," Commander Telles greeted. "Welcome to Porto Santo."

"Thank you, Commander," Abby replied. "It is good to see you again."

"These marines will see you and your family to secure quarters. Are any of you in need of medical care?"

"No, I think we're okay," Abby said. "Just a bit shaken up."

"Understandable."

"Ma'am, if you'll follow me, we have a vehicle waiting," the marine sergeant said, offering to lead Abby and her family away.

Abby turned to Jessica. "Thank you, Jessica," she said, giving the lieutenant commander a hug.

"My pleasure, Abby." Jessica watched Abby and her family as they walked away and boarded the waiting vehicle. "What's the plan?" she asked, as two vehicles full of Ghatazhak soldiers pulled up behind the Mirai, and men immediately began to dismount.

"Reports from Tanna indicate that local security

forces have lost control of the population," the commander explained. "Tannans are *buying* their way onto jump shuttles ferrying them to Tanna's three jump-capable cargo vessels in orbit. My men and I will travel to Tanna in the Mirai. We will secure and monitor those operations, and take control of those cargo ships, as well as the evac ops at the Cobra production plant. Boxcars and troop jumpers will follow us in, carrying additional marines to aid with the evacuation effort."

"Great," Jessica said, "I'm going with you."

"Only as far as the Aurora," Commander Telles corrected as his men headed up the Mirai's cargo ramp.

"No, I'm going back to Tanna. I need to find Synda and her family."

"*My* orders are to transfer you back to the Aurora, at the recharge layover point. *Your* orders are to return to your duties on board the Aurora, not to return to Tanna."

"I don't give a shit what my orders are," Jessica said angrily. "I'm going..."

Commander Telles raised his hand. "You need to stop this behavior right now," he insisted.

"What?"

"There is a crisis. Millions of people are about to die, and your ship is about to go into battle in the hope of protecting them. Your place is on that ship, not running around on the surface of Tanna looking for your friend."

"That *friend* has two newborn babies, and a hus..."

"If you cannot follow orders and perform your duties as instructed, you do not belong in that uniform, Lieutenant Commander."

"There are three other tactical officers on board the Aurora," Jessica argued.

"And you trust them to perform their duties as well as you?"

"That's not the..."

"It *is* the point," Telles insisted, interrupting her. "How will you feel if the Aurora and her crew are lost because of errors made by the tactical officer who took your place because *you* decided to ignore the orders of your superiors in order to save *one* insignificant family?"

"She is *not* insignificant!" Jessica protested.

"Perhaps not to you," Telles replied. "But you cannot deny that in the grand scheme of events, they are."

Jessica stood there, staring at Commander Telles, fury in her eyes.

"Consider this decision carefully, Jessica," Commander Telles warned.

"*The men are loaded and ready to go,*" Master Sergeant Jahal reported over the commander's comm-set.

"Very well," Commander Telles replied, his gaze still fixed on Jessica's defiant eyes.

"If she dies..." Jessica said in a low, determined tone.

"Give me her pertinent data, and I will try to locate her and bring her to safety."

"Don't make promises you can't keep," Jessica warned.

"I make no promises," Telles replied. "I said I will *try.*"

"Try hard."

"The Ghatazhak always do."

Jessica turned and headed up the cargo ramp.

Commander Telles watched as she disappeared into the back of the Mirai. His left eyebrow went up and he shook his head as he started up the ramp, tapping his comm-set. "Pilot, Telles. Take us to the Aurora."

* * *

Brill brought the vehicle to a stop at the edge of the crowd. "I cannot go any further," he told Captain Dubnyk, who was in the passenger seat next to him. "There are too many people."

"Press forward," Captain Dubnyk insisted. "They will part, or they will be run over."

"There are too many of them," Brill objected.

"Brill, if we do not get onto a shuttle soon, before Alliance forces arrive to take control, it will be too late."

"How do you know they will come?"

"You must trust me on this," Captain Dubnyk assured him. "They will come, and soon." The captain reached over and turned the young man's face to look at him. "I once told you that for every man there will come a day when he must do the unthinkable in order to survive. Today is that day. You know this to be true."

Brill reluctantly nodded agreement. He depressed the accelerator pedal ever so slightly, inching the car forward, forcing those in front of him to move aside. As the mob slowly parted, the occasional man beat angrily on the side of their vehicle, threatening to break the windows.

After several minutes of slowly breaking through the crowd, Captain Dubnyk was frustrated with their lack of progress. "Kino, Elaz. Get out of the vehicle and work your way to either side and ahead of us. Go maybe twenty or thirty meters, then fire

427

your weapons in the air. When the crowd begins to disperse, fire into them to create even more panic."

"What?" Kino exclaimed, surprised by the captain's instructions.

"The crowd will attack them," Brill warned.

"No, they *will* scatter," Captain Dubnyk said confidently.

"But why fire into the crowd?" Elaz asked.

"If you do not show them that you are capable of killing them, they *will* attack you, and you *will* die," the captain explained.

"Why can't we just take our chances in here?" Fayla asked.

"The crowd will become even more dense as we get closer to the shuttles," Captain Dubnyk explained. "If we do not do this, we will be left behind and we will all surely die. Is that what you want? Because if it is, I have chosen the wrong students to follow me to glory."

A determined look came over Elaz in the back seat. He opened the door, pushing it against the crowd that was pressing on it from outside, and climbed out. Inspired by his friend's determination, Kino did the same, exiting the vehicle to the right and disappearing into the crowd.

"They will be killed," Fayla said in despair.

Captain Dubnyk turned to look back at his followers. Their faces revealed their fear and their uncertainty. "If they should die, then we shall respect them for their sacrifice so that we might live."

* * *

Jessica entered Nathan's ready room without warning.

"Glad you made it back," Nathan said, looking up from his data pad.

"I need a shuttle and your authorization to take it to Tanna," she said abruptly.

"Why?"

"It's chaos, there, Nathan. I need to find Synda and her family and get them off that planet."

"I'm afraid I can't allow that," Nathan told her, setting the data pad down.

"Can't, or won't?" Jessica demanded.

"Excuse me?" Nathan said, not caring for her tone.

"You heard me."

Nathan leaned back in his chair, folding his hands across his lap calmly. "Close the hatch," he instructed.

Jessica did not respond, only continued to stare at him.

"Sergeant!" Nathan called. A moment later, the guard appeared at the hatch. Nathan motioned for him to close it.

"Would you like to rephrase your question, Lieutenant Commander?" Nathan suggested politely.

"Oh, don't play that rank bullshit on me, Nathan," Jessica warned.

"Fine. How's this. Shut your fucking mouth and stand at attention...Lieutenant Commander...or I'll have the good sergeant out there *arrest* you and throw you in the brig for the duration of this mission, after which you'll be handed over to command to face charges of insubordination. Is that more to your liking?"

Jessica stared at him for several seconds. Finally, she stiffened up and assumed the position of attention, her eyes fixed straight ahead instead of trying to stare him down.

"I'm going to speak now, Lieutenant Commander,

and you're going to listen. Not talk, but listen. Is that understood?"

"Yes, sir." Jessica replied, her eyes still looking straight ahead.

"Your attitude has become increasingly worse since you returned from Kohara. I've noticed it, Telles has noticed, the admiral has noticed it... Hell, even Vlad has noticed. I've cut you some slack because you're a valuable member of this crew, and you've been through a hell of a lot recently. Also, because you are my friend. But this bullshit of storming about and making demands, saying whatever you want has got to come to an end, right here and now. Is *that* understood?"

"Yes, sir," Jessica replied.

Nathan sat there for a moment, observing his officer, his friend. He knew how angry she was at him at the moment, but she had left him little choice, as she was setting a bad example for the rest of his relatively young and inexperienced crew, as well as undermining his authority as captain.

"As captain, I do not owe you an explanation," he said. "However, as your friend, it is the least I can do. I cannot give you a shuttle to go look for your friend, because command has ordered all our shuttles, as well as the Celestia's, to head for Tanna in order to assist in the evacuation. All we have left are two SAR shuttles, and we need to ensure that *those* remain available to retrieve pilots during battle." Nathan sighed. "Now, go to your quarters, get cleaned up, and get some rest. We jump to Tanna in just under three hours, and I *need* you at my tactical console."

"Yes, sir," Jessica replied, her anger subsiding.

"Telles is a man of his word, Jess," Nathan added as she turned to exit.

Jessica paused, closing her eyes for a moment. Finally she spoke. "Thank you, sir," she said quietly before opening the hatch and exiting the ready room.

* * *

Commander Telles walked down the Mirai's cargo ramp onto the tarmac at the Cobra gunship production plant on Tanna. All around him, people were running away as his Ghatazhak soldiers spread out to secure the area. To his left, a shuttle was lying on its side, on fire, with a number of bodies scattered nearby. The scene was grim, but not unexpected. The commander's experiences had taught him that when faced with significant risk of death, humans could do just about anything. The chaos he and his men had been sent to control was proof of that.

"Troop jumpers have put down along all sides of the compound," Master Sergeant Jahal informed his commander. "Marines are establishing an outer perimeter, Ghatazhak will secure the flight line. Boxcars are holding in orbit until we give them the go ahead to land."

"Very well," Commander Telles replied. "Begin loading personnel as soon as the area is secure. No one gets on board a transport without presenting an ID and being searched and scanned."

"Understood. I tasked Sergeant Lazo and a squad of his marines to locate the lieutenant commander's friend, assuming she is still at her place of residence."

"Tell the sergeant to do what he can to find her."

"He has the coordinates of her residence, along with her comm-unit number, and images of the woman and her infant children. I have assigned him a combat jumper as transport."

"Very well," the commander replied. "Let's get to work."

* * *

Elaz pushed his way through the crowd of people trying to get closer to the two jump shuttles in the middle of the square. He had never in his life seen Tannans behaving like such madmen. They seemed truly insane...yelling and screaming, pushing and shoving. Grown men were even pushing women and children out of their way, forgetting everything they had been taught as Tannan men.

When Captain Dubnyk had first spoken of the ugly side of men, Elaz had not taken it seriously. Like many of the things of which the captain often spoke, they seemed to be from days long past. He knew that humanity had been more advanced technologically back then, but he found it hard to believe that they were still just as barbaric then as they were now.

But what he was seeing today affirmed his belief in *everything* Captain Dubnyk had *ever* told them.

Elaz stopped, turning around to look back at the vehicle containing the captain and his friends. People bumped into him constantly, sometimes forcefully, as he stood there, trying to find the vehicle he had left only minutes ago. But the vehicle was nowhere in sight. All he could see was the ever-pulsing crowd of people.

There was a loud roar of engines. Elaz turned to his left, and saw one of the shuttles lifting off. It was barely above the crowd and pulling away as it rose. Elaz watched it for several moments, until it disappeared in a flash of blue-white light.

There is only one shuttle left, Elaz realized. He had to act, before it was too late. He reached in his pocket as people continued to push up against him, taking hold of the handle of his weapon, but he was too afraid to pull it out and use it. He closed his eyes, trying to find the courage, all the while cursing himself for his cowardice and wondering if the captain had chosen the wrong man for this horrendous task.

The screech of energy weapons fire cut through the voices of the crowd. The sound caused Elaz's eyes to open with a start. People were screaming and yelling, running in all directions and knocking one another over.

Elaz pulled out his weapon and pointed it skyward, firing repeatedly. The crowd of people around him began to flee, seeking to escape the gunfire. He fired several more times. He heard the sound of an electric vehicle engine suddenly surging to full power, and the thud of metal against bodies.

Elaz looked to his right and saw the vehicle accelerating toward the last shuttle, running over anyone who failed to get out of its way in time.

Out of the corner of his eye, Elaz saw several men running toward him. Elaz lowered his weapon, pointed it at them, and fired... over and over again, until all of the men had fallen. He kept firing into the fleeing crowd, shooting people in the back as they escaped. He could hear Kino firing as well. Blast after blast, along with the sickening thud and sizzle as the energy blasts found human flesh.

Elaz felt a tremendous blow against his back, knocking him forward onto his belly. Something struck him in the head, then in the neck, back, and head again. He felt the air leave his lungs as more blows struck him in the back and sides. A terrible pain in his head, warm fluid coming from his mouth, and finally a searing pain in his head followed by blackness.

Two of the four men guarding the shuttle ran toward the sound of the second shooter, firing their weapons as they ran. Just as they left, an electric vehicle rammed into the barricade, crashing through and almost hitting the last remaining shuttle. The other two guards held their energy rifles high, urging those Tannans brave enough to still be in line to quickly board the cargo jump shuttle so they could depart before the crowd got completely out of control. The guards took aim at the vehicle, moving slowly into better firing positions, suspicious of what had transpired.

Fayla practically fell out of the vehicle as the door swung open. "Help me!" she cried out in anguish. "My grandfather! He is injured!"

The first guard saw the attractive young woman in apparent distress, and automatically moved to provide assistance. He was so distracted, that he did not notice the other two men falling out of the open doors on the other side of the vehicle.

The other guard did.

The second guard immediately opened fire, shouting warnings to the first guard as he fired again and again.

Tahri was the first hit, taking a blast to his chest, sending him flailing backwards. Ranin, who had come out right behind him, tried to raise his weapon to fire, but took two shots to his head and neck, killing him instantly.

Brill, staying crouched behind the open driver's door, eliminated the second guard.

The other guard pushed Fayla aside and brought his weapon around to shoot Oray and Toma as they climbed out of the vehicle, guns in hand. Oray fell to the guard's first blast, but his second shot went wide as Fayla kicked the man in the knee, causing him to fall. Toma jumped over and shot the second guard in the face, then climbed over his body and charged toward the shuttle, following Brill and firing toward those trying to board the shuttle.

Fayla turned to help Captain Dubnyk out of the vehicle, but instead was handed a weapon.

"Go!" Captain Dubnyk ordered, shoving the weapon in Fayla's hands. "Help them take the shuttle! It is our only hope!"

Fayla's eyes widened when she looked at the weapon.

"GO!" Captain Dubnyk repeated.

Fayla turned and headed for the shuttle, shooting at anyone who was not Brill or Toma. She charged to the shuttle's rear loading ramp, only to find Toma standing inside. There were at least twenty dead bodies around him. Men, women, even children. Toma turned and looked at her, a crazed look in his eyes.

"Toma!" she cried out, as if to ask what had happened.

"*The shuttle is ours!*" Brill yelled from the cockpit. "*I have the pilot!*"

"Get the captain," Toma instructed Fayla.

Fayla spun around to return to the vehicle, but stopped dead in her tracks after the first step. There before her was Captain Dubnyk, standing taller and more proudly than she had ever seen the old man stand before.

"We must depart quickly," Captain Dubnyk said. "We are not yet safe."

"What about the others?" Fayla asked. "What about Kino and Elaz?"

"They are all dead," Captain Dubnyk said as he walked past her and headed slowly but surely up the shuttle's loading ramp.

* * *

"*Falcon One, Telles,*" the commander called over the comms.

"Telles, go for Falcon One," Loki replied.

"*Falcon One, Telles. We have a fleeing cargo shuttle, believed to be hijacked. It left the surface and is climbing to orbit, but has not jumped. Intercept and destroy.*"

"Did you say *hijacked*?" Loki asked.

"*Affirmative,*" the commander replied, sounding a bit impatient. "*Intercept and destroy, before they figure out how to activate the jump drive.*"

"Yes, sir," Loki replied.

"Holy shit," Josh exclaimed, surprised at the request. "I don't believe it."

"Neither do I," Loki said as he scanned the atmosphere of Tanna.

"Who the hell would hijack a cargo shuttle?"

"I have no idea," Loki replied. "All I know is that we have orders to shoot it down."

"But what if it's a mistake?" Josh wondered as he turned to the intercept heading that Loki had just sent to his flight display. "What if..."

"Not for us to worry about," Loki interrupted. "Telles says shoot, we shoot."

"Jump this ship, or I will kill you!" Brill demanded, the barrel of his weapon pressed firmly against the shuttle pilot's head.

Something beeped.

"What was that sound?" Toma asked.

"It came from there!" Fayla said.

Captain Dubnyk came forward and looked at the console. "It is another ship. Most likely an interceptor, judging by its speed. They mean to destroy us." Dubnyk looked at the frightened pilot. "I would suggest you do as the man asks."

"I will not," the pilot said defiantly.

Brill shoved the barrel of his weapon into the pilot's mouth. "One last chance." When the man still did not comply, Brill pressed the trigger, sending the back of the pilot's head splattering across the aft bulkhead of the cockpit.

Fayla screamed, blood spraying across her face and chest.

"What the hell, Brill!" Toma yelled. "Now what are we going to do?"

"Get the body out of my way," Brill demanded, pulling the dead pilot's body up out of the seat and heaving him into Toma's arms. "I will jump the ship myself."

Captain Dubnyk looked at the sensor screen. "The interceptor is closing rapidly, Mister Daymon."

Brill climbed into the pilot's seat, studying the controls.

"You *do* know how to jump this ship, don't you?" Captain Dubnyk asked.

"I have seen it done during training. It is not difficult." He looked around the console frantically. "All such ships have an emergency escape jump feature, to get out of trouble quickly...in case the Jung ambush them. If I can just find the..."

"A wise feature," the captain interjected, trying to engage the young man in conversation to help calm him down.

"...Wait... I think this is it." Brill's eyes went wide with recognition. "Yes...first these up here," he said, flipping several switches. "Then these." Several red lights turned green. "Yes! Yes! I remember. The jump drive is active."

"The interceptor has fired missiles," Captain Dubnyk warned. "The time to jump is now."

"I think... I think..." Brill repeated, nearly paralyzed by uncertainty. He pressed the emergency escape jump button, but nothing happened. A look of confusion washed over him. "It should have worked."

"Why didn't it?" Toma demanded.

"I don't know..."

"The interceptor's missiles are closing on us," Captain Dubnyk warned.

"Wait!" Brill yelled, the answer coming to him. He turned to look at Toma. "Quickly! Cut off the pilot's right index finger and give it to me! Hurry!"

———

"Five seconds to impact," Loki announced from Falcon One's cockpit. "Three......two... Wait! The target has jumped. Telles, Falcon One. The target has jumped away."

"*One, Telles. Pursue, pursue.*"

"Falcon One, pursuing," Loki replied. "Josh, turn to one seven five, up five, and match the target's speed."

"One seven five, up five. Accelerating," Josh replied as he initiated a turn and brought up the throttles.

"Stand by to jump."

"On course and speed," Josh reported. "Jumping."

———

"They have returned," Captain Dubnyk warned. "Jump us again, quickly!"

Brill pressed the pilot's severed finger against the emergency escape jump button again. "Jumping!"

Captain Dubnyk glanced at the sensor screen, as the interceptor reappeared behind them. "They are jumping along with us," he realized. "How often can this ship jump?"

"As often as we like," Brill replied.

"Then jump us again, three times!" Captain Dubnyk ordered.

Brill did not ask questions, only did as the captain ordered. He pressed the dead pilot's severed finger against the emergency escape jump button again. He waited a few seconds for the jump to complete, then repeated the cycle two more times.

"Turn hard to port, then jump six times!" Captain Dubnyk ordered.

Brill initiated the turn, then began jumping again as instructed. "When the pilot's finger cools down, this may no longer work," he warned in between jumps. "Once the system realizes that unauthorized use is being attempted, it may lock us out for good, or worse."

"Worse, meaning, blow us up?" Captain Dubnyk surmised.

Brill said nothing and kept jumping the ship.

"That is why we have Toma," Captain Dubnyk replied.

"The pilot's finger will not be enough to unlock and take control of the system," Brill warned. "It will require the pilot's authorization code as well. It is how they hand command of a shuttle from one crew to the next. I have seen it."

Captain Dubnyk turned to look at Toma. "Can you crack the code?"

"I believe so, yes," Toma replied.

"That's six jumps," Brill reported.

"Continue jumping until we are out of the system, and away from both the interceptor *and* the Jung fleet," Captain Dubnyk instructed. "Make random turns, left and right, and up and down, every so often. And whatever you do, keep that finger warm."

Brill nodded.

Captain Dubnyk turned back to Toma. "It's all up to you now, Toma."

"I will do my best," Toma promised.

"I'm sure you will," Captain Dubnyk replied. He turned back and looked out the window to his right, catching brief glimpses of space as the window cycled from clear to opaque and back again with each jump. Soon, the first step in his resurrection would be complete.

———————

"I've lost them," Loki finally admitted. "They must have started executing turns in between jumps, so we'd lose their trail."

"What do we do?" Josh asked, looking at his partner.

Loki sighed. "What else *can* we do? We jump back to Tanna and report to Commander Telles."

* * *

Captain Nash had been pacing the floor of the Cobra command center for more than half an hour. He started five minutes prior to the earliest moment that the Jung could come out of FTL and hadn't stopped since. With each passing moment, he wondered if the Jung were traveling slower than their top FTL speed, or if they were planning to come out as close to Tanna as possible, in order to strike immediately.

A third thought kept nagging at the back of the

captain's mind. *Could they have decided that the system wasn't worth expending ordnance over?* It was a ridiculous thought, to be sure, but it kept nagging at him, nonetheless. On one hand, the Jung had demonstrated on several occasions their propensity to punish worlds that defied them. However, if, as some suspected, the Jung had their sights set on expansion *outside* the Sol sector, the ships currently passing through their system *could* have more important matters to deal with. So, as ridiculous as it seemed, it still *was* possible...at least remotely.

A young lieutenant stepped up behind Robert, coming to attention and offering a salute. "Lieutenant Elgar, sir," the young man announced. "I was told you wished to speak with me?"

"You're a pilot, right?"

"Yes, sir," the young lieutenant replied.

"How many sim hours do you have?" Captain Nash wondered.

"One hundred and forty, sir."

"But no actual."

"Incorrect, sir," the lieutenant replied. "I have thirty-two minutes of actual flight time."

Captain Nash looked surprised at first, figuring it out a moment later. "You flew Cobra Three Zero up from the surface, didn't you?"

"Just trying to be accurate, sir."

"How's your crew?" the captain asked. "They doing okay in their simulations?"

"There is room for improvement, sir," the lieutenant admitted.

"Your crew get any group time in the full ship simulator?"

"A little."

Captain Nash's eyebrow went up. "How little?"

"Three hours, but they also have thirty-two minutes of actual, sir."

"Of course." Captain Nash sighed. "Have you run any of the standard attack maneuvers?"

"Legally, only the alpha and beta series," the lieutenant replied. "But we have run most of the others during our open sim time."

"Good, you're going to need it."

"Sir?"

"You and your crew are taking Cobra Three Zero into battle."

Lieutenant Elgar didn't respond.

Captain Nash looked at the lieutenant. "Are you alright, Lieutenant?" he asked, noticing the young man's pale complexion.

"Uh, I'm not sure, sir."

"You don't think you're ready for it?"

"I'm not sure that's my call, sir."

"Actually, it is."

"Then I'd have to say no, sir, we're probably not ready to go into combat," the lieutenant confessed, "but that doesn't mean that we aren't willing to go."

Captain Nash nodded. "Well, at least you aren't full of shit, Lieutenant. Get your crew to your ship, and get out there. Control will vector you to your attack group." Captain Nash reached out and shook the young man's hand. "Good luck, Lieutenant."

* * *

"How did this happen?" Commander Telles asked his master sergeant.

"The jump shuttle was attached to one of the cargo vessels that regularly run passengers and resources between Earth and Tanna," Master Sergeant Jahal explained. "My understanding is that the crews took it upon themselves to start evacuating people, possibly even for profit."

"Most *likely* for profit," the commander agreed. "Despite how *wonderful* everyone thinks these Tannans are, I find them no different than any other human culture, complete with the same flaws and weaknesses inherent to all." The commander took a deep breath as he looked out across the orderly flow of evacuees to the boxcars waiting on the tarmac at the Cobra gunship production plant. "What about Tannan security?" he wondered. "Where were they?"

"They were en route at the time. Apparently they were delayed due to roadway congestion."

"These people don't have airships?"

"Apparently not," the master sergeant replied.

"Were the shuttle crews at least armed?" the commander wondered.

"They were, and they did kill several of the assailants. However, the attack was well coordinated. They fired into the crowd, killing at least twenty innocent people, causing them to disperse, so that they could ram the barricades with their vehicle. There was a young woman involved as well, as a diversion..."

"Of course," Commander Telles said, shaking his head.

"*Telles, Falcon One,*" Loki called over the commander's comm-set.

"One, go for Telles."

"*The shuttle got away, sir. We tracked them jump for jump for the first few, but they must have started doing multiple jumps, possibly even turning between jumps, in order to evade our pursuit. Recommend we take a few more Falcons and start a grid search, while there is still time.*"

"Those shuttles are protected against such things," Commander Telles commented.

"They are," the master sergeant agreed. "Could they have been hacked?"

"Doubtful, but not impossible. More likely the pilot was a willing accomplice."

"However, the maneuvering the ensign described *would* suggest a level of training above basic cargo shuttle operations," Master Sergeant Jahal pointed out.

"Indeed," Commander Telles agreed with the master sergeant's observation. "*That* is what I find most curious." Commander Telles tapped his comm-set. "One, Telles. Take three more Falcons with you and conduct your search. If you do not find that shuttle within two hours, return to Tanna, understood?"

"*Will do, sir,*" Loki acknowledged. "*Sorry, Commander.*"

"Just find that shuttle, Ensign."

"*Yes, sir.*"

Master Sergeant Jahal looked at his commander. "You do not believe this was just a bunch of Tannans wanting to escape certain death."

"We cannot afford to," the commander replied. "Vector Lazo to collect the bodies of those attackers and bring them back here. We will attempt to identify them later. That may bring us some answers."

CHAPTER TWELVE

"Multiple contacts," the sensor officer at the Cobra command center announced. "Eleven FTL signatures."

"Position?" Captain Nash asked.

"Six hundred kilometers and closing. They're on course for standard orbits over Tanna." The sensor operator paused for a moment to verify the data, then turned to Captain Nash. "Their shields are up, sir."

"The cruisers are separating from the battleship," the tactical officer added. "They appear to be headed for lower orbits. Frigates are headed for higher orbits."

"The cruisers will conduct the bombardment, and the frigates will fly cover," Captain Nash surmised.

"They're going to have a tough time hitting our gunships with missiles, Captain," the tactical officer insisted. "They should know that by now."

"They do," Captain Nash agreed. "What they *don't* know is whether or not we have anything *other* than gunships...like something bigger."

———

"Break into six-element groups," Cobra command instructed over the comms. *"Five groups total. First element in each group takes lead. New group designators are One-One through One-Six; Two-One through Two-Six; and so on. Frigates first. Transmitting target designators and assignments now."*

Commander Rano looked at his new copilot, Lieutenant Borru. "Are you ready, Lieutenant?"

"Yes, sir," the lieutenant replied, swallowing hard.

Captain Nash was next on the comms. *"All gunships, keep your jumps tight, no more than ten light seconds. There's going to be so much traffic, we don't need to be adding comm-buoys to the mix. And for God's sake, keep your time in the kill zone as short as possible... Good hunting."*

Commander Rano glanced at the tactical screen on the center console as the target designations came up. "One Leader to Group One. We've got frigate one. Fly the attack patterns assigned by command. We'll start with pattern beta seven, offset splits, fore and aft, with variable intervals between five and ten seconds." Commander Rano took a deep breath. "Follow me in, gentlemen."

———

Alert sirens began to blare all across the Cobra gunship production plant on Tanna.

"Commander Telles, Cobra command," the voice called over the commander's comm-set.

"Go for Telles," the commander replied.

"Jung ships have come out of FTL. ETA to orbit is fifteen minutes. Recommend you clear the area immediately."

"Understood." Commander Telles turned to Master Sergeant Jahal. "How long until those boxcars finish loading?"

"Fifteen, maybe twenty minutes."

"Tell them to hurry it up. I want them off the ground in twelve, and jumping one minute after that."

"They won't be full," the master sergeant warned.

"I don't care. Wheels up in twelve...period. I don't care if they have people hanging off their ramps.

Anyone left in Tannan skies after fifteen will be a target."

"What about the troop shuttles? When that last boxcar leaves, the crowd is going to rush the shuttles, just like last time."

"Just before the last boxcar launches, have the Ghatazhak fall back to the troop shuttles and the Mirai and hold. Once they secure those ships, have the marines on the fence line fall back to the shuttles for evac."

"And if the crowd doesn't cooperate?"

"Anyone who doesn't do what they are told, dies... understood?"

"Yes, sir," the master sergeant replied without hesitation.

"Captain," the sensor operator called. "The Jung battleship is launching fighters."

Captain Nash moved to get a closer look at the tactical display. "How many?"

"At least fifty of them, sir."

"That battleship is still twelve minutes out," the tactical officer commented. "That's a long ways out to be launching fighters from, isn't it?"

"Yes, it is," Captain Nash agreed.

"Besides, we don't have any surface defenses, or interceptors. Why do they need fighters?"

"To assert their dominance," Captain Nash realized. "It's not enough to destroy Tanna. They want to scare the crap out of anyone who might survive, so others will know what the Jung are capable of doing to those who stand against them."

"All gunships are starting their attack runs," the tactical officer reported.

"Here we go," Robert mumbled to himself grimly.

447

"I'm picking up at least fifty of them," Loki told Josh. "It looks like they're all headed for the planet."

"*Cobra command to all Falcons,*" one of the controllers called over their comms. "*Intercept and destroy all enemy fighters.*"

"*All* of them?" Josh repeated in disbelief. "All fifty of them?"

"*Transmitting target designations now,*" the controller added.

"Relax," Loki said. "That's only six or seven fighters per Falcon."

"In that case, no problem... Piece of..."

"Don't you dare," Loki interrupted. "Adjust course ten degrees to port and five down relative."

"Ten to port and five down," Josh replied as he adjusted their Super Falcon's course.

"Selecting four targets."

"On new course," Josh reported as he finished his turn.

"Dial up eight hundred thousand clicks," Loki instructed. "As soon as we come out of the jump, turn hard to starboard, forty degrees, dial up one hundred and jump again. I'll launch, and then you pitch up twenty and jump ten more clicks. That will put us passing over them, fore to aft..."

"And I pitch over and fire at whoever is left," Josh finished for him. "I know what a right dogleg with overhead cleanup is, Lok."

"Jump point in three..." Loki began.

Josh dialed up the first jump's distance and pushed the selector switch straight up and held it, his index finger barely touching the jump button.

"Two..."

Then he put his hand on the throttle and waited for Loki to finish the count.

"One..."

As the word 'jump' came out of Loki's mouth, Josh pressed the jump button, holding it a full two seconds before releasing. As the windows cleared, he pushed his throttles to full power and put the Super Falcon into a tight right turn. As the ship turned, he dialed up one hundred kilometers for the next jump. "Turn complete," he reported as he rolled level. He pulled his throttles back to zero, killing the main engines. "Jumping." He pushed the jump button again. The windows cycled.

"Weapons bay doors open," Loki reported. "Four good locks. Launching four chasers."

Josh changed the jump range to ten kilometers as Loki fired the missiles.

"Four chasers...away," Loki reported.

Josh pushed his throttles to full power again and pitched the Super Falcon's nose up twenty degrees. He watched the navigational display for several seconds, waiting for his ship's actual course to match the direction their nose was pointing. The gently curving magenta line flattened out and turned green.

"Four missile impacts," Loki reported.

Josh pulled his throttles back, pushed the jump button again, then pulled back hard on his flight control stick. His ship's nose came up and over as they jumped forward ten kilometers along their direction of flight. He continued pitching over as the windows cleared, until the cross hairs on his targeting display went from red to green. He pressed the trigger and held it, sending red-orange plasma torpedoes speeding toward the Jung fighters passing under them. Two fighters exploded, adding to the four other fireballs that were rapidly dying in the vacuum of space as the oxidizer in the Jung fuel was used up.

"Roll us over so I can get the turret on the rest of them," Loki suggested.

Josh had started the maneuver as soon as he heard the word 'roll' come out of his partner's mouth. Two more Jung fighters came apart as Loki fired on them with the Super Falcon's nose turret.

"Hell yeah!" Josh exclaimed. "That's eight! On the first pass, no less!"

"*One, Six!*" another Super Falcon pilot called over the comms. "*Roll left! Roll left!*"

Josh didn't ask why, snapping his ship into an immediate roll to port. As the ship entered its third roll, a bright yellow fireball lit up the inside of their cockpit. The next revolution revealed chunks of Jung fighter streaking past them.

"*Sorry about that,*" the pilot of Falcon Six apologized. "*I didn't know you guys were going to get greedy. I nearly took off your starboard wing!*"

"No problem, Jory," Josh replied. "I guess they didn't break as much as we thought they would when they saw our missiles coming."

"*Who says they saw them coming,*" another pilot chimed in playfully.

"Cut the chatter," Loki instructed. "Eight of them got through and are headed into the atmosphere..."

"*Command to all Falcons,*" the controller at Cobra command interrupted. "*More fighters being launched, from the cruisers. All four of them. Twenty fighters from each cruiser, headed for the surface. Break into two-element groups and intercept. Target designators on their way.*"

"What about the eight that got away?" Jory wondered from Falcon Six.

"I have a feeling we're going to be chasing a lot of fighters today," Loki replied.

———

"Turn complete," Cobra Two's copilot reported. "Jump point in three seconds."

"That damned frigate should've been dead on the second pass," Captain Annatah declared. "What kind of shields do they have on that thing?"

"Jumping."

Captain Annatah watched as the auto-flight system initiated the jump. Two seconds later, their windows cleared and the Jung frigate that they were about to make their third attack run on appeared before them. This time, however, her shields were not shimmering from the power drain of recent plasma weapons impacts.

"Yes!" the copilot cheered, realizing that the frigate's shields were finally down, and the kill was theirs.

"Firing forward tubes!" Captain Annatah announced as he pressed the trigger on his flight control stick to fire the plasma torpedoes. "Light her up, gentlemen!" Captain Annatah continued to make tiny adjustments to his gunship's pitch, keeping his nose pointed at the enemy ship as they passed under it. Balls of plasma from the gunship's four torpedo cannons and bolts from her two side-mounted, quad-barreled turrets tore the target's hull apart, sending debris flying in all directions. Secondary explosions from deep within the frigate soon followed, as each wave of plasma torpedoes found their way deeper into the enemy ship's hull. Finally, the frigate broke apart in the middle. The

451

main propulsion section at the aft end of the frigate exploded, causing the remaining portion of the aft half of the ship to slam into the broken forward section.

"*Oh, yeah!*" the pilot from Cobra Three cried out as he came out of the jump and witnessed the destruction of the Jung frigate. "*Nicely done, Nolan!*"

Red bolts of energy blasted into the tarmac at the Cobra gunship production plant, sending debris flying across the pavement.

Commander Telles and Master Sergeant Jahal were already tracking the attacking Jung fighters with their shoulder-mounted, mini-laser turrets. As the first four Jung fighters dove toward them, the commander and the master sergeant activated their lasers, and raised their rifles to open fire.

Commander Telles ran to the left, the master sergeant to the right. Two of the diving fighters altered their trajectory to follow the commander, as he sprinted across the tarmac, leaping over destroyed vehicles and the bodies of the dead and dying. The diving fighters fired again, sending red bolts of energy into the ground behind the fleeing commander.

Commander Telles dove for cover, flying a good five meters through the air, twisting over, and firing at the fighters as he soared over the generator truck. His shoulder-mounted laser cut swaths across the nose of one of the attacking fighters, but caused little damage. Bolts of plasma energy from his rifle tore into the diving fighter's left wing, causing gray smoke to trail from it, but the fighter kept on going.

As the commander flew over the top of the truck,

he rolled back over, tucking and rolling as he landed, coming right back up to his feet. "Fire!" he ordered.

Two Ghatazhak soldiers who had been hiding behind the truck, out of the view of the attacking fighters, stepped up, raised their shoulder-fired, chaser missile launchers, and fired.

The two Jung fighters, unaware of the threat, had entered a lazy turn to the left, making them easy for the missiles to track. One of the Jung fighters became aware of the threat and dropped several brightly burning countermeasures, pulling into a vertical climb with his engines roaring. The other fighter only managed to get two countermeasures out, having made the mistake of turning as he climbed. One of the chaser missiles found the turning fighter's starboard engine, and the fighter exploded in a bright orange fireball.

Another explosion sounded to the commander's left. He turned and saw another fighter falling from the sky, brought down by Master Sergeant Jahal's team. "Jahal?"

"*Still here.*"

"Mirai, Telles. You loaded?"

"*Last ones are coming up the ramp now, Commander.*"

"Get out of here before those other two fighters circle back. You're an easy target on the ground."

"*What about you?*" the Mirai's pilot wondered.

"We're not ready to leave yet," Commander Telles replied. "The fun's just started."

"*Remind me not to attend any Ghatazhak parties, Commander.*"

"We'll catch a ride with the marines, as soon as the last boxcar departs."

"*Good luck, sir.*"

Telles turned and looked at the other two Ghatazhak soldiers. "How many more missiles do you have?"

One of the soldiers smiled. "Plenty, sir."

"Good. Feel free to light those other two fighters up when they come back around."

"Our pleasure, Commander."

Commander Telles started running across the compound toward the last boxcar. A long line of Tannans headed toward the ship, still seeking to escape the attack. "Boxcar still on the deck, this is Telles. You need to get your ass in the air before those two fighters come back around."

"*We're not even half loaded, yet,*" the pilot replied over the comms.

"You can be half loaded and jumping your ass back to Sol, or you can be burning to death in a half-loaded pile of boxcar on the ground. Your fucking choice."

"*Closing up now,*" the pilot replied quickly.

To the commander's right, the Mirai's engines fired, and she began to ascend. He watched the ship climb and accelerate as he continued running toward the last boxcar on the other side of the tarmac.

"All troops around the last boxcar," the commander called over his comms. "If anyone tries to interfere with that boxcar taking off, take them out."

The roar of the Mirai's engines went silent as she disappeared in a flash of blue-white light.

"Jahal! As soon as we get those last two fighters off our backs, get our men to secure the extraction point. Then call in the troop jumpers and order the marines to abandon the perimeter and join up for extraction."

"*Yes, sir,*" Master Sergeant Jahal replied.

"Any word from Lazo?"

"*No luck at the subject's residence. Lazo conducted an aerial search of the area using the jumper's sensors, even had it check for women carrying one or more infants, but came up with nothing. The subject must have left before we even arrived. Do you want him to widen the search area?*"

The commander slowed his pace. Something wasn't right. He stopped and looked around the compound, his eyes eventually drifting skyward. High above the far horizon, he could see orange streaks of light heading toward the surface. "Negative," he told the master sergeant. "Recall Lazo. Recall everyone. It's time to go."

———————

"Another frigate has been destroyed!" the Cobra command center's tactical officer declared.

"Reports of nuclear detonations on the surface of Tanna!" one of the communications officers reported.

"Where?" Captain Nash inquired.

"The Bellaweise continent, east of Lorrett."

"How many?"

"Three so far. The detonations suggest an east-to-west pattern, along the middle latitudes."

"The cruisers," Captain Nash realized.

"Captain!" the tactical officer called. "The rest of the frigates have gone to FTL!"

"Order all gunships to attack the cruisers!" Captain Nash instructed. "Comms, get me Falcon One."

"Aye, sir."

"I've got the frigates again," the sensor officer reported. "They FTL'd to the far side of Lorrett."

"They appear to be standing off," the tactical officer added.

"Shall I retask the gunships back onto the frigates?" one of the communications officers asked.

"No, they'll just go back into FTL," Captain Nash replied. "They know that their frigates are too vulnerable. They want our gunships to go after their cruisers."

"Then perhaps it is a bad idea to do so?" the tactical officer suggested.

"You're probably right," Captain Nash admitted. "But what choice do we have? If we do nothing, those cruisers will glass the entire planet."

"Even if we manage to destroy all four cruisers, we'll never destroy that battleship, sir," the tactical officer reminded him.

"I know," Captain Nash replied.

"I've got Falcon One for you, Captain," one of the communications officers announced.

Captain Nash tapped his comm-set. "Falcon One, Captain Nash. The cruisers are targeting the surface with nukes. Can you intercept them before they reach their targets?"

"*We can try,*" Loki replied.

"Jump point in three..." Lieutenant Borru began.

Commander Rano gave his flight control stick a slight push forward, bringing Cobra One's nose down slowly as the gunship continued coasting along on its attack course.

"Two..."

As the gunship approached a thirty-degree pitch below its flight path, the commander countered with opposite thrust to stop the ship's pitching motion.

"One..."

The commander pushed the selector switch on his flight control stick all the way up and held it, setting the stick's trigger button to activate the jump drive.

"Jump."

Commander Rano pressed the trigger button, activating the jump drive. Through his front window, he could see the pale blue light flow out in all directions from emitters on the forward section of their hull. He never saw the light completely cover the hull, as the windows turned opaque to protect their eyes against the jump flash.

A second later, the windows cleared, and a Jung cruiser slid down into view from above, as Cobra One began to pass over the enemy target. The commander did not wait for confirmation of a target lock. At this range, he was going to hit the Jung cruiser's midship dorsal shield no matter what.

The commander tapped his flight control stick, edging it forward slightly to resume a slow but steady decrease in pitch relative to their flight path. He then slid the selector switch on his flight control stick all the way down, selecting the forward plasma cannons, and held it. He pressed the trigger, holding it down as well. "Firing."

Red-orange flashes of light filled the gunship's cockpit, announcing the departure of plasma torpedoes. From such close range, the balls of plasma energy struck the Jung cruiser's shields less than two seconds after leaving their tubes. The target's shields flashed a bright yellow-orange with each impact, sending shimmers of light out across the shield in all directions. All four plasma torpedoes struck the same shield, as did the next four, and the four after. At the same time, both his gunners opened up on neighboring shield sections with their quad-barreled plasma cannon turrets, while his tactical officer used the gunship's eight mini-turrets to target various points across the enemy cruiser. Not a single one of their shots would get past the enemy ship's shields, but they would add to the cumulative weakening that those shields would experience as each gunship followed suit. As long as his ship was within firing range of a Jung target, he would fire every weapon he had.

Cobra One's nose continued to pitch down to stay pointed at the target as they passed over it. Their own shields began to shimmer in pale blues and whites, as rail gun slugs from the cruiser's point-defense turrets found them.

A blue-white flash on the opposite side of the enemy ship, and forty-five degrees to Cobra One's right, announced the arrival of the second gunship in the attack group. Cobra Two would conduct a similar attack pass on the same shield section, but from a different angle.

"Time to go," Commander Rano said as he pushed his selector switch up and pressed the trigger to execute their escape jump.

The pale blue light again began to spill out across their hull as the windows turned opaque. As they jumped, the commander pressed the auto-flight engage button on the side of his flight control stick, allowing the system to put them on the next attack course by flying them through a series of turns and jumps. It was a repetitive style of attack, composed of a few minutes of automated maneuvers, followed by twenty seconds of terror. It seemed easy to execute, but the cycle of adrenaline-filled tension and relaxation was surprisingly tiring, as each jump into the kill zone was not only an opportunity for them to kill their enemy, but also for their enemy to kill them.

———————

"New target! Bearing one seven zero, forty clicks! Just entering the atmosphere!" Loki reported.

"I'm on it," Josh replied as he pulled the Super Falcon into a sharp right turn. He quickly dialed up thirty-five kilometers on their jump range setting, pushed the selector switch up, and pressed the trigger. The Super Falcon's windows turned opaque then clear again, and Josh pulled their nose up sharply, bringing his throttles up to full power.

"Reacquired," Loki reported. "Four clicks and closing *really* fast! Going to nose turret."

Josh instinctively rolled the ship over, giving his partner a better field of fire. Loki wasted no time, tapping the target on the screen to select it and then activating their nose turret. Bolts of red-orange plasma streaked from below their nose, hurtling skyward in search of the Jung weapon falling toward them.

"Four bandits, inbound from the north!" Loki reported as their nose turret continued to fire.

An explosion only a few hundred meters ahead of them lit up their cockpit. Josh immediately snap rolled the ship another ninety degrees and pulled the interceptor to port, pushing his nose down and reducing his throttle at the same time.

"Fly three four seven," Loki instructed.

"We got it, right?" Josh asked, wanting to be sure.

"Yeah! Yeah! We got it!" Loki replied. "Bandits are ten clicks out, climbing up from twenty-two five. Intercept in fifteen seconds."

Josh rolled the ship one last time to get level, as

459

he ended his turn exactly on the intercept heading his partner had given him. "Can you tag them with missiles?"

"Closure's too hot!" Loki warned. "They're all yours."

"Sweet."

"I've got six more bandits descending from orbit off our starboard side, sixty kilometers and closing."

"How about them?" Josh asked as he flipped his selector switch to torpedoes.

"Break right after your first pass and hold on the second group for ten seconds so I can launch on them," Loki instructed.

"How many missiles we got left?" Josh asked as he fired the plasma torpedo cannons at the rapidly approaching Jung fighters.

"Two," Loki replied. "Four, One!" Loki called over the comms. "How many chasers do you have left?"

"One, Four is full up."

"I'm about to launch two on the six bandits north of us! Can you tap the other four?"

"One, Four. Can do."

Two explosions appeared less than a kilometer in front of them. Josh broke into a right turn. "Ten seconds."

Loki tapped two of the six icons on his targeting screen, then pressed the launch button. "Launching two!" he announced. "Falcon One! Two chasers away!"

Josh immediately reversed his turn, dialed up his jump range to ten kilometers, then pushed the selector up and pressed the trigger to jump the ship.

"Falcon Four! Four chasers away!"

"One, Six! I've got your other two locked! Disengage!"

"One, disengaging!" Josh replied, pulling the Super Falcon's nose hard right and upward as he slammed his throttles forward.

"*Falcon Six! Two chasers away!*"

Loki watched as the four bandits to the north disappeared from his screen, as did the two below them. Before he could report the destruction of the last six enemy fighters, more targets appeared on his screen. "Shit! Multiple targets! Fighters and nukes! Who besides us is empty?" Loki asked over the comms.

"*Six is empty!*"

"*Five is empty!*"

"Six, One, take the nuke to our north!" Loki instructed. "Five, take the one to our south! We'll take the ones directly ahead of us. Everyone else go after the fighters and keep them off of us!"

"Fuck, this is fun," Josh exclaimed.

"No kidding," Loki replied. "Command, Falcon One. It's getting a bit sporty down here!"

"Debris! Dead ahead!" Lieutenant Borru exclaimed as they came out of the jump.

Commander Rano glanced at the display in the center console, noting the debris field almost upon them. He pushed the base of his flight control stick to the left, causing the gunship to fire its starboard translation thrusters. He pulled their nose to starboard and pitched down to bring the gunship's nose onto the Jung cruiser passing below them.

"It's Cobra Eight!" the tactical officer reported. "I'm picking up their emergency beacon!"

"That's four ships lost!" the copilot exclaimed. "On *one* cruiser!"

Commander Rano paid no attention, his

concentration focused on the enemy cruiser just beyond the debris field passing between them.

"Her shields are down!" the tactical officer reported.

"Open up!" the lieutenant ordered.

Commander Rano pressed his trigger, sending four balls of plasma into the unprotected hull of the cruiser. The hull tore open, exposing her secondary hull underneath. The commander fired again, and again. Each wave of torpedoes plowed deeper into the enemy ship, setting off additional explosions.

The commander kept firing as his ship passed over and cleared the target. His nose still pitching to stay on the cruiser, he continued firing until a jump flash announced Cobra Two's arrival. The commander ceased firing and pushed his selector switch upward into the jump position, but did not press the trigger to execute the jump. Instead, he stared at the cruiser as they drifted away from it. He watched as Cobra One's shields shimmered from rail gun impacts. Cobra Two fired every weapon she had at the damaged area of the cruiser's hull.

"What are you waiting for?" the copilot wondered. "Jump!"

The commander just kept staring. "Wait for it..."

The Jung cruiser split in half just forward of her main propulsion section. More secondary explosions rocked both halves of the crippled ship, setting off an unstoppable chain of events leading to her complete destruction.

It was an awe-inspiring sight to behold. A handful of tiny gunships had brought down a Jung warship more than two kilometers in length. A day ago, he never would have believed it possible, but now, it gave him hope. He knew they could not destroy the battleship, not even with fifty gunships, let alone the twenty-six they had left. However, if they could destroy everything else, it would take hours for the battleship to fully destroy the surface of his world. And the Aurora was less than an hour away.

———

"Got it!" Josh exclaimed as the weapon exploded a few hundred meters in front of them.

"Break right and dive!" Loki ordered. "Two bandits on our six!"

Josh rolled the Super Falcon to the right and pulled the nose up, forcing the ship into a tight right turn, as energy weapons fire streaked past them to starboard.

"*One, Three! I'm on them!*"

"Make it quick!" Loki exclaimed. "One of the nukes got past us and is heading for the surface!"

"No fucking way," Josh said as he twisted the interceptor back around to chase the Jung weapon below them.

Energy weapons fire slammed into the port shields, shaking the ship and causing her shields to flash bright yellow. A nearby explosion lit up the cockpit.

"*Splash one!*" the pilot of Falcon Three cried out over the comms.

"Where is it?" Josh wondered.

"Five more to port! Three thousand meters below us!" Loki replied. "Impact in ten seconds! It's too late, Josh! You gotta break off and jump clear, or we'll..."

Josh knew what Loki was going to say, and had already begun to pull out of his dive. Just as he leveled off, there was a brilliant white flash below them. Josh pushed the selector switch on his flight control stick up and pressed the button, jumping clear of the blast a split second before it reached them.

There was a moment of silence after the jump.

"FUCK!" Josh shouted.

"I've got eight bandits to the west, twelve to the north, and six more to the east," Loki announced. "Anyone got any chasers left?" he asked the other Super Falcons.

"*We can still go after them with guns and plasma torpedoes,*" the pilot of Falcon Three suggested.

"How many cruisers are left?" Loki wondered.

"*Last I heard, two were left.*"

Loki looked at the tactical display. Among the numerous icons representing Jung fighters coming after the Super Falcons were six more nukes descending rapidly toward the surface of Tanna. "This is never going to work," he realized.

"*Cobra command to all Falcons,*" the controller called over the comms. "*The last evac ship has departed. Falcons One and Two, provide cover for the Cobra plant until the Ghatazhak get clear. Falcons Three through Eight, climb to orbit and try to draw the fighters away from the gunships.*"

"But they'll glass the whole fucking planet!" Josh exclaimed.

Loki looked at his friend sadly. "They know, Josh. They know."

———

"How many ships do we have left?" Captain Nash asked.

"We're down to eighteen gunships!" the tactical officer replied.

Captain Nash studied the tactical display on the console in front of him, quickly flipping through the tracks of the previous attack runs on the first two cruisers. "There's not enough variation," he concluded. "Those damned cruisers have so many point-defense turrets they can cover at least three different engagement areas at once." He turned to the communications officer. "Order all gunships to combine into a single attack group and concentrate on the third cruiser...the one closest to the Cobra plant. Split into three groups of four, and one group of six. Attack from six different angles, and make all turns so that they stay clear of each other's engagement areas. Stagger the attacks of each group a full thirty seconds apart, so the cruisers have time to swing their guns away from the next attack group. That may reduce the rate at which we're losing ships."

"Attack jump in three..." Lieutenant Commander Jahansir's voice announced over Specialist Sennott's helmet comms.

Taji flipped the safety off on his quad-barreled plasma turret.

"Two..."

He looked out the side of his turret canopy at his world below him. He could see at least six massive mushroom clouds rising from the surface, marking the locations where nuclear weapons had detonated on the surface of Tanna. Weapons that had been dropped from orbit by the very ship they were about to attack.

"One..."

Two more flashes of light on the surface announced another pair of nuclear detonations.

"Jump."

Taji turned his attention forward as his turret

canopy turned opaque. A second later, the canopy cleared, and the Jung cruiser was directly in front of him again. The sight used to scare the hell out of him, though he was used to sitting at the end of the long protrusion out of the middle of the gunship. But he had gotten over it.

"Fire away!" the lieutenant commander ordered, as if they needed to be told.

Taji pressed his trigger and held it, moving his gun control yoke to rotate his turret and keep his stream of plasma bolts trained on the same spot on the Jung cruiser's midship port-side shield.

The ventral shield protecting Cobra Two's underside suddenly failed, and several rail gun slugs tore into the gunship's port side. Taji flinched as pieces of the ship's hull flew upward, passing between his turret and the ship itself.

"Ventral shield is down!" Ensign Saari reported from Cobra Two's tactical console.

"We're taking fire!" Lieutenant Crist reported, his voice sounding panicked. *"Hull breaches! Port side! We're losing..."*

The lieutenant's voice was overpowered by the sound of explosions aft of Taji's turret. He was suddenly jerked in his seat, his restraints digging deep into his shoulders and his head snapping to the left. He twisted his head around to look aft, and caught a glimpse of their port side. "Holy shit! A big section of our port drive is gone!"

Taji looked forward again, noticing that the gunship was in a flat spin. *I've got to get out of this thing and back inside the ship,* he realized.

"Port engine is dead!" the lieutenant continued. *"Jump drive is off line!"*

A blue-white flash of light appeared out of Taji's line of sight.

"Cobra Three just jumped in behind us!" the copilot reported.

Taji saw flashes of red-orange as Cobra Three fired at the Jung cruiser, unaware of Cobra Two's plight. The flashes repeated three more times as Taji's ship continued to spin.

"Target's shields are down!" the tactical officer cried out.

Taji held on tight as the ship spun. The power inside his turret went dead. More flashes of red-orange light cast eerie shadows within his turret. He pressed the release button on his restraints, and was thrown against the canopy to his left. More flashes of red-orange light.

"Direct hits!" the tactical officer reported. *"Three scored direct hits!"*

All Taji could hear was the sound of his own breathing as he struggled to pull himself across the turret toward the tunnel that would take him back into the heart of the gunship and to safety.

Another flash of blue-white light.

"Taji!" Specialist Turchin called from the starboard gun turret. *"Get back out of your turret! Quickly!"*

Taji pulled himself across the turret and pressed the hatch control mechanism. Nothing happened. "The hatch control doesn't work!" he cried out.

"Use the manual override on the hatch!" Turchin yelled over the comms.

Another flash of blue-white light.

"That's Cobra Four!" Captain Annatah said.

"Oh, fuck!" the copilot exclaimed.

"Four! Two! Break right! We're right in front of you! Dead stick!"

Taji swung the hatch open, but it was too late. He was suddenly flung back across the turret, slamming into the canopy and then bouncing back across toward the open hatch.

But the tunnel on the other side didn't lead back to the safety of the gunship.

His comm-set crackled. He thought he heard screams, but then it went dead. He fumbled to get control as he bounced around inside his turret. Then he saw it. Outside his canopy. His ship, broken in half, the pieces drifting away from him. He also saw Cobra Four, its entire front section, crumpled and torn, its cabin open to space.

Oh, God!

Another jump flash, followed by red-orange flashes. A few seconds later, brilliant yellow flashes. Then something slammed into his turret, breaking it apart.

Taji gasped for air, but found none. A bitter cold washed over him. Then blackness.

"You've got about three minutes before you take a nuke!" Captain Nash warned the commander over the comms.

"Understood," Commander Telles replied. "Telles to all ground forces! Fall back to the troop jumpers! It's time to leave!"

"Telles, Lazo! These people are advancing on us! Are we clear to fire?"

"Mow them down, Sergeant!"

"Behind you!" Master Sergeant Jahal warned.

Commander Telles spun around, spotting an armed Tannan charging in his direction, weapon aimed right at him. Telles leaned to his left as the man fired, the energy bolt passing to his right. He drew his sidearm and placed a single shot into the man's face. The man stumbled, his momentum carrying him forward onto the tarmac. The commander continued firing into the charging crowd.

"Combat One, Telles! Ready for extraction!"

"*Telles, Combat One! Thirty seconds!*"

"Bulldogs One and Two, depart as soon as you get the last man on board!" the commander instructed as he continued to fire into the crowd, barely holding them at bay.

"Ten bandits, dead ahead!" Loki announced.

"Where the hell are they going?" Josh wondered.

Loki studied his tactical display, examining the course of each group of fighters in the area. "I think they're heading back to their ships. Command, Falcon One. I think the fighters are returning to their ships."

"*We're seeing the same thing, Falcon One.*"

"Do you still want us to pursue?"

"*Pick off any that you can, but stay out of their defense perimeters.*"

"Falcon One copies."

"You don't think they're bugging out, do you?" Josh wondered hopefully.

"Not a chance," Loki replied. "More likely they're getting them out of harm's way, before they really start pounding the surface."

"*Command! Two-Four! We've lost all power and maneuvering! Our shields are...*"

The transmission ended abruptly. Lieutenant Elgar looked as his copilot, Lieutenant Tolamay, sitting on the other side of Cobra Three Zero's cockpit. "Is that ten, or eleven?" he wondered.

"Nine ships left," his copilot replied. "Jump point in five seconds."

Lieutenant Elgar took in a deep breath as he prepared to execute what would be his fifteenth attack run of the day. He hadn't even finished his simulator training.

Six months ago, he was working as a carpenter in a small shop that made tables, chairs, and benches. Now, he was flying a gunship in defense of his world.

"Jump," his copilot said, having completed his countdown.

Lieutenant Elgar pushed the selector switch on his flight control stick up and pressed the trigger. The gunship's windows turned opaque, and a second later, when they cleared, the last Jung cruiser was about to pass over him again.

The lieutenant pushed his selector switch down to the torpedo position and held the trigger in. He stared out the front window as balls of red-orange plasma spitting out of the torpedo cannons under them slammed into the enemy ship's shields, causing them to flash and shimmer. After two rounds of plasma torpedoes, his ship began to shake violently.

"Incoming fire!" his tactical officer warned.

"Jump us out!" Lieutenant Tolamay urged.

"Forward shields have failed!" the engineer reported.

The ship lurched to starboard as Lieutenant Elgar pushed the selector switch up to the jump position and pressed the trigger.

Nothing happened.

He tried again. The ship lurched.

"Hull breach!"

"Jump!"

"I did!" Lieutenant Elgar replied. "It's not working!"

"Jump drive is offline!" the engineer reported. "No maneuvering on our entire port side!"

"Target is firing again!"

Lieutenant Elgar scanned his console, looking for a solution. He only found one.

"Cobra Three Zero is hit!" the tactical officer at the Cobra command center reported. "She's firing her mains!"

"Why aren't they jumping?" Captain Nash wondered.

"Impact!" the sensor office announced. "Cobra Three Zero has rammed the cruiser. The target's port forward shields are down!"

"How many ships do we have left?" Captain Nash asked. He already knew the answer, but was hoping that somehow he had lost track of a few.

"Eight gunships left, sir," the tactical officer replied. "And six Super Falcons."

Captain Nash sighed. "Evacuate all remaining personnel."

The communications officer looked confused. "This facility is not under direct attack, sir."

"It will be shortly."

"Firing!" Commander Rano announced as Cobra One came out of its jump only a few hundred meters from the last Jung cruiser in orbit over Tanna. Both he and Lieutenant Borru looked out the forward windows as their plasma torpedoes tore into the hull of the fourth and final Jung cruiser. Four rounds of torpedoes later, the cruiser came apart, her aft section erupting in a brief fireball of propellant before the vacuum of space extinguished it.

"Command, Cobra One," Commander Rano called over the comms. "Cruiser four is destroyed. Proceeding to engage the battleship."

"*Cobra One, Command, negative. Do not engage the battleship. Jump to rally point hotel four.*"

"Command, One, say again?"

"*One, Command. Do not engage the battleship. Jump to rally point hotel four. Once all gunships have rejoined, proceed to Sol.*"

"Command, One..."

"*Cobra One, Command, Nash,*" Captain Nash called over the comms. "*It's over, Commander. We can't win this.*"

Commander Rano couldn't believe what he was hearing. "We cannot run away while our home is destroyed..."

"*We've already lost more ships than I was authorized to expend,*" Captain Nash explained. "*You can't take out that battleship, Izzu. Not with eight ships. Not with eighty ships.*"

"I don't care how many ships you are authorized to expend," Commander Rano argued. "That's my world down there, Robert. I'd rather die defending it than run away."

"*I hear you, Izzu, but my orders come directly from Alliance Command...*"

"I do not care about your Alliance!" Izzu yelled. "I am a Tannan! And my world is burning!"

———

"He switched off his comms, sir," the communications officer told Captain Nash.

Captain Nash took a deep breath.

"Cobra One is jumping," the Cobra command center's tactical officer reported.

"I've got new contacts!" the sensor officer reported. "Inbound missiles. Coming from the frigates. They're headed straight for us. Impact in three minutes."

"The other Cobras are following him, sir," the tactical officer said. "I can't say I blame them, either."

"I know how you feel," Robert said.

"Do you?" the tactical officer replied accusingly.

Robert turned and looked at him. "I watched my world fall to the Jung, and I was helpless to do anything about it. I had my orders, and I followed them. I took my ship into hiding...for months. So I know what it feels like...trust me."

"With all due respect, Captain, your world wasn't being destroyed, only conquered."

Captain Nash had no reply. He turned back to the tactical display on the console before him, watching as the last eight Cobra gunships jumped in to attack the Jung battleship bombarding their world. One by one they jumped in close to the target to fire, and one by one, they were destroyed.

"Missile impacts in two minutes," the sensor operator updated.

The tactical officer watched as the last Cobra gunship disappeared from his screen. He looked up at Captain Nash. "I'm sorry, Captain. No disrespect was intended. I just couldn't leave my post while my brothers were still out there fighting."

Captain Nash turned and looked at his tactical officer. The Tannans were passionate people, sometimes to the point of being extreme. But they were also fiercely loyal and proud. So proud, he had often wondered how the Jung had managed to hold control over their world for as long as they had.

Captain Nash took a deep breath and sighed. "Everyone, to the evac shuttles."

Combat One appeared in a blue-white flash of light no more than ten meters above their heads. The shock wave caused by the sudden displacement of air would have knocked anyone else to the ground, but the Ghatazhak's motion-assist undergarments stiffened appropriately to hold them steadfast against the rush of air.

Commander Telles, Master Sergeant Jahal, and the last two Ghatazhak soldiers ran to the combat jump shuttle as it settled onto the tarmac. Behind them, several hundred terrified Tannans chased after them in a final, desperate attempt to escape certain death.

The first two Ghatazhak soldiers jumped up into the port door to the combat jumper as Sergeant Torwell brought his top-mounted weapons turret around to the port side and opened fire on the charging crowd.

Commander Telles and Master Sergeant Jahal stood on the port side of the combat jumper, firing away at the crowd, determined to keep them far enough away that they could safely take off.

"*Twenty seconds to impact!*" Ensign Latfee called over the commander's helmet comms from the combat jump shuttle's copilot seat.

Both the commander and the master sergeant took a step backward toward the combat jumper. Master Sergeant Jahal stopped firing and climbed inside. Once inside, he opened fire again, while Commander Telles climbed up into the shuttle.

"*Ten seconds!*" Ensign Latfee warned.

"Let's go!" the commander ordered as he climbed into his seat.

The combat jump shuttle's engines screamed back up to takeoff power, lifting the shuttle from the tarmac. Commander Telles continued to look outside as the shuttle climbed and accelerated forward. The doors slid closed, and the sergeant in the topside turret stopped firing. The commander gazed out the window as they passed over the raging crowd. As they passed over them, something caught the commander's attention. A young man and a young woman, crouched down behind the corner of one of the line shacks, each of them clutching something wrapped up in small blankets. Something small, about the size of...

Oh, my God, the commander thought. "Wait!" he exclaimed. "Put us down!"

There was a bright flash of white light from behind them.

"Nuclear detonation!" Ensign Latfee reported.

"There's no time!" Lieutenant Kainan insisted, as the combat shuttle's windows turned opaque.

* * *

Jessica stood at the forward end of the Aurora's port hangar bay, watching Combat One roll out of the mid-bay elevator airlock. As the shuttle rolled out, its port side door slid open, revealing the four Ghatazhak and the shuttle's crew chief in the back. Two Ghatazhak soldiers stepped down out of the shuttle as it rolled, followed by Commander Telles and Master Sergeant Jahal.

Jessica looked at Commander Telles' face, locking eyes with him. She knew by his expression that he had been unable to retrieve her friend and her friend's family. She turned and headed back toward the forward hatch.

Commander Telles continued walking toward the forward end of the hangar bay, his trusted master sergeant at his side.

"You're not going to tell her?" the master sergeant asked.

"It would serve no purpose," Commander Telles replied.

"She will find out...somehow, someday."

"Perhaps, but hopefully she will be in a better state of mind then. She is too close to the edge now."

"You got that right."

Commander Telles spotted Captain Scott coming out of the forward hatch. "See to the men," he instructed the master sergeant. "Get them fed and rested. We will be needed for search and rescue, once the remaining Jung ships are driven from Tanna."

"Yes, sir," Master Sergeant Jahal replied.

Commander Telles walked up to Captain Scott.

"Commander," Nathan greeted. "A rough one?"

"It was not pleasant," the commander admitted. "Did any of the gunships survive?"

"I'm afraid not."

"That is unfortunate. They were a valuable asset," the commander said. "What about the people on the asteroid base? What about Captain Nash?"

"They made it out just before a missile strike took out the entire asteroid."

Commander Telles looked surprised. "That is illogical. To destroy a valuable fuel depot."

"They probably figured we'd blow it before we'd hand it over to them anyway," Nathan said. "Which is true, of course."

"Of course."

"I take it you were unable to retrieve Lieutenant Commander Nash's friend," Nathan surmised.

"That is correct," the commander replied. "I sent a team to her residence as soon as we arrived, but she was not there. The team conducted an aerial search, but to no avail."

Nathan sighed, looking back toward the corridor where he and Jessica had passed without words a moment ago.

"How do you think she will handle this?" Commander Telles asked.

Nathan was surprised by the commander's genuine concern. "We will see. I suspect she'll still be able to do her job. We had a *talk*."

The commander's eyebrow went up. "Indeed." Commander Telles thought for a moment, then spoke. "Captain, when we were departing, I saw a man and a woman huddled behind a small building on the tarmac. I believe they were each holding an infant wrapped in blankets. I know it sounds highly unlikely, considering the Cobra plant is a highly secure area..."

"Synda's husband worked at the plant," Nathan told him, a grim look on his face.

Commander Telles was at a loss for words. "She did not tell me. If I had known, I would have had my men search the crowds trying to get on the evacua..."

"Not your fault, Commander," Nathan interrupted. "Did you tell her?"

"I did not think it was an appropriate moment," Commander Telles explained. "The lieutenant commander and I have not been on the best of terms since the battle of Kohara."

"You were probably right not to say anything

right now," Nathan agreed. "But you *will* have to tell her someday."

"I understand."

"Very well," Nathan said. He patted the commander on the shoulder. "Get some food and rest," he told him. "We jump to Tanna in forty-five minutes."

* * *

"Two minutes to jump point," Mister Riley announced.

"General quarters," Nathan ordered.

"General quarters, aye," Naralena replied.

Nathan rotated his command chair to face aft, as the trim lights all about the Aurora's bridge turned red to indicate her change in level of readiness. "Lieutenant Commander, do you have the updated orbital tracks from Falcon One?"

"Affirmative, sir," Jessica replied. "They should be halfway around the planet by now. Last count was four frigates and one battleship. No fighters or gunships in the area. All updated targeting data has been provided to the Celestia's tactical officer."

"One minute," Mister Riley updated.

"All departments report general quarters," Naralena reported. "XO is in combat, COB is in damage control. Flight ops reports all combat and SAR birds are ready for launch."

"All shields are up, all weapons are charged," Jessica reported.

"Very well," Nathan replied.

"Thirty seconds," Mister Riley said.

"Jump flash," Mister Navashee reported. "Falcon One."

"Incoming message from Falcon One," Naralena

told Nathan. "Ensign Sheehan reports no change in any of the targets' orbital tracks."

"Very well."

"Celestia reports general quarters, ready to jump," Naralena added.

"With those Falcons jumping in and out to keep an eye on them, those Jung ships have got to suspect something is coming," Jessica warned. "They'll be ready."

"They won't be ready enough," Nathan said with conviction.

"Coming up on first jump point," Mister Riley informed them.

"Execute both jumps as planned, Mister Riley."

"Jump one, in three......two......one......jumping."

The subdued jump flash lit up the interior of the Aurora's bridge for the briefest of moments, as the ship transitioned from the recharge layover point nineteen light years from the 72 Herculis system, to a point only five light years out.

"Jump complete. Verifying jump two plot. Jump drive one down to seven point five percent of max energy." Mister Riley checked his console. "Forty seconds to attack jump."

Nathan sat as patiently as he could, knowing that every moment they spent here was another moment that a nuclear weapon could be detonating on Tanna. He also knew that no matter what he did in the next hour, Tanna was doomed. The Jung ships had already dropped enough nuclear weapons on the planet to eventually wipe out all life on the surface, and make it uninhabitable for centuries to come. And for what reason? Because the Tannans had rejected their rule? It was a ludicrous thought, considering that the Jung's only interest in the system had been as a fueling stop on their way out of the sector. They could have just as easily struck up a mutually beneficial deal with the Tannans that did not require conquering them.

Of course, none of that mattered now. All that mattered was that the Jung ships that put the final nail into Tanna's coffin were going to be destroyed, and with as much force and aggression as he could muster.

"Jump plot verified," Mister Riley reported. "Twenty seconds to jump."

"Celestia reports ready for attack jump," Naralena reported.

"Execute attack jump as scheduled," Nathan instructed.

"Aye, sir," Mister Riley replied. "Attack jump in ten seconds."

Nathan closed his eyes, clearing his thoughts and emotions as his navigator counted down the last few seconds to the jump. This battle would be personal.

The inside of Nathan's eyelids glowed brightly for a split second.

"Jump complete," the navigator reported.

Nathan opened his eyes.

"Five contacts," Mister Navashee announced. "Four frigates, one battleship. Targets one and two, dead ahead. Five kilometers, and two thousand kilometers."

"Plotting jump to second target," the navigator said.

"Locking onto primary target," Jessica announced. "Give me two down and one to port, Mister Chiles."

"Two down, one to port," the helmsman replied.

"Battleship is three thousand kilometers to port," Mister Navashee continued.

"I've got a firing solution," Jessica announced from the tactical station.

"Fire all forward tubes," Nathan ordered, "singles only."

"Single shots, all forward tubes, aye," Jessica replied.

"Jump flash," Mister Navashee added. "Celestia is making her run on frigate three."

"Jump to second target is plotted and ready," Mister Riley said.

"Torpedoes away," Jessica reported, as the Aurora's bridge lit up with red-orange flashes.

"Battleship is locking missiles on us," Mister Navashee warned.

"Torpedo impacts," Jessica reported.

Nathan watched the main view screen as the first Jung frigate, still three kilometers away, exploded behind a barrage of red-orange impact flashes.

"Snap jump us to the second target," Nathan instructed calmly.

"Battleship is firing missiles," Mister Navashee warned.

"Snap jumping to second target," Mister Riley replied.

"Jump complete," Ensign Sperry reported.

"Second frigate, dead ahead," Ensign Kono reported from the Celestia's sensor station. "Three kilometers."

"I have a firing solution," Luis reported from the tactical station.

"Fire when ready," Cameron instructed from her command chair.

"Firing singles, all forward tubes."

"Aurora has destroyed frigate two," Ensign Kono announced. "They're jumping away."

"Message from the Aurora just before she jumped," Ensign Souza reported from the comm station. "They're setting up for phase two."

"Target four is destroyed," Ensign Kono confirmed.

"Mister Hunt, climbing turn, forty degrees to starboard."

"Climbing turn, forty to starboard, aye."

"Mister Sperry, make ready a two-light-minute jump."

"Jump complete," Mister Riley reported. "Intercept angle is perfect, sir."

"I have a firing solution on the battleship," Jessica said.

"Very well," Nathan replied. "Stand by to snap jump to next firing position. Tactical, two rounds of triplets, full power, all forward tubes. Fire when ready."

"Full power triplets, all forward tubes...firing," Jessica reported.

The Aurora's bridge again lit up with red-orange light as two rounds of triplets, a total of forty-eight plasma torpedoes, headed for the distant Jung battleship.

Nathan glanced up at the time display on the tactical display screen to the right of his helmsman.

"All torpedoes away," Jessica reported.

"Ready on the jump," Mister Riley added.

Nathan watched the seconds count down, waiting for the plasma torpedoes they had just launched to travel approximately half the distance to their target. "Snap jump... Now."

"Jumping."

"Two more rounds of the same," Nathan ordered. "Fire on my order."

"First rounds will pass us in fifteen seconds," Mister Navashee warned.

"Give me four degrees up, one to starboard," Jessica instructed the helmsman.

"Four up, one to starboard."

"That's it," Jessica said. "I have a solution."

"Five seconds," Mister Navashee warned.

Nathan turned his head to the right to look at the starboard edge of the Aurora's spherical main view screen, waiting. Two seconds later, two groups of twenty-four plasma torpedoes streaked past their starboard side.

"Fire," Nathan ordered.

"Firing," Jessica replied.

The bridge flashed red-orange again as forty-eight more plasma torpedoes headed for the Jung battleship.

"All torpedoes away!" Jessica reported.

"Ready on the next jump?" Nathan asked his navigator.

"Aye, sir," Mister Riley replied. "Plotted and ready."

"Picking up Celestia's plasma torpedoes now," Mister Navashee reported from the sensor station. "All torpedoes, theirs and ours, should strike the target within a thirty-second period."

"That should shake them up a bit," Jessica commented.

"Ninety-six plasma torpedoes over thirty seconds?" Nathan said. "I should hope so."

"First impacts in twenty seconds," Mister Navashee reported.

"Execute your next jump, Mister Riley," Nathan ordered.

"Jumping."

"Executing turn to parallel course with target and decelerating," Mister Chiles reported as the Aurora's jump flash subsided.

"You're sure about this, right?" Nathan asked, turning to look over his shoulder at Jessica.

"Hey, it wasn't my idea," Jessica defended, "it was Delaveaga's. But yeah, it makes sense. Our shields are more effective when the angle of incidence is shallow. If we nose up to her midship, she won't have a single gun that can fire directly on our forward shields."

"Turn complete," Mister Chiles reported. "Pitching ninety to port, forty-five up."

"Jump is plotted and ready," Mister Riley added.

"First torpedoes should be striking the target now," Mister Navashee updated.

Nathan glanced at the time display on the starboard tactical view screen. "Execute jump on my mark, Mister Riley."

"Standing by to jump on your mark."

"Celestia reports she is ready to jump in high as planned," Naralena announced.

"Very well."

"Pitch maneuver complete," the helmsman announced. "Our nose is now perpendicular to our flight path, with a forty-five-degree up angle."

"All forward torpedo tubes are charged and ready," Jessica added. "Forward plasma cannon turrets are also charged and ready. All forward shields are at full power."

"Coming up on initial impacts plus thirty," Mister Navashee announced.

"Jump us in," Nathan ordered.

"Jumping."

Nathan closed his eyes briefly as the jump flash illuminated the bridge for a split second.

"Jump complete."

Nathan opened his eyes.

"Range to target, one hundred meters!" Mister Navashee reported. "Her midship shields are down to twenty percent!"

Nathan stared at the main view screen as the Jung battleship's starboard side slid across, filling it from side to side.

"Those are some impressive shields!" Jessica commented.

"Jump flash! The Celestia jumped in above us," Mister Navashee reported.

"Firing position in five seconds," Jessica added.

"Fire when ready," Nathan instructed.

The Aurora slid sideways alongside the massive Jung battleship, approaching from her stern, forty-five degrees below her. The Celestia was sliding sideways as well, but approaching from the battleship's bow, sliding aft, forty-five degrees above the enemy vessel.

The Aurora was the first to open fire, firing triplets from her forward mark three plasma torpedo cannons, as well as her new mark five torpedo cannons under her bow. In addition, all four of her forward, quad-barreled, plasma cannon turrets opened up, sending a constant stream of plasma bolts pouring into the battleship's starboard midship shield.

The enemy ship's shields turned a bright yellow as both ships continued to pound away at her failing shield. The battleship swung every gun it had onto its attackers...their dorsal guns taking aim on the Celestia, and their ventral guns firing at the Aurora. But both ships were nose-toward-target, giving the battleship very poor firing angles which greatly reduced the effect of their rail gun slugs on the Alliance ships' shields.

All three ships' shields glowed and shimmered as their strengths were tested. The Jung's a brilliant yellow, and the Alliance ships' a pale blue.

———————

Nathan watched as the flashing shields of both ships lit up his bridge. Never before had he brought his ship so close to an enemy target in order to sit there and slug it out. The view was almost mesmerizing, filling the entire spherical view screen. He looked up, and could barely make out the Celestia high above him as she fired away, her image obscured by both ships' shimmering shields.

Then there was a brilliant white flash of light.

"Target's shield is down!" Mister Navashee reported.

Nathan's attention returned to the middle of the view screen, as the Aurora's plasma torpedoes tore into the hull of the battleship, as it began to slide to the right.

"Target is accelerating!" Mister Navashee said. "She's making a run for FTL! She's charging her mass-canceling fields!"

"Celestia has ceased firing!" Jessica added. "They're yawing to starboard! We're losing our firing solution!"

"Full translation to starboard, Mister Chiles!" Nathan ordered.

"Starboard translation at full!"

The rate at which the Jung battleship slid to their right decreased almost immediately, but did not stop.

"Keep our tubes on them!" Nathan insisted.

"Celestia is firing her mains!" Mister Navashee reported. "She's accelerating past the target. She's... She's moving in *front* of the battleship, sir!"

"They're trying to block them from running!" Nathan realized.

"We can't translate fast enough to keep up with her," Mister Chiles warned, "and if I yaw to keep our tubes on her, we can't use our translation..."

"The broadside cannons!" Jessica yelled.

"Helm! Return our nose to flight path and fire up the mains!" Nathan instructed. "Bring us level with the target and bring our port broadside cannons in line with her midship!"

"Aye, sir!" the helmsman replied.

"I'll bring in all our portside guns as well," Jessica said, "top and bottom!"

"Fire at will!" Nathan ordered.

The Celestia pulled ahead of the fleeing Jung battleship and turned to put herself directly in the path of the ship, about eight hundred meters ahead of her and matching her speed. She then swung her nose around, flying backwards, and used her deceleration thrusters to accelerate at the same rate as the Jung battleship.

"Target is still accelerating," Ensign Kono reported from the Celestia's sensor station.

"Doesn't matter," Cameron replied. "As long as we're in front of her, she can't go to FTL."

"Are you sure about that?" Lieutenant Delaveaga

challenged as he continued to fire the Celestia's plasma torpedo cannons.

"She's right!" Ensign Kono confirmed. "We've got too much mass! If they go to FTL, they'll collide with us, and their mass-canceling fields will fail! The result would be catastrophic!"

"Yeah, for us as well!" Luis replied.

"They're closing on us," Ensign Sperry warned.

"We're already at full power on decel engines!" Ensign Hunt added.

"Can we flip back over and go to our mains?" Cameron asked.

"No, sir!" Ensign Sperry replied. "She'd ram us before we completed our end-over."

"That's what she wants," Cameron realized. "How badly will they be damaged if they collide with us at our current closure rate?"

"Plenty of damage," Ensign Kono replied. "But I'm pretty sure we'll get the worst of it."

"She's right!" the systems officer confirmed. "Our forward shields are at fifty percent and falling!"

"Target's forward shields are at eighty-four percent, and falling slowly," Ensign Kono added.

"The Aurora is pulling alongside the target!" Lieutenant Delaveaga reported from the Celestia's tactical station. "They're going to broadside guns!"

"How long before they ram us?" Cameron asked.

"Ninety seconds!" Ensign Kono replied.

"Be ready on that escape jump, Mister Sperry."

"We'll be jumping along the same course as the target, sir!" the navigator replied. "If we execute a standard escape jump, and they go to FTL..."

"Set your escape jump range to one light hour!" Cameron ordered. "That will give us plenty of time to get out of their way!"

"The target is still accelerating toward the Celestia!" Mister Navashee reported from the Aurora's sensor station. "Target has dropped all shields except for those around her bow! She's channeling all her power into her forward shields!"

"Keep firing everything you can, Jess!" Nathan ordered. "We've got to crack her open before she goes to FTL! She's betting she can win this race!"

"I am, sir!" Jessica replied. "But that bitch has got one thick-ass hull!"

"At her current rate of acceleration, the target will collide with the Celestia in one minute!"

"She'll jump out of the way, right?" Jessica wondered.

"I sure as hell hope so," Nathan replied.

"Jump flashes!" Mister Navashee reported with excitement. "Six Super Falcons! Aft of the target, three kilometers and closing!"

"Comms!" Nathan called. "Tell them to fire on her main propulsion!"

"Aye, sir!" Naralena replied.

"Our port shields are down to fifty percent across the board!" the systems officer warned, as the enemy ship continued to pound the Aurora's shields with her massive rail guns.

"Falcons are firing!" Mister Navashee announced. "Target is bringing her aft guns around to target the Falcons."

"Oh, fuck!" Loki exclaimed. "They're bringing their aft guns around! Two and Three! Target those guns! Quickly!" Loki instructed over the comms. "Everyone! Take evasive actions, but keep firing!"

Josh began maneuvering the Super Falcon about

wildly, while keeping their nose pointed at the target, as he continued to fire their plasma torpedoes at the Jung battleship's main propulsion section. "We gotta slide in close!" Josh insisted. "They won't be able to touch us!"

"We'll be in the thrust wash, Josh!"

"It's better than being in their cross hairs! Besides, we've got shields, remember!" Josh didn't wait for Loki's agreement, dialing up a jump range of two and a half kilometers and pushing his selector switch up.

"Falcons have jumped!" Mister Navashee reported. "They jumped in closer to the target!"

"They're getting in tight so the target's aft guns can't get a solution on them!" Jessica realized.

"They did it!" Mister Navashee exclaimed. "The battleship has lost main propulsion! She's no longer accelerating!"

"Comms, tell them to keep firing!" Nathan ordered. "Mister Navashee, how long until they collide?"

"She's still closing on them," Mister Navashee replied. "Maybe fifty seconds now."

"They might have enough time to flip over and use their mains," Jessica suggested.

"Secondaries!" Mister Navashee reported. "Several of them!"

"Target's losing all forward shields!" Jessica added.

"They're losing main power!" Mister Navashee continued.

"Keep firing," Nathan ordered with determination. He slowly rose to his feet, staring at the main view screen as it displayed the view from the portside cameras. Chunks of the Jung battleship's hull flew in every direction as balls of plasma fired from the Aurora's broadside cannons tore into the target. More secondary explosions deep within the battleship ripped her apart, from the inside out.

The Aurora's shields suddenly stopped flashing and shimmering.

"Target is no longer firing," Mister Navashee reported. "They've lost all power, Captain. Main and secondary."

The nose of the great battleship suddenly exploded, destroying the entire forward quarter of the ship.

"The Celestia hit their missile bays!" Mister Navashee reported. "The target is slowing. Collision is no longer imminent."

"Cease-fire while we bring our tubes back onto what's left of her," Nathan instructed. "Comms, tell the Falcons to disengage and stand clear. Same goes for the Celestia."

"Aye, sir."

"Forward cameras, please," Nathan instructed as he stared at the main view screen.

"They're doomed, Captain," Mister Navashee said. "That explosion slowed them down enough that their orbit will decay in a few days. They'll burn up in the atmosphere."

"I don't care," Nathan replied coldly, as he watched the battleship slide to the middle of the main view screen once again. "Helm, back us away to avoid debris. Tactical. All forward tubes and guns. Full power, singles. Let's finish this."

"Full power singles on all forward tubes. All forward guns. Firing," Jessica replied.

Nathan stood there and watched, along with everyone on the Aurora's bridge, while the Jung ship that destroyed Tanna broke up, and finally exploded under the Aurora's heavy bombardment.

* * *

Nathan entered the Aurora's main hangar bay located directly below her main flight deck. Normally full of Super Eagles, Super Falcons, and various types of jump shuttles, it was now full of evacuees from Tanna. Medical teams, jump-shuttled in from both Earth and Tau Ceti, triaged Tannans and Terrans alike as they unloaded the shuttles still sitting in the elevator airlocks. The triage started with radiation scans meant to separate those with lower dosages who could wait for treatment, from those with higher dosages who needed immediate nanite therapy to prevent death. Once categorized by the radiation teams, they went to medical triage. Those who could walk moved under their own power through the registration line where volunteers provided food, water, and comfort while the identities of the refugees were logged. Those whose injuries prevented them from walking were further divided into immediate and delayed treatment groups.

It had been less than two hours since the last Jung ship bombarding Tanna had been destroyed, after which the search and rescue operations on the surface of Tanna had begun in earnest. The Jung had only managed to bombard two thirds of the planet, but it was enough to guarantee that it would be uninhabitable for decades to come, if not centuries. Boxcars were already shuttling Tannans from the one third of Tanna that had not been directly attacked, back to Earth as quickly as possible in order to return and load up again. There were still tens of thousands of people on the surface who, although not directly attacked, were at great risk of radiation exposure if not evacuated in short order.

Two hours, and the Aurora had already taken more than one thousand wounded onto her decks. Troop and cargo jump shuttles, hastily converted into medical transports, were ferrying the wounded stable enough to survive a few more hours without treatment back to Earth, while those in immediate need were being treated anywhere they could. In the medical departments of the Aurora and the Celestia, in the corridors, even in the hangar bay itself...the wounded were everywhere. The goal was simple: stabilize them enough to move them to Earth.

Nathan couldn't imagine how Earth was reacting to the events on Tanna. Every Alliance world was offering help. Food, shelter, clothing, water, medical care, housing...anything and everything they could share, they were willing to provide to the people of Tanna.

Although the scene in his hangar deck seemed like a chaotic mess, Nathan knew that it was anything but. His medical staff, led by Doctor Chen, had recently conducted such mass casualty drills, and in this very bay. They had a system, and they had rehearsed it. Now those efforts were paying dividends that could not be adequately measured.

Jessica suddenly ran past him. Nathan watched her run toward the starboard, forward elevator airlock as it opened. A cargo shuttle was inside, its aft end pointing toward the bay so that its passengers could be offloaded down its cargo ramp and directly into the hangar bay.

Commander Telles came walking down the ramp, carrying an injured young woman.

Nathan headed toward the commander, breaking into a run within a few steps.

Jessica ran up to the commander as he stepped out of the elevator airlock and carefully placed the injured woman onto the deck. "Oh, my God, Synda," Jessica gasped, kneeling down next to her and brushing Synda's hair back from her eyes. A nearby medical team noticed that the commander had carried in the wounded girl himself, and immediately ran to her side to provide aid. They pushed Jessica back out of the way and started working frantically on the badly wounded young woman.

Jessica knelt down a meter beyond the medical team, her hands cupped over her mouth, her face twisted with anguish as she watched them try to save her friend's life.

As Nathan stepped up behind Jessica, he saw Synda turn her head toward Jessica and open her eyes. Synda looked at Jessica and tried to speak, but could only cough, small amounts of blood and tissue spewing from her lips as she did so. Synda's eyes were pleading for help.

Nathan looked down at Jessica, as she lay face down on the deck straining to reach her friend's hand. Despite the objections of the medical team, Jessica finally managed to take Synda's hand and squeeze it firmly. As she did so, Synda's eyes went blank and motionless. Her breathing stopped. Jessica watched as the light in Synda's eyes faded away, and her grip on Jessica's hand went limp. The medical team worked frantically to revive Synda, but her injuries were too severe, and there were so many others who needed their help...others who had a chance to live, if they received care in a timely fashion. For Synda, all hope was gone.

Jessica's face fell, her arms wrapped around her head, as she lay motionless on the deck.

Sergeant Lazo came down the ramp from the cargo shuttle, carrying an infant wrapped in a medical blanket. The baby started crying, startled as it came from the more quiet environment of the small cargo shuttle, into the noisier environment of the massive hangar bay bustling with activity.

Jessica heard the baby's cries and raised her head. She spotted the sergeant, and immediately got to her feet and moved quickly toward him, taking the baby from his arms. Jessica looked at the child, recognizing the tiny face. "Give her to me," she said softly.

Sergeant Lazo handed the crying infant over to Jessica.

"There, there," Jessica cooed. She looked at the sergeant. "Where's the other one?" she asked.

Sergeant Lazo looked at Commander Telles, unsure of what to say.

"The other child did not survive," Commander Telles told her. "This one lived only because her father attempted to shield them all from the blast with his own body."

Jessica's eyes were welling up with tears as she rocked the baby in her arms, trying to calm the terrified child down.

"I am so sorry, Jessica," Commander Telles said.

Jessica looked at the commander, then turned to look at Nathan as he moved closer to her. "I don't even know which one she is," Jessica whispered, choking back her tears. "Ania or Esma. I think it's Ania," she said, starting to weep, "I'm just not sure."

Nathan put his arm around her, and led Jessica and the infant slowly toward the exit.

CHAPTER THIRTEEN

Admiral Dumar sat at the head of the conference table in the command briefing room deep inside the Karuzara asteroid base, listening to representatives from each of the Alliance worlds within the Sol sector.

"The fact is, this could happen to any of us," the representative from Weldon insisted. "Once routine communications are lost with a Jung world, it is only a matter of time until a fleet of ships comes to investigate."

"The only reason a *fleet* of ships arrived in the 72 Herculis system was because they were on their way out of the system," the representative from Beta Hydri argued. "Until a few years ago, we never had more than a single Jung ship in our system."

"You don't know that for sure," the representative from Weldon replied. "They could have been responding to a report made when the first Falcon appeared in the system. More than enough time has passed since then for..."

"Gentlemen," President Scott interrupted, "we are arguing over details that can never be proven one way or the other. Yes, the Jung could show up in any system, at any time, with any number of ships. However, Tanna was the *only* world that was outside of our one-minute jump range, *which*, I might add, could be extended to forty-two light years, given a few more months. *If* the Jung should suddenly arrive in any of our systems, the Alliance *will* be able to respond, in force."

"That's easy for you to say," the representative

from Weldon said irritably. "The Alliance is *based* in your system."

"Weldon is a mere seventeen light years from Sol, Mister Paulson," The representative from Tau Ceti pointed out. "You have little to worry about."

"Said the man whose system has *two*, soon to be *three*, warships parked at home."

"You are only twenty-five light years from Tau Ceti," President Kanor replied. "Short of a battle platform showing up on your doorstep, *all* of the Alliance ships would arrive before the Jung made it into orbit over your world!"

"Please, gentlemen," President Scott urged as the men raised their voices to be heard over one another.

"How many lives were lost defending Tanna?" Mister Paulson asked in a louder voice.

"What does that have to do with anything?" President Kanor asked, irritated.

"What would you suggest, Mister Paulson?" President Scott wondered. "Would you like to offer your world back to the Jung? Beg their forgiveness?"

"That is not an option, and you know it," Mister Paulson said in an accusatory tone. "After all, the Alliance liberated my world without consent."

"How were they supposed to get consent?" President Kanor wondered. "Jump in and ask the Jung for permission to conduct a planet-wide poll, or something?"

"Do not mock me, sir," Mister Paulson warned.

"Sit down, Paulson," President Kanor said, waving him off.

"And what if a battle platform *did* show up in one of our systems?" the representative from Delta Pavonis questioned. "What would the Alliance do?"

"Battle platforms come out of FTL several hours sub-light travel time from inhabited worlds," Admiral Dumar said. "In fact, they usually stay a considerable distance out. It would be quite easy to launch a jump KKV attack against a target at such a position."

"But that takes time," the representative from Delta Pavonis argued. "An hour, if I remember correctly. Those battle platforms have gunships inside. Gunships that could be used against any of our worlds while you are preparing your jump KKV attack."

"Gunships that could easily be handled by Super Falcons, or our own gunships, not to mention our larger ships," Admiral Dumar explained.

"You don't *have* any more gunships," Mister Paulson reminded the admiral.

"We have already begun planning a new gunship manufacturing plant on Sorenson," President Kanor assured them. "In six months, we will have at least fifteen to twenty new gunships, fully crewed and ready for action."

"Six months?" Mister Paulson said indignantly. "I'm talking about right now! We have to take action, and we have to take it now!"

"What would you have us do, Mister Paulson?" President Scott inquired.

"We need to attack!"

"We have been," the president replied patiently.

"I'm talking about the Jung homeworld! We need to show the Jung that we can take the fight to their home system, the same way that they have taken it to everyone else's!"

"Are you mad?" President Kanor asked, almost laughing. "You saw the preliminary intelligence reports, Paulson. The Jung have more than one hundred ships in their home system, many of them battleships *and* battle platforms! It would be suicide." President Kanor looked at Admiral Dumar for support. "Tell him, Admiral!"

Admiral Dumar said nothing.

President Kanor stared at the admiral. "Admiral?"

"*Mad* is a strong word," the admiral replied. "It implies an impulsive act, one without forethought, one without a specific, tangible goal in mind. Aggressive? Yes. Risky? Most definitely. However, risk can be mitigated."

President Kanor continued to look at the admiral, waiting for him to continue. "You're serious, aren't you?"

"The question you must ask is, 'Why?'" Admiral Dumar said. "What would you hope to accomplish with such an attack? What message would you like to send?"

"That we can hurt them as much as they can hurt us!" Mister Paulson declared.

"That is an untrue statement," Admiral Dumar disagreed in his usual calm demeanor. "The Jung outnumber us by a sizable margin. Granted, we may have technology on our side, but if they were to gather their numbers into a unified force, and then go on a rampage, there would be no stopping them."

"Then you don't believe we should attack their homeworld?" President Kanor surmised.

"I did not say that. I said you must be fully aware of what it is you wish to accomplish by attacking their homeworld."

"To show them that we *can*," Mister Paulson said.

"*That*, sir, is a stupid reason, by itself."

President Scott took a moment to consider his

words. "Admiral, if you decided to attack the Jung homeworld at this time, what would *you* be trying to accomplish?"

Admiral Dumar stared at the others for a moment, considering his answer. It was a question he had asked himself many times before. "Attacking the Jung homeworld for the purpose of destroying as many of their ships as possible would be a foolish waste of time and resources. Yes, destroy as many ships as possible, but more importantly, we *must* show them that we are able, *and willing*, to take innocent human lives, in the same fashion as they have demonstrated, time and time again. So far, they have seen us fight when our backs were against the wall, and we had no choice. They have also seen us go on the offensive, using the element of surprise to minimize our losses, in order to secure a safe perimeter around our worlds. What they have *not* yet seen, is that we are willing to go above and beyond, to take that extra step, to cross the furthest line... that we are willing to do what other men cannot do... what the Jung *already* do. *That* is a valid reason to attack the Jung home system."

"You want us to target the innocent citizens of the Jung Empire?" Mister Paulson exclaimed, outraged. "Kill innocent women and children?"

"Of course I do not *want* to do such a thing," the admiral defended. "But I do recognize that such a thing must be done in order to send the correct message. And for the record, we do not have to directly target the innocent. We simply have to ignore concerns of collateral damage, which, I might point out, is still a far sight better than what the Jung themselves do."

500

"Using the same moral measure as the Jung would not serve us well," President Kanor warned.

"Of course," Admiral Dumar agreed. "Which is why we should not directly target non-military targets. However, if the Jung chose to locate their military assets in the middle of heavily populated areas, that is their own problem. We should not make it ours."

Neither President Kanor nor Mister Paulson had a response.

"Do you believe you can successfully execute such an attack?" President Scott wondered.

"Without incurring losses that would put us at further risk?" Mister Paulson added.

"I do," Admiral Dumar replied, without hesitation. "However, there is another question to ask, before considering such an attack. 'How will the Jung react?'"

Those assembled exchanged concerned glances.

"Will they request a cease-fire, or will they become so enraged that they set out to destroy all our worlds?" Admiral Dumar continued.

"Assume the latter," President Scott suggested. "How would they go about it? Could we defend against it? What kind of time frame are we talking about?"

"All legitimate questions, yet all of them irrelevant to this discussion," Dumar replied. "There are only two ways to prevent the Jung from eventually destroying us all. Either we must destroy them, or we must convince them that *our* destruction would guarantee their own."

* * *

Nathan entered his quarters and closed the door behind him. The last five days had been grueling for him and his crew. In fact, it had been difficult for everyone throughout the Alliance. Every member world had pitched in to help the Tannans in any way that they could. But even with all that help, there was nothing that anyone could do to save their world. Tanna was lost.

That fact was what weighed on Nathan's mind the most these days. It wasn't the one point five million people who had died, or the tens of thousands who were now fighting to recover in hospitals all over the Alliance. It wasn't even the Tannans who were now homeless. It was simply the knowledge that they all lived in a galaxy where someone could do this to an entire world, and feel justified in doing so.

It wasn't the first time that Nathan had experienced this feeling. The Ta'Akar Empire had been just as heinous in some of their acts. That made it even more difficult. It might be easier for him to accept that a single, evil empire was willing to commit such atrocities. But seeing *two* completely unrelated empires, each of them unaware of the other, and both capable of such acts, it left Nathan with little hope for humanity as a whole.

Nathan tossed his uniform jacket on the chair in the corner of his bedroom and sat down on the edge of his bed. After untying and removing his boots, he fell backward onto his bed, his arms spread wide. All he wanted to do was sleep—for days if he could— perhaps to dream of anything other than his current reality.

Perhaps a mountain cabin, on the edge of a lake, he thought, his eyes closed. *No spaceships, no comm-sets, no Alliance. Just peace and quiet.*

Just as he was about to drift off to sleep, his door buzzer sounded. He ignored it. It sounded again.

"Oh, for crying out loud," he said, sitting up. The buzzer sounded a third time.

Nathan rose from his bed and headed back into the living room. The buzzer sounded a fourth time. "Unbelievable," he said as he reached for the door latch. He swung the door open, and found Vladimir standing on the other side, a bag in one hand, and a bottle in the other.

"I'm not hungry," Nathan said as he turned around and headed for the couch.

"Of course you are," Vladimir disagreed.

"How would you know?"

"Your cook told me you haven't been eating," Vladimir said, closing the door and following Nathan to the seating area in the middle of the living room. He sat down in one of the chairs, opened the bag, and pulled out something wrapped in plastic and tossed it to Nathan.

"What's this?" Nathan wondered, catching the item.

"Dollag steak sandwich," Vladimir answered, as he pulled out one for himself as well.

"Oh," Nathan drooled. "With the spicy green paste?"

"And tomato and onion."

"Damn," Nathan said, opening the wrapper. "I thought we ran out of dollag steaks months ago."

"You should check your own pantry," Vladimir said. "You've still got several kilograms of it in the freezer."

Nathan bit a large piece off his sandwich and chewed it with vigor. "You are such a good friend."

"I know," Vladimir agreed as he took a bite of his own sandwich. He set his food down on the coffee table and picked up the bottle from the floor, opening it. He took a healthy swig, then passed it to Nathan. "Drink this."

Nathan took the bottle from him, held it up to his nose and sniffed it. "Whoa. What the hell is this? It smells awful."

"Better you don't smell it," Vladimir instructed.

"What is it?"

"Better you don't know."

"I'm not going to drink it, if I don't know what it is," Nathan said stubbornly.

"Just trust me."

"That's why I want to know what it is."

"It's homemade beer, alright?"

"In whose home was it made?"

"A good friend."

"A good friend?" Nathan sniffed it again. "Damn, the smell makes my eyes water. Who the fuck made it, Vlad?"

"Okay, I did," Vladimir finally admitted. "I made it."

"On board?"

"Actually, no. Well, yes and no. The first couple of batches I made on Porto Santo. This batch, I made in my quarters."

"You have a brewery in your quarters?" Nathan took a swig.

"In my head, actually."

"How big is your head?" Nathan asked as he took another drink of the foul smelling beer. "Mine's barely big enough for me."

"For some reason, my head is twice the size of every other head on this ship," Vladimir told him. "It is very odd. There is this big empty space between the toilet and the shower. Almost enough room for a second shower."

"So you decided to put a brewery in there instead."

"It made sense, especially since this stuff smells like shit," Vladimir said, a grin on his face.

Nathan laughed. "Yes, it does. Exactly like shit, in fact." He took another drink. "It doesn't taste like shit, though." He handed the bottle back to Vladimir. "It actually tastes pretty good."

"That's the alcohol in it talking," Vladimir told him, then took a good long drink himself.

"How much?" Nathan asked, taking another bite of his sandwich.

"Eighteen percent, I think."

"Holy crap," Nathan replied, shocked. "You realize this is totally against regs, right?"

"It is okay," Vladimir said. "The captain and I are close friends."

"Give me that," Nathan insisted, taking the bottle from Vladimir and taking another drink. "I should confiscate this, you know."

"You can keep it," Vladimir told him. "I have more."

Nathan laughed, placing the bottle on the table and leaning back on the couch as he took another bite of his sandwich. He let out a long sigh.

"It has been a difficult week," Vladimir commented, noting his friend's general melancholy.

"I've had worse, I suppose," Nathan replied. "Not *much* worse, of course."

"It is not your fault, Nathan. You know this."

"I never said it was my fault."

"You didn't have to," Vladimir replied. "I know you. You think everything is your fault."

"I do not."

"Well, maybe not that *everything* is your *fault*, but you do always wonder if you could have done something different, something that would have prevented something bad from happening."

"Perhaps, but that's not the same thing."

"No, but it is close. I know you," Vladimir reiterated.

"Oh really? Then what am I thinking?"

Vladimir took another swig from the bottle, looked at Nathan, and thought. "You are thinking, 'If only I had never struck up that deal with Tanna, and helped them get rid of the Jung, then all of this never would have happened.'"

"Not bad," Nathan admitted, as he took another bite of his sandwich. "And it's true, by the way. The entire planet, and everyone on it, would still be alive today, if I had never agreed to help them."

"And if you hadn't helped them, we would have run out of propellant. The Jung would have captured the Celestia, or at least, the Celestia would no longer exist, and Earth would probably still be under Jung control. You were doing what you thought was the right thing to do for your people, just as that Tannan... What was his name?"

"Garrett."

"*Da*, Garrett. Just as Garrett thought he was doing at the time. It was just as much his decision as it was yours."

"That's the thing," Nathan said. "Did I really have the right to make such a decision? Did I have the right to put so many lives in jeopardy?"

"You didn't know you were putting their lives at risk at the time, Nathan," Vladimir argued. "You thought you were *improving* their lives, by giving them their freedom."

"But I was wrong."

"No, you weren't wrong. You simply could not

have foreseen all the possibilities. Your decision to get involved with the Tannans, to help them achieve their freedom from the Jung... It is not the reason they died. They died because the Jung attacked them."

"Because we helped them overthrow the Jung," Nathan reminded him.

"I ask you which shirt looks better on me, the red or the blue, and you say the red, and then a madman kills me because he doesn't like red shirts, is that your fault?"

"That's not the same," Nathan argued. "There's no way for me to anticipate that a madman hell bent on killing people wearing red shirts is going to see you and kill you."

"And at the time that you struck the deal with Garrett, you had no idea that the Jung routinely glassed worlds that defied them, did you?"

Nathan shrugged his shoulders. "I suppose not."

"You can only do what you think is right, based on the information you have at the time that you make your decision," Vladimir explained. "When are you going to get that through your head, Nathan?"

"Get what through my head?"

"What?"

Nathan smiled. "Must be the beer," he said, taking another swig. "I get what you're saying, Vlad, I really do. It's just that being the captain, you sometimes get put in situations where you have to make decisions that affect far more people than you could imagine. You know it when you make the decisions. But you make them anyway, and then you have to live with the consequences. It's damned tiring, sometimes."

"Then quit," Vladimir suggested.

Nathan looked at him, confused. "I can't quit."

"Sure you can," Vladimir insisted. "I mean, you can't quit the EDF, you enrolled for a ten-year term..."

"Actually, the EDF doesn't exist anymore, so technically..."

"*Da, da, da,*" Vladimir replied. "That is a good point. It is also another discussion entirely. What *I* mean is that you could step down as captain, take some other job. Something less stressful, like, flying a cargo shuttle, perhaps?"

"I can't do that," Nathan said, taking another swig from the bottle. "I have to see this through, all the way to the end."

Vladimir chuckled, taking the bottle back from Nathan. "*That,* is *why* you are the captain." Vladimir took another drink from the bottle, then handed it back to Nathan. "Because you have ethics."

"They have a cure for that, don't they?" Nathan asked as he took the bottle back and took another drink.

"They do," Vladimir replied. "You're drinking it."

* * *

Admiral Dumar sat at his desk, studying the intelligence analysis on the Jung home system. He had reviewed it nearly a dozen times over the past five days, ever since the Alliance council had asked him to submit a plan to attack the Jung homeworld. It had taken him less than a day to put together the plan and submit it to the council. That was four days ago, and with each passing day, he could not help but continually review his plans, looking for the slightest mistake that could snatch victory from their hands. In all those days of review, he had yet to find an error.

It was a daring plan, one that made a lot of assumptions about how the Jung would react, but there was no way around that. Although they had tested the Jung tactics many times in battle, military forces tended to behave differently when defending their home turf, as opposed to foreign battlefields.

A knock came at the admiral's door. The admiral looked up and saw President Scott, standing in the doorway. "Mister President," the admiral said in surprise. "I was not aware you were coming."

"It's a surprise visit," the president said. "However, I would have expected your staff to at least alert you of my arrival."

"I left strict orders not to be disturbed unless we were under attack," Admiral Dumar explained as he rose from his chair. "But I am surprised they didn't feel your presence was worthy of interruption. I shall have to speak to them."

"I'm kidding," President Scott said. "I actually never told anyone I was coming. I didn't even use the presidential shuttle. My security team and I just caught a ride on one of your personnel shuttles. Your staff didn't even know I was here until I entered the command wing. So, go easy on them."

"Of course. Please, have a seat, Mister President," the admiral offered, coming around his desk to sit on the same side as the president. "So, why all the secrecy?"

"The media loves to make a big deal out of every move I make these days," President Scott explained. "Especially with Galiardi and his people squawking at anyone with a camera. Besides, I wanted to talk to you in person, and I know you're a busy man."

"No more so than you."

"Nevertheless."

"What is it you wish to speak to me about?" the admiral wondered.

"I'll get straight to the point," President Scott said. "Several members of the council are concerned about how the Jung will react, *if* we attack their homeworld. Now, I know what you told us when you presented your plan. But I also know that you were playing it safe, taking a middle ground, so to speak. I don't blame you, considering all the pressure from Galiardi's group. So I decided to come to you, and ask you straight up. How do you think the Jung will react? And don't worry, I won't hold you to it. I just want to know what you really think."

"I see," the admiral replied. "I'm afraid my answer will not be as simple as you might have hoped. You see, the Jung are not as simple and straightforward of a society as you might think. They have many factions, or 'castes'. Each of these castes has different branches and layers. And each of them will react differently."

"Try to simplify it for me, Admiral," President Scott suggested.

"Well, take the three main factions within the ruling caste," the admiral continued. "First, you have the Isolationists. I speak of them first, because they are the original Jung Empire. They couldn't care less about conquering the Sol sector, or any other part of the galaxy. Their primary concern is the Jung home system, and the nearby systems that made up their empire for the first five centuries after the bio-digital plague. Their reaction will be to withdraw and protect their own core. They will likely call for a cease-fire, and offer to enter into negotiations. They might even do that *without* us having to attack them. Then there are the Core Expansionists. They are the ones who pushed to expand and conquer the Sol sector. Their original justification might have been to ensure the safety of the original Jung Empire, which they felt was threatened by the resurrection of the core worlds of Earth, but their true goal is to grow the core empire in traditional fashion, from its center outward."

"And how might they react?" President Scott wondered.

"I expect their pride to be the biggest problem. It's bad enough that we've been wiping them out all over the core the past few months, but when we attack their home system, they're going to want revenge, and in a big way. *They* are the ones who will be the biggest threat. *They* are the ones who will want to rally their forces and send everything they've got to destroy us. Fortunately, they are not the controlling party. *That* would be the Isolationists."

"That's good for us, then," the president surmised.

"Yes, and no," the admiral corrected. "You see, although the Isolationists control the government of the Jung homeworld, they do not control the military, or the worlds that the military has conquered. At least not directly. So, it is entirely possible that the Core Expansionists would ignore a decision by the Isolationists to call for a cease-fire. In fact, they might even attack during peace negotiations, without the Isolationists' foreknowledge."

President Scott sighed. "Not simple at all."

"Indeed," Admiral Dumar agreed. "And finally, we have the Conquerors, whose goals have very little to do with the core empire, or the Jung worlds in the Sol sector. The Conquerors are aware that there are many human-inhabited worlds further out in the galaxy, and they want to go out and establish their *own* empires. They would likely still align themselves with the Jung empires of old, but that is not guaranteed. It is almost impossible to predict how they will react. They may side with the Core Expansionists, in which case we will be in even greater peril. On the other hand, they may simply decide that it is not their concern, and go about their escapades further out in the galaxy."

"So, that is why you want a fail-safe, a way to guarantee that the Jung will *not* attack *any* Alliance member world, lest they risk their own destruction."

"Precisely," the admiral replied. "It is the only way to exert *any* level of control over all three main factions. Imminent threat of destruction."

President Scott leaned back in his chair. "Well, Admiral, the council did like your attack plan. They thought it was bold enough, and destructive enough to make the Jung think hard about continuing their activities in the Sol sector, but conservative enough to maintain a reasonable level of post-attack defense. However, they still did not want to commit to such an all-out attack against the Jung homeworld."

"I see," the admiral replied. Although part of him was disappointed, another was relieved.

President Scott stood. "However, what swayed their vote was the fact that the loss of the Tannan propellant pipeline represents a serious short-term reduction in not only our own propellant supplies, but also the financial resources that have made us able to procure so many of the basic resources that many of the member worlds, Earth included, still desperately need. In other words, as much as we dislike the idea of provoking the Jung further, we feel we have little choice. The Jung attack on Tanna must not go unanswered. Your attack on the Jung home system has been approved. Furthermore, you are instructed to carry out the attack at the earliest possible date, so as to capitalize on the fervor of support the destruction of Tanna has generated for the Alliance across all worlds."

"Thank you, Mister President," the admiral said as he stood up to see the president off.

"I only hope we are doing the right thing, Admiral. To be honest, it feels very much like we are about to poke a hibernating bear with a very pointed stick."

* * *

The captains and lead tactical officers, as well as the CAGs from both the Aurora and the Celestia, were gathered in the Karuzara's main mission briefing room. None of them had been told the topic of the briefing, but they all had their suspicions.

Captain Nash and his lead tactical officer were the last to arrive, making their way over to sit next to Jessica and Nathan.

"I was wondering if you were going to make it," Jessica said under her breath as her brother sat down next to her.

"Captains," Robert said in greeting to both Nathan, and to Cameron, who was sitting to Nathan's left, along with her lead tactical officer, Lieutenant Delaveaga.

"Did you get to fly your new ship here?" Jessica asked in jest.

"Nope. Took a shuttle, like everyone else." He gestured to his tactical officer. "Jess, this is my lead TO, Nessa Monath. Lieutenant, this is my sister, Jessica, her CO, Nathan Scott, the Celestia's CO, Cameron Taylor, and her lead TO, Luis Delaveaga."

"A pleasure to meet you all," Lieutenant Monath greeted.

"Koharan?" Jessica asked, recognizing her accent.

"Yes, sir," the lieutenant replied.

"How'd you end up as TO?"

"Just lucky, I guess."

"The lieutenant was trained by the Jung as a weapons systems engineer," Robert explained. "That, and her high scores on the tactical improvisation simulations got her the spot. Not luck. Any idea why we're here?"

"Nope," Jessica replied. "But I'd bet a month's pay that it's got something to do with attacking the Jung home system."

"It's about time," Nathan mumbled.

"It's only been nine days," Cameron retorted.

"Eight days too long," Nathan replied.

"No argument here," Jessica agreed.

Admiral Dumar entered the briefing room, followed by several assistants, as well as Commander Bowden.

"Admiral on deck!" the guard at the door announced, causing all in attendance to rise to their feet and stand at attention.

"Seal the room," the admiral ordered as he walked to the podium in the corner of the room. The guards at both entrances closed and locked the doors, after which, one of the admiral's assistants activated the sound curtain.

"Everything discussed from this point forward is considered classified, and is not to be discussed with anyone outside of this room, unless otherwise directed by myself. Not even amongst yourselves." The admiral looked around the room, making sure everyone had heard him. Satisfied that everyone understood his last words, he spoke. "As you were."

As they sat back down, the admiral pressed the control pad on the podium, causing the lights to dim and the main view screen to come to life, displaying a system chart that was unfamiliar to most of the officers in the room.

"CP-60 424," the admiral began, "Otherwise known as *Patoray*, a variation of the Jung word for 'home'. It is a G8 star, slightly smaller than Sol with about half the luminosity, and is roughly sixty-four light years away. It has only four worlds. Three of them rocky, and a single gas giant. The Jung homeworld is the second planet in the system. They call it, *Nor-Patri*. If you are interested in the specifics of their homeworld, they will be available on your secure data pads, which are being updated as we speak. The Jung homeworld has four satellites, the biggest of which they have turned into a combination shipyard, spaceport, and military base. We believe that Jung command is located here. The satellite itself appears to be an asteroid. It is unknown if it orbits the Jung homeworld naturally, or if it was moved there by the Jung. The asteroid itself, which the Jung call *Zhu-Anok,* has a mean radius of four hundred and fifty kilometers and is composed of water-ice and rock. Although we were not able to use active sensors to scan its interior, there is evidence on the surface of interior excavation, which is most likely quite extensive."

The admiral changed pictures, showing a close up of the asteroid. "*Zhu-Anok* is encircled by a massive ring-like structure that ranges in width from two kilometers, to as much as ten kilometers in some places. The structure is connected to the surface of the asteroid by a series of evenly spaced

515

columns, each of which is several hundred meters in diameter."

"Damn," Nathan said under his breath.

"We believe this structure contains shipyards, complete with pressurized dry dock bays, docks, support facilities, fabrication shops, and of course, defensive systems." Admiral Dumar looked up from his notes. "*This*, is our primary target."

"What type of defenses are we talking about?" Captain Roselle asked.

"Three layers of rail guns," the admiral replied. "The larger the guns, the fewer and more widely spaced they are. Of the largest, there are more than one hundred, and of the smallest, there are nearly ten times that number. They also have thirty missile launchers. However, it is unknown if they employ long or short range missiles, or if their warheads are nuclear or conventional."

"If it is that heavily defended, then perhaps we should just use jump KKVs and take out the entire asteroid," Captain Poc suggested.

"I have considered that option. However, based on the lack of shuttle traffic between the Jung homeworld and the asteroid base, we believe that the asteroid itself is a shell containing hundreds of levels, and quite possibly hundreds of thousands, if not millions, of people. Again, the reduced shuttle traffic would indicate that these people both live *and* work within this asteroid, and the structure encircling it. Even a single KKV strike would be catastrophic, and would likely kill hundreds of thousands of innocent people."

"It didn't seem to bother the Jung," Nathan commented under his breath.

Admiral Dumar heard Captain Scott's comment,

but decided to ignore it, despite the fact that he sympathized with the captain's position. "We believe that our usual hit and run tactics, using primarily plasma weapons, should do enough damage to the structure to send a clear message to the Jung leaders."

"Message?" Jessica wondered aloud. "You want to send a message?" Jessica turned to Robert. "How about payback's a bitch, asshole."

Robert wanted to laugh, but controlled himself.

Jessica felt Nathan's elbow in her side, and stopped chuckling at her own remark.

Admiral Dumar paused, sending a disapproving glare at the lieutenant commander, followed by a quick glance at her commanding officer next to her. "Do not misunderstand," the admiral continued. "Our intent is not to destroy the Jung. We're not even trying to take out all their military assets within their home system. Our goal is to arrive unannounced, cause as much destruction as possible, and then leave, all without losing a single ship."

"What the hell kind of message does *that* send?" Jessica asked.

"Jess," Nathan scolded quietly.

"That we are both willing, and able, to visit as much death and destruction onto them, as they have brought onto us *and* our allies," the admiral replied.

"Could that not be accomplished through the use of JKKVs?" Captain Poc reiterated.

"We will be using jump KKVs, Captain," Admiral Dumar assured him. "However, we must demonstrate the abilities of our ships as well as our standoff weapons of mass destruction. They must witness the full range of our abilities. That is also why we are using their own ships against them...to show them that we can capture their vessels and make them our own."

"Haven't we demonstrated these facts already?" Lieutenant Delaveaga wondered. "Surely by now Jung command has received word about at least *some* of the systems we've liberated."

"Indeed they have," Admiral Dumar agreed. "But we have seen that the Jung are quite adept at the use of propaganda. There is no reason to think that they do not do the same with their own people. Therefore, we need to demonstrate our abilities and resolve by an attack within their home system, where their own people can witness the horror directly."

"You're hoping to turn the Jung population against their own leaders, aren't you?" Nathan realized.

"Not so much *against* their leaders, but rather to put pressure on them to change their plans in regard to the Sol sector."

"You're looking for a cease-fire," Nathan surmised, "not a victory."

Admiral Dumar looked Nathan in the eyes. "I'm looking for a way to save us all, Captain Scott. By our estimates, the ships currently within the Jung home system represent only a quarter of their total forces... Perhaps even less. If they were to rally even half their total numbers to make another run at Earth, they would roll right over us, and then over every member system."

"But it would take years for them to rally so many ships and send them our way, possibly even decades," Jessica argued. "During that time, we can build more ships, create better..."

"How many ships do you think you can build

in ten years' time?" Admiral Dumar asked. "Ten? Twenty? A formidable force, yes, but against several hundred warships? And what if, during that ten years, the Jung manage to develop their own jump drive, and retrofit every ship in their fleet? What then?"

"All the more reason to throw everything we've got at them," Jessica argued. "Now, before they have a chance to improve their defenses to protect against our jump weapons."

Admiral Dumar stared at Jessica for several seconds. "Sometimes, it is more effective to show an enemy your weapon, to instill fear and to make them wonder just how badly they will be hurt should you use it. For if you *do* use it, and you fail to kill your enemy, they will know that they can survive your weapon. They will know that the pain it creates is not as bad as they had feared. More importantly, they will become enraged, and will seek vengeance, just as you are now, Lieutenant Commander."

Jessica settled back down and considered the admiral's words. As much as she wanted her revenge, she knew, just as the admiral knew, just as everyone in the room knew, that there was far more at stake.

"There are more effective ways to win a war than to simply destroy everything your enemy possesses or holds dear," Admiral Dumar assured everyone in the room. "The Jung have demonstrated their lack of understanding of this concept time and time again. Most recently, by their destruction of Tanna." The admiral took a breath. "*We* are about to educate them."

Admiral Dumar looked around the room, briefly locking eyes with every person in attendance, before continuing. "Now, let us discuss the details of the attack."

* * *

Nathan sat in his ready room, studying the admiral's battle plan on both his data pad and the large view screen on his wall.

"What do you think?" Jessica wondered, as she lay stretched out on the couch, studying her own data pad.

"I think it's a good plan. Not too much, not too little, minimal risk to our ships."

"It's based on a lot of assumptions, though," Jessica pointed out. "Like assuming the battle platforms never change their orbital paths around the parent star. How the hell did he come up with that one from just a five-minute recon?"

"Probably because it takes so much propellant to change the course of something that large," Nathan explained.

"Well, sure, if you're going to go all 'orbital mechanics' on me."

"Plus, there is no reason for them to do so, since they still think that no one would ever attack them."

"Well, how do we know their shields will all be down?" she challenged.

"Because they were then, and again, they have no reason to suspect that anyone would attempt a direct attack on their homeworld."

Jessica shook her head. "Still a lot of assumptions in here."

"I thought we aren't supposed to talk about it?"

"He said we could only discuss it with our senior staff, and even then only a few hours before go time," Jessica reminded him. "So, I guess it depends on your definition of 'a few'."

"I'm pretty sure twelve hours is more than a few, Jess."

"All right, define 'go time'."

"Maybe we should just shut up and stop talking about it," Nathan said.

"Maybe." Jessica continued looking at her data pad. "I still don't think it's enough."

"You don't think destroying six battle platforms, twelve destroyers, a few cruisers and frigates, and taking a few chunks out of their shipyard ring with jump KKVs, is enough?"

"No, I don't," Jessica replied in a matter-of-fact tone. "And I'm betting you don't either."

"Then what do you think would 'be enough'?" Nathan wondered.

"Destroy everything *and* glass their fucking world," Jessica replied, her voice heavy with malice. "*That* would be enough."

"And then every Jung ship still out there eventually hears about it, and heads for Earth," Nathan said. "And *they* all want to do the same to us, and all our friends. Where does it stop, Jess?"

Jessica sat up on the couch and looked at Nathan. "Are you seriously going to sit there and lie to my face and tell me that you *don't* want to see every last one of them fry? Really?"

"You're damned right I want to see them fry!" Nathan replied. "Every last one of them!" Nathan paused a moment to regain his composure. "But like I said, that won't solve anything. It might make you and me feel better, at least for a moment, but it won't solve anything, and it probably *will* make matters worse, just like Dumar said."

Jessica sighed. "I still don't buy it."

"You don't have to. Neither one of us does. We

521

do have to follow orders, and carry out the mission as designed. And that's exactly what I'm going to do. I'm assuming that you will too." Nathan waited several seconds for an answer. "You will, won't you?"

"Of course I will, Nathan," she finally replied. "Don't be an idiot."

"I'm never too sure about you these days," Nathan commented. "Half the time, I wonder if you're going to turn around and pop me in the mouth."

"And get thrown in the brig for the rest of my days?" Jessica replied. "Sorry, you're not worth it."

"Gee, thanks."

Jessica stood up and stretched. "Well, since we're headed for the proverbial hornet's nest tomorrow, I guess I'd better get some sleep."

"It's going to take us nearly twenty-eight hours just to get to the JKKV launch point, Jess," Nathan reminded her. "I think there's time."

"Oh, that's right," Jessica replied. "Well, in that case, maybe you and I should go for a tumble or two between the sheets. You could try that line on me again. You know, how you're shipping out tomorrow, and it could be your last night on Earth. It worked before, remember? At your father's party?"

Nathan sat dumbfounded, his eyes wide and his mouth open. "Uh..."

"Jesus, look at you," she laughed. "I was kidding, Nathan," she added as she headed for the exit. She stopped at the hatch and turned back to him. "Hey, at least I didn't punch you in the face."

CHAPTER FOURTEEN

The intercom buzzer in Nathan's ready room sounded. Nathan pressed the button. "Go ahead."

"*Helm reports we're completing our big turn,*" Naralena reported over the intercom.

"On my way," Nathan replied. He rose from his chair and headed for the exit.

"Captain on the bridge!" the guard announced as Nathan stepped through the ready room hatch onto the Aurora's bridge.

They had been within a few light years of the outer edges of the Jung's home system for seven hours now, during which time he had been hesitant to go any further than his ready room.

"About time, Mister Chiles," Nathan said in jest as he passed by Jessica at the tactical station and headed for his command chair.

"Sorry, sir," Mister Chiles replied. "Coming about at three quarters light takes a while."

"How much propellant have we used so far?" Nathan asked as he took his seat.

"About half our normal capacity," the systems officer replied.

"Our next three turns are all only a few degrees each," Mister Riley reminded the captain, "so we won't be using much propellant. The decel burn is a different story."

"We'll use up an additional twenty-five percent when we decelerate," the systems officer added. "But I've already started transferring propellant from the extra propellant bladders in the cargo bays, so we should be back up to half capacity by the time we make our first attack jump."

"Very well," Nathan replied.

"Turn complete," Mister Chiles reported from the helm.

"Jump to fourth deployment point is plotted and ready," Mister Riley added.

"Port and starboard flight decks report first waves of JKKVs are loaded and ready to deploy, and second waves are standing by," Jessica announced.

"Very well. Mister Riley, execute your jump."

"Aye, sir. Jumping to JKKV deployment point four... In three..."

As his navigator counted down, Nathan glanced at the mission status display on the port auxiliary view screen to his left. Since they were running silent during the deployment phase of the attack, the display could only verify what steps the Aurora had completed. It was, however, able to estimate what tasks the other ships should have completed, based on elapsed time since the mission clock had started nearly eight hours ago. According to the display, the Celestia—which had started much later than the Aurora due to the fact that she did not have to execute a big turn—was about to deploy her fourth group of JKKVs as well. According to mission protocol, no news from the other ships meant everything was going according to plan. However, Nathan would have preferred direct data links, even the asynchronous ones they used during coordinated battles over wide areas.

The jump flash washed over them, and Nathan's attention turned to the main view screen. It was a habit he had never been able to break: feeling the need to immediately *see* where they were, even though the stars themselves rarely moved enough to notice.

"Jump complete."

"We are at launch point four," Mister Navashee reported. "No contacts."

"Deploy JKKVs," Nathan instructed.

"Aye, sir," Jessica replied.

———

A catapult tech in a full pressure suit checked the hookup on the forward gear of the jump KKV on the outboard catapult in the port launch bay. Satisfied that it was ready to go, he gave a thumbs-up to the controller on the other side of the window to the port launch control room. After receiving both visual and audio confirmations from the controller, he quickly moved to the side of the launch bay, where he disappeared behind a safety wall.

The tech at the inboard catapult did the same, followed by the tech at the center JKKV, sitting between and behind the inboard and outboard JKKVs, each of them running to the sides of the launch bay to take refuge behind their safety wall.

Seconds later, the launch alarm sounded, and the inside of the launch bay turned red. There was a swoosh of air as the massive door at the front of the launch bay began to rise, sucking the last bit of atmosphere out into space. The door quickly disappeared into the ceiling, and the launch tube was open to space and ready to launch.

The outboard JKKV accelerated quickly down the wide launch tunnel, riding a glow of blue light at the base of the catapult sled as powerful electro magnets pulled both toward the exit. The inboard JKKV was next, surging forward and accelerating in the same manner only seconds after the first JKKV had exited the launch tunnel. Finally, the center JKKV departed, racing down the launch tunnel and into space, to join the others that had preceded it.

The massive door lowered again, dropping from its slot in the ceiling. It took only five seconds for the door to fully close and seal off the launch tube again. There was a sudden whoosh of air as the launch bay began to repressurize. In thirty seconds, the bay would be back to normal air pressure. Then the next three JKKVs, waiting just outside the launch bay would also be rolled in and hooked up to the catapults for launch.

"First six jump KKVs are away," Jessica announced.

"Translating to port," Mister Chiles reported from the helm.

"Next six will be ready to launch in two minutes," Jessica added.

"Very, well," Nathan replied. After the next wave was launched, they would start the process again, making a slight course change and short jump between the next two deployment points.

Another glance at the mission display told Nathan they were on schedule. In less than fifteen minutes, they would be jumping into the Jung home system of Patoray.

* * *

"They only know that we have *two* jump-capable ships," Cameron corrected her tactical officer. "And as far as they know, we have no shields, and just medium-powered plasma torpedoes."

Luis stood behind the Celestia's tactical console, doubt clearly written on his face. "They know we were able to take down a battle platform. That, by itself, should make them worry."

"But they still think we do not know where their homeworld is located," Cameron reminded him. "That's why it was so important to use one of their shuttles to peek inside their system, so as not to raise suspicion."

"First group of JKKVs is away," Luis reported, temporarily interrupting their conversation. "Second group in two minutes." He looked back at his captain, facing him in her command chair. "So, you don't think an FTL shuttle, with a broken transponder—one which they probably have no record of, no flight plan, or *anything* for—isn't going to raise any suspicions?"

"Surely they've had undocumented flights before," Cameron said. "Besides, they've been able to keep their location a secret for centuries. I doubt they'd put *all* their forces on alert just because of *one* mysterious flight of one of their *own* shuttles."

"I suppose you could be right," Luis finally admitted. "After all, the Jung are nothing if not arrogant." He sighed. "Still, I find it hard to imagine that we can take out a significant portion of their fleet in a single attack."

"Just think of all the ordnance being put onto multiple targets at the same time," Cameron pointed out. "It's mind boggling, to say the least."

"Just the seventy-two jump KKVs is hard to wrap my mind around, let alone all the jump missiles."

"Exactly," Cameron agreed. "This very well could be the Alliance's greatest victory."

"Let's hope," Luis replied. "The second group of JKKVs is away, Captain. We're clear to decelerate."

"Very well," Cameron said, rotating in her chair

to face forward again. "Mister Hunt, you may begin our deceleration to combat speed."

"Beginning deceleration burn, aye," the helmsman confirmed.

* * *

"Falcon crews, you'll be launching immediately after the briefing," Major Prechitt explained to the flight crews in the mission briefing room. "You'll fly to your rally points and meet up with the cargo shuttles you're escorting. You'll jump into the atmosphere of the Jung homeworld at an altitude of twelve hundred meters. Since you'll be jumping in at the same time as the JKKV strikes against the battle groups, you should not encounter any defenses, air or surface based. As long as the cargo shuttles jump in, drop their loads, and get out, you should be fine. As the entire surface of Nor-Patri is urban, it doesn't matter where the drops occur as far as distribution is concerned. Therefore, we chose the jump-in points so that you can lock onto your primary surface targets *and* launch *while* the cargo shuttles are conducting their drops. As soon as they finish their drops and jump away, you will jump to your secondary surface targets and engage them as well. After that, you jump back up to orbit and engage anything small that you find. Fast-attack shuttles, gunships, patrol ships, fighters...you can even take a run at a frigate if you can do so without putting your ship at undue risk."

"What are the cargo shuttles dropping?" Josh asked.

"Leaflets," Major Prechitt replied.

"You're kidding," Josh said.

"Isn't that a little, uh..." Loki began hesitantly.

"Archaic?" Major Prechitt finished for him.

"I was going to say inefficient, but…" Loki let his words trail off.

"Don't worry, they'll be broadcasting the same message," Major Prechitt explained. "From a series of simple comm-sats being deployed by a flight of twelve utility jump shuttles."

"Won't the Jung just shoot them down?" Josh wondered.

"Of course they will," Major Prechitt responded. "Sooner or later. But considering all they'll have to deal with in the first few minutes of the battle, I doubt they are going to get around to a dozen com-sats broadcasting unwanted messages to their citizens for at least five or ten minutes. That's plenty of time for the message to be heard by billions."

"Then why the leaflets?" Josh asked.

"Mostly, because it scares them."

"But, they're only pieces of paper, sir," Josh reminded the major.

"Yes, but an enemy was able to suddenly appear over their heads, and drop millions of those pieces of paper on top of them," the major replied. "What if that paper was infected with some highly contagious disease?"

Josh's eyes grew wide with shock. "Are they?"

"No, but they don't know that. It's all about panic, gentlemen. Panic among the citizenry puts pressure on the political leaders. If the people of Nor-Patri do not feel safe, they may pressure their leaders to call for a cease-fire with us. It's all a mental game."

"That our butts are being put on the line to play," Josh muttered under his breath.

"Eagle drivers, your first task will be to harass surface targets. Infrastructure, mostly. Power plants, communications, water supplies, sewage treatment facilities...anything that will make their life miserable. Now, while we've identified a handful of targets from the limited recon data that Ensigns Hayes and Sheehan so bravely acquired for us..."

Josh waved modestly at the crowd from his seat. "It was nothing, really..."

"...You will likely have to identify many targets on your own," the major continued. "Again, try to keep collateral damages low, whenever possible. Now, within minutes of the attack, we expect the Jung to launch fighters to come after you. You may engage them, if you feel you have the advantage. However, do not press a bad situation. That's what a jump drive is for. Never stay in one place for long, and always vary your jump distances and patterns. Stir up some shit, get them to chase you about for a bit, then jump up to orbit and start harassing anything you can find up there. That will force the fighters in the atmosphere, which have already been burning propellant, to burn even more of it to follow you up to orbit."

"Understood," Commander Goodreau replied with a nod.

"We'll try to leave something in orbit for you guys to shoot at, Commander," Josh joked.

The commander did not respond.

* * *

"Sixteen missiles away," Commander Jento reported from the Kent's tactical station.

"Ensign Vitko, take us to the next launch point," Captain Poc instructed from his command station.

"Jumping to launch point two," the navigator announced. "In three seconds."

Captain Poc watched calmly as his navigator counted down, and then jumped the frigate to their next missile launch point. Just like the first one, it was just inside the outer borders of the Jung's home system, Patoray. They would launch missiles from four different locations, against six different target groups. All of their missiles, just like those of their sister ship commanded by Captain Nash, would execute their jumps simultaneously along with the jump KKVs deployed by the Aurora and the Celestia. Together, their weapons would wipe out half the Jung forces in the Patoray system in the blink of an eye.

"Jump complete," the navigator reported.

"All missiles loaded," the tactical officer reported. "Aligning launchers."

"Stand by to execute your turn, Lieutenant Serra," Captain Poc instructed.

"Aye, sir," the Kent's helmsman replied.

"All missile launchers aligned. All jump missiles ready for launch."

"Launch."

"Launching all missiles," the commander replied.

Captain Poc watched the tactical display on his console as twelve missile tracks appeared and started moving away from the center of the display.

"Twelve missiles away," the commander reported. "Reloading."

"Executing turn to next jump line," the helmsman reported.

"Jump to launch point three, in one minute," Ensign Vitko reported.

The attack was a well-choreographed series of jumps and launches, by multiple ships, and at multiple targets, with every weapon timed to jump in and strike its assigned target at the same moment in time. So far, it was going like clockwork.

* * *

"Are the SAR shuttles ready?" Captain Roselle asked his XO.

"Loaded and ready," the commander replied. "We even put Lieutenant Commander Bowden's ex-Jung cohorts on them to handle comms, just in case."

"Remember, they are not to use the jump drives unless absolutely necessary. If the Jung don't tag them as unfriendlies the moment they come out of our shuttle bays, they sure as hell will when they see them jump. So if they do, they'd better make damn sure they jump their asses all the way out to the pickup point."

"I've been over it with them, Gil," the commander assured him. "Stop worrying."

Captain Roselle leaned back in his ready room chair. "Who's worrying?" he said casually. "I'm just double-checking, that's all."

"That's what I'm here for, Gil."

"Okay, maybe I am worrying, but only a little. Can you blame me? We're about to attack the whole damned Jung system."

"Yeah. Thank God we've got the biggest ship in the fleet," the commander said.

"Biggest and toughest," the captain added with conviction. "I can't wait to start picking off those damned ships. Their captains won't know what the hell is going on."

"The smart ones will figure out we're not on their side pretty quick."

"At least they won't see our jump flash," Captain Roselle said. "That was a pretty good idea to jump in five light minutes out, and then FTL it the rest of the way to Nor-Patri. By the time they see our flash, we'll already be sitting between the Jung homeworld and that damned ring station of theirs, blasting away at both."

* * *

"All jump missile targeting data has been confirmed," Lieutenant Monath reported from the tactical station directly behind Captain Nash's command station. "The missiles are programmed, and their auto-jump sequencers are running. We are ready to start deployment."

"Helm?" Captain Nash called.

"We are on course and speed for the first launch point, sir."

Captain Nash looked at the mission status display on the console in front of him. There were only thirty seconds left until they had to jump into the outer edges of the Jung home system and start launching their jump missiles. "Very well. Mister Poschay, jump us in on schedule. Lieutenant Monath, stand by to launch the first wave."

"Jumping in three..." the navigator announced.

"Aye, sir," the lieutenant replied from the tactical station.

"Two..."

"Today, we seek vengeance for the people of Tanna," Captain Nash stated proudly.

"One......jumping."

Captain Nash briefly remembered the faces of the men and women he had trained, and had subsequently sent to their deaths in defense of their world, as the new Alliance frigate 'Tanna' jumped into the enemy's home system.

* * *

Captain Iniga climbed the ladder into the flight deck of the old boxcar. "Damn, Hal, when are you going to fix the gravity in that tube so we can shoot up it without any effort like the rest of the tubes on this bucket?" he asked his engineer as he stepped onto the flight deck.

"Oh, I'll get right on that, Captain," the engineer replied sarcastically. "Assuming we get back alive from this bullshit assignment."

"How the hell we went from hauling Ancotan grain and Palean engines to launching planet busters I will never understand," the captain said as he took his seat.

"Just promise me you'll get us back to the Pentaurus cluster eventually," the engineer asked.

"You bet your ass," the captain replied.

"Coming up on deployment time," the ship's navigator announced.

"Ready on bay one," the engineer reported.

"Open the bay doors, Hal," the captain instructed.

"Bay one, doors coming open. Weapon one, maneuvering thrusters show ready."

Captain Iniga watched the view screen as the bay doors opened, revealing the view outside.

"Bay one doors are open."

"Deploy KKV one," the captain ordered.

"Deploying KKV one."

Captain Iniga switched camera views to the external camera facing away from the boxcar's converted cargo pod. The nose of the old Takaran comm-drone turned jump-enabled kinetic kill vehicle appeared, growing longer as it left the bay. In less than a minute, the device was clear of the boxcar. "Light her up, Hal."

"Aye, sir," the engineer replied.

The captain watched his monitor as the comm-drone's main propulsion system came alive, and the vehicle rapidly accelerated away from them. "Kiss your little refinery goodbye, you Jung bastards," the captain muttered. He took a deep breath and sighed.

"The weapon is burning hot and normal," Hal reported. "She's on course and accelerating rapidly. She should be at launch velocity in ten minutes."

"Very well," Captain Iniga said. "Let's get the second one out there and on her way, just in case they decide to launch her as well."

Hal looked at his captain. "You don't really think they'll launch the second one, do you?"

"I have no clue," the captain admitted. "But if they do, there are going to be about a million Jung who are going to have a really bad day."

* * *

A massive Jung tanker ship loomed low over the refinery moon of Promittel. Her engines burned silently at full thrust as she struggled to lift her fully loaded storage tanks off the surface, to take them back to the ring base at Zhu-Anok.

As the tanker ship rose from the surface, there was a brilliant flash of light that lit up the entire horizon of the small moon. Then a wave of destruction swept over the moon's surface as the moon broke apart. The wave quickly reached the propellant storage facility. There was a flash of burning propellant, several hundred thousand kilotons of it, which only lasted an instant due to lack of sufficient oxidizer in the non-existent atmosphere of Promittel.

The wave of debris slammed into the rising tanker, tearing it apart. Seconds later, the tanker exploded. Seconds after that, all that was left of Promittel was an expanding cloud of dust and debris spreading out in all directions, lit by the lavender light reflecting off the gas giant it had once orbited.

———

At the stable gravity point between Nor-Patri and Zu-Anok, the Jung battle platform Ton-Emora and her accompanying fleet of ships sat quietly in space. Other than the occasional training exercises, the Ton-Emora battle group had been stationed here for nearly forty years, ever since the Ton-Emora herself had been completed. She was the last of the battle platforms to be built by the Jung, and there was much speculation as to what design might someday replace what the Jung considered to be an invincible weapon. With fifty of them in service all over the Jung and Sol sectors, and beyond, there seemed little need to continue spending resources on ships of such mammoth scale.

Today, that perception of invincibility would be forever shattered.

The Ton-Emora's shields flashed brightly as unknown objects struck them at great velocity. Her shields quickly failed, overcome by the kinetic energy of the relativistic objects colliding with them.

Three cones of debris suddenly shot from the Ton-Emora's third, fourth, and fifth arms. Secondary explosions rocked her central core, and quickly spread out to the remaining undamaged arms. In fewer than twenty seconds, the Ton-Emora was completely destroyed.

A the same time, the shields of the Jar-Torigor, only twenty kilometers ahead of the platform, also flashed as two objects slammed into them at similar speeds. A third object struck the battleship's now unprotected hull, blasting her stern apart. She was quickly enveloped by a wave of secondary explosions from deep inside her hull that rushed forward, consuming the entire ship. Within seconds, the battleship was obliterated.

A split second later, a dozen flashes of blue-white light appeared less than a kilometer away from the remaining cruisers and frigates. Having the weakest shields of the group, the four frigates immediately exploded as nuclear warheads riding on the tips of missiles, which appeared from behind the flashes of blue-white light, quickly reached their targets and detonated. The cruisers were also hit, but with four missiles each instead of two. They too were blown apart by the detonations.

The Jar-Aniram strike group had arrived in low orbit no more than a few hours ago. After two weeks of exercises on the outskirts of the Patoray system, her crew, and the crews of the cruisers and frigates that made up her strike group, were looking forward to returning to Nor-Patri to visit friends and family.

As the first few liberty shuttles left the Jar-Aniram, the ship suddenly came apart, debris spraying in all directions. Her bow was the first to go, then her midship. With her shields down, it took only two impacts to take the ship apart.

The rest of the ships in her group faced a similar fate, as flashes of blue-white light appeared no more than a kilometer above the strike group. Missiles appearing from the flashes rained down on them, enveloping them with nuclear detonations. None of the ill-fated ships had their shields up, and every one of them fell to the missile barrage.

The shields surrounding the asteroid moon, Zhu-Anok, and her massive ring base, were the crowning achievement of Jung shield technology. It had proven that it was possible to envelope something of such size with a shield just as they had done with their ships and battle platforms. The big difference, and the most significant one to the Jung, was the fact that this shield did not hug the landscape of the moon, or the hull of the ring base, as it did with their ships. This shield was a dome that surrounded the entire, nine-hundred-kilometer-wide asteroid, as well as her ring base. The Jung military saw it as the ultimate in protection for their precious ring base, as well as all the manufacturing and living facilities inside the asteroid itself. The Jung people saw it as a stepping stone to their true dream. A shield that could protect their entire world.

Today, the shield around Zhu-Anok would be tested. It too flashed brilliantly nearly a dozen times, as unknown objects traveling at near-relativistic speeds slammed into the shield.

But the shields around Zhu-Anok did not fall.

"Coming up on strike plus twenty seconds," Mister Riley reported.

"Take us in on schedule," Nathan instructed.

"Aye, sir. Jumping to Nor-Patri in ten seconds."

"Flight ops reports all fighter launch tubes are ready to shoot," Naralena reported.

"Three......two......one......jumping."

The view screen flashed a subdued blue-white as the Aurora transitioned from her position outside of the Patoray system, into orbit above the Jung homeworld of Nor-Patri. When the screen cleared, Nathan could not only see the planet below, but also debris fields in the distance where a Jung strike group had once been positioned.

"Jump complete."

"Debris field ahead," Mister Navashee warned.

"Maneuver up range of the debris path," Nathan instructed.

"Aye, sir," the helmsman replied.

"Green deck," Nathan instructed.

"Green deck, aye," Naralena replied.

"Holy..." Mister Navashee exclaimed, excitement in his voice. "Captain, I have never seen this much debris at once. In orbit, at gravity points... I'm even starting to pick up signs of destruction from Nor-Patri's gravity points... One, Two, Four, and Five."

"Are you saying we killed them all?" Nathan asked in disbelief. "In a single strike?"

"No, sir," Mister Navashee replied. "Not all, but a whole lot of them, sir. I'm only picking up about twenty frigates, and ten cruisers...and some of them are pretty badly damaged as well."

"First wave of fighters is away," Naralena reported.

"What about Zhu-Anok?" Nathan asked.

"One moment," Mister Navashee replied. "No, sir, she appears to be undamaged."

"Are you sure?" Nathan asked, concern in his voice.

"No, sir, I'm not. That whole battle group that was at Nor-Patri's first gravity point is obscuring my sensors. I'm basing my findings strictly on the fact that I'm *not* seeing any debris behind that group. The ring base *could* have taken damage from the JKKVs *and* the jump missiles, and I might not be able to see it yet." He turned to look at the captain. "The Jar-Benakh should have just arrived, sir. They should be able to get a better read on Zhu-Anok."

Commander Goodreau set his jump selector to altitude mode as he pitched his Super Eagle down toward Nor-Patri's surface. Behind him were seven

539

more Super Eagles, for a total of eight ships in his flight. The next group of eight was loading into the Aurora's launch tubes and would be en route to attack a different location on the surface of the Jung homeworld shortly.

He activated the jump control link system on his display, slaving the jump systems of the rest of the Super Eagles in his flight with his. "Blue Flight, Leader. Sync-jump in ten, down to one thousand." He checked his jump link and verified that the other seven Super Eagles had good links to him, then he activated the jump sequencer at the five-second mark. As the sequencer counted down, he cut his throttle and armed the plasma cannons that protruded from the side fairings on either side of his ship's nose.

His canopy turned opaque as all eight Super Eagles jumped down into the atmosphere, coming out in a row of eight, simultaneous blue-white flashes, only one thousand meters above the planet-wide city.

At an entry speed of twenty times the speed of sound on Nor-Patri, the sonic booms were a frightening scene to behold. At such speeds, the booms would come several seconds after their jump flashes. By the time the citizens on the surface of the Jung homeworld had overcome their initial shock and looked up to the skies, they would already be several kilometers downrange.

"Blue Flight, Leader. Break now." The commander rolled his ship onto its left side and pulled on the nose, taking it into a gentle turn. With his throttles closed, he immediately started losing speed. However, it would take a lot of turning to bring him down to normal maneuvering speeds, and until then, he had to keep his turns wide to avoid tearing off the Super Eagle's wings.

He quickly activated his targeting systems, which immediately locked onto a sewage treatment plant still two hundred kilometers away. The system automatically canted his plasma cannons down to their maximum deflection of five degrees.

He executed two more wide turns as he closed on the first target, gazing out the sides of his canopy as the endless expanse of cityscape slid past him in a blur. Never had he seen a world so entirely covered by urban and suburban sprawl. He found it hard to believe that there were no open spaces left on this world, but he had yet to be proven wrong.

The distance to his first target closed to atmospheric firing range in less than a minute. His auto-flight system took over, making tiny adjustments to his course to ensure a direct hit. His plasma cannons fired four pairs of plasma bolts in rapid succession, which struck the plant still twenty kilometers ahead of him.

The auto-flight system released control of his Super Eagle, and the commander entered another wide turn to bring his speed down even further.

"*Leader, Three. Bandits, fifty clicks, bearing one four. Looks like they just took off.*"

"Three, with me, forty-five from target's right. Two and Four, from target's left. Five by five, in ten." Commander Goodreau watched out of the corner of his eye as the acknowledgment lights for the other three ships in his flight lit up for a few seconds, indicating they had received and understood his instructions. It was a feature that the commander had insisted the Alliance technicians add to their

Super Eagles, as it saved considerable time, and was standard procedure for Takaran fighter pilots.

Another shallow turn and a short jump, and the targets were forty-five degrees off to their right, just over five kilometers away. The commander turned to the right, bringing his nose in line with the targets, then jumped again, putting all of them directly in front of him.

The commander and his wingman opened fire, walking their plasma cannons across the flight of enemy fighters, breaking them apart before they even realized their attackers were on top of them. The other two Super Eagles did the same from the opposite direction, tearing apart what few Jung fighters remained of the group that had taken off on their intercept mission only a few minutes ago.

Per procedure, the commander and his wingman pulled up to pass over the doomed formation of enemy fighters, veering slightly left as they climbed. The other two Super Eagles dove slightly and veered right, eventually coming onto the same course as the commander and his wingman. It was a perfect intercept.

"Two and Four, rejoin," the commander instructed.

"Just below you, and two back, boss."

Commander Goodreau did not respond, but simply called up his next target.

———

"Are you secure back there?" the copilot of the cargo jump shuttle called over the helmet comms.

"Almost," the crew chief replied from the back of the cargo shuttle. He reached over and removed the cover from the last pallet of leaflets, and stowed it inside the forward gear locker, along with the rest of the covers. He looked back at the twenty large stacks of leaflets, all standing neatly, uncovered and ready for distribution.

"Come on, Chief, we jump in thirty seconds," the copilot warned.

The crew chief squeezed between the most forward stack of leaflets, knocking several of them off, and took his seat in the forward port corner of the shuttle's cargo bay. He fastened his restraints, then gave them a tug to be sure he was secure. "I'm good," he announced as he plugged the life-support umbilical back into his pressure suit, going back on the ship's oxygen. "Suit pressure looks good. Let's do this."

"Jumping in five seconds," the copilot announced from the cockpit above the cargo bay.

The crew chief placed his hand on the door control panel to his right, putting his finger on the open button as the copilot counted down.

"Jumping."

A small amount of blue-white light passing through the few small windows of the shuttle's cargo bay illuminated the compartment for a brief moment.

"Jump complete," the copilot reported. *"Open her up!"*

The crew chief pressed the open button, causing the back door to slowly drop open. At twelve thousand meters above the surface of Nor-Patri, the decompression of the cargo bay was enough to suck most of the leaflets right out the back of the shuttle. Within twenty seconds, ninety percent of the pamphlets were gone, slowly falling to the surface as the high altitude winds spread them out over the endless cityscape below.

The crew chief pressed the open button for the front door, opening it just enough to create a wind tunnel effect that pushed the remaining leaflets out of the cargo bay. With only a few leaflets still swirling about, refusing to exit, the crew chief pressed the close buttons for both doors. As soon as the status lights for both doors turned green, he called out over his helmet comms. "We're closed up! Let's get the hell out of here!"

* * *

"*Falcon One, Heavy Three is empty, jumping out.*"

"Roger Heavy Three, see you back at the rally point." Loki watched the sensor display on his console as the icon representing the cargo shuttle disappeared.

"How far out are they now?" Josh asked.

"The first group is gone," Loki said. "So is the second. Super Eagles took care of them. But there are four more groups still climbing up from the surface. The closest ones are still three minutes out."

"*Falcon One, Heavy Two is empty. Jumping out.*"

"Roger, Heavy Two," Loki replied.

"*Heavy One is also empty. Jumping out.*"

"Roger, Heavy One," Loki replied. "That's all the heavies in our coverage zone. New course, two four seven, down five."

"Two four seven, down five," Josh replied as he changed course and pitched their nose down slightly.

"Jumping to next target area."

The Super Falcon's windows turned opaque for a brief moment, and Josh and Loki found themselves fifteen hundred kilometers downrange and two thousand meters above the city.

Loki quickly selected their next four targets,

locking the tracking systems of their last four missiles onto the targets. "Opening bay doors." He pressed the launch button. "Four boomers, away."

Josh waited until he could see all four missile contrails stretching out in front of them, then pitched up as he brought his throttles to full power. He quickly dialed up a new jump range to get them to orbit. He then looked at Loki and smiled. "Let's go shuttle hunting."

———————

"Out of FTL," the Jar-Benakh's navigator reported.

"Multiple contacts!" Ensign Marka reported from the sensor station. "Two battleships, five cruisers, fifteen frigates..."

"Jump missiles," Captain Roselle ordered.

"Assigning targets," the tactical officer replied.

"Captain!" the sensor officer called out urgently. "The ring base is still intact! She's still got full shields!"

"What?" Captain Roselle exclaimed, instantly rising to his feet. "Are you sure?"

"Damned sure, sir," Ensign Marka replied. "She's bringing her guns and missile launchers on us now."

"Tactical!" the captain called. "New target! Put everything you have on that ring base! Jump missiles, big guns, the works! All point-defenses on those missiles! Helm, turn into the Zhu-Anok. I want to put our plasma torpedoes on her."

"Turning into the ring base," the helmsman replied.

"Forward guns are firing!" Lieutenant Commander Kessel reported from the tactical station. "Locking jump missiles on the ring base!"

"Captain, I'm picking up a large energy spike

on the asteroid base. I believe their shield is even more powerful than a battle platform's." The ensign turned toward his captain. "If that's the case, it's going to take every gun we have to even make a dent."

"You heard the man," Captain Roselle said. "Get every damned gun you can on that thing. That's their main base, where they make the majority of their ships. We take that out, and we buy the Alliance decades of time to build up our fleet!"

"Taking rail gun fire!" the tactical officer reported. "The big stuff!"

"Forward shields are taking a pounding," the systems officer warned. "They're already down to ninety percent."

"New contact!" Ensign Marka reported. "Coming around the back side of Nor-Patri. It's the Kent, sir!"

"Mas! Call the Kent. Tell them to dump everything they've got into that ring base. Target the center of it."

"Aye, sir!"

"If we can put everything into one shield section, we might get it to drop so we can get some nukes inside of that shield!"

"First wave of missiles away!"

"Captain, their shields are already showing some strain from just our cannons," the sensor operator reported, perplexed.

"That's a good thing, Weedge," Captain Roselle commented.

"You don't understand," Ensign Marka replied. "That power surge is still there, and it's building! If it isn't going into their shields... Oh, my God! I've got movement on the asteroid's upper pole! It's a gun of some sort! A big one! It's charging! Captain! You gotta jump!"

"Snap jump!" Captain Roselle ordered. "NOW!"

"Missiles away!" the Kent's tactical officer reported. "Sixteen clean launches. Impact in thirty seconds."

"The Jar-Benakh just jumped away!" Lieutenant Todson reported from the sensor station.

"What?" Captain Poc replied. "Why would they..."

"Huge power spike on the... INCOMING!"

A thick red beam of laser light, made visible only by the dust and wreckage debris drifting across the beam's path, reached out from the top of the distant asteroid, slamming into the Kent's forward starboard shields. Her shields glowed for a moment, then failed as emitters overloaded and exploded on the side of her hull. With her shields down, the laser blast sliced into the Kent's bow, finding her forward missile bay. The intense energy of the laser detonated several of the missiles, causing a chain reaction of detonations that tore the Kent apart from stem to stern as it came over the horizon of Nor-Patri.

"Captain, the Jar-Benakh just jumped!" Mister Navashee reported from the Aurora's sensor station. "And I've got a massive power surge coming from the asteroid base."

"Flight reports all fighters away," Naralena reported.

"Then it's still intact?" Nathan asked his sensor operator.

"Yes, sir! Something is firing from her upper pole. It's a laser! It just fired!"

"Did it hit anything?" Nathan asked urgently.

"No, sir. Not that I can see. I think they were shooting at the Jar-Benakh. That must be why they jumped. The angle on the weapon indicates the laser probably passed by the other side of Nor-Patri."

"Message from the Jar-Benakh," Naralena announced. "Transmitted just before she jumped. They're calling on all ships to attack the center point of the ring base, directly in line with Nor-Patri. They mean to overload at least one section of shields."

"Where are those two cruisers?" Nathan asked.

"Off our port side, and closing fast," Mister Navashee replied.

"Helm, turn into those cruisers. Put on an overhead pass, five hundred meters, and prepare to jump us in close. Angle down on the bow to fire," Nathan instructed. "Jess, be ready on all forward tubes. I want to take both those ships out in a single pass, then we'll have a few minutes to pound that ring station before those battleships get within firing range of us."

"On course for attack run," Mister Chiles reported. "Bringing the bow down now."

"Ready on all forward tubes."

"Triplets on all of them," Nathan ordered. "Full power."

"Full-power triplets, aye," Jessica replied.

"Ready on the jump," Mister Riley announced.

"Snap jump us in," Nathan ordered.

"Snap jumping," the navigator acknowledged.

The jump flash washed over the Aurora's bridge as the ship transitioned from their orbit over Nor-Patri to a position less than a kilometer away from the two approaching Jung cruisers, and only five hundred meters above their flight path.

"Jump complete."

"Firing all forward tubes!" Jessica reported. "Torpedoes away!"

The Aurora's bridge flashed red-orange several times as the first round of torpedoes slammed into the nearest enemy cruiser. The mark three plasma torpedoes overwhelmed the cruiser's shields and caused them to buckle. The shots from their mark five torpedoes brought the shields down, and allowed the third group of triplet shots to tear into the target's hull, breaking her wide open.

"One down," Jessica reported. "Second target in five..."

"The Jar-Benakh is back," Mister Navashee reported.

"Firing on target two," Jessica reported.

"Incoming message from the Jar-Benakh," Naralena announced as the bridge flashed red-orange again. "They're warning us about the laser weapon."

"Target two is destroyed," Jessica reported as the second cruiser on the main view screen exploded.

"Captain!" Naralena continued. "The Kent is down! Jar-Benakh reports the Kent is completely destroyed. She was hit by that laser."

"Where are the Celestia and the Tanna?" Nathan demanded.

"The Celestia jumped away four minutes ago after deploying her fighters," Mister Navashee reported. "She just attacked several cruisers and frigates at Nor-Patri's opposite gravity point."

"And the Tanna?"

"Unknown, sir," Mister Navashee replied. "She's not on my sensors."

Nathan glanced at the tactical display to the right of his helmsman, taking note of the Celestia's position.

"She should have seen that laser shot," Nathan surmised.

"Celestia just jumped, Captain. Given the time delay, she might not have seen it before she jumped."

"Comms, as soon as you see either ship, broadcast a warning about that damned laser," Nathan directed.

"Aye, sir."

"How much time before those three battleships get within attack range?"

"Ten minutes at maximum FTL, sir," Mister Navashee replied. "And they went to FTL one minute ago."

"Helm, turn into that ring base," Nathan directed. "Put our nose on that center point the Jar-Benakh was referring to, but keep an open jump line in case they try to target us with that laser."

"Aye, sir," the helmsman reported.

"Comms, warn the Jar-Benakh that we're starting our attack run from their port side and astern of them. Transmit our attack plot as soon as you get it from Mister Riley."

———————

"Four Jung gunships just came out of FTL directly to our starboard, five kilometers out," the Tanna's sensor operator reported. "They're firing rail guns!"

"Escape jump, Mister Poschay!" Captain Nash ordered.

"Escape jump, aye!" the navigator replied as he initiated the jump.

"Tactical, feed the coordinates and profiles of those gunships into four jump missiles and fire when ready. Calculate for last known..."

"Course and speed, yes, sir," Lieutenant Monath finished for him.

"Helm, hold your course until she fires," Captain Nash added.

"Holding her steady," the helmsman replied.

"Message from the Aurora," the comm officer announced. "They need all ships to attack the ring base. They're sending targeting data. They're also warning of a laser weapon on Zhu-Anok. It got the Kent, sir."

"The Kent?" Captain Nash repeated reflexively. "Are there any survivors?"

"Firing missiles," Lieutenant Monath announced.

"No, sir," the comm officer replied.

"Missiles away."

Captain Nash sighed. "Turn us toward Zhu-Anok and prepare to jump to a point ten million kilometers above that asteroid. I want to launch everything we've got and be long gone by the time they can fire on us."

———————

"Breaking orbit," Ensign Hunt reported from the Celestia's helm.

"On course and speed for Patoray gravity point one," Ensign Sperry added. "Jump plotted and ready."

"Execute your jump," Cameron ordered.

"Jumping in three..."

"All forward tubes are charged and ready," Lieutenant Delaveaga reported from the tactical station.

"Two..."

"Triplets on the mark threes, singles on the mark fives, if you please," Cameron instructed.

"One..."

"Triplets and singles, aye."

"Jumping."

The jump flash washed over the Celestia's bridge. When it cleared a moment later, a damaged but still operational Jung battleship nearly filled their main view screen, as it slid from top to bottom.

"Jump complete."

"Firing all forward tubes," Luis reported.

Cameron watched as twelve mark three, and four mark five plasma torpedoes raced away from her ship and slammed into the hull of the battleship. The enemy vessel broke apart, explosions from within triggered by the massive amounts of thermal energy imparted by the impact of highly concentrated plasma against her hull. Her helmsman kept the Celestia's nose on the target by continually pitching down as they passed over the target at a distance of only a single kilometer. Because of this, her tactical officer was able to continue pummeling the Jung battleship with plasma torpedoes.

The battleship was now upside down on the Celestia's view screen, and getting smaller as they coasted away from the target, flying stern-first. Two more rounds of plasma torpedoes served as the enemy vessel's final executioner, and the five-kilometer-long battleship broke in two. The sections drifted apart as more explosions rocked her insides. The forward half split yet again, and the stern section exploded.

"Target destroyed," Ensign Kono reported from the sensor station.

"Next target?" Cameron asked.

"Two frigates and a heavy cruiser at Nor-Patri's fourth gravity point," Luis suggested. "Frigates are nearer, and the cruiser is about ten clicks beyond them."

"The cruiser's power readings are fluctuating, Captain," Ensign Kono added. "They may be having shield problems."

"Very well," Cameron replied. "Mister Sperry, plot an intercept jump to those targets."

"Aye, sir," the navigator replied.

"Comms, any updates from our other ships?"

"No, sir."

"Ensign Kono?"

"The Aurora and the Jar-Benakh should be on the far side of Nor-Patri. I have no fixes on either the Kent or the Tanna. We should get a better picture as soon as we jump to Nor-Patri's fourth gravity point."

"Very, well," Cameron replied as she studied the new targets on the tactical display. "Lieutenant, we'll jump in between the frigates and hit them with our broadside cannons as we pass. That should also give us a good firing line on the cruiser with our forward tubes."

"Aye, sir," Luis replied.

"On course and speed, ready to jump," Ensign Sperry reported.

"Take us in," Cameron instructed.

"Jumping in three..."

Cameron glanced at the tactical map again. The Jung homeworld was directly between them and the asteroid ring base. She had been on the opposite side of that planet from the rest of the Alliance forces for the entire ten minutes that the Celestia had been in the system, and she really wanted to know the status of that ring base.

She would have to wait.

The jump flash washed over the Celestia's bridge.

The Celestia passed directly between the two Jung frigates, about two kilometers away from each. She fired her broadside cannons repeatedly, sending groups of eight balls of plasma toward the targets. As she did so, she also fired all eight of her forward torpedo tubes, sending waves of sixteen plasma torpedoes each, racing toward the Jung heavy cruiser still ten kilometers ahead of them.

The two frigates came apart as the first round of plasma shots, fired from the Celestia's broadside cannons, overwhelmed their shields and caused them to collapse. The second round tore the ships apart, leaving only debris behind.

"Both frigates are destroyed," Ensign Kono reported.

"Cease fire on all forward tubes," Cameron directed. "Helm, change course to pass over the cruiser, then pitch us down. I want to be ready to jump the remaining distance and finish her off if the first two rounds of mark fives..."

"Impacts!" Ensign Kono reported. "I was right! Her shields had to be damaged already. She's coming apart!"

"Captain!" Ensign Souza called from the comm station. "Message from the Aurora. Ring base is intact. Heavily shielded. Laser weapon on top pole. Kent is down. No survivors. Attack center point of ring base nearest Nor-Patri."

A solemn look came over Cameron's face. They had lost a ship...a crew. "Mister Hunt, put us on course for that ring base."

"We are *not* getting through," the Jar-Benakh's tactical officer reported in frustration. "That damned shield of theirs is too strong!"

"Have we made *any* headway?" Captain Roselle asked.

"The shield section over that laser weapon is down to ninety percent, sir," Ensign Marka replied.

"Then we just have to keep pounding her," the captain insisted.

"The laser weapon is targeting us again, Captain," Ensign Marka added. "The weapon is charging."

"Damn it! Escape jump!"

"Escape jump, aye!" the navigator replied.

"Comms, message to all ships!" Captain Roselle barked. "Screw the ring base! Attack that damned laser first! Once we kill that thing, we can take down that ring!"

"I'm detecting several ships coming out of the ring base, sir," Ensign Marka reported. "Cruisers, frigates, and gunships."

"Bring us about again," the captain ordered. "We'll do another pass standing on our heads, firing our forward tubes as we pass over the weapon. Kes, put as many of our forward guns as you can on the shield section covering that laser. Sugar... Flash... Use the rest of our guns on anything coming out of that ring base."

"Message from the Celestia," the comms officer announced. "They've received the Aurora's update and are going to attack the center point of the ring."

"Raise them and tell them to go after the laser weapon instead," Roselle ordered.

"Too late," Ensign Marka interrupted. "The

Celestia just jumped into Nor-Patri's first gravity point!"

———

"Firing all forward torpedoes," Luis reported from the Celestia's tactical station. "Firing forward plasma cannon turrets."

"Captain! Multiple ships coming out of the ring base!" Ensign Kono reported with urgency. "Cruisers, frigates, and gunships."

"Hit as many of them as we can with the rest of our guns," Cameron ordered.

"Message from the Jar-Benakh," Ensign Souza announced. "They want us to attack the shield section protecting the laser weapon from above. Jar-Benakh is making lateral passes. Aurora is making forty-five-degree dives from Nor-Patri's side. They want us to come from the opposite side, on even minutes only."

"Helm, pitch up forty-five and prepare to jump five light minutes out," Cameron instructed. "We'll then pitch up more and to port, so we can jump over to an apex point."

"I see where you're going, sir," Ensign Hunt replied.

"I knew you would," Cameron said. "Lieutenant. We'll dive in on our port side, sliding by Zhu-Anok at twenty clicks. We pitch in, put a few rounds of triplets from all forward tubes, then hold attitude and slap them with the port broadsides before we jump."

"Understood," Luis replied.

"First turn complete," the helmsman reported.

"Jumping five light minutes," Ensign Sperry announced as the jump flash washed over the Celestia's bridge. "Jump complete."

"Executing next turn," the helmsman announced.

"Aurora just jumped for her attack run," Ensign Kono reported. "She's picking up some fire from the ships that just came out of the ring base." The ensign turned to look at her captain. "If they launch any more ships, it's going to get awfully crowded around Zhu-Anok, sir."

"Turn complete."

"Executing next jump."

"Just keep your eyes on those ship tracks," Cameron told the ensign. "If you think our jump line is about to get blocked, speak up."

"Yes, sir," Ensign Kono replied.

"Executing final turn," Ensign Hunt announced from the helm.

Cameron studied the tactical display as it updated the status of all known targets in the Jung's home system. Where there had once been mostly red triangles, there were now red Xs with growing circles around them to indicate the dead ships' expanding debris fields. By all indications, the attack was already an overwhelming success. The joint JKKV and jump missile strikes on the six battle groups alone had scored nearly forty-eight kills, with the combination strikes on the groups of Jung ships in closer to Nor-Patri resulting in at least thirty more enemy ships being destroyed. But it still wasn't enough. They had to destroy that ring base, or, at the very least, do considerable damage. Otherwise, the message that they were trying to send the Jung would not be as strong as they desperately needed it to be. The leaflets had provided a simple message: 'The Alliance and the Jung can live in peace together, or we can all die together.' They had to prove to the Jung that it was not a bluff.

"Turn complete," Ensign Hunt reported.

"Attack jump plotted and ready," Ensign Sperry added.

"Roll us on our port side, and yaw us twenty degrees in, Mister Hunt," Cameron instructed.

"Roll to port, and yaw twenty to port," the helmsman acknowledged.

Cameron waited, watching the ship's attitude display before her on the pedestal between her navigator and her helmsman. Once the attitude change was complete, she gave the order. "Execute attack jump."

"Jumping in three..."

"All forward tubes are charged and ready," Luis reported.

"Two..."

"All forward turrets are ready."

"One..."

Cameron glanced at the mission clock, verifying that they were still in an even minute.

"Jumping."

The jump flash washed over them. The Zhu-Anok asteroid appeared on the main view screen, sliding from right to left as they passed over it.

"Firing all forward tubes," Luis reported. "Firing forward turrets."

Cameron watched as waves of plasma torpedoes poured out of her ship and headed for the upper pole of Zhu-Anok.

"The laser weapon is charging," Ensign Kono reported.

"Is it targeting us?" Cameron asked.

"No, sir. It's pointed twenty degrees off our departure course. I think it's trying to anticipate the Aurora's next attack line."

"Losing our angle on the bow," Luis reported, "switching to quads and port broadsides."

"Pitching back to course," Ensign Hunt reported.

"Captain!" Ensign Kono shouted in warning. "Two cruisers! Dead ahead! They just came out of the ring base! They're trying to block our path!"

"Evasive!" Cameron ordered. "Get us a clear jump line!"

"The laser weapon is moving!" Ensign Kono warned. "Toward us!"

"Get us out of here, Mister Sperry," Cameron urged.

"Taking evasive," Ensign Hunt confirmed.

Cameron looked to the tactical display as the ship started to change course to get a clear jump line. There were two cruisers, one behind the other, moving from left to right in an attempt to stay in front of them as they turned. There was insufficient space to pass between them. To make matters worse, yet *another* ship was coming out of the ring base behind them.

"The laser has a lock on us!" Ensign Kono warned.

"Pitch up!" Cameron ordered.

"They're firing!"

"Snap jump!" Cameron ordered.

"Our jump line isn't..."

"NOW!"

On the main view screen, Cameron could see the pale blue light as it quickly poured out of the emitters and spread across the hull. Within a second, it solidified and began to flash. Then there was a sudden red flash of light that encompassed the entire screen. Jump emitters started exploding all over their forward hull, as well as shield emitters.

"We're hit!" Ensign Kono reported.

"Cascade shield failure!" Luis warned.

"Jump drive is offline!" the system's officer added.

The main view screen flickered twice and then went black.

"Do we still have maneuvering and propulsion?" Cameron asked urgently.

"Yes, sir!" Ensign Hunt replied.

"Full power to the mains!" Cameron ordered.

"Full power, aye!" the ensign replied.

"Those ships are still in our path!" Ensign Kono warned.

"Ram them if you have to!" Cameron replied. "Just get us below the asteroid's equator and out of that laser's firing line! We can't take another hit like that!"

"Captain!" Mister Navashee called from the Aurora's sensor station. "The Celestia's been hit!"

"How bad?" Nathan asked, rising from his command chair.

"She's lost all shields! She's got dead emitters all over the place! She may have lost her jump drive as well! She's in a full power run for Zhu-Anok's equator!"

"They're trying to get out of that laser's firing line," Jessica realized.

"They've got three cruisers making a run to block their path and force them to turn before they get clear," Mister Navashee continued. "It looks like they may collide."

"Helm, turn into the lead cruiser and jump us in," Nathan ordered. "Jess, be ready to fire everything at that cruiser."

"Turning to intercept," Mister Chiles confirmed.

"I'm on it," Jessica assured him.

"Jump ready," Mister Riley reported.

"Snap jump," Nathan ordered.

"Snap jumping," the navigator responded as the jump flash washed over them.

The Jung cruiser suddenly appeared directly ahead of them, with the Celestia to the far right of the spherical screen, practically to Nathan's side, firing desperately at every ship around her.

"Fire!" Nathan commanded.

"Firing all forward tubes!" Jessica replied.

"The laser has a lock on the Celestia," Mister Navashee warned. "It's firing!"

Nathan turned his head to the right, and watched in horror as the laser cut into the top of the Celestia's stern section, just forward of her antimatter reactors. The laser energy tore through her unprotected hull, setting off secondary explosions that tore her in half, sending her forward section into a slow tumbling motion as both sections continued to drift across the asteroid's landscape on their way to the ring station at the asteroid's equator.

"The laser is still tracking the Celestia!" Mister Navashee warned.

"First cruiser destroyed!" Jessica announced. "Give me five to port for the second target!"

"The laser is charging again," Mister Navashee added.

"Five degrees to port, aye," Mister Chiles confirmed.

Nathan felt a sick feeling in his stomach as he stared out the right side of the main view screen at his friend's mortally wounded ship.

"Lock on the second target!" Jessica announced. "Firing!"

"Jump flash!" Mister Navashee reported. "It's the Jar-Benakh! She's moving in to shield the Celestia!"

"Second target destroyed!" Jessica announced.

"Helm! Slow us down and match the Celestia's course and speed! Then bring our nose back around so we can fire torpedoes into the third cruiser!"

"Incoming missiles from two frigates!" Mister Navashee warned.

"Point-defenses are spinning up to intercept the missiles," Jessica reported.

"The laser is charging again!" Mister Navashee warned.

"How long until the Celestia is out of that laser's firing line?"

"One minute!"

"Captain! The Jar-Benakh is swinging her nose to starboard," Jessica reported.

"The laser is firing!" Mister Navashee announced. "Holy shit! It hit the Jar-Benakh in her stern!"

"How bad?" Nathan asked, his eyes wide.

"You don't understand. Her angle! She deflected most of the laser's energy away. Her stern starboard shields are down to twenty percent, but she suffered no real damage."

"Can she do that again?" Nathan wondered.

"She won't have to, Captain," Mister Navashee exclaimed. "We'll be across the equator and out of that damned laser's firing line in twenty more seconds."

"I've got a shitload of incoming here," Jessica warned. "I don't know how long I can keep up with them."

"Jump flashes!" Mister Navashee reported with excitement. "Dozens of them! Jump missiles! Oh, my God! They're hitting everything!"

"It's got to be the Tanna!" Nathan exclaimed.

"Damn right it is," Jessica commented proudly.

"She just took out every ship in the area, Captain!" Mister Navashee shouted gleefully.

"How long until the next closest ships get within attack range?" Nathan asked.

"Assuming no more come out of that ring, about ten minutes!"

"Comms! Raise the Celestia! Green deck! Launch all SARs and shuttles! And tell them not to bother bringing anyone back here, just jump straight to the departure rally point! Then contact the Jar-Benakh and ask them to do the same."

"Aye, sir," Naralena replied.

"And dispatch a jump comm-drone to the launch boxcar," Nathan added. "Tell them to launch the second KKV! Target is Zhu-Anok! Impact in ten!"

"Captain!" Jessica objected. "That KKV will..."

"You have your orders!" Nathan demanded.

"Aye, sir!" Naralena replied. "Dispatching jump comm-drone."

Nathan stared at Jessica.

"I hope you know what you're doing," she muttered.

Me too, Nathan thought.

The Celestia's bridge was dark, lit only by the dim emergency lighting and the occasional sparking of electrical arcs from behind consoles. An acrid haze filled the air, and the sounds of alarms filled the bridge. Cameron looked around. Without the main view screen, the bridge seemed remarkably cut off from the rest of the universe. She had a flashback of the bridge of the Aurora, nearly two years ago.

"Any contact with engineering?" Cameron asked.

"No, sir," Ensign Souza replied frantically. "We've lost contact with everything aft of midship."

"I'm not getting any data from main propulsion or power generation," the systems officer said. "I'm barely getting any data at all, Captain."

"Sensors are dead," Ensign Kono reported.

"I've lost all propulsion and maneuvering," Ensign Hunt added.

"All nav and jump systems are down as well," Ensign Sperry said. He looked at Captain Taylor. "We're dead-stick, sir. Dead-stick and blind."

"Captain! Fighter Launch Control!"

Cameron tapped her comm-set. "Go for Captain."

"Sir, I'm looking out the aft observation window! Our whole drive section is gone! We've been cut in half just aft of midship!"

"Oh, my God," Cameron exclaimed.

"We're done, Captain," Luis realized.

"Can you see the aft section?" Cameron asked over her comm-set.

"Yes, sir, but barely. We're in a slow end-over. She's battered, but intact. She looks dead as shit, though."

"Understood."

"I've got the Jar-Benakh on ship-to-ship local," Ensign Souza reported from the Celestia's comm station. "They've launched rescue shuttles. So has the Aurora! They're on either side of us, trying to cover our evac!"

Cameron took a deep breath. "Give the order. All hands, abandon ship. Send everyone aft of the forward primary bulkheads to the port and starboard flight decks. Everyone forward, go to the bow escape pods. They're set to auto-jump to the departure rally point."

"Aye, sir," Ensign Souza replied, as the evacuation alarms began to sound.

"Two more cruisers coming out of the ring base, far side," Ensign Marka reported from the Jar-Benakh's sensor station. "They'll have range on us in two minutes."

"Tanna reports she's all out of missiles, Captain," Ensign Jullen reported from the comm station.

"Be ready to pound those cruisers," Captain Roselle ordered.

"Aye, sir," the tactical officer reported.

"Our first wave of rescue shuttles is on its way back, Captain," Ensign Marka reported.

"Ring base is launching fighters!" the tactical officer reported.

"Mas! Recall all Eagles and Falcons from orbit! Tell them to fly cover for the Celestia!"

"Aye, sir."

"Tactical," Captain Roselle continued. "Until there are more missiles headed our way, put our point-defenses on those fighters. I don't want them harassing our SAR ops. Understood?"

"Yes, sir."

"Shoot and scoot! Shoot and scoot!" Loki instructed. "Don't stay in one place long enough for them to get a lock on us!"

"I'm scootin'!" Josh replied as he executed his fifth single-kilometer jump in the last two minutes, ever since they had jumped from orbit over Nor-Patri to cover the Celestia's evacuation.

"Two more, ten high!" Loki warned. "They're firing!"

"And I'm scootin'!" Josh said again, activating

the jump drive. As the windows cleared, he pulled their nose up hard, bringing it around to face aft as he pressed the trigger and fired his plasma torpedo cannons. He waved their nose back and forth, spraying the flight of fighters behind them, destroying three of the five pursuers in the process.

"Four more, four high!" Loki warned. He glanced at his tactical display, looking for friendlies. "Eagles at one one four by twenty-eight, Falcon One! Attack the guys to your left and get them off our ass, so we can go after the guys to our four high!"

"Falcon One, Blue Leader. Engaging."

Josh pushed their nose back around and fired the main engines again, steering toward the gap between the Celestia's forward section and the Aurora to her left.

"Two dead ahead!" Loki reported. "They're going after one of the SAR shuttles!"

"I'll take those two," Josh said. "You handle the ones at our three with the nose turret."

"Got it!" Loki replied.

"Fuck," Josh muttered as he looked out the forward windows. The Aurora was to his left, and the forward two thirds of the Celestia was to his right. He glanced out the right windows, looking past Loki, and saw the battered propulsion section of the Celestia. He looked at Loki, exchanging glances. "This is insane."

"I know."

Josh turned his attention forward again, as four shuttles departed the Celestia and made a run for a clear jump line out of the system. Two Jung fighters turned to attack the fleeing shuttles. "I don't think so," Josh said as he turned the Super Falcon toward them and pressed his firing button. Plasma torpedoes shot out on either side of the cockpit, passing behind the attacking fighters moving from his left to right. Josh continued firing as he tightened his turn, walking each successive round of plasma torpedoes closer to the Jung fighters. Finally he tagged the trailing fighter. But before he could tag the leading one, it exploded in a fireball, after which two Super Eagles flashed past their starboard side in the opposite direction.

"Shit!" Loki yelled.

"Cutting it a little close, aren't they?" Josh muttered.

———

"*We'll take care of your jump drive,*" Nathan insisted over the Celestia's bridge loudspeakers. "*Just get off that ship! The KKV will strike in two minutes!*"

"Copy that," Cameron replied over her comm-set. "We're leaving now." She rose from her command chair. "All right, people! Time to go!" Cameron stood and watched as her bridge staff left their posts and headed out for the exits. As soon as they were all gone, she followed Luis out the starboard exit.

As they stepped into the starboard airlock corridor, the ship suddenly lurched, throwing them against the left wall.

"*Breach! Flight deck! Starboard side!*" a voice called over her comm-set. Cameron struggled to follow the others. She could feel the gravity fluctuating under her feet as she stepped from the airlock corridor into the main corridor.

"The ramp auto-sealed!" Ensign Souza yelled from ahead.

"Around the corner, back this way!" Cameron yelled. "Down the ladder to B deck, then forward to the escape pods!" she explained, turning to lead the way. She ran as best she could, her gait thrown off by the variance in gravity fields from deck plate to deck plate.

Cameron rounded the corner to her left, ran a few more steps forward, then turned right and continued to the end of the short corridor. She popped open the hatch, revealing a microgravity tunnel that stretched from the fighter deck above to the lowest deck in the Celestia. "Here!" she ordered. "Down two decks to C, then forward through the primary bulkhead. Escape pods should be on your right as soon as you pass through the bulkhead!"

Luis stopped and looked at her. "You first, Captain!"

"No way!" Cameron objected. "The Captain is the last one off the ship!"

"Then I'm the second to the last!" he insisted.

"Suit yourself, Lieutenant!"

They watched as the other eleven members of the bridge staff dove down the microgravity tunnel, pulling their way quickly along the ladder. After the last one dove in, Luis followed, and then Cameron.

Cameron pulled herself along, rung by rung, at a steady pace, following the line of crewmen down to C deck. Finally, she came out of the tunnel onto the deck in a prone position, again being held by the deck's artificial gravity plating.

Luis grabbed Cameron and helped her to her feet, pushing her through the bulkhead hatch. He stepped through after her, swung the hatch closed, and locked it.

They ran nearly all the way forward before they found the one escape pod that had not yet been launched.

There was a terrible twisting noise, followed by the screeching sound of metal being twisted and torn. The deck shifted, and the gravity plating failed, sending them spiraling in all directions. Cameron grabbed the railing and pulled herself toward the hatch to the escape pod, following the others. She looked behind her. Luis was only two meters away, struggling to make it to the hatch. Debris, tearing away from the decks and walls of the corridor swirled about, careening off the walls and ceiling.

Cameron managed to pull herself inside the escape pod hatch. She turned around to look for Luis, just as something tore through the bow of the ship with incredible force. There was a rush of escaping air, and Luis shot down the corridor with the rest of the debris, as everything was sucked out into space through the breach.

"LUIS!" Cameron cried out, reaching for him as the air around her was sucked out into space. Ensigns Souza and Kono grabbed their captain and pulled her into the escape pod, while Ensign Sperry closed the hatch behind them.

Seconds later, the Celestia's last escape pod ejected.

"Direct hits on her bow!" Mister Navashee reported from the Aurora's sensor station. "The last escape pod is away!"

"Kill that son of a bitch!" Nathan ordered.

"Give me ten to starboard and two down!" Jessica ordered the helmsman.

"Ten starboard, two down, aye," Mister Chiles replied as he executed the change in course to bring their tubes to bear on the Jung cruiser that had just put a few hundred rail gun slugs into the bow of the Celestia.

"Firing all forward tubes!" Jessica reported.

"Mister Navashee! Tell me you have a data link with the Celestia's self-destruct system!" Nathan said.

"Yes, sir, I do!"

"Target destroyed!" Jessica exclaimed.

"How long until the KKV hits?" Nathan asked.

"Thirty seconds!"

"Set it to blow in twenty!" Nathan ordered. "Helm, put us on a run out of here, full power! Don't jump us until my order!"

"Yes, sir!" Mister Chiles replied.

"Comms! Tell all ships to jump to the departure rally point! NOW!" Nathan instructed.

"*Aurora to all Alliance ships!*" Naralena's voice called over Josh and Loki's comm-set. "*Jump to Foxtrot One, immediately! Jump to Foxtrot One!*"

"That's it," Loki declared. "Time to go!"

"Don't gotta tell me twice," Josh replied as he brought his throttles to full power and turned away from Zhu-Anok and toward open space.

"Jumping in three..." Loki began.

"Fuck that!" Josh replied, pushing the selector switch on his flight control stick up and pressing the jump button.

"Five seconds to detonation," Mister Navashee announced from the Aurora's sensor station.

Nathan watched the rear camera view on the Aurora's main view screen as Nor-Patri, Zhu-Anok, and what was left of the Celestia, shrank away from them as they accelerated out into deep space.

There was a bright white flash where the Celestia's propulsion section had once been, as her antimatter reactors dropped their containment fields right on cue, destroying the jump drive along with everything within two thousand kilometers of it.

The flash only lasted a few seconds, and then it was gone. Five seconds later, the super jump KKV appeared from a flash of blue-white light, and slammed into Zhu-Anok, breaking the asteroid apart and taking the ring base along with it.

In the blink of an eye, Nathan had just killed close to a million Jung, and he didn't feel the slightest bit of remorse. *Is this what I've become?*

Nathan stared at the destruction on the view screen for several seconds, then gave the order. "Jump us to the departure rally point, Mister Riley."

CHAPTER FIFTEEN

"General Bacca?" the ship's pilot called from the doorway to the general's quarters.

"Commander," the general replied, looking up from his data pad.

"I hope I am not disturbing you, sir."

"Not at all," the general said, setting his data pad down on the table beside him. "In fact, you are a welcome distraction. I have been studying these signals from Earth too much. It is refreshing to speak Jung with someone. English is such a boring, utilitarian language, nowhere near as rich as our native tongue."

"Of course."

"What's on your mind, Commander?"

"You asked me to inform you when we are only a few days out from Sol."

"Indeed I did."

"We are currently two point five Earth days from our planned drop-out point."

"Excellent. Please, take the ship out of FTL long enough to put the high-speed comm-drone that we intercepted *back* on its way to Sol."

"If you don't mind me asking, General, to what end?"

"I wish the leaders of this *Alliance* to receive our leader's so-called 'call for peace' prior to our arrival."

"I was under the impression that you wished to deliver the message yourself," the commander said.

"I had considered doing so, yes," the general admitted. "However, considering the situation, and our recent history with the Terrans, they are more likely to, as they say, 'shoot first and ask questions later.' Not a very good way to start off a peace negotiation, wouldn't you agree?"

"Indeed, sir," the commander agreed. "What speed would you like the comm-drone to travel at?"

"Whatever speed gets it there at least a full day ahead of us, Commander."

"Of course. I will see to it immediately." The commander turned to depart, then stopped. "Pardon me, General. If I might make another inquiry?"

"Please."

"You spoke of a 'call for peace'? Does this mean that Jung Command is accepting defeat at the hands of the Terrans?"

"Doubtful," the general replied. "It is more likely a ruse, a ploy intended to buy time so that Command can move more ships into the area so we can put these annoying people in their place, once and for all."

"Then, there is still a chance?"

"A chance?" the general wondered.

"For us to save face, to avoid bringing shame to our caste."

"You view failure as something to be ashamed of, Commander?"

"Of course."

"Shame is cast by failure, only if those who failed did not learn from their mistakes, brush themselves off, and try again. You see, one can either accept defeat, or reject it and continue to try. While the latter does *not* guarantee honor, the former *does* guarantee disgrace."

"But, I was taught that the Jung never surrender, that we fight to the death. We either succeed, or we die in the attempt."

"Who is to say that the *attempt* is over, Commander?" the general said, a small smile on his weathered face.

The commander thought about the general's words for a moment before leaving. "I will dispatch the comm-drone immediately, General."

General Bacca picked up his data pad again. "Thank you, Commander."

* * *

Nathan sat in his ready room doing nothing. His morning staff meeting was complete, his inspections of the post-battle repairs still in progress had been conducted, and the daily intelligence briefing from Karuzara had been read. He literally had nothing to do.

Or at least, nothing that he *wanted* to do.

It had been four days since they had attacked the Jung home system, and while it had been heralded as a major victory by all the worlds of the Alliance, the cost had been far greater than anticipated. Two ships had been lost, and a third badly damaged. Countless friends had died, including two of Nathan's oldest and dearest.

He felt guilty for dwelling on the loss of two close friends, when several hundred members of the Alliance had also been lost. But it was the loss of Luis and Devyn that had hit him the hardest. Cameron would survive. She would be in the hospital for a few weeks, and would face at least a month of rehabilitation, but she would be back to her old self again. He only hoped that she would agree to be his executive officer again, now that she no longer had a ship, and since Commander Willard would soon be given command of the refurbished Scout One, to be called 'Recon One' instead.

Another thought had crossed his mind as well. Resignation. Once Cameron returned to duty, he could tender his resignation. He could leave the service and return to Earth. His grandfather's home was still intact, for the most part. Even his old plane was there. It, like the house, was in need of repair, but it would be therapeutic for him. The fresh air, the hard work. And the idea of flying again...real 'stick and rudder' flying. That appealed to Nathan as well.

But it was still not over. It was true, they had dealt a devastating blow to the Jung, but no one yet knew what the Jung's response to their attack would be. And until they knew, until he could be sure, he could not find peace.

The intercom panel in his desk beeped. *"Flash traffic from Command,"* Naralena said, a sense of urgency in her voice. *"Long-range sensors have detected an object headed for Earth at eighty percent light. It just dropped out of FTL. Command suspects it could be a Jung weapon. They are requesting that we jump out to intercept."*

"General quarters. Break orbit and prepare an intercept jump," Nathan ordered as he stood. "I'm on my way."

"Aye, sir."

Nathan moved quickly out of his ready room and onto the Aurora's bridge. "Status," he queried as he moved quickly from the back of the bridge toward his command chair located at the center.

"Breaking orbit now," Miser Chiles reported from the helm.

"Jump point to intercept in twenty seconds," Mister Riley added.

"Anything more on the object, Mister Navashee?" Nathan asked.

"No, sir. I've got the feed from the Karuzara's long-range sensor array, but the object is so small, and so distant..."

"How distant?"

"About eighteen billion kilometers, sir," Mister Navashee clarified. "It came out of FTL just inside the heliopause."

"Could it be a weapon?" Nathan wondered.

"If it is, whoever sent it doesn't know how to use it very well," Jessica said as she entered the bridge and went straight to her usual station at the tactical console.

"On course and speed for intercept jump," the helmsman reported.

"All departments report general quarters," Naralena announced. "XO is in combat, chief of the boat is in damage control."

"All weapons systems are charged and ready," Jessica added.

"Very well," Nathan said. "Mister Riley, jump us out there."

"Aye, sir," Mister Riley replied. "Jumping in three......two......one......jumping."

Nathan slowly took his seat as the jump flash briefly illuminated the interior of the Aurora's bridge.

"Jump complete," Mister Riley reported.

"Contact," Mister Navashee said. "I've got the object. One million kilometers and closing fast. It appears to be a Jung comm-drone."

"Is it on a collision course with Earth?" Nathan wondered.

"No, sir," Mister Navashee replied. "Captain, it's changing its attitude. It's flipping end over."

"I've got locks on it with both forward plasma cannons, Captain," Jessica reported.

"It's firing its main engines," Mister Navashee added. He turned to look at the captain. "I think it's decelerating, sir."

"Captain," Naralena called from the comm station at the back of the bridge. "The object is transmitting. Omnidirectional, all frequencies... It's in Jung."

Nathan stood again, turning around to look at Naralena as she listened to the message. After a few seconds, he grew impatient. "Well?"

"I believe the message is from the Jung High Command... It could be 'council', the words are very similar. They are asking to begin negotiations... Captain, I think they're offering a cease-fire."

"Of course they are," Jessica said. "We just kicked their ass."

"No," Nathan disagreed. "Their top comm-drone speed is one hundred times light. There's no way in hell that thing was launched *after* we attacked them. This thing must've been in flight for..." Nathan snapped his fingers several times. "Help me out with the math, here, Mister Riley."

"Two hundred and forty-seven days, sir."

"Like I said, it was sent before we attacked their homeworld. *Long* before we attacked." Nathan thought about it for a moment. "Double that number for a round trip... This call for a cease-fire is probably in response to our retaking of Earth."

"How the hell do we know if they still mean it?" Jessica wondered.

"There's more," Naralena interrupted. "They say they've already sent an envoy to begin negotiations, and that they will arrive shortly."

"Did they say *how* soon?" Nathan asked.

"No, sir," Naralena replied. "They also say that the probe is programmed to enter into a stable orbit around Earth, so that we may use it to send a message back to the Jung, if we wish."

"No way in hell we're letting that thing anywhere near Earth," Jessica insisted.

"Agreed," Nathan said. "Is that it?" he asked Naralena. "Nothing more?"

"No, sir. They clearly announced the end of the message."

"Take it out," Nathan ordered, stepping up to the front of the tactical console.

"Gladly," Jessica replied. "Firing forward plasma turrets."

"Comm-drone is destroyed," Mister Navashee confirmed.

"Conduct a full sweep of the area," Nathan ordered. "I want to be damned sure that drone wasn't some kind of a Trojan horse."

"A what?" Mister Navashee inquired, unfamiliar with the term.

"It's a history thing," Nathan replied. "Comms, load that message into one of our jump comm-drones and send it back to Command. Let them know we're sweeping the area before we return."

"You know what this means," Nathan said to Jessica.

Jessica just looked at him and shrugged.

"It means we didn't *need* to attack the Jung home system. All those people... All of *our* people... None of them needed to die." Nathan turned and headed for his ready room without saying another word, his face pale.

"Nathan," Jessica said, wanting to reassure him, to comfort him.

He did not respond. He just disappeared into his ready room without another word.

* * *

Nathan entered the bridge through the port entrance, as he pulled on his uniform jacket.

"When the message said an envoy will arrive shortly, I didn't think they meant the next day," he said to Naralena as he entered.

"Ship is at general quarters," Naralena replied as Nathan passed. "XO is in combat, chief of the boat is in damage control."

"All weapons are charged and ready," Jessica reported.

"Intercept jump is plotted and ready," Mister Riley added. "The ship is on course and speed."

"What is it?" Nathan asked. "Another comm-drone?"

"No, sir," Mister Navashee replied. "Too big for a comm-drone. It's a bit bigger than a Jung gunship. It did, however, come out of FTL at the same location as the comm-drone, only at a greatly reduced speed."

"No other contacts?"

"No, sir."

Nathan sighed. "Well, let's go say hello, shall we? But keep your finger on the escape jump button, Mister Riley."

"Aye, sir. Jumping in three......two......one...... jumping."

Nathan moved to his command chair as the jump flash washed over the bridge. His eyes stayed fixed on the main view screen.

"Jump complete."

"Target reacquired," Mister Navashee reported. "Eight million kilometers and closing. They'll pass on our port side, about six thousand kilometers out, twelve degrees down relative."

"Green deck," Nathan ordered. "Launch the ready birds."

"Green deck, aye," Naralena replied.

"Target is indeed a ship," Mister Navashee continued. "Her only weapons appear to be mini-rail gun turrets, one top, one bottom. My guess is that she's some kind of long-range FTL shuttle, Captain."

"That's it, though? Just mini-rail guns. No antimatter reactor, no nuclear warheads, nothing like that?"

"No, sir."

"Does she have shields?"

"Unknown," Mister Navashee replied. "But if she does, they aren't raised."

"Flight ops reports four Super Eagles away," Naralena announced. "Time to intercept is two minutes."

"Relay your sensor readings to those fighters," Nathan instructed.

"Already on their way, sir."

"How long until she reaches us?" Nathan wondered.

"At present closure, about ten minutes," Mister Navashee replied. "But the target is decelerating, just like the comm-drone did."

"Then she means to make orbit as well," Nathan surmised.

"Mister Chiles, come about, nice and easy, and come in behind the target on a standard intercept."

"Standard intercept, aye," the helmsman acknowledged.

"One minute to fighter intercept."

"Receiving transmission," Naralena reported.

"From the fighters?" Nathan asked.

"No, sir. From the Jung ship."

"Put it up," Nathan instructed.

"The transmission has video as well," Naralena warned.

"Fine," Nathan replied. "Might as well see who we're talking to."

A moment later, an elderly, yet distinguished looking man, wearing a perfectly pressed Jung uniform, appeared on the main view screen.

Nathan had to control his surprise at the identity of the Jung officer. "General Bacca."

The general smiled. "*Captain Scott. Well, this is a pleasant surprise. I see you're looking well.*"

"Apparently Jung Command has a sense of humor, sending the same man I ran out of the system as a peace envoy."

"*Well, it just so happened that I was still in the neighborhood, and, what with travel between distant stars being so time-consuming for those of us without jump drives, I guess our leaders chose expedience over decorum. Apologies if my presence offends you.*"

"Your *presence* has precious little *effect* on me," Nathan assured the general. "State your intentions, General. My patience is in short supply these days."

"*I humbly request an audience with your leaders in order to negotiate a cease-fire, so that both our worlds can live in peace.*"

"Don't you mean, *all* our worlds?"

"*You have others?*" the general inquired, appearing surprised.

"Alliance membership in the Sol sector has grown somewhat during your absence," Nathan explained with great satisfaction.

"*I see. Well, I suppose that makes this negotiation*

even more necessary. So, will you grant me an audience?"

"I'll have to speak with my superiors," Nathan replied.

"Muted," Naralena announced. "Captain, our fighters are in position behind the target, and have missile locks. They can destroy her in seconds, if ordered."

"Very well," Nathan replied. "Unmute." Nathan took a breath before continuing. "In the meantime, General, continue on course and rate of deceleration. Make no changes to either without permission. If you do so, the four fighters on your six will destroy you in the blink of an eye. Raise your shields, charge your rail guns, or attempt to spin up your mass-canceling fields, and you will meet the same fate. Is that clear, General?"

"Quite clear, Captain. I will see you at the negotiations."

"It is doubtful that I will be there."

"But why?" the general asked.

"I am just a ship's captain," Nathan explained. "One of many. I shall leave the negotiating to our leaders."

"Oh, but I insist," the general drawled. *"I do so prefer to have a familiar face across the table from me."*

"I'll leave that decision to my superiors," Nathan replied, unfazed.

"I shall emphasize the need for you to attend," General Bacca said. *"I so look forward to finally speaking with you, face to face."*

Nathan made a gesture to kill the connection, then turned to face Jessica at the tactical station behind him. "Can't say that I feel the same."

* * *

General Bacca was led into the room by four heavily armed Ghatazhak, and placed unceremoniously into a small conference room.

A minute later, Admiral Dumar, President Scott, Commander Telles, and Captain Scott all entered the room and sat across from the general.

"Ah, Captain Scott," General Bacca greeted, rising to his feet to acknowledge him.

The two Ghatazhak guards closest to him raised their weapons, immediately taking aim at the general.

General Bacca noticed their change in stance, but chose to ignore them. "And the captain's father, President Scott. So good of you both to come. But, where is Eli?" the general wondered. "I hope he is well."

Nathan felt a surge of anger welling up inside of him. His father felt it as well, and looked at his son as if to caution self-control.

"I'm afraid I haven't had the pleasure," General Bacca said, turning to Admiral Dumar and offering his hand in friendship.

"Admiral Dumar, commander of all Alliance forces in the Sol sector," the admiral replied, ignoring the general's hand. "This is Commander Telles, commanding officer of all Ghatazhak forces within the Sol sector."

Commander Telles offered only a polite nod.

"The Ghatazhak," the general said, holding his chin up to offer more dignity to the name. "Impressive name. I assume these are yours?" he said, pointing to the two Ghatazhak soldiers flanking him on either side. "Not very talkative, are they?"

"Please, be seated," President Scott instructed.

583

"I have to say, I am surprised that our meeting place is so...drab. But I suppose this chamber is *not* normally used for such purposes," the general surmised.

"We have chosen to keep you, and your ship, in a secure area at the extreme outer edge of this base, away from critical areas, just to be safe," Admiral Dumar explained.

General Bacca tilted his head slightly. "You believe me to be a ruse? An ambush of sorts? That my ship, perhaps even my very person may be a weapon meant to destroy your leaders?" The general laughed. "Gentlemen, the Jung do not operate in such ways. If we want someone dead, we point a weapon at them and shoot, face-to-face, so to speak."

"I believe the admiral's concern was more about one of our *own,* killing *you,*" Nathan said coldly.

General Bacca's face broke into a wide smile. "I'm *so* glad you were able to attend, Captain Scott. I *knew* that I would like you."

"Your message spoke of peace," President Scott interrupted. "State your terms."

"Straight to the point, I see. Myself, I prefer the common pleasantries, but, since I am a guest here." General Bacca took a breath, adjusting himself in his seat. "In exchange for a promise *not* to destroy your world, the Jung Empire requires that you agree to the following terms. First, you must not attempt to expand your influence outside of the Sol system. Second, your forces shall not fire upon any Jung forces, unless first fired upon by said forces, and then, only as needed for reasonable defense. There, you see? We are not asking much."

Admiral Dumar's eyebrows went up. "Are we *allowed* to travel outside the Sol system?"

"Of course," the general replied. "The Jung are not unreasonable."

"I'm afraid there's going to be a problem with some of what you propose," Admiral Dumar began, "the first of which is what the Jung see as our sphere of influence. You see, it has expanded beyond the boundaries of the Sol system."

"Ah, yes. What was it called? The Pentaurus cluster? I'm sure that won't be a problem, especially since it is well beyond our current range of travel. I'm sure we can amend that part to include them as well."

"How generous of you," the admiral replied dryly. "However, my concerns lie with the Sol sector. More specifically, a sphere at which the Sol system is the center."

"I see," General Bacca replied, his left eyebrow rising in surprise. "And how big is this proposed 'sphere'?"

"Thirty light years," the admiral said.

General Bacca was quiet for a moment, his expression unchanged. "In radius, or diameter?"

"Radius, as measured outward from Sol."

General Bacca chuckled. "And you expect the Jung to withdraw all forces from this sphere? That would be more than a dozen systems."

"Eighteen, to be exact," Admiral Dumar corrected. "And the Jung do not have to *withdraw* from those eighteen systems. We have already removed them."

Again, the general was silent. His normally confident and condescending cheer had turned sour. "By *removed*, you mean..."

"Destroyed," Admiral Dumar replied, barely able to hide the pleasure he took in saying the word.

"All space-going assets, and all surface assets. Completely destroyed."

"As in, no survivors," General Bacca concluded.

"There *were* survivors," Admiral Dumar replied. He looked at Commander Telles. "They are being held in a secure facility. There are what, about..."

"Three thousand seven hundred and fifty-three Jung prisoners," Commander Telles replied, "at last count."

General Bacca's demeanor also changed, becoming more adversarial. "Assuming your claims are accurate, this changes things considerably. In fact, I may need to contact my superiors before continuing further. Unfortunately, that will take time, during which, incidents will undoubtedly occur." General Bacca sighed. "I'm afraid you have greatly complicated the matter, gentlemen. Such losses will be difficult for the military castes to accept...my own included."

"Then it appears a cease-fire is not possible," Admiral Dumar surmised, appearing quite willing to accept the inevitable. He leaned away from the table and raised his hand to signal the guard. "We will return you to your ship and escort you out of the system. Feel free to report our discussion to whomever you wish. Meanwhile, we will continue to..."

"Admiral," the general interrupted, "I'm shocked."

Admiral Dumar looked at the general, a curious expression on his face.

"You know how these negotiations go. I offer you something, you counteroffer, and so on. Over time, we forge a compromise that both parties can live with. To give up now would only demonstrate your complete lack of interest in a cease-fire, and I find it hard to believe that you would rather continue a war than discuss a possible peace between us."

"Of course, a peace would be preferable," Admiral Dumar admitted. "However, you indicated that the losses suffered by our removal of your forces from nearby systems would be impossible to accept. Therefore, I concluded that continued discussion would be a waste of our time."

"I said *difficult*, not *impossible*," the general corrected.

"My mistake," the admiral acquiesced gracefully. "How would you like to proceed, General?"

"Make a counteroffer," the general suggested. "Tell me what *your* terms would be."

Admiral Dumar looked to President Scott.

"Immediate withdrawal of all Jung forces from the Sol sector," the President stated. "The boundary of which will be a sphere of fifty light years in radius, measured outward from Sol. Furthermore, there will be no passage of Jung warships within the Sol sector, without express permission of the Alliance."

"So, it seems that we only differ in twenty measly light years," the general said. "How about this? We will give you your thirty light year sphere of influence, as apparently, you have already *taken* it. In addition, we will release control of any inhabited system that lies within the Sol sector, as you define it, but lies beyond your current thirty light year bubble, provided that the occupants of those systems *wish* us to relinquish control back to them."

"I'm afraid it's even more complicated than you realize," Admiral Dumar said.

"How about this?" Nathan began, taking it upon himself to join the negotiations. "We keep cleansing systems of Jung assets, expanding ever outward, while *you* spend the next two hundred and forty-seven days high-tailing it back to Nor-Patri, or more accurately, CP-60 424, and await an answer from your leaders." Nathan noticed the sudden change in the general's smug expression. "That's right, we know where your homeworld is located," he said, leaning forward, a satisfied smirk on his face. "So, round-trip...throw in a week for debates by your leaders, that's what? Five hundred days?"

"Five hundred and one," Commander Telles corrected.

"How much further do you think we can expand our 'area of influence' in five hundred and one days, General?" Nathan asked, leaning forward even more, his voice growing more menacing. "Fifty light years? Sixty? Seventy? One hundred? How many Jung-controlled systems would that be? I know of at least one, about sixty-three point eight light years away that we've already beaten up on pretty badly. I admit, we haven't taken it *completely*, but given time, I'm sure we..."

"Enough," President Scott intervened, pulling Nathan back in an attempt to dial down the rising emotions in the room.

"You're bluffing," General Bacca stated confidently, refusing to be shaken by Captain Scott's outbreak.

Admiral Dumar placed a data pad on the table, turned it on, spun it around to face the general, and then slid it across to him. "This data pad contains everything we know about the Jung home system. It also contains estimated enemy casualties and losses, as well as after action reports from all ships. If that is insufficient, there is also plenty of video footage from the battle. My apologies if the information is a little one-sided. Your people were not in a sharing mood at the time."

General Bacca studied the data pad, scrolling through screen after screen, his mouth agape, his expression one of disbelief, bordering on horror. After several silent minutes, he pushed the data pad back across the table, leaned back in his chair, and attempted to regain his composure. Finally, he spoke. "I suspect you will wish to transfer me to wherever you are holding the other Jung prisoners."

Admiral Dumar cast a curious look at the general. "You are no longer interested in negotiating a cease-fire on behalf of your empire? Not even with the generous terms *we* have offered?"

"As you said earlier, Admiral. It would be a waste of both our time."

"I don't understand," President Scott said. "Surely your people would want to avoid further attacks on their home system."

"I'm afraid I *do* understand," Admiral Dumar said. "The general believes that the Jung will be too outraged to accept a peace forced upon them. Their military castes will not accept such disgrace. They will want revenge."

"You understand the Jung well, Admiral," General Bacca said.

"I have known men like you my entire life," Admiral Dumar said, disdain in his voice. "Men whose entire reason for being is to spill the blood of others. Who can only prove their worth through aggression and acts of utter violence, rather than through acts of intelligence, compassion, and understanding. I have news for you, General. Empires built by such men *always* fall."

"You do *not* understand," the general replied,

589

seething with anger. "Your alliance has willingly crossed a line..."

"We were pushed over that line," Nathan defended.

"Captain," Admiral Dumar scolded, looking at Nathan out of the corner of his eye.

"General Bacca," President Scott began. "It is true that our peoples hate one another. But it is also true that both our peoples wish to survive. We want our two sectors, one of which, by your own admission, is too far away to be of concern. You want the rest of the galaxy. By such comparisons, we are but a grain of sand on an endless beach. Surely, a man as experienced as yourself can see the logic in a peaceful coexistence."

"There can be no peace between us," General Bacca said with a scowl. "Not after what you have done. It is not only the military that will cry out for vengeance, it is the people themselves. Had you limited yourselves to only military targets..."

"Well, now you know how it feels," Nathan muttered.

"Captain Scott, I will not warn you again," Admiral Dumar scolded. He turned back to the general. "Let me lay this out for you, General. You see, you have one chance to save your homeworld, quite possibly your entire empire. We may only have a few ships right now, but the commander here...well, let's just say that he and his men are quite adept at boarding and capturing Jung ships. Don't forget, we have already cleared a thirty-light-year perimeter around Sol. That means we have at least one and a half years in which to build more jump weapons, more ships, train more troops, and destroy more Jung assets as we grow our *own* empire. Then again, we already have enough weapons to wipe out your entire homeworld, without any of our ships ever entering it again. Will all your forces *outside* your home system rally and come at us in a massive attack? Undoubtedly. But that will take years to coordinate, possibly even decades, during which time we will continue to build our forces and diminish yours, as we jump from system to system, picking your ships off one by one."

Admiral Dumar took a breath. "Luckily for you, the Terrans are not an overly aggressive people. They are willing to forgive and forget, as long as they have guarantees that such transgressions shall never happen again. To be honest, *my* people would not be so forgiving. So, I suggest that you at least bring our terms back to your leaders, and let them decide for themselves. Let's see if your empire is smart enough to recognize its own mistakes, and learn from them."

"It will do no good," General Bacca insisted. "By the time I get back to Nor-Patri, the *Tonba-Hon-Venar* will be well under way."

Admiral Dumar and the others listened for the translation in his comm-set. *"Tonba-Hon-Venar roughly translates as 'battle for vengeance and honor',"* Naralena reported over their comm-sets.

"Bowden here, Admiral," Gerard chimed in. *"Tonba-Hon-Venar is a call to fight, regardless of the consequences. The purpose is not necessarily to win, but rather to die trying. The best comparison to Earth culture I can give you is a 'holy war', but without the religious element."*

"How long does it take your people to commit to such a campaign?" Admiral Dumar wondered.

"That is difficult to say," General Bacca admitted. "There has not been such a call in centuries."

"Are we talking days or weeks?" the admiral pressed.

"Considering the ferocity of your attack, the debate amongst the caste leaders will not take long," the general guessed. "A week, at the most, especially if public rallying is strong, which it undoubtedly will be."

"The attack was five days ago," Admiral Dumar stated.

"I can get him back to Nor-Patri in thirty hours," Nathan suggested.

"A jump shuttle could do it in an hour," the admiral countered.

"It must be the Aurora," General Bacca insisted, rather eagerly.

"It could be a trap," Commander Telles said. "A way to lure the Aurora into Jung hands."

Admiral Dumar thought for a moment. "Unlikely," he finally decided. "The logistics would be impossible. However, I am curious as to why the general thinks the Aurora should deliver the message."

"Simple," the general explained. "The Aurora is the original jump ship. We have known about it since the project began. Why do you think your world was crawling with spies? If you truly wish a peace between us, it *must* be the Aurora that delivers the terms. A shuttle would be a sign of weakness, of fear, but to fly the very ship that led the attack only days earlier into the heart of the Jung home system? *That*, my dear admiral, is a show of strength and resolve, one that will be taken seriously by my leaders."

Admiral Dumar looked at Commander Telles. "Commander?"

"His logic rings true, Admiral," Commander Telles

admitted. "However, taking the Aurora back into the Patoray system constitutes a considerable risk."

"If you truly wish this peace, Admiral, it must be the Aurora," General Bacca reaffirmed. "And it must be now."

* * *

"They will have their remaining ships spread out all over the system," Jessica warned. "Random spacing, constantly changing course, speeding up and slowing down…anything they can do to make themselves difficult to target."

"I am aware," Nathan replied. "Would you stop pacing?"

"They'll fire the moment we jump in. Missiles, guns, the works."

"There's a nice comfy couch right there," Nathan pointed out. "You love that couch, remember? Maybe you should try sitting on it."

"Are you even listening to me?"

"Of course I'm listening to you, Jess," Nathan replied. "It's just that you're making me nervous, and I don't need help in that department."

Jessica stopped pacing. "This is insane," she said to herself. She turned to Nathan. "I told you that this is insane, right? Jumping in, shields down, weapons cold… It's actually *beyond* insane. What if it's a trap?"

"That's logistically impossible, Jess, and you know it."

"I'm not talking about some grand scheme cooked up by Jung Command. I'm talking about Bacca playing you. He could be making this whole *Tonba-Hon-Venar* thing up, for all we know."

"Gerard already knew about it."

"That doesn't mean anything."

"You're right, they could have fed him the information years ago, so that he would corroborate the general's story..."

"I'm being serious, Nathan..."

"I know you are, Jess. What makes you think the general is trying to play me, anyway?"

"Because that's what I would do in his shoes!"

The entry buzzer sounded. "*Admiral Dumar to see you, sir,*" the guard announced over the intercom.

"How the hell does an admiral come on board without me knowing?" Nathan wondered.

"Or me," Jessica added. "I'm in charge of security, after all."

"Send him in," Nathan instructed as he stood. He noticed Jessica stopped pacing. "Finally."

The hatch opened, and Admiral Dumar stepped inside. "Captain, Lieutenant Commander," the admiral greeted.

Jessica and Nathan both raised their hands in salute, which the admiral returned.

"Lieutenant Commander, if you don't mind, I need to speak with our captain in private."

"Of course, sir," Jessica replied, moving toward the exit, exchanging glances with Nathan on the way out.

"How can I help you, sir," Nathan said, gesturing for the admiral to sit.

Admiral Dumar waited for the hatch to close before taking a seat across the desk from Nathan. "I wanted to speak with you before you departed."

"Not that I don't welcome the visit, sir, but you could have just called over the vid-link."

"Some things are better done in person," the admiral said. "I'm sure I do not have to remind you how dangerous this mission could be."

"No, sir. My chief of security has been reminding me of this for the last hour," Nathan replied wearily.

"Well, she is right in doing so. Commander Telles has spent the last hour interrogating the more cooperative prisoners in regards to this whole *Tonba-Hon-Venar* thing, trying to get a feel for it, trying to understand how the Jung public mindset plays into it and all."

"And what did he find out?"

"That you will likely be the target of their hatred," the admiral explained, "perhaps even more so than the Earth itself."

"Why me?" Nathan wondered.

"A lot of reasons, really. You're the one who formed the Alliance to begin with. You're the one who got the Aurora back to Sol, and you're the one who retook Earth. More importantly, you're the one who led the attack on the Patoray system."

"I was just the captain of one of five ships in that attack," Nathan said. "I was just following a battle plan, like the rest of them. A plan that *you* devised, Admiral."

"And you were the one who decided to launch a jump KKV against that station. According to Telles, *that action*, not the attack itself, is what will push the *Tonba-Hon-Venar* through the Jung leadership."

"You *told* me to do whatever it took to ensure that our message would be heard by the Jung...loud and clear. Just before we left..."

"I remember," the admiral admitted. "I'm not placing blame, Nathan. You did what you had to do. I likely would have done the same thing in your place. Telles *definitely* would have done the same thing...perhaps even worse."

"We had already lost the Kent," Nathan said,

pleading his case, "and we were losing the Celestia as well. Had I not fired those KKVs, not only would the Jung have seen the battle as a victory, but we might have lost everything."

"I know, Nathan. Like I said, I am not passing judgment on you. I *agree* with your decision. If I could take the blame for the attack, if I could shift the hatred of the Jung from you to me, I would gladly do so. But I cannot."

"I wouldn't ask you to, Admiral."

"I know you wouldn't," Dumar replied. "That's why you're 'Captain of the Aurora'." Admiral Dumar sighed, leaning back in his chair. "And now, you have to fly your ship back into the Patoray system, where there will be millions of eyes on you, each of them burning with absolute hatred. Millions of people who want nothing more than to see you die a thousand deaths. I'm not sure how I can ask someone to do such a thing."

"You're not making this any easier, sir," Nathan replied nervously. This time, it was Nathan who sighed. "Look, if things go south, I can jump out and head home, and we'll be no worse off than we were, correct?"

"Correct."

"And I guarantee you, Mister Riley will have his finger on that escape jump button."

"I should hope so."

"However, if for some crazy reason, the Jung *are* willing to talk, what do I do? How far am I authorized to go with the negotiations?"

"I'm afraid I can't help you there," the admiral said. "Just follow your instincts, Nathan. Trust them. I do. Casimir did."

"The thing is, I've been thinking about this whole

scenario, and I can't for the life of me figure out *why* the Jung would agree to a cease-fire. Especially one that requires them to give up even more territory than we've already taken from them. They greatly outnumber us, and they know it. Even if they do not attack for another twenty years, they will still outnumber us. Yes, we can build ships, perhaps many, but so can they, and in greater numbers. There is *no way* for us to win this. None. The Jung must know this. That's why they have built *so* many ships over the centuries, to ensure that they will *always* outnumber their enemy by a sizable margin."

The admiral looked at Nathan. "I've known this for some time."

Nathan just looked at him, dumbfounded.

"Sometimes, in war, neither side wins," the admiral said. "There are only two ways that this can happen. Either both sides are destroyed, or they reach a stalemate."

"A stalemate," Nathan replied. "I wasn't aware that you played chess, Admiral."

"Oh yes. A fascinating game."

"And how do we convince the Jung that a stalemate exists, when it doesn't?"

"Ah, but it does, my boy," Dumar said, a smile on his face. "That's why I came to speak to you, to explain how."

* * *

"Captain!" General Bacca greeted enthusiastically in the corridor. "Wonderful ship you have here. The decor is a bit bland, what with all the grays and such. If it weren't for all the yellow, orange, and red warning signs, this ship would have no color at all."

"It's a warship, General, not a cruise ship."

"Ah, yes, those sea-going vessels your people love

to sail leisurely about your tropics. I never really understood the whole concept. I mean, can't you just go to a nice resort and do all the same things?"

"These will be your accommodations for the duration of the journey," Nathan explained, pointing to the entrance to the guest quarters.

One of the four Ghatazhak soldiers escorting the general opened the door to the quarters and let the general enter.

"Sleeping area, head, living area, kitchenette, stocked with snacks," Nathan explained. "Even an entertainment system to help you pass the time."

"Wonderful, I have missed your world's numerous video plays," the general said. "What is it you called them? Movies? Such a quaint name."

"You will be restricted to this space for the duration," Nathan continued, ignoring the general. "There will be two guards stationed outside your door at all times. Should you try to leave without permission, they will kill you. You will receive four meals during the journey. If you require any other sustenance or services, use the intercom."

"There's an intercom? How wonderful."

"It only connects to the steward, no one else," Nathan told him.

"Before the final jump into the Patoray system, the guards will bring you to the bridge, as I suspect your presence will be required." Nathan looked at the general. "Will there be anything else, General?"

"I don't suppose you want to meet to discuss Jung negotiating procedures? Perhaps, over dinner? I so hate to dine alone."

"I don't think so," Nathan replied, turning to exit.

"You know, your brother was much better company."

Nathan turned back around and stepped closer to the general. Closer than usual. "Let me make one thing perfectly clear. I despise you, and I wish nothing more than to see you dead. So, you'd better hope that your people are willing to listen, otherwise I will leave you in the Patoray system..."

"Wonderful..."

"By pushing you out an airlock, without a suit, just before we jump clear." Nathan offered a fake smile. "Enjoy your stay."

Nathan turned and headed out the door without another word.

"Not exactly the forgiving type, is he," the general said to the Ghatazhak sergeant still standing at the doorway looking at the general.

The Ghatazhak sergeant smiled, then turned and departed, closing and locking the door behind him.

* * *

Nathan opened the door to his quarters wearing nothing but his underwear and a t-shirt. Standing in the corridor was Vladimir, holding another bag and a bottle. "Why is it every time I'm trying to get some sleep, you show up with beef and booze?"

"Because I am a wonderful friend," Vladimir said, entering Nathan's living room. "But it's not beef, it's dollag."

"As close as we're going to get these days," Nathan said as he closed the door and followed Vladimir to the sitting area. "Besides, I can't really tell the difference."

"Dollag is more tender, and has a richer, deeper flavor to it," Vladimir insisted as he unwrapped the sandwiches.

"Smear that green shit on it, and I don't really care," Nathan said as he took the sandwich from

Vladimir's hand and plopped down in the chair next to him.

"Careful, Nathan, I may test that theory someday," Vladimir replied as he took a bite from his sandwich.

The two of them sat there for several minutes, chewing their dollag, and taking turns drinking from the same bottle.

"Are you nervous?" Vladimir finally asked.

"Why? Because in eight hours we're jumping into a system full of billions of people who hate me, and is crawling with dozens of ships whose captains would all *love* to be the one who killed 'Nathan Scott, Captain of the Aurora'?" Nathan took a long drink from the bottle of home-brewed beer. "What's there to be nervous about?"

"Just wondered," Vladimir said, taking the bottle back from Nathan.

They continued chewing in silence for a few more minutes, before Nathan finally spoke.

"Let me ask you a question, Vlad. When you think about what you are fighting for, what do you think of?"

"I don't know. Our crew, I suppose. Russia, maybe? I don't think I have ever considered this question." Vladimir took another drink. "What do you think about?"

"Beaches."

"Beaches. Why beaches?"

"I don't really know," Nathan admitted. "But I also think about dogs, running on the beach."

"You or the dogs?"

"The dogs," Nathan replied. "I'm just sitting there, my feet up, drinking a beer or something."

"Perhaps that beach represents something?" Vladimir suggested.

"Like what?"

"Freedom? Life? Solitude?" Vladimir suggested. "What do you think it represents?"

Nathan thought for a minute, taking another bite of his sandwich while he pondered his choices. He took the bottle back from Vladimir and took another drink. "Happiness," he finally said. "No responsibilities, no dangers, no work to do... Just sitting there watching the dog run around on the beach, and listening to the seagulls squawking, and the sound of the waves crashing."

"I think I understand," Vladimir said, trying to imagine it for himself. "I have only been to the ocean one time in my life."

"Really?" Nathan said, surprised.

"*Da*! I know! I have been to the other side of the galaxy, so to speak, but I have only been to the ocean one time. And it was cold."

"Then I guess my beach image doesn't work for you."

"*Nyet*." Vladimir thought for a moment. "But for me, it would be the forest. One with a river winding through it, or a lake. *Da*, a lake. A *dacha* by a lake, high in the mountains, surrounded by forest. No one for kilometers. Hunting, fishing, cleaning, and cooking your daily catch, a good woman to keep you warm at night. And a massive stone fireplace, with a roaring fire every night." Vladimir took another drink. "But it would have to be self-cleaning. I hate cleaning up fireplaces. Very dirty work."

"You know what? That works for me too," Nathan said. "Even the self-cleaning fireplace. But I'd want a seaplane to be able to fly in and out from the lake. And a sail boat, so that I could spend windy days crisscrossing the lake in the afternoon sun." Nathan placed the last piece of sandwich into his mouth and leaned back in his chair. "But we don't really fight for *those* things, do we," he observed. "We fight for the right to *have* such things, just the way we want them."

"*Da.*"

Nathan sat there, staring at the gray ceiling of his quarters. "After all that has happened over the past two years, after all this time in space, what do you miss the most?"

"Russian women," Vladimir said. "Actually, any woman who isn't wearing a uniform and carrying a gun or a data pad."

"Why am I not surprised," Nathan laughed.

"What do you miss, Nathan?"

Nathan thought for a moment. "You're not going to believe this, but I miss my parent's place...the place I grew up."

"I thought you joined the EDF to get *away* from your family?"

"So did I," Nathan admitted. "But after all this time, and after everything that *has* happened, I realize now how much a part of me they all were. Even Eli."

"This is true," Vladimir agreed. "We are all products of our upbringing, both good and bad." Vladimir picked up the bottle and finished off the last bit of beer. "*Konyets.* Wait here. I will get another bottle."

"Don't bother, Vlad," Nathan insisted. "I've gotta get some sleep anyway."

"Are you sure? I could get more dollag as well?"

"No, I'm good. Just burp me and put me to bed."

"I am not your mother," Vladimir said with a

dismissive wave as he rose and headed for the door. "I will let you sleep."

"Hey, Vlad," Nathan called after him. "Have I told you recently how much these talks mean to me?"

"*Nyet.*"

"Good, because I hate lying to friends," Nathan said, a smile creeping onto his face.

"*Spakoinoi nochi,* Nathan," Vladimir said as he reached for the door.

"You're supposed to salute your captain on departure, you know!"

"I told you, Nathan, I will follow your orders, but I will not salute you."

"I could have you thrown in the brig, you know."

"Here, how is this?" Vladimir asked as he exited, flipping his middle finger at Nathan.

"There's still room for improvement!" Nathan yelled as the door closed. He took in a breath and sighed. "Good night, my friend."

* * *

"Are all these guards really necessary?" General Bacca asked as he met Nathan and Jessica at the entrance to the Aurora's bridge. He looked at Jessica. "I don't believe I've had the pleasure," he said.

"Drop dead," Jessica replied immediately. She glanced at Nathan, half expecting a scolding gaze, but received none. "I still don't think we should let him on the bridge. He's full of nanites, you know."

"Of course I'm full of nanites, young lady," the general said cheerfully. "They keep me healthy."

"And make you into zombie spies."

"The guards stay, General," Nathan said, turning to the Ghatazhak sergeant. "He makes one false move, you shoot him...dead. Understood?"

"Beyond doubt," the Ghatazhak sergeant replied.

General Bacca ignored the Ghatazhak sergeant's menacing tone, and leaned in toward Jessica. "Just between you and me, the nanites work all sorts of wonders in the body, if you know what I mean."

There was a sudden, high-pitched whine. It went from a low pitch to a higher one in a few seconds, and then disappeared completely. The general felt something poke him in the groin, and slowly looked down to find the barrel of Jessica's energy pistol against his crotch, and her finger on the trigger. He looked back up at Jessica's face as a smirk came across it.

"I'll take this to mean you're not interested, then."

"Good read, grandpa," Jessica replied. She switched off her weapon and holstered it, then stepped through the outer hatch into the port bridge airlock corridor.

Nathan grinned. "You'd really better hope this works, Bacca, or getting tossed out an airlock is going to seem like heaven." Nathan turned to follow Jessica into the airlock corridor. "Bring him."

Jessica stepped through the inner hatch onto the Aurora's bridge, followed by Nathan.

"Captain on the bridge!" the guard announced.

The Ghatazhak escorted General Bacca onto the bridge, as Jessica went to her tactical station, and Nathan went to his command chair. The Ghatazhak moved the general into the space left of Naralena's comm station, just in front of the entrance to the captain's ready room. Two of the Ghatazhak stood close on either side of the general. The other two took up positions on either side and slightly aft of the captain, facing the general so as to have a clear shot at him should the old man somehow manage to overpower the two Ghatazhak standing next to him.

"We're on course and speed for the jump," Mister Riley reported as Nathan took his seat. "Insertion jump into the Patoray system is plotted and ready."

"Set general quarters," Nathan instructed. "Shields down and weapons cold," he added, just in case Jessica had forgotten the plan. He also wanted to make sure that General Bacca knew the ship was going into the Jung home system in as non-threatening a posture as possible.

"Do you think that's wise, Captain?" General Bacca said.

"Do not speak unless spoken to, General," Nathan instructed, his right hand up with his index finger pointing upward.

"Pardon me."

"Mister Riley, Mister Chiles," Nathan began. "Same standing orders as last time. Should you see our escape route becoming blocked, do not wait for me to give you orders to maneuver. Furthermore, if we are about to be hit by anything larger than medium-sized rail gun fire, do not wait for me to give the command to jump, just jump. While we're on the subject, Mister Riley, all our escape jumps should take us *outside* the Jung home system, unless instructed otherwise. We don't need to jump *into* trouble when we're trying to jump *out* of it, is that clear, gentlemen?"

"Aye, sir," Mister Chiles acknowledged.

"We know the drill, sir," Mister Riley assured his captain.

"Yes, you do."

"All departments report general quarters, Captain," Naralena announced. "XO is in combat, and the chief of the boat is in damage control."

After a few seconds of silence, Nathan turned around slowly to look at Jessica.

"Yes, all shields are down, and all weapons are cold," Jessica reported. "Still say this is a stupid idea," she added under her breath.

"Broadcast ready?" Nathan asked Naralena.

"Yes, sir."

"Start broadcasting the moment we come out of the jump," Nathan reminded her.

"Yes, sir."

Nathan took a deep breath. "Very well. Mister Riley, you may execute the insertion jump into the Patoray system."

"Executing insertion jump in five seconds," the Aurora's navigator announced.

Nathan tried to breathe normally as his navigator began the countdown.

"Three..."

Once again, he was about to take his ship deep into the Jung home system.

"Two..."

Only this time, his ship would be defenseless...

"One..."

And they would not have the element of surprise on their side.

"Jumping."

The Jung would be ready to attack.

"Jump complete," Mister Riley reported as the jump flash subsided.

"Incredible!" General Bacca exclaimed, witnessing an actual jump for the first time.

"Transmitting message."

"Multiple contacts..."

"Something in our jump line..."

"Turning two degrees to starboard..."

"Battleship, two cruisers, four frigates," Mister Navashee continued. "The frigates are launching missiles..."

"How many?" Nathan inquired.

"Thirty-two missiles inbound!" Mister Navashee replied. "Closest one will impact in fifteen seconds!"

"I can intercept them with point-defenses," Jessica reminded Nathan.

"Keep those weapons cold!" Nathan ordered.

"Five seconds!" Mister Navashee warned.

"Mister Riley!"

"Escape jump!"

The jump flash immediately washed over the bridge, as the Aurora jumped clear of the Patoray system.

"Jump complete."

"Sensors are clear," Mister Navashee reported. "No threats in the area."

"Jesus!" Jessica exclaimed. "A few more degrees to starboard and I could have taken out two of those frigates!"

"That was absolutely amazing!" General Bacca declared in excitement. "All those missiles right on top of you, and you simply vanished. I must say, I'm surprised you didn't manage to destroy every ship in the system last time you were here! I might also add, that is the fastest I've ever seen any Jung ship open fire. Your Alliance must have really made an impression on them during your last visit."

"What part of *don't talk* did you *not* understand?" Jessica barked.

"You're right, I'm sorry," the general apologized. "It's just that, well, it was quite exhilarating."

"Shut the hell up, Bacca!" Jessica snapped. "Comms, were you broadcasting the message?"

"Yes, sir," Naralena assured him. "Every frequency, every language, and at full strength."

"Helm, bring us about. Let's try this again," Nathan instructed.

"Coming about, aye."

"Mister Riley, put us in a different part of the system."

"Yes, sir."

"Mister Navashee, did you get a snapshot of their ships' locations?"

"Yes, sir, I did."

"Great, give Mister Riley a location with the least number of Jung ships nearby."

"That's not going to be easy, sir," Mister Navashee warned.

"Well, let's at least jump to somewhere we can hang out long enough for the entire message to get out before we're blasted all to hell."

"Yes, sir."

"If you'd just let me use the point-defense systems," Jessica begged.

"No way," Nathan said, cutting her off. "We are not firing a single shot."

"Maybe we can just send in a jump comm-drone?" Naralena suggested.

"They'd just destroy it even faster," Nathan said. "Besides, there's no way I'm sending an unmanned jump-enabled vessel anywhere near them."

"Turn complete," Mister Chiles reported from the helm.

"Insertion jump, plotted and ready," Mister Riley added.

Nathan took in another deep breath and sighed. "Let's try this again, people. Jump us in, Mister Riley."

"Jumping in three......two......one......jumping."

"My God, that never gets old, does it?" General Bacca exclaimed.

"Jump complete."

"Multiple contacts," Mister Navashee reported.

"Transmitting message," Naralena announced.

"Three cruisers, eight frigates, all within firing... FTL signatures!" Mister Navashee exclaimed. "Three of the cruisers just... Wait! All three cruisers just came out of FTL! Two kilometers and closing fast! They're firing rail guns and missiles! Five seconds!"

"Jumping," Mister Riley announced as the jump flash washed over them.

"Damn it!" Nathan cursed. "You'd think they would at least respond with a 'drop dead' or something." Nathan turned to Naralena. "Were we in there long enough for them to receive the message?"

"It's a burst transmission, Captain. It only takes a few seconds to transmit a ten minute recording."

"You're transmitting digitally," General Bacca realized. "She's right," he said, pointing at Jessica. "This is a stupid plan."

Nathan scowled at the general.

"Don't you see, Captain? They're not going to allow a digital signal from a known enemy ship to enter their systems," General Bacca explained. "They think you're trying to transmit a virus or something, so you can take down their shields, or take their weapons offline so that you can easily destroy them. If you want them to hear you, you need to transmit an *analog* message. *Radio*. You do have *radio* transceivers, don't you?"

Nathan looked at Naralena for an answer.

"We do," she told him. "But an analog message

will take a lot longer to send. Ten minutes, if we transmit the entire message."

"Can you edit the message?" Nathan asked. "Maybe just transmit the portion in Jung?"

"Which dialect?" Naralena asked. "There are thirteen of them, that I know of."

"Actually, there are more than forty," the General corrected. "But only three that are used here. Besides, you only need one to speak with the caste leaders. May I?"

Nathan looked at Jessica, who shrugged. Nathan shrugged toward Naralena as well. "Give him a comm-set."

Naralena handed a comm-set to the Ghatazhak soldier between her and the general, who then handed it to General Bacca.

"Shall I just start talking after we jump, or would you like to prerecord the message?"

"Prerecord it," Nathan instructed.

"As you wish." The general looked at Naralena. "Should I just start talking?"

"Whenever you are ready," she replied.

General Bacca began speaking Jung in an authoritative tone. He spoke for at least thirty seconds before finishing.

Nathan looked at Naralena for a translation.

"He said, 'This is General Bacca, commander of the sixth brigade of the Mogan caste.' He then gave an authentication code, followed by, 'Hold your fire, this is not an attack. The people of Earth wish to speak to the caste leaders, to discuss terms of surrender.' Then he repeats the last part about not firing and wanting to speak to the caste leaders."

"Who said anything about surrendering?" Nathan wondered.

"I didn't say *who* was surrendering," General Bacca pointed out.

"I'm pretty sure they're going to assume that *we're* the ones offering to surrender," Nathan replied.

"Let them," the general insisted. "It's the only way you're going to get them to talk to you. You have to remember, *every* Jung citizen on Nor-Patri will hear this broadcast."

"Everyone on Nor-Patri uses radio transceivers?" Naralena asked.

"Alright, not everyone, but there will be at least a few, and within seconds, the message will be repeated digitally around Nor-Patri, through the sat-net. Using the word *surrender* will help the caste leaders save face. Trust me, Captain, it is the *only* way you will get to speak with them."

"*They* sent an invitation to discuss a cease-fire to *us*, remember?" Nathan said.

"That invitation was sent over two hundred and fifty days ago, Captain, *before* you attacked their system," the general pointed out. "Trust me, this is the only way. Otherwise, you might as well push me out the airlock now, because you're just wasting both our time."

Nathan sat in his chair, thinking.

"The message will still take time to send," Naralena warned.

"Bring us back around, Mister Chiles," Nathan ordered.

"Coming about, aye."

"What was our time in the system?" Nathan asked.

Mister Riley looked at his console. "Thirty-two seconds the first time, twenty-five the second."

"And right now, every ship is on full alert, their

weapons are hot, and they are actively scanning every square meter of that system," Jessica explained. "If you let me use the point-defenses, I can give us the time we need to send the full message."

Nathan looked at General Bacca for direction, despite the fact that the very idea of consulting with the man on anything, short of how best to execute him, was sickening.

"At this point, I don't think it really matters one way or the other," the general admitted. "Just as long as you don't shoot directly at any other ship," he added, looking right at Jessica.

"I'll try to control myself," she replied dryly.

"Very well," Nathan said. "Spin up our point-defenses, but leave our shields down for now."

"Turn complete," Mister Chiles reported.

"I've plotted a jump to a spot that will give us at least forty seconds," Mister Riley said, "assuming they don't anticipate our jump and shoot before we get there."

"Very well. Jump us back in."

"Jumping in three......two......one......jumping."

General Bacca stared at the main view screen as the jump flash washed over the bridge, enjoying every moment of it.

"Jump complete."

"Transmitting new message, analog format via radio transceivers," Naralena announced.

"Multiple contacts. One cruiser and three frigates within firing range," Mister Navashee reported. "Two more cruisers and a battleship will be in firing range in thirty seconds. The near cruiser and frigates are launching missiles. Eighteen inbound. First impact in thirty seconds."

"Firing point-defenses," Jessica announced. "One down, two, three..."

"Twenty seconds in system," Mister Riley reported.

"The message has played once in its entirety," Naralena added.

"Twelve down, thirteen, fourteen..." Jessica continued reporting as the Aurora's point-defenses destroyed the incoming missiles, one by one.

"The cruiser is firing another wave of twelve missiles," Mister Navashee warned. "She's firing rail guns as well. First impacts in twenty-four seconds."

"That's eighteen," Jessica reported. "Concentrating on the second wave now."

"Forty seconds in system," Mister Riley reported.

"The other ships are in firing range," Mister Navashee warned. "The battleship is launching missiles. Forty-eight inbound, Captain. Impact in thirty seconds."

"The message has played twice now, sir," Naralena reported.

"Eight down, nine down, ten down..."

"The additional frigates have also launched missiles," Mister Navashee warned. "Those impacts will be in twenty-eight seconds."

"Second group of incoming destroyed," Jessica announced. "Targeting the third group of forty-eight, but it's going to be close, sir."

"One minute in system," Mister Riley reported.

"Incoming message, from the Jung battleship," Naralena said. She immediately put it on the loudspeaker. The Jung officer spoke in his native tongue, and he did not sound happy.

"What did he say?" Nathan asked after the officer finished speaking.

"Not the response we were looking for, sir," Naralena replied.

"She's correct, Captain," General Bacca confirmed. He leaned forward slightly to look around the Ghatazhak soldier to his right, trying to make eye contact with Naralena. "Your Jung is quite good, my dear."

"I'm not sure I'm going to be able to intercept all of these missiles, Captain," Jessica warned, her voice sounding tense.

"Get us out of here, Mister Riley," Nathan instructed.

"Aye, sir," the navigator replied.

Nathan turned back around to face Jessica and General Bacca, as the jump flash washed over them.

"Jump complete."

"Why didn't it work *that* time?" Nathan wondered. "I'm pretty sure they heard us."

"Oh, yes, they heard you," General Bacca agreed. "I just think they didn't *believe* you."

"Why would we lie?" Nathan wondered. "What could we possibly have to gain?"

"Think like the captain of a Jung ship," General Bacca suggested. "Your job is to keep any and all enemy ships as far away from Nor-Patri as possible. Failure to do so would likely result in disgrace, imprisonment, or even execution. In fact, I would not be surprised if most of the men commanding the ships you just encountered were first officers a week ago, if you get my meaning."

"They think we're lying to try to get past them... to attack Nor-Patri," Jessica surmised.

"We don't need to lie to them to get past them," Nathan reminded her. "We can *jump* past them anytime we'd like."

"They are brand new captains, recently promoted due to the failures of their previous commanding officers. They don't even understand what a jump drive is," General Bacca explained.

"Then what do we do to convince them?" Nathan wondered.

"You already answered your own question, Captain," General Bacca said. "You jump past them."

"To where?"

"To Nor-Patri," General Bacca told him. "In orbit, directly over the senate chambers. Then your message will go directly to the caste leaders."

"What about surface defenses?" Jessica wondered. "They had them on plenty of other Jung worlds. They're bound to have a ton of them here."

"Surprisingly, they do not," General Bacca admitted. "No one expected an enemy would develop something like a jump drive. Their massive number of ships was their primary defense."

"But you said the Jung knew about the jump drive project when it first started," Jessica said in an accusatory tone. "That was twelve years ago. Why didn't they start building them then?"

"At first, no one believed it possible. Later, when it appeared not only possible, but likely, they chose not to do so for fear of creating public doubt in our own military might," the general explained.

"Jesus," Nathan exclaimed in frustration. "Everywhere you go, politics is the same old bullshit."

"If you jump in directly over the senate, you will have plenty of time to transmit your message and get a response," General Bacca insisted.

"He's right, Captain," Mister Navashee confirmed. "Their ships are spread across the system, and in random patterns. The only common denominator is that they are *all* at least two hundred million kilometers away from Nor-Patri. When we jump in, it will take at least ten seconds for those ships to even see us, let alone change course and come back to engage. We'd have at least a few minutes."

"Unless they go to FTL to get back," Nathan pointed out.

"It is forbidden to come out of FTL any closer than one hundred million kilometers to Nor-Patri," General Bacca told them. "It has been a standing order for as long as anyone can remember. There is simply too much traffic near the homeworld."

"Even if they think their beloved senate and all their caste leaders are under attack?" Nathan challenged.

"Like I said, none of them were captains a week ago," the general reminded him. "However, I suppose you have a point. Although unlikely, it *is* possible."

"It sounds like something you'd do," Jessica said, one eyebrow raised.

Nathan sighed again. "Can you jump us in over the senate?" he asked his navigator.

"If someone shows me where it is, sure."

Nathan looked at Jessica. "Do we even have a map of Nor-Patri?"

"Between the first recon and scans taken during the attack, we were able to piece one together," Jessica replied.

"General?" Nathan asked.

"Of course."

"Jess?"

"Coming up," Jessica replied. A moment later, a rough map of Nor-Patri's landmasses was on the clear view screen panel protruding from the middle of the back of Jessica's tactical console. General

Bacca moved in closer, coming to stand next to Jessica, as he studied the image.

"Not entirely accurate, but close enough, I suppose," the general said. "There," he added, pointing at the display. "The senate chambers are there, at the confluence of those three rivers. Arrive anywhere within line-of-sight of that river junction, and the caste leaders will hear your message, I am sure of it."

"Very well," Nathan said. "Bring us back around and prepare to jump to orbit, over that river intersection."

"Aye, sir," Mister Riley acknowledged.

"No one is ever going to believe this," Jessica muttered.

"Hell, *I* don't believe it," Nathan said.

"How do you think I feel?" General Bacca said, stepping back to his spot near the entrance to the captain's ready room.

"Turn complete," Mister Chiles reported.

"Jump to Nor-Patri orbit, directly over the senate chambers, plotted and ready," Mister Riley advised.

Nathan sighed again. "Jump us in."

"Jumping in three......two......one......jumping."

"If this doesn't work, someone's going out an airlock," Nathan muttered as the jump flash washed over them once more.

"Jump complete."

"Transmitting message, analog form, over radio transceivers," Naralena reported.

"No ships within firing range," Mister Navashee announced.

"Are we in the right place?" Nathan asked, looking at Nor-Patri on the main view screen.

"That intersection of three rivers is coming up now," Mister Navashee confirmed.

"Nicely done, Mister Riley," Nathan congratulated.

"The entire message has been transmitted," Naralena announced.

"Keep playing it until we get a response," Nathan ordered.

"Aye, sir."

"Captain," Mister Navashee said, concern in his voice. "Something is not right."

"What *something*?" Nathan asked.

"The planet surface," the sensor operator explained. "There's a *lot* more damage than there should be."

"We attacked the surface as well, remember?"

"We attacked infrastructure, communications, power generation, defenses," Mister Navashee pointed out. "I'm detecting *massive* amounts of damage. Impact craters the size of..." Mister Navashee turned to look at Nathan. "Sir, I think pieces of that ring station fell onto Nor-Patri. Maybe even pieces of Zhu-Anok itself."

"That's impossible," Nathan insisted. "The attack angle should have taken the debris *away* from the planet."

"I understand that, sir. But there *are* impact craters on the surface of Nor-Patri," Mister Navashee insisted. "Dozens of them, in fact."

Nathan rose from his seat, staring at the Jung homeworld rotating slowly beneath them, noticing large dark areas of the surface that he did not remember being there before. Indeed, there were dozens of them. "Magnify," he ordered.

"If the force of the impact was enough, *some* debris *could* have been pushed toward the planet,"

Mister Navashee theorized. "There's still a lot of what looks like debris, from both the ring station *and* Zhu-Anok, in orbit around the planet."

When the main view screen refocused, Nathan could see the destruction more clearly. Gigantic areas of the planet-wide cityscape had been wiped clean as if nothing had even been there. On the edges of the craters, he could see the remains of buildings, roadways, tramways...all of them ripped apart by shockwaves.

He thought about the glassing of Tanna. The captains of those ships probably had a similar view of the planet as they were bombarding it. Until this very moment, Nathan had wanted nothing more than to do the same thing to this world, to scorch its surface, and to make it forever uninhabitable. But now, even though he was looking at only a fraction of the damage that had been done to Tanna...it sickened him.

What have we done? he asked himself.

"Captain," Naralena called, pulling Nathan's attention away from the devastation on the view screen. "I'm receiving a message from the caste senate." Naralena closed her eyes, listening intently. "They have agreed to speak with us, but only by vid-link."

"Are they going to order their ships to stand down?" Nathan asked.

"Yes, they claim to be sending that order now. However, they suggest that we raise our shields and keep them up, for they cannot guarantee that the commanders of their ships will comply."

Nathan continuing staring at the main view screen in disbelief.

"I would do as they suggest, Captain," General

Bacca said, his voice seething with anger from what he too was witnessing on the view screen. "Especially considering what you have done to our world."

"Yes, of course," Nathan replied. He looked at Jessica. "Raise our shields."

"*Finally,*" Jessica exclaimed. "All shields are coming up."

"Four ships inbound," Mister Navashee warned. "Two cruisers and two frigates."

"How long until we can talk with the caste leaders?" Nathan wondered.

"They should all be in session," General Bacca said. "I would expect they have been in session nonstop since your attack a week ago."

"I'm getting another message, Captain," Naralena reported. "A hail, from the senate communications officer. They are requesting a vid-link."

Nathan turned forward and straightened his uniform jacket. "General, front and center if you please."

General Bacca moved forward and came to stand beside Nathan, to his left.

"Open the connection," Nathan instructed.

A rectangular window appeared in the middle of the main view screen, revealing a stately chamber. In it were four men and four women, seated behind a long, curved table that hid their lower halves behind lacquered wood. Along the wall behind them were the flags of all the castes of the Jung.

"I am Captain Nathan Scott, of the Earth-Pentaurus Alliance ship, Aurora. I am auth..."

"*State your terms of surrender, and we shall consider your fate,*" the woman sitting in the center of the room said, interrupting the captain.

"There appears to be a misunderstanding,"

Nathan said. "Possibly a translation issue, as we have only recently learned your language. We were not coming here to surrender. We came in response to the message sent by you...a call for peace."

"*That was before,*" the woman explained curtly. "*This is now.*"

"I do not understand," Nathan replied.

"*Your unprovoked attack on our homeworld has triggered a public outcry for Tonba-Hon-Venar. There can be no peace.*"

"The attack was hardly unprovoked," Nathan defended.

"Captain," General Bacca warned.

"You invaded our world, killed millions of our people, and when we fought back, you tried to destroy our planet. You glassed Tanna, one of our allies, and you cracked Kent in half, killing everyone. How can you sit there and claim that our attack on your world was unprovoked?"

"*The Jung take what the Jung need to thrive,*" the man next to the women stated. "*It is the way of the strong. Did your people need to destroy Zhu-Anok in order to thrive?*"

"Did your people *need* to glass Tanna in order to thrive?"

"*Worlds are cleansed when their populations prove uncooperative and require too many resources to manage, thus interfering with the expansion of the Jung Empire.*"

Nathan turned to look at Jessica behind him. "That almost makes sense, in a twisted sort of way," he said under his breath. Nathan turned around to face the main view screen. "Defending Earth, and our allies within the Sol sector, was taking up too many *resources*, thus interfering with the recovery and safety of our people. The attack on your world was meant to send a message."

"And what message was it meant to send?"

"That a continuation of hostilities between the Jung Empire and the Earth-Pentaurus Alliance would consume many resources, and cost countless lives. That it would interfere with the prosperity of both our peoples. We wanted to show you that we could destroy your world just as easily as you can destroy any of ours, in the hopes that you would agree to a cease-fire, while we negotiate a way to peacefully coexist, and perhaps even help one another prosper."

"You've got to be kidding me," Jessica mumbled.

"Unless your people surrender now, the demands of the Jung people for a Tonba-Hon-Venar will be approved, and the call will be sent out to every ship in the fleet. The order will be to destroy Earth, and any world that allies with it."

"That will take years," Nathan said, "during which we will build more ships and more weapons. And we will seek out your ships, destroying them one by one, as we have already been doing. You will have a hard time gathering together enough ships to destroy any of our worlds."

"It takes but a single ship to destroy a world, if her crew is willing to commit to the Tonba-Hon-Venar."

"Captain," Naralena called from her comm station.

"Your world will end."

"Muted," Naralena reported. "Sir, I believe Tonba-Hon-Venar means fight to the death. However, the use of the suffix 'ba' on the end of the root word 'ton', followed by 'hon', which means honor..."

"Get to the point," Nathan insisted, still looking forward.

"Tonba-Hon-Venar *could* mean 'To give your life with honor for vengeance.'"

"Oh, you *are* good," General Bacca cooed.

"Unmute," Nathan ordered. "Then your world will end as well," Nathan replied.

"Although much damage was done, your attack failed to destroy our world, Captain. You lost nearly half of your forces in the process. The fact that you attacked a massive force with so few ships would indicate that you have no others."

"We don't need others. Had we wanted to destroy your world, we would have. We have the means. As you said, it takes but one ship. We took it one better. We have created weapons whose only purpose is to destroy worlds, and from great distances. As I now speak, there are eight such weapons, jumping around the stars at random. Each day, they move to a new location that only they know. Each day, they send a jump comm-drone back to Alliance Command asking a single question. 'Should I postpone the attack?' As long as they receive orders to postpone the launch of their weapons, your world survives another day. Should you attack Earth, or *any* of our allies, those weapons *will* launch, and your world *will* end."

The vid-link disappeared.

"What happened?" Nathan asked, spinning around to look at Naralena.

"The transmission was terminated at their end, Captain, not ours."

"It appears you have 'rattled their cage'," General Bacca observed.

"I'm hoping that's a good thing?" Nathan replied.

"Possibly. Then again, possibly not. Right now, I imagine they are discussing the situation among themselves."

"Captain, those ships are coming into firing range, and closing fast," Mister Navashee warned.

"How many?"

"One battleship, two cruisers, with about eight frigates a few minutes further out. The battleship will reach firing range first...in about two more minutes."

"Keep that escape jump warm, Mister Riley," Nathan instructed.

"My finger is on the button, sir."

"You cannot leave, Captain," General Bacca urged. "You must demonstrate your resolve if you want them to take your threats seriously."

"How can they not take the threat of planet-busting weapons set to fail-safe as a serious threat?"

"They are still stuck in the mindset of FTL. The idea that such weapons can suddenly *appear* out of nowhere, and they would have no defense, borders on unbelievable in their minds. I saw your ships jumping about in battle, and had I not experienced your miraculous jump drive technology first-hand, I too would have a hard time wrapping my mind around its tactical advantages. Give them time."

"One minute until that battleship reaches firing range on us."

"I've only got a minute to give them, General," Nathan reminded him.

"Take a few shots, if you must, but stand your ground, Captain. The military castes respect strength and honor, the Isolationists just want to survive."

"What about the other castes?" Nathan wondered. "What do they want?"

"It does not matter. The Isolationists outnumber the other castes."

"Combined?"

"No, but the Expansionists and the Conqueror castes would never team up to overrule the Isolationists, who are the most senior and most respected caste in all of the Jung. They are the founders of the empire, after all."

"Twenty seconds," Mister Navashee warned.

"Are they targeting us?" Nathan asked.

"Yes, sir, they are."

"Channel shield power to our threatened sides," Nathan ordered.

"Aye, sir," the systems officer replied.

"The problem is the military caste," General Bacca continued, moving closer to the captain and speaking in hushed tones. "They require something to appease their honor. Some sacrifice...something of meaning."

"Like what?"

"I do not know." The general's face lit up with an idea. "Perhaps, if you offered to share your jump drive technology with them?"

Nathan looked at the general in surprise. "You've *got* to be kidding."

"Then, what?"

"Battleship is ten seconds out," Mister Navashee warned. "They are spinning up missiles for launch."

"Point-defenses, Jess," Nathan instructed.

"Point-defenses, aye."

"You must think of something, Captain."

"Incoming message," Naralena announced. "The Jung senate is requesting another vid-link."

"Battleship has launched missiles!" Mister Navashee reported. "Twenty-four inbound. Impact in two minutes."

"I'm on it," Jessica assured Nathan.

"Put them up," Nathan instructed Naralena.

The vid-link appeared on the main view screen again, showing the same scene.

"*We are willing to entertain the idea of negotiations,*" the woman at the center of the table began, "*but we fear the military caste will be difficult to convince.*"

"Five down," Jessica reported, as the Aurora's point-defense turrets fired away at the incoming missiles.

"*Your attack has brought disgrace upon them in the eyes of the other castes. If they are not allowed to seek revenge, to spill Terran blood, the vote to initiate the Tonba-Hon-Venar will end in a tie, in which case the people will decide. The same people whose homes and families your Alliance destroyed.*"

"Ten down," Jessica updated.

"You must think of something," General Bacca whispered. "They will only be satisfied with blood. Terran blood...the blood of a leader, or a great warrior..."

"Then take mine!" Nathan offered to the Jung senate.

"What?" Jessica exclaimed.

A satisfied smile crept onto General Bacca's face.

"I am a great warrior of Earth. I command her greatest ship, and I alone ordered the launch of the weapon that destroyed Zhu-Anok, and killed millions of people on Nor-Patri. So if you must spill more Terran blood, spill mine, and let it end here, for both our peoples' sake!"

"MUTE!" Jessica ordered.

"Muted," Naralena replied.

"What the hell are you doing, Nathan!"

"I'm saving us all!" Nathan replied. "Mind your console, Lieutenant Commander!" Nathan raised his hands and snapped his fingers, pointing at the view screen.

"*You are offering to sacrifice yourself?*" the female caste leader asked to clarify.

"I am, if you agree to an immediate cease-fire, *and* you agree to begin formal negotiations for a lasting peace."

"All incoming missiles destroyed," Jessica reported, her voice highly stressed.

"*An impressive offer.*"

"Are they firing again?" Nathan asked his sensor operator, in hushed tones.

"No, sir. That battleship has not launched any more missiles," Mister Navashee replied.

"One other thing," Nathan said to the caste leaders. "I demand a fair trial."

"*Trial?*"

"I assume you are charging me with war crimes against the people of the Jung Empire?"

"*You shall have your trial.*"

"Yeah, right!" Jessica scoffed.

Nathan snapped his fingers.

"Muted," Naralena reported.

"One more, and I'll have the Ghatazhak toss you in the brig," Nathan warned Jessica with absolute conviction. He snapped his fingers again. "Then we have a deal?"

"*It will have to be put to a vote. Remain in orbit. We will contact you shortly.*"

"Order your ships to stand down. Our destruction will trigger yours," Nathan warned.

"*Understood.*"

The video screen disappeared again.

Nathan looked at Mister Navashee. "What are those ships doing?"

Mister Navashee turned back to his console and studied his displays. "The battleship is no longer targeting us, and they have begun their deceleration for orbital insertion. I believe they mean to parallel us."

Nathan sighed.

"I believe you have just saved both our worlds," General Bacca congratulated. "Well done, Captain Scott."

Nathan recognized the sound of gloating when he heard it. "Return this man to his quarters," he ordered, a look of contempt on his face. Nathan headed aft, toward his ready room. "Remain at general quarters," he instructed Jessica. "You have the conn."

* * *

Nathan sat in his ready room, staring at his data pad on the desk in front of him. He had tried several times to write a letter to his father, and to his sisters, but he couldn't find the words.

He picked up the remote and turned on the view screen on the forward bulkhead above the couch where Jessica loved to stretch out and relax. A few more button presses, and the scene that Captain Roberts had always liked to run on the view screen began to play.

Nathan stared at the video of the view from Captain Robert's beach house. The waves crashing in the background, the golden retriever running on the beach, the seagulls squawking. He had played this video on many occasions, and it had always made him feel better. But not this time. That's when Nathan realized. It was not *his* happiness, it was someone else's.

Nathan's happiness was this ship. This crew. This job. He had spent his entire childhood doing what his parents wanted him to do. Even his young adult years had been spent being groomed for something that was not of his choosing. And when he had finally broken free and made his own career choice, he had chosen the one thing that he could possibly think of, that was the complete opposite to what his family had wanted him to do.

Funny thing was, it had worked. He had never been more proud to be a part of something in his entire life. Here, he had made a difference. Here, he had faced challenges and overcome extreme adversity. Here, on this ship, he had become a man.

His ship and his crew meant everything to Nathan, and it seemed only fitting that he would give his life to save not only them, but his entire world, as well as the lives of all the member worlds of the Alliance. His decisions had already saved millions of lives, but also cost millions of others, so in a way, the sacrifice he had offered seemed a fitting punishment.

Of course, there was still a chance...

The intercom buzzer sounded. Nathan pressed the button. "Go ahead."

"*Message from the Jung caste senate,*" Naralena said. There was a long pause, as if she was having trouble saying the words. "*They have accepted your terms. They are sending a shuttle for you and General Bacca.*"

Nathan said nothing, only closed his eyes as the reality set in.

"*Sir?*"

"Understood," Nathan replied, his voice broken. He cleared his throat. "Alert flight to expect the shuttle. I'll meet them on the port hangar deck. Notify Doctor Chen, and call Commander Willard to the bridge."

"*Aye, sir.*"

Nathan took in a deep breath, and let it out in a long sigh. He watched Captain Roberts' video a few more minutes, wondering if he would see another ocean before he died.

Finally, he opened the desk drawer, and picked up the bullet that had killed his brother, Eli...the bullet Nathan himself had fired. He put the bullet in his pocket, rose, and headed for the exit.

Nathan stepped through the hatch from his ready room, onto the bridge.

"Captain on the bridge!" the guard barked.

Nathan looked about at his staff, each of them already standing at attention. Commander Willard was standing next to the tactical station. Nathan stepped up to him. "As soon as I'm gone, jump away and head home. Let the admiral deal with the negotiations. You just get everyone safely back to Sol."

"Yes, sir."

"The ship is yours, Commander. Take good care of her, and take good care of her crew."

Commander Willard stared into his captain's eyes, unsure of what to say. "I don't think I'm ready," he admitted in a quiet voice.

"You're more ready than I was," Nathan reassured him. "You'll do fine." Nathan shook Commander

Willard's hand, then turned to Jessica. She threw her arms around him, holding him tight, like she would never let him go. "You'll never know how important you are to me," she whispered in his ear. After another minute, she pulled back slightly, kissed him softly on the cheek, then released him and stepped back, wiping her tears away quickly.

Nathan turned around to face forward, staring at the big, wrap-around, spherical view screen and the image of the Jung homeworld below them. He looked at the faces of his bridge staff. These were the men and women he had fought side by side with. They had counted on him, and he on them, and together they had done great things. And now, they were about to bring peace to the Sol sector.

Nathan took a deep breath, fighting back his emotions. "It has truly been an honor to be your captain. Thank you for all that each of you has done. Without you, I never would have made it this far. No matter what you do with the rest of your lives, because of the things you have done on this ship, you will forever be heroes."

Nathan turned and headed for the port exit.

"Company, A-ten-SHUN!" Jessica barked. The bridge staff stiffened, coming to attention as commanded. "SA-LUTE!"

Nathan slowly turned back around to find every person on the bridge holding a perfect salute. Nathan came to attention himself, returned the salute, and then left the Aurora's bridge for the last time.

He walked down the corridor and headed for the ramp. On either side of the corridor were the men and women of the Aurora's crew...his crew, and they were all standing at attention, their hands at their brow to salute their departing captain. Nathan came to the head of the ramp and found Major Prechitt, the Aurora's CAG, saluting and standing at attention at the top of the ramp. Nathan wanted to say something to the man, but the major was paying his respects in the way that best conveyed how he felt about his commanding officer. Nathan exchanged glances with the major, saying more in one look than they could with a thousand words.

Nathan headed down the empty ramp, finding the main corridor on the next level down also lined with the members of his crew.

Doctor Chen met him at the bottom of the ramp, a pneumo-ject in hand. She looked up at him, staring into his eyes. "Are you sure about this, sir?"

"I don't have a choice," he replied solemnly. He looked straight ahead, preparing himself for the injection.

The doctor pressed the pneumo-ject to Nathan's neck and pressed the button, emptying its contents into his jugular vein. "I am so sorry," she whispered.

Nathan looked back down at her. "Thank you for everything, Doctor."

"Good luck, sir," she replied softly, stepping back out of his way.

Nathan walked proudly down the corridor, his eyes forward as he headed for the port hangar deck. At the main hatch, he found Josh and Loki, standing on either side of the hatch, both of them assuming the same posture as the rest of the crew.

Nathan smiled. "That uniform never did look right on you, Josh. I also think this is the first time I've ever seen you issue a proper salute." Nathan tipped his head. "I'm honored," he said, as he returned Josh's salute.

"I'm probably gonna break out in a rash any second," Josh cracked, "but it'll be worth it."

Nathan smiled as he patted Josh on the shoulder. He then faced Loki, returning his salute as well. "That uniform *does* look good on you, however."

"Thank you, sir," Loki replied quietly. "For everything."

"I could say the same to both of you." Nathan took a deep breath. "Clear skies, gentlemen."

"Same to you, Captain," Josh replied sadly, as Nathan stepped through the hatch.

Nathan stood just inside the forward end of the port hangar bay. The Jung shuttle was already pulling out of the midship elevator airlock. General Bacca was standing a few meters ahead of him, watching the shuttle as well.

Nathan looked around. Other than the few deck hands who were directing the Jung shuttle, everyone else was standing at attention in honor of their departing captain.

"A touching sign of respect," General Bacca said.

Nathan looked at the General, barely containing his rage. "As I'm most certainly facing execution sometime in the near future, I have *zero* to lose by snapping your fucking neck, right here, right now... General. So I suggest you keep your mouth shut until we get on board that shuttle. Is that understood?"

The four Ghatazhak guards assigned to escort General Bacca smiled at Nathan's remarks. The sergeant then shoved the general in the direction of the waiting shuttle.

Nathan followed the Ghatazhak and the general to the shuttle. Halfway there, he stopped and looked to his right. There, standing in front of the port side hatch, was his friend, Vladimir. He was standing at perfect attention, holding a salute, also struggling to control his emotions. Nathan turned toward his chief engineer, returned his salute, and nodded at him. Nathan turned back toward the Jung shuttle. The Ghatazhak soldiers had released the general and allowed him to board the shuttle, then had taken up positions on either side of the boarding ramp to face Nathan as he approached. In unison, all four of the Ghatazhak soldiers drew their hands up in salute.

Nathan could feel his heart pounding, his temples throbbing, and his breath quickening as he returned their salute. Finally, he turned, walked up the boarding ramp, and disappeared into the Jung shuttle.

Vladimir, the Ghatazhak, and the rest of the deck hands all stood there in silence, as the Jung shuttle raised its boarding ramp, closed its hatch, and began to roll back into the elevator airlock.

"Aurora... Departing," Naralena's voice announced over the ship's loudspeakers.

Thank you for reading this story.
(*A review would be greatly appreciated!*)

COMING SUMMER 2016

**Part II
of
The Frontiers Saga**

Visit us online at
www.frontierssaga.com
or on Facebook

Want to be notified when
new episodes are published?
Join our mailing list!
http://www.frontierssaga.com/mailinglist/

Made in the USA
Middletown, DE
10 May 2018